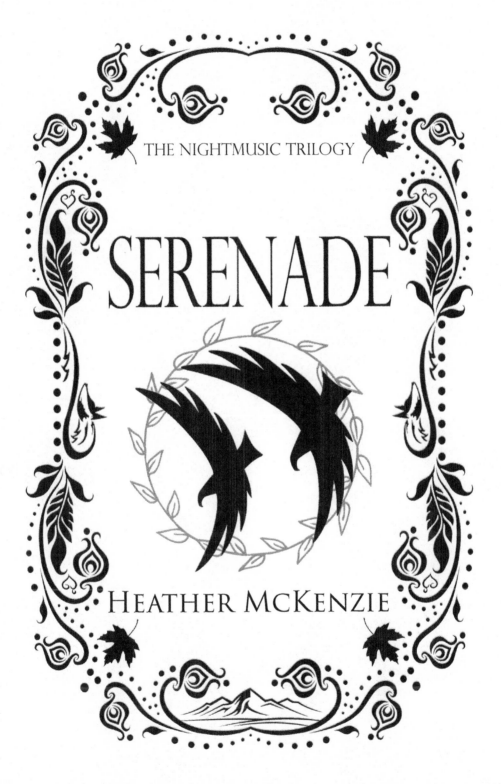

THE NIGHTMUSIC TRILOGY

SERENADE

HEATHER MCKENZIE

For Haley, Emily and Joshua

We might be small,
Our tiny blip in the cosmic ocean is just that
a blip…
But what an incredible blip it is.

Serenade
Copyright ©2017 Heather McKenzie

ISBN 978-1-63422-220-4
Cover Design by: Marya Heiman
Interior Design by: Courtney Knight
Edited by: Courtney Whittamore & Cynthia Shepp

For more information about our content disclosure, please utilize the QR code above with your smart phone or visit us at www.CleanTeenPublishing.com

SUMMER, 2014
KAYA

1

CATCHING MINNOWS

MY LUNGS BURNED, SWEAT STUNG MY EYES, AND EVERY MUSCLE screamed, but running was an escape from my over-controlled life and the rush of adrenaline and fresh mountain air a drug I couldn't get enough of. It kept me sane. It made me feel normal—or close to what I dreamed normal might be.

As my feet hit the trail, dewdrops fell from the canopy of trees and landed on my overheated skin. It was pure bliss out here in the woods. The only place where I could take my mind somewhere else and pretend I was far away from my home nestled in the midst of one of Canada's most beautiful national parks. I wanted to daydream that I was free to go wherever I wished without bodyguards glued to my sides, but that wasn't going to happen today; Oliver was unusually quiet, which meant something was wrong, and Stephan was wheezing as if he were about to die. And as much as I would have liked, I couldn't pretend I didn't care about either of them.

My male nanny since birth was red faced and stumbling. His husky frame was stuffed into the same spandex outfit he'd worn yesterday, and his hair was left in its natural state of salt-and-pepper curls. His lack of attention to his appearance was out of character, as was his inability to keep up with Oliver and me.

"Hey Stephan, should we stop for a bit?" I asked with a sideways glance, hoping I wasn't offending his manliness by showing concern. "You're scaring the wildlife."

He tripped and almost fell. "No," he said, coughing. "I'm… made of steel. Invincible."

I'd heard that a million times. "Well, Superman, there must be kryptonite in your mismatched socks this morning," I joked. "Really though, there's no harm in resting for a minute or two."

"No," he snapped.

I told myself not to worry. He really was tough as nails. Like one of those rugged cowboys in a western movie who wore his scars like medals.

All that was missing was the hat and chaps—thank goodness.

The trail opened up onto the white beach of Spring Lake. It had sparkling blue water so irresistible I couldn't help but sprint toward it. I kicked off my sneakers, yanked my yoga pants up over my knees, and waded into water so clear you could drink it.

"Kaya, you're going to get pneumonia. Get out of there," Stephan nagged from the shore, still sounding winded.

"It's fine. Really, it's not that cold," I lied.

Truthfully, the mountain-fed lake was just a hair over the freezing mark and had a good sting to it. Teeth chattering, I stood perfectly still, staring at my reflection in the crystal-clear water. My hair was too long and dark—the blue-black shade and green color of my eyes courtesy of my dad—and my body was too thin. My pale cheeks could use some color aside from the odd dusting of freckles across my nose, but that would mean wearing makeup, and that wasn't my thing. I felt plain looking, if that was even a feeling, but I figured that was okay since I stood out enough just by being the daughter of Henry Lowen—one of the world's wealthiest and most-hated men. My last name might as well have been a neon sign stuck to my forehead. Everyone knew about the billionaire's daughter who was locked away in the creepy castle—I was a modern-day Rapunzel in the majestic resort-town of Banff Alberta.

I swirled a finger across the glass-like surface of the lake and my reflection disappeared along with a school of minnows circling my legs. I wanted to dive under with them and then swim as hard and fast as I could to the other side to explore the shoreline, *alone,* but the cold was turning me numb. Reluctantly, I waded back to the beach where Stephan had collapsed against a pile of driftwood, still catching his breath, and Oliver stood next to him holding out my shoes with an impatient look about him.

"Time to go," he said.

The sun hit his broad shoulders just right, giving his skin a glow that was impossible to ignore. His glorious shape seemed as if he'd been sculpted from the hands of a master artist, and I'd never understood why someone as beautiful as him would take the job as a bodyguard.

"Not yet. Please." I begged, dropping down to the soft sand.

My pink shoelace dangled between his massive fingers as his gaze shifted to Stephan then back to me. His deep brown eyes studied mine for a moment, and then with a heavy sigh, he shook his head. "Fine."

Dropping down on the sand across from me, he took my frozen toes in his hands. I noticed his full lips were slightly pursed, and the concentration wrinkle on his forehead was a bit deeper than usual. "Is there something wrong?" I asked.

In the past, it wouldn't have occurred to me to ask this sort of question because, truly, I didn't care. In fact, what I'd felt toward him for a long time was borderline hatred. But, over the last year, things had started to change. Oliver was becoming *different*. Or was it me?

He tilted his head and arched an exquisite eyebrow. "Wrong with me? Why do you ask?"

"I guess because you seem a little withdrawn, and…" *Should I say it?* "Because I don't hate you anymore."

A crooked smile spread across his face. He looked at me with a thoughtful expression on his face. "Well, Kaya, I'm just—" He paused, as if searching my eyes for his words. "Hungry."

There was something more on his mind than his stomach. I could see it. But it was probably best not to pry. Instead, I savored his gentle touch as he rubbed warmth back into my toes, giving me shivers that had nothing to do with being cold. I imagined *my* fingers running over his hands and forearms, then across the seams of his white T-shirt —it made such a striking contrast against his chocolate-colored skin. He was so…

What was wrong with me? I wasn't supposed to be thinking *that*.

I closed my eyes and concentrated on the hum of the forest instead. The sun on my face. The breeze coming off the lake, and the smell of flowering trees in the air. It was heaven, far from the buzz of people and the confines of the estate. I was grateful the family doctor insisted these daily runs were important to my psyche because Dad would have preferred to keep me locked up day and night. Sometimes, I was sure Oliver felt the same—he was always so serious, so controlling, and so filled with worry every time I was out of the confines of my room. This kept my anxiety level on a constant upswing—which he always took great pleasure in trying to subdue.

The gentle movements of his hands gradually slowed my pulse, my nerves untangled, and my thoughts drifted to a faraway place. I basked in his heavenly touch… until a loud snapping sound came from the trees.

"What was that?" I yelped, jerking away with a now-pounding heart.

Oliver leapt to his feet just as three quick flashes of light burst from within the shadows of the trees. "Oh, it's just *them*," he said casually and brushed the sand off his shorts before sitting back down again, this time right next to me.

Them. Twenty or so armed guards. Hidden in the trees.

"Relax, Kaya. It's okay," he added, his massive hand reaching for mine.

How many times had he said that to me in the last year? And was everything okay? *No.* I had a group of men following my every move to protect me—to keep me alive. Things were never *okay...*

Absentmindedly, I touched my neck. I could still feel the scar that ran from my ear to my collarbone made from a knife that did more than just damage my skin. My sixteenth birthday was over a year ago, but it was as clear in my mind as yesterday. Oliver saved my life that day, using his body to shield mine. He would have died for me. And I wasn't sure if that realization was why I'd started to like him, or if I'd decided I *owed* it to him.

He checked his watch and then tipped his face toward the sun. At that angle, I could freely stare at his profile. He looked far different from when I first met him. His hair used to be an unruly halo around his head and his body thin and lanky. I thought back to when I was seven and the estate was in lockdown. Stephan and Dad had rushed me to the basement gym where we waited among a hundred or so men who all seemed intimidating and tall. I was annoyed with the boy in a too-big uniform who had dark, piercing eyes that barely blinked. He kept staring at me as if I were a monster. I asked Dad about the men, why they were there, but I was mostly curious about the boy.

"They are guards in training. They'll work here on the estate or at one of our companies someday. That one right there was plucked off the street not too long ago. He's the youngest one we have. Probably only sixteen," Dad had said. *"His whole family was taken from him and the poor kid witnessed the whole thing. Tragic. Anyway, he is showing remarkable potential. Maybe he'll be one of your guards in a few years."*

At the time, that thought had made me wiggly from my hair to my toes. *"I don't like him,"* I said. *"He's gross and creepy."*

I remembered Dad zeroing in on Oliver's unwavering gaze aimed in my direction, and my uncomfortable disgust because of it. There was a wicked look in Dad's eyes when they returned to mine.

I shivered.

"What's going on in that crazy head of yours?" Oliver asked, bringing me back to the lake, the blue sky, and his molasses-colored irises.

"Just thinking that I could stay here all day."

"Oh."

"Not you?" I asked, drawing a daisy in the sand with a twig.

"Nope. There are no pancakes out here."

"Ah. The almighty pancake. It rules your life, doesn't it?' I teased.

"We all know *exactly* what rules my life."

Of course, he was referring to me. "Aren't you lucky then?" I asked.

He grinned as if he did feel lucky, which was completely ludicrous. "Do you want to run the long way back?" he asked, brushing over what was about to be an awkward moment.

I always wanted to push myself to the limit—to run as hard as I could or work out until I puked. The sore muscles were confirmation that I had *done* something—that I was *alive* in my otherwise-numb life. But Stephan, now resting against some driftwood and oblivious to the world, seemed a bit too pale for another hour and a half of running. The dark shadows under his eyes were darker than usual, and, once in a while, a cough erupted from his chest. Maybe he'd caught a bug from the maid yesterday; she'd been sneezing and spewing germs all over the place.

"I think Stephan's sick. We should call for a car to meet us up at the highway."

Oliver wasn't listening. He'd leapt to his feet and had his hand to his earpiece. Stephan had also sprung to life and was now staring down the beach on high alert.

"What?" I asked, getting ready to run. My anxiety kicked into over-drive and I imagined the worst, envisioning my sixteenth birthday all over again.

Stephan pointed down the beach to where a small, dark shape was moving low to the ground. "Three cubs. Momma bear is in the trees. We'll have to cut the running short today."

I breathed a sigh of relief. It was just bears and they couldn't give a rat's ass about me. One of the little fuzz balls scurried to the water's edge and gave it a sniff. Moments later, a sibling joined, smaller but braver. He put all four paws in and then playfully romped in and out of the water. They were so happy and free. I envied them.

"Cute little things, aren't they?" Stephan said, now at my side and reaching protectively for my hand. His eyes were bright, cheeks pink again, and I wound my fingers through his, grateful as always for his affection. There was no warmth from my dad, ever, and Oliver would only be completely smothering if I let him.

"Their fuzzy 'lil bear butts look like your face," I teased, giving Stephan's greying beard a playful tug.

"You're such a brat."

I smiled up at his gruff face and noticed something shifting behind him. The light changed among the massive evergreens, bushes swayed, and before I could say anything, two men in head-to-toe camouflage popped out of the shadows.

Stephan clutched his chest. "Why do you guys always have to sneak up like that?" he said with a gasp.

"We have orders to escort Miss Lowen back to the estate," said a very clean-shaven man. A 'Lowen Security' badge was sewn to his jacket, and his expression was so serious I had to laugh. He reminded me of Oliver when he first became my guard. I'd teased him about the stupid outfits he wore until they were replaced with cargo shorts and T-shirts. Although Oliver's uniform had changed, his serious expression hadn't.

The three of us followed the guards, crashing and stomping up the old logging road toward the highway like a stampede of drunken teenagers. This was supposed to keep mama bear away, but it was hilarious. My giggles got worse every time Stephan gave me 'the look', and became almost uncontrollable when the sides of Oliver's mouth lifted too. By the time we made it to the car, I was wiping tears from my eyes. It felt good to laugh. We didn't do that much.

But my giddiness dissolved when, sandwiched between Oliver and Stephan in the back seat of the limo, the Bow Springs Estate's towering spires came into view. They poked up into the sky like the mountains themselves, a structural marvel that was impossible to miss.

Home sweet home.

Built 150 years ago on the edge of an impressive cliff, it looked like a castle. On the east side, a massive jagged rock face dropped down to meet the Bow River, and on the South side miles of forest stretched up the side of a mountain to snow-covered peaks. The valley sprawled out in front, sloping gradually down toward Banff and miles of winding trails and pristine lakes. It had been a hotel when my grandfather owned it and gave it to my parents as a wedding gift. Dad closed it shortly after Mom's death and made it our private residence. Now the priceless art, crystal chandeliers, stained glass windows, and immaculate gardens were hidden from the public eye, just like me.

It hadn't always been so bleak. From what I'd heard, when Mom was around, the place was warm and inviting. It used to be buzzing with actors, politicians, and royal families, the elaborate architecture loved and admired. People even liked my dad back then. But when Mom died, power and greed took over his brilliant mind and within two years, he was in *Forbes Magazine's* "The Forbes World's Billionaire List". If there were most-hated list, he'd have been on that too.

The car pulled up to the first gate, and a massive iron structure large enough to keep out Godzilla opened with motorized arms. After a series of commands and verifications, we made our way to the lobby. I wished the old revolving doors still worked because they were great to drive

Stephan crazy with. Now big, bulky metal monstrosities were in their place and two large men were stationed permanently on either side just to open and close them. I wondered, as I glanced at their bored faces, if that was their career choice: big, metal door openers.

A maid greeted us in the foyer. She was a plump woman with ginger-colored hair and a genuine smile. I handed her my jacket, the pockets filled with shells and stones.

"So, how was the run, Miss Kaya?" she asked as the doors locked behind us.

"It was fine until the zombies came out of the ground and tried to eat us," I replied nonchalantly.

"Oh, how unfortunate. Good thing your spaceship was fueled up."

I smiled. It was rare for staff to play along with my feeble attempts at humor.

"Breakfast is being served on the second terrace," she added, "but unfortunately, your father won't be joining you. He got called away on business."

"Shocker," I said sarcastically.

"Or, maybe the zombies ate him," she joked.

"I'm not that lucky."

Oliver's eyebrows drew together and he cleared his throat. "Really, Kaya, you know he'd be here if he could."

I would have argued, but Oliver would have defended Dad until the cows came home—and we had no cows. My father was pretty much nonexistent in my life. Affection never emanated from his perfectly polished, self-centered, wildly corrupt heart. I was fiercely protected and guarded, living under a million rules and regulations for my own safety, but I was beginning to question whether it was out of love. When he moved me to the opposite end of the estate, started missing my birthdays, was gone for months, and returned with new girlfriends without so much as a hello, it started becoming obvious that he didn't care about *me*. I was just an object to him.

Like I did a hundred times a day, I pushed him out of my mind and followed Oliver and Stephan up the marble stairs, through the observatory hall, and out onto the second terrace. The aroma of breakfast wafted in from the patio, a place with a view that I'd admired since I was a kid. The scenery still took my breath away. Hundreds of feet below us, the river gently flowed through miles of untouched forest, and above, snow-topped mountain peaks met an endless sky. The birds sang as we ate, some brave enough to steal crumbs from beneath the serving table while the staff bustled about in crisp black-and-white uniforms. I took my usual chair next to Oliver and attacked a loaded plate of potatoes and pancakes—the one good thing about living here was the food. Dad was adamant that we only eat vegetarian, organic ingredients. In fact, he was completely neurotic about it. Sugar might as well have been the devil in his mind.

"So, what's on the schedule this morning, Kaya?" Stephan said between mouthfuls. "French? English? Snake charming? Deep-sea diving?"

I avoided paying attention to my schedule to remain ignorant of the monotony. Oliver, however, was a walking day planner.

"Nope. She's got Ms. Elms for swimming, and then piano and theory lessons all afternoon."

Stephan had a twinkle in his eyes as he flared his nostrils in disgust. "Bach and that nasty Mozart? Why does your father insist you learn that classical crap? I don't get paid enough to sit through it. Why not study the blues? Now that's *real* music."

I knew he secretly enjoyed Bach and Beethoven. He always pretended to read while I practiced, but the pages of his books never turned.

"And for heaven's sake, fencing and Japanese? Is he training you to be a ninja?" he added, reaching for a glass of water. His hand shook as he took a sip, water dribbling down his chin. He was about to say something more, but a harsh cough burst from his lungs and his whole body jerked like a bee had stung him.

"Are you okay?" I asked.

He coughed again, causing water to spill over the sides of the glass and onto the crystal butter dish. As he struggled to clear his throat, the wind picked up, fluttering the edges of the white tablecloth and rocking the vase of fresh-cut flowers in the middle of the table. I reached to steady them.

"Yeah, just ate too fast," he said softly.

"Are you sure? You look a little... *off*," Oliver asked anxiously.

Stephan didn't reply. His cheeks turned a horrible shade of grey, and then the glass slipped from his hands and shattered into a thousand bits on the stone patio.

"Stephan!" Oliver yelled, bolting from his chair.

But before Oliver could get to him, Stephan's eyes rolled back in his head and he collapsed face-first onto his breakfast.

2

◊TUMBLE

THE CLOCK ON THE SICKLY-GREEN HOSPITAL WALL TICKED SO
slowly I thought time itself had stopped. The minute hand
passed twelve thirteen times while Stephan's heart monitor kept
setting off alarms and bringing nurses running into the room.
They'd push buttons and reset devices, then casually wander off
like it was no big deal. Every time it happened, it felt like my own
heart had stopped too.

I sat at his bedside and rubbed the back of his hand with my thumb.
Every scar, mole, and blue-green vein was familiar and clearly memorized from the many times his hands had comforted me. For as long as I
could remember, Stephan had been at my side. He said once that he held
me as a newborn before even my own mother did, and I didn't doubt it.
He taught me how to fish and how to ride a bike, got me on ice skates
when I was terrified, and spent every holiday with me—and many times,
it was just the two of us. We shared an intense love of nature, a passion
for science fiction books, and a mutual dislike of almost all the other
nannies. The scar between his thumb and forefinger was there from saving me from a dog attack and the others scattered across his palm were
from four thwarted abduction attempts. He was my bodyguard, mother,
father, best friend—*everything* to me. If I lost him…

Oliver was worried too. His pacing next to the foot of Stephan's bed
had made little black trails of scuffmarks on the polished, white floor,
and he'd probably cracked his knuckles a hundred times. Usually, he
answered to Stephan, who was his superior, but now he was in charge—
talking to the doctors, calling family, increasing security, hovering over
me…

"We need to get some fresh air and something to eat, Kaya," he said
for the fifth time.

I ignored him for the fifth time.

He crossed the room to grip my shoulder with a subtle demand of
obedience. "Are you listening?"

I nodded my head numbly, squeezing Stephan's hand a bit tighter.

"Let's go across the street for a quick bite. I'll give the nurse my phone number so she can call us if he wakes up."

I could have been completely stubborn, which was my default, but his brown, bloodshot eyes were weary, and the look on his face was a mixture of sadness and concern. Oliver was normally so stoic that seeing him emotional in any way tugged at my heartstrings. Reluctantly, I obeyed.

We left the hospital, followed by *them*. Although they tried to be discreet, the odd trio of 'golfer', 'businessman', and 'drug dealer' tagging along so closely was as discreet as toilet paper trailing from your shoes. I hadn't left the safety of the estate since my birthday, and under the yellow glow of the streetlights with my strange entourage in tow, it hit me that I was out *in public*. Part of me was scared to death. Another part was… excited and devious—if Dad had been around, this would never be allowed. I reached for Oliver's hand and noticed a slight upturn in the corners of his mouth as he laced his fingers through mine.

The Derrick Bar was the only place with an open sign in the window. We found a dimly lit table in the corner and went unnoticed by the patrons, who were completely immersed in the slot machines. By the look of the near-empty place, eating the food here was the real gamble.

A pink-haired waitress with an orangey, fake tan didn't even bother to check if I was underage. She was just eager for a tip. She handed us menus, and I felt as if I were in a dream inquiring about the strange food… Was everything deep fried? Was there anything vegetarian? The strawberry tattoo on her arm had me asking if they had any organic fruit. She laughed like I'd told a joke.

Oliver suggested I get fries. "They're strips of potatoes boiled in oil," he explained. I trusted him, but I secretly wondered if starving might be better than putting something Dad would have called poison in my mouth.

"So, a healthy plate of deep-fried taters for the lady and two BLTs with extra bacon for you, sir. Will that be all?" the waitress asked in an accent I couldn't place.

"Pie. Don't care what kind," Oliver said wearily, and I felt oddly jealous as he watched our shapely server stroll away.

"Man, I must look like a disaster," I muttered, suddenly inexplicably worried about my appearance. I could feel the puffiness around my eyes, and I was sure my red nose—raw from tissue overuse—rivaled Rudolph's.

"I don't know. I never look at you," Oliver said with a grin that made butterflies dance in my stomach. I tried to drown them with coffee.

"She's pretty, isn't she?" I said.

"The waitress? Sure, but she's got nothing on you."

I laughed. "Liar."

His eyes settled on mine. I should have looked away, but I didn't. The look on his face was intense—too intense—and it stirred up feelings in me that were wrong on every level. I absolutely could not, *must not*, have a crush on my bodyguard.

Swigging back the rest of the vile coffee, I faked needing to visit the ladies' room. My reflection in the bathroom mirror was horrifying; I was still in my running clothes from earlier that morning, and my tank top was smudged with dirt. I pulled off the baseball cap Oliver had used to try to disguise me—an ugly purple thing purchased in the hospital boutique—and undid the messy braid beneath. Tangled waves fell to my waist and I wondered what I would look like with short hair—or maybe pink hair like the waitress…

I rinsed my face with cold water but my cheeks remained paper white. At least the hospital smell was gone from my hands. Desperately trying to untangle my mop of hair, I wished I had a hairbrush or at least a tube of lipstick so I didn't look so… terrible. But really, what did it matter? It was only Oliver getting a close look at me… the same guy who saw me every single day for the last five years. But I had to admit, today felt different for some reason, and as much as I didn't want to, I *cared*, and that sucked.

Our food—if you could call it that—was on the table when I returned.

"Did you hear from the nurse?" I asked.

Oliver sighed. "No, Kaya. Everything is all right. Just eat something."

I dragged a mangled French fry around my plate, completely unable to bring the horrid, greasy thing to my mouth. I tasted the ketchup; it made a better paint than a condiment. I swirled it into macabre circles on the chipped plate.

"You sure adore Stephan, don't you?" Oliver asked bluntly.

Did I detect a tinge of jealousy in his voice? "Yes. I adore him," I answered truthfully. "I love him more than anyone in the world. He has been with me since I was born. I mean, I've had lots of nannies, but Stephan was the one who always went above and beyond. Without him, there'd be no love in my life. So, yeah I adore him. It really hit me today that he's… he's all I've got."

Saying those words made my chest hurt, and the ketchup and fries became even more repulsive.

"I know how you feel, Kaya," he said softly and his eyes became watery, "you don't always realize how much you love someone until things like this happen."

I knew what it was like to lose a parent, but Oliver had lost his entire family. All of them—mom, dad, two sisters and a brother—killed right before his very eyes. He had experienced the worst kind of sadness imaginable and refused to talk about it. A few times, late at night when there was nothing on TV and we were both wide awake, I would gently bring it up. I would ask what his mom looked like or fish for a name of one of his sisters, but I would get nothing. Zero. Zip. We could share our love of Radiohead and Renoir or have heated debates on politics, but discussing anything about his life before he came to work at the estate was off the table.

"You can talk to me about *that,* you know," I said cautiously.

His brown eyes fluttered. "Talk to you about what?"

"You know… about what happened to your family. You can talk to me."

"Oh," he said, clearing his throat, "there is nothing to talk about. You're my family now."

He reached across the table and placed his hand over mine. I didn't pull away. Our hands contrasted beautifully, mine pale and small, his coffee-colored and strong. I stared hard at him, like I'd never really looked at him before, and he reeled me in on an invisible line with his sleepy brown eyes. With his other hand, he reached for my cheek and brushed aside a lock of hair, and then I couldn't resist—I turned my palm over to touch his… I felt his warm skin with my thumb and then wound my fingers through his. All the air left his lungs. He blinked rapidly. Then, as if I had suddenly developed a flesh-eating disease, he yanked his hand away and almost knocked our coffee off the table.

"It's time to go," he said abruptly.

"Sorry, I won't ask about it again. I promise," I said, seeing his flustered face.

But I knew it wasn't my bringing up his family that had thrown him for a loop. It was because our hands wound together in a way that felt far different than it ever had. He stood, staring down at me while I fished for something to say, but thankfully, we were interrupted by the phone ringing in his pocket. I watched his face while he said barely more than two words to whoever was on the other end of the phone.

"That was the nurse. Stephan is awake," he said, hanging up.

I bolted out of my chair so fast I stumbled backward. Oliver lunged for my arm, reached around my waist, and pulled me close—his lightning-fast reflexes preventing me from an embarrassing fall. The scent of cigars and citrus surrounding him made my head swim, and as he held me longer than necessary, everything about the look in his eyes made me tremble.

"You need to be more careful," he said in a breathy whisper. "You're all I've got."

What?

My world came to a grinding halt. *You're all I've got?* His arms briefly tightened around me, my body feeling so light that I feared it might soar up and away, and when he let go, I felt like I'd fallen back to earth. His words swam around in my head like a bunch of piranhas gnawing at the shield I'd built to keep words like that out. Dammit. It was becoming impossible to dislike him.

But now I was on the receiving end of a silent treatment that made the five-minute walk back to the hospital torture. I snuck in a few sideways glances, but couldn't read the expression on his face. Was he embarrassed about what he'd said? Was it an insignificant slip of the tongue? Or was it a confession of deeper underlying feelings? I suspected the latter, and that was terrifying.

To add tension to my inner turmoil, my bossy, over opinionated, ex-nanny was waiting for us at Stephan's bedside when we got back. Anne had received my texts but couldn't remember how to reply, so she decided to come and talk to me in person instead. I stared in awe at her outfit, which was a head-to-toe lavender pantsuit with kitten appliqués that looked like it had been made by the Easter bunny. There were brightly colored peacock pins artfully placed on the lapel of her blazer to pull the whole 'look' together, and a heady perfume clung to her curly, grey hair like smoke from a pack-a-day habit.

"You look tired, dear," she said.

I noticed her eyes were bloodshot when she pulled away from my respectfully distant hug. The clock over the door said three-thirty in the morning. "Yeah, I'm exhausted. I didn't want Stephan to be alone." He was sound asleep again, the crisp, white sheet pulled up under his chin. He looked like he was dead. I was grateful for the reassuring, steady blip of the heart monitor.

Anne inspected the dismal room through thickly framed designer glasses, her grey hair shifting around like a helmet on her head. "This place is dreadful. Your father should put some money into this hospital." Then her eyes drifted to my chest and widened in alarm, and she lowered her voice into an angry whisper. "Kaya, we had a deal. You promised not to wear that necklace. Why must you always defy me, girl?"

The only connection I had to my mother was dangling from my neck—the same place it had been for the last year. The odd red stone encased in ornately decorated silver was impossible to miss, and I'd always been careful to hide the pendant under my clothes. In the craziness of the day, I forgot to conceal it.

"I'm sorry," I muttered.

Anne growled. Oliver feigned disinterest and headed to the window.

"I just... well... I couldn't take it off," I said meekly.

I wasn't one to break promises, but the necklace was a gift from my mom. She'd trusted Anne to hold on to it and, for sixteen years, it had been safely tucked away in the old nanny's safe. There were secrets surrounding it, and Anne wasn't ready to divulge them. I just prayed that she would share them before the Alzheimer's gnawing at her mind completely took over.

She wrung her spotty hands as if she were wringing my neck. "Kaya, your father can *never* see that." She hissed.

"Why?" I asked, even though I knew I wouldn't get an answer.

Anne crinkled her nose, her voice slightly rising in pitch. "We've discussed this. Your mother made me promise before she died and Henry can never find out about it. She said it was 'insurance' and that you'd know what to do with it someday. Now *take it off.*"

The poor old broad looked like she was about to crack. Stephan's ragged breathing and limp body covered in tubes was enough stress for the old woman. I felt horrible. "I'll be more careful. Dad will never see it, I promise," I said as I flipped the necklace around so it was under my hair and hanging down my back. The cold silver with Mom's initials etched on the backside was now resting between my shoulder blades. Someday, I'd figure out why it was so important to keep this strange piece of jewelry hidden, but now wasn't the time. I'd just keep pretending it had superpowers, housed a tiny universe, or was the key to a spaceship Mom buried in the garden.

Anne sighed heavily, eyeing Oliver's looming shadow next to the window. "Take her home now," she ordered, clearly still angry. "I'll look after Stephan. Neither of you are needed here anymore."

I was about to protest, but then I heard the voice I had been longing to hear all day.

"Yeah, go home, you assholes," Stephan croaked. "This attention is really pissing me off."

I lunged toward him and almost tripped over his heart monitor to plant a kiss on his damp forehead. His voice, no matter how grumpy, was a blessing. I held back tears, feeling relieved. "I love you, Stephan," I said, "you're going to be all right."

"Well, of course I am—I'm made of steel, remember?" His words were strong, but his delivery was weak. "How 'bout you, my sweet petunia. You okay?"

"I am perfectly fine."

"Good. Then get your butt home."

"No. It's my turn to look after you for a change."

He sighed heavily. The look in his eyes was one I'd seen a million times—no matter what the argument, I wasn't winning. "Now is not the time to be stubborn, okay?" he said softly. "I'm not asking—I'm telling. *Go home.*"

He was hurting. I wanted to take away his pain or lessen it somehow but the only thing I could do was leave so he wouldn't worry about me. I hugged him for as long as he would tolerate, told him I loved him, and then said it again close to his ear so his beard brushed my cheek. It was difficult to leave the room, but knowing he was safe in Anne's bossy but capable hands made it a little easier. She'd never admit it, but she cared for him, maybe as much as I did.

Once out in the hall with Oliver glued to my side, I felt it necessary to ask him something important that was weighing on my mind. I also needed to break the tension between us before we both snapped.

"Hey, Oliver?"

"Yeah," he answered, sounding sleepy while we waited for the slowest elevator in the world to come to our floor.

"Can you promise me something?"

He turned to face me. "I'll promise you anything," he said eagerly with a slight hint of anxiety in his tone.

I considered telling him that when he said sweet things, stared at me too long with his dreamy brown eyes, or put his hands on my cheek… it was inappropriate. It was unwanted. And I was trying desperately not to like it.

But I couldn't.

"Promise me that no matter what, you will never allow me to wear matching polyester pant suits like Anne's— *ever,*" I said in complete seriousness.

He laughed with relief, clearly not expecting this request. "Hell, yeah. How about this: I promise that when we get old, I'll buy you a whole bunch of those nice stretchy, velvet pants with the elastic waist and the zippered jackets to match. You'd rock that look with a granny bun, sittin' on the balcony knitting for our grandbabies."

I stopped dead in my tracks. *Our grandbabies?* Did he see a future for us… him and me… *together?*

Suddenly quiet, he reached for my hand as the grey doors of the elevator opened. My mind reeled as he pulled me ahead. Would I grow old with my bodyguard—with Oliver—living out my days confined to the estate? I couldn't imagine being with him that long, but then again, I couldn't imagine being *without* him. In fact, I couldn't picture the future at all; it was nothing but an empty, blank space. Past today, it was just blank.

Just… blank.

3

RATTLE THE CAGE

FOR FIVE DAYS, OLIVER AND I SPENT EVERY WAKING MOMENT AT Banff General Hospital. The room was dreary and always cold, but that wasn't why I was shivering. Today, the doctors were explaining Stephan's surgery while he lay there nonchalantly, like he was about to get a haircut. Apparently, angioplasty was a common and rather non-invasive method of opening blocked arteries to increase blood flow, but it sounded absolutely dreadful; a tube with a deflated balloon was going to be threaded up through an artery in Stephan's leg to where the blood flow in his heart was reduced, then pumped up to widen the area.

I was going to have a breakdown if I didn't leave the room.

Stephan's replacement stuck to us like glue as Oliver and I made the short walk to The Derrick Bar. The sun was shining on the bustling streets of Banff as busloads of tourists and locals flocked to the many boutiques and world-class restaurants. The sweet aroma of chocolate drifted out from the candy shops, and the gem store windows sparkled with locally mined jade and ammolite. Oliver held my hand, his grip tightening when we passed a street vendor selling scarves, but it was purely professional. We hadn't broached the "you're all I've got" statement he'd made the first night Stephan was in the hospital, so I just acted as if I hadn't heard it. And that was just fine with both of us.

The summer air wafting in through the open patio doors of the bar calmed my mind. Thankfully the new guy, Stephan's temporary replacement—emphasis on *temporary*—stayed outside on the patio to smoke—I'd threatened to choke him with his Iron Maiden T- shirt if he didn't. Dumping six packets of sugar into my coffee because I could, I pretended to enjoy it while the pink haired, overly tattooed waitress, whose name we now knew was Angela, flashed her signature mega-watt smile.

"Don't you guys ever get sick of this place?" she asked, handing over the plastic menus, "I mean, biking, canoeing, hiking, fishing… tree hugging… I'm dying to do something that doesn't involve a backpack and running shoes. In no way are laces, or anything with Velcro, fashionable."

Angela was so likeable and different from anyone I'd ever met. I felt drawn to her even though she kept trying to flirt with Oliver—he was so disinterested it was embarrassing.

"You guys into live music?" she asked, straightening her fifties-style skirt that was completely out of place in the rugged bar. "I hear there's a club down the street where indie bands play."

Oliver had become focused on a woman a few tables away. "Why don't you ask that broad glaring at us? She looks like she could use a night out," he said irritably.

Angela turned to see an older woman with crisp brown hair and hideous orange lipstick who looked like she was trying to shoot daggers at us with her eyeballs. "Ugh. That's Karen, the boss's girlfriend," she said, shoulders slouching. "That woman is a huge pain in the ass and she hates me."

"Well, if her nostrils flare any wider, her entire face might cave in," Oliver said.

Coffee—now more like syrup—shot out of my nose, and I couldn't contain the snorting laughter that escaped with it.

"God, I love it when you smile," Oliver said, and suddenly it was as if everything in the room had faded from existence and it was just him and me. "I just want to make you happy all the time," he added.

Angela lifted an eyebrow and backed away, giving Oliver the opportunity to move his chair closer to mine. Now side by side, thighs touching, he twisted around to face me and reached for my cheek—a move he'd been deploying too often lately. What the hell had gotten into him? I had been completely ignored for days and only receiving Oliver's business side, and now he was staring at me as if I were a roast beef sandwich and he hadn't eaten for days.

"So pretty…" he said.

Was he high? Had he gotten into Stephan's pain meds? Had he been drinking? "What the hell, Oliver? Stop it," I said harshly.

His hand fell from my face and he looked completely crushed. When he realized *they* were watching—our undercover posse only sitting a few tables away—a slight tinge of red flushed his dark cheeks. "I'm sorry. I shouldn't have done that. It's time to go," he said with a break in his voice.

"Oliver, I just meant…" I felt terrible. I didn't want to hurt his feelings and was about to apologize when Angela returned with coffee pot in hand.

"Refill?" she asked tentatively, sensing the tension.

Neither of us replied.

"Okay then," she said. "Well hey, why don't you guys come by and visit me Saturday night? We'll go dancing." She playfully swung her hips. "I'm off at nine if you're interested."

Oliver wasn't listening. He clenched his hands into fists, turned away with a huff, and marched off, leaving me alone with my new friend who looked entirely defeated.

"Um, I think you might have made him blush." I lied.

Angela sighed. "Yeah right. I know it's probably a complete waste of time, but I just can't help it. He's stunningly gorgeous—solid muscle head-to-toe..."

I nodded my head in agreement.

"Wait a minute... you're not *with* him, are you?" she stammered, "I mean, I just assumed... I'm sorry... but, you're not *together*, are you?"

"No. We're just good friends," I said.

She exhaled in relief. "That's what I thought. He's got a thing for you, though. You know that, right? I mean, I'm wearing my one-hundred-dred-percent guaranteed man-catching dress, but he couldn't take his eyes off you for even a second, and I was *workin'* it."

"I think he just forgot to put in his contact lenses... and it's kinda dim in here... and you know how it is with men and fashion... there's also a lot of... sandwiches and... other distractions."

Angela laughed, causing her silky pink hair to swish around her face. "You're adorable," she said with a wink. "Come by Saturday. We'll have a good time, I promise. But leave Mr. Serious behind; we'll have way more fun without him."

I didn't get a chance to reply. Mr. Serious had returned to possessively grip my arm and guide me toward the door. "That will *never* happen," Oliver said.

BACK AT THE HOSPITAL, STEPHAN LOUDLY EXCLAIMED THAT HE WAS SICK to death of all our faces, so while he bathed, Oliver, the new guy, and I occupied the sitting room nearby. I settled into a decrepit old chair while Oliver paced in front of a viewless window and watched me out of the corner of his eye. Both of us were pretending the metaphorical elephant stomping around in the room was just a little furry mouse. He had let his guard slip, and it was clear that his increasing devotion and possessiveness of me wasn't because of a paycheck. Truthfully, I was beginning to feel something for him too... and whatever that *something* was, it was getting harder to deny, so I had to keep reminding myself that besides Stephan and Anne, guards and nannies came and went. Allowing any emotional attachment to one of them would just be setting myself up for heartbreak—because at some point, Oliver would leave too.

I turned on an ancient TV and leaned back to numbly listen to an articulate voice predict that the coldest winter in years was just around the corner. A news anchor from the town's local station reported the most recent hockey scores, the upcoming election, the increasing price of chairlifts and resort fees... and it was all static in my ears until an all too familiar name caught my attention; *Henry Lowen... medical breakthrough... Eronel Industries...* They were talking about my dad and his company.

I sat up straighter, giving the images flashing across the TV my full attention. It showed a massive factory on fire and emergency crews moving frantically around the structure, battling black plumes of smoke billowing out of windows. Sirens could be heard in the background as a reporter narrated the scene:

"Today in Montreal, a protest organized by The Right Choice Group against the medical giant Eronel Industries turned deadly when a fire broke out. The blaze has claimed the lives of at least eight employees and has left five unaccounted for. The cause of the fire has yet to be determined, but three suspects have been detained for questioning. The Right Choice Group has been actively demanding the recall of Eronel's fertility drug Cecalitrin, claiming that the drug causes damage to the brain, resulting in psychosis and sometimes death. However, all further investigations are inconclusive at this time. Henry Lowen, CEO of Eronel Industries, addressed reporters during a press conference this afternoon."

And there he was—smiling as lights flashed and field reporters hurled questions in rapid fire. Polished and effortlessly captivating, Dad spoke and the crowd grew quiet. His charm and good looks were weapons that he knew how to use effectively. The sound of his lilting voice turned my stomach. "An alarming number of women are unable to conceive naturally, and the number is steadily increasing," Dad said, running a jeweled hand through his jet-black hair. "Cecalitrin is a safe treatment that has allowed many women to conceive when they otherwise would not have been able to do so. The accusations claiming that our company would put women in danger are ludicrous. Eronel was created by my late wife's brilliant father, John Marchessa, and has been a family owned and operated business helping people all over the world for over fifty years..."

Although the name *John Marchessa* rolled off his tongue easily enough, I could clearly detect the hatred. Dad and my grandfather were enemies of epic proportions.

I couldn't continue to listen to any more of his lies, so I clicked off the TV.

"Hey, I was watching that," said Stephan's replacement, who I would only refer to as New Guy—he wouldn't be around long, so I wouldn't bother with learning his name. Sprawled out in the plastic chair next to me, his leg bounced up and down while his jaw worked at a glob of gum. He looked more like a wannabe rock star than a guard with his tattooed arms, his long hair in a ponytail, and a smug smile that I found wildly irritating.

"Well, you're not watching it anymore," I said shortly. I was rude, but I didn't care.

"Don't you want to hear what your dad has to say?"

I didn't need to hear his speech to know what he would say: business—lies—business—lies—repeat. It was all my dad *ever* said.

"Nope," I said defiantly and marched back toward Stephan's room with Oliver and New Guy in tow—I was—eager for my best friend's company whether he wanted it or not. But when I arrived at his door, I could tell something wasn't right; the guards posted outside were standing and on full alert, and my undercover entourage wasn't even trying to be undercover. The large man who had been pretending to be a golfer— still in the same clothes from nine days ago—ushered us quickly inside the room and shut the door.

The room was filled with daisies. Hundreds of perfect, yellow-and-white blooms dangled on thin stems in pretty vases. They were everywhere. Glass containers overflowing with the delicate flowers were set on the floor, the windowsill, taking over every available space and lighting up the room. They were stunning in comparison to the mint-green walls and Stephan's completely horrified expression.

"Stephan, do you have an admirer?" I asked, but I was ignored.

His hair was sopping wet and his jaw was clenched in agitation. I turned to Anne for answers, but she was in the corner mumbling to herself and twiddling her thumbs. I noticed she had on mismatched shoes and a crazy pantsuit the color of key lime pie; I patted my chest to make sure the necklace was concealed.

"What's going on, Stephan?" Oliver asked.

"The flowers were delivered a few minutes ago. The delivery boy was questioned but knew nothing."

"And what's wrong with getting flowers?" I asked, but I was ignored yet again.

Stephan sat up a little higher on his bed, wincing. "Oliver, backup will be here to assist you in getting Kaya back to the estate, which you must do immediately."

The veins around Oliver's temples pulsated as his whole body tensed. I had to laugh. This was ridiculous. What were they worried about? They were just flowers. As I picked up a bouquet of the pretty yellow petals, key lime pie came flying at me from the corner. Anne lunged at the vase in my hand and knocked it to the floor, slicing open my palm as the glass shattered. Blood instantly gushed from my sliced skin.

"What the hell is wrong with you, Anne?" Oliver yelled as he dove to my side.

The wound stung wildly, but I was mostly in shock. "Anne?" I said, staring at my old nanny's white face, and then at the shards of glass embedded in my skin. Her cheeks had turned paper white and her eyes had glazed over.

Next to me, Oliver was seething and so filled with anger I thought he might explode. Through gritted teeth, he yelled for a nurse while gripping my wrist like a vice.

"I'm okay, Oliver," I said feebly.

Anne made a move toward me. "I'm so sorry," she said as Oliver protectively stood in front of me, staring her down until she backed away. New Guy calmly took Anne by the arm and guided her to a worn recliner in the other corner while she kept mumbling and repeating her apologies. Had she lost her mind? Had the Alzheimer's progressed that fast? As she sank down into the leather-upholstered chair, I started to worry about her sanity more than the drops of blood seeping from my wounds.

Soon, a smiling, young nurse was next to me cleaning and removing the shards of glass from my hand. A janitor tossed all the flowers in a bin and swept up the broken vase. His broom left red streaks on the floor and the sight made me woozy—I didn't do well with blood, especially my own.

"You okay, my butter bean?" Stephan asked.

He was so frail and now appeared to be so worried about me I thought he might faint. The majority of the tubes were gone but the IV line in his arm remained. He was still sick. I was supposed to be looking after him and here I was bleeding all over the place. "I'm fine," I said with as much reassurance as I could muster.

"Nurse, you got two minutes," he said impatiently to the woman digging around inside my hand.

"Relax, Sir. We don't want you to have another heart attack," she said sweetly.

He swore at her under his breath.

"Geez, it's amazing what a bunch of flowers can do to a guy," I said jokingly to the nurse, who nodded in amusement, and silence fell over the room like the calm before the storm. Stephan tapped his finger anxiously on the bedrail, New Guy chewed his gum, and Oliver fumed.

Thankfully, Anne broke the silence. "Listen Kaya," she said, "I'm sorry. I didn't want to upset or scare you, but we have reason to believe these flowers are from John Marchessa."

As the nurse nudged a piece of glass, I flinched—not from the pain, but from the mention of my grandfather. John Marchessa made himself very clear years ago. An eye for an eye, a daughter for a daughter. He blamed my dad for the death of his only child—my dear, sweet, suicidal mother—so he wanted me dead too. It was safe to say there were no warm and fuzzy family reunions in our future.

New Guy straightened up, obviously up to speed on the family drama, and checked the door to make sure it was locked. The tension in the room suddenly made the air seem dense and uncomfortably hot.

"Why do you think they are from *him*?" I asked, starting to sweat.

"Because daisies were your mother's favorite flower," said Anne. "The day your mom went into labor, John Marchessa sent thousands of them to the estate. She was so happy she wanted to name you Daisy."

"Shut up, old woman." Stephan hissed, looking like he might leap from the bed and rip her eyes out.

Anne ignored him and continued. "Your dad wouldn't let her name you *Daisy* because you already had a name."

This made no sense. "Did Dad choose to name me Kaya, then?" I asked.

Anne bit her lip. "No—someone else did."

"Annie, stop it," Stephan barked, now squeezing a corner of his bed sheet into a crumpled ball.

"She isn't a child anymore, Stephan. It's time to tell her what we suspect."

"Not what *we* suspect, what *you* suspect, which is completely irrelevant because *you're bat-shit crazy*."

Anne wasn't even remotely fazed by Stephan's insult. She stayed remarkably calm, and her eyes drifted to my chest where she knew I was concealing the necklace. She didn't seem mad, or crazy, or unreasonable, and I felt like I was listening to the Anne from my childhood—the sensible woman who made me eat my porridge and say my prayers.

"Your father didn't name you," she said, "neither did your mother. I think you were—"

"Anne, there are no facts!" Stephan interrupted. "No solid, black-and-white evidence for any of this *nonsense* rolling around in your head!"

"Stephan, you can turn a blind eye all you want, but you know as well as I do what a newborn baby looks like, and Kaya looked to be a least a week old when they put her in your arms. She was not a newborn. I realize that, yes, Lenore was pregnant—we know she went into labor—but we didn't *witness* the birth. I guarantee that stocky, brown-eyed, redheaded Lenore Marchessa did not give birth to this fine-boned, green-eyed girl!" Anne's finger hung in the air, pointing at me, and with a wink, a smile came over her face.

My mind reeled. My mother, the one who abused me and died by her own hand, wasn't really my mother? Suddenly, a sense of relief washed over me like a tidal wave. That would make sense as to why I never had an emotional connection to the woman I barely knew. Even though Stephan was adamant that Anne was crazy, her words felt like the truth— like they were the most real thing I'd heard in years.

The room was silent again except for Stephan's heavy breathing—he was avoiding my eyes and gritting his teeth. I was about to throw a thousand questions at him, but a staccato popping sound silenced the words not yet off my tongue.

I knew that sound.

"Get down!" Stephan yelled.

A woman started screaming in the hall, accompanied by the gut-wrenching sound of gunshots. Oliver and New Guy flipped the empty metal bed over onto its side and then pushed the nurse and me to the floor behind it. Stephan pulled a gun out from under his pillow, flung himself off his bed, and crouched down, his IV line taut as he aimed for the door.

I could hear the thud of large bodies hitting the floor in the hallway, and then the door burst open and bullets ripped through the air. I put my hands over my ears while Oliver pinned my body tightly to the metal bed frame. Out of the corner of my eye I watched New Guy's shoes gripping the floor, jerking as he pulled the trigger, and it was as if I had been transported back to my sixteenth birthday... *the pink restaurant... the windows shattering as a waiter held a knife to my throat... four guards dead, and my own blood a warm pool spreading beneath me...*

Then, the noise stopped. I felt something wet dripping down my cheek and Oliver dropped to his knees to face me. "Are you hurt?" he asked frantically.

"What? No, I'm fine," I stammered, staring at a wound on his hand.

The mattress was riddled with bullet holes, some big enough to see through. Had I been three inches to the right, one would have gone through my forehead. Suddenly, I felt faint.

Oliver stood and pulled the frightened nurse to her feet, then reached for me, his blood mixing with mine from the cuts on my palm. I forced my knees to extend, and then I looked up; there was blood everywhere—on the walls, the floor—and I pleaded with my stomach to not get sick.

"I got one, wounded two others," Stephan said breathlessly, his open hospital gown leaving nothing to the imagination. "Now get Kaya the hell out of here before more of those cockroaches come crawling in."

As Oliver guided me around a body that was blocking the doorway, the room started to spin. In the hall, the guards and the 'golfer' were sprawled out on the floor, creating a pattern that only death could design. Someone was screaming, an old man was hyperventilating in his wheelchair, and a doctor was calling 911.

Then I heard a voice repeating Anne's name frantically. I pulled away from Oliver and turned to see Stephan on his knees before her, shaking her, pleading with her…

"*Annie?*" he was saying, as if trying to wake her.

I wanted to go to him, but Oliver caught me by the waist and held on.

"Stephan, is she okay?" I asked, desperately trying to see through the doorway.

Stephan shook his head and crumpled to the floor. Then, I saw her, slumped over in the chair, her hair loose and hanging over her face with her hands resting on her lap like they were catching raindrops—only they were filled with blood from a hole in her chest—made by a bullet meant for me.

4

Bang Your Head

THERE WERE NO FLOWERS ON HER CASKET, ONLY LARGE GREEN-and-white hosta leaves I'd plucked from the garden. It was a small gathering, and Dad was not among us. My anger toward him and his unbelievably messed up priorities distracted me, which helped me get through the funeral—and I held onto those feelings of anger until they lowered Anne's coffin into the ground. Then, I thought my heart might break; the woman who was the closest thing I had to a mother was gone.

The whole estate was on lockdown, but I didn't care. I had no intention of leaving my room anyway. I wanted to be alone—to grieve, cry, scream—but Oliver wouldn't budge an inch from my bedside and the maids wouldn't stop prodding. So I buried myself deep under the covers, hiding and hoping to sleep away the sadness, but it lingered like one of those nightmares when you're trying to run for your life, but your legs don't work.

For days, voices drifted in and out of the room. I ignored them successfully, until one found its way through the thick, wool blanket covering my ears. The cocky, self-assured tone turned my sadness into anger, compelling me to sit upright. I blinked to make sure what I was seeing was real as a figure stood in front of the window, sunlight surrounding him like a halo—only this was certainly no angel.

"Hello, Kaya," said Dad.

He had a worried look on his face, and this pleased me to no end. His jet-black hair, the same inky color as mine, was freshly cut, and he was tanned a light golden brown, making his green eyes stand out even more underneath his heavy lashes. I placed my hand on my chest—thank goodness, the necklace was still hidden under my flannel pajamas.

"I'll leave you two alone," Oliver said politely, and he left, closing the door behind him. I stared blankly at the man I hadn't been alone with in years.

"Are you okay?" he asked.

"You missed the funeral," I snapped, hoping my voice had an edge to it.

"I'm so sorry about that, really I am. I feel terrible that I couldn't be there for you, but business…"

I put my hand up. "Yep. I get it."

He sat down on the bed next to me, sinking lightly into the floral-patterned comforter, but his posture was still straight as an arrow. Then, totally out of character, he reached out his arms and pulled me in for a hug. I stiffened with shock; I couldn't remember the last time I'd received any sort of affection from him. His arms were far nicer than the stuffy sheets and blankets I'd been using as a substitute for all these years. The smell of expensive cigars and cologne around him brought me back to my childhood. I felt myself relax, and I placed my head against his chest. All my anger disappeared. "I missed you," I admitted.

"I missed you too," he said, hugging me a little tighter. "I'm sorry I haven't been there for you, lately. I'm truly sorry."

How I needed to hear that.

He pulled away and put his hands on my shoulders, looking at me with laser focus. "I know it's been hard for you, but I promise things will get better. I'm working to get everything under control. Our lab is close to an incredible breakthrough that could change everything, Kaya. It's—"

"Stop," I said impatiently, "I don't care about business. I just care about finding out who killed Anne."

His eyelid twitched, and his left nostril flared slightly. I knew what those little ticks meant—*lying…*

"I don't know," he said flatly.

"Tell the truth," I demanded.

He dropped his hands from my shoulders and shook his head slightly in defeat. "You're a smart girl; you can see right through a lie, can't you?"

I nodded. "Yep, and with you, they occur often."

"Such a valuable gift," he muttered. As he turned his head, I noticed a new scar than ran from the middle of his jawline to his ear. How long it had been since we were in the same room? Two months?

"John Marchessa is determined to destroy me; he's aiming right for my heart…" he said, pointing a manicured finger at my chest, "which is you."

"So I've heard," I said dismally.

"Anne was in the wrong place at the wrong time."

"So, her death was courtesy of dear ol' Gramps? You're sure?"

"Police are investigating."

I knew there was something he wasn't telling me, but I also knew that when he clasped his hands together, like he had now, there was no chance of learning any more information. So I moved on to another topic—one that had been eating away at me like a slow-eroding acid. "Anne said something to me before she died—something about Mother wanting to name me Daisy, after her favorite flower..." Dad raised his eyebrow, but I took a breath and pressed on, "but you wouldn't let her because I already had a name."

His expression darkened, as if turned to stone, and he pulled away to rake his fingers through his hair. My heart sped up; Anne wasn't crazy. Dad's discomfort at the mere mention of the topic was confirmation enough.

"Just the ramblings of an old woman. Be thankful your crazy mother didn't name you Gertrude or Buckwheat," he said, feigning lightheartedness.

"Yeah," I muttered.

Dad's face softened. "Listen, I'm sorry you lost your mom at such a young age—it's not fair—but you have to know that I tried to cure her, Kaya," he said, staring out the window. "I spent a fortune on research and new treatments, but nothing worked. She didn't commit suicide because of me—no matter what Marchessa claims. She was sick. She did it to herself."

"It's not your fault," I said automatically.

"I know. But John Marchessa blames me for her death."

"Yes. *An eye for an eye.*"

"Uh hmmm." He nodded absently, and then he stood, smoothing the front of his thousand dollar pants. "Listen, Kaya, I actually came here to talk to you about something very important."

I knew it. His visit to my end of the estate wasn't to check on my mental health—that would have been too good to be true. I considered burying myself under the blankets and covering my ears to avoid hearing whatever he had to say, but he was nervous—lip twitching, nostril flaring, hands running through his hair repeatedly—and I was intrigued.

"By law I am required to inform you of a few things, and my lawyer insists that there's no time like the present," he said coolly, as I fidgeted on the edge of the bed, embarrassed that I couldn't remember the last time I'd changed my clothes. "So here goes..." He cleared his throat nervously. "Everything is yours. This estate, Eronel Industries, and its sister companies. All of it is yours. I've only been acting as the executor of the estate until you become of legal age, and then you will subsequently take over."

"What? What the—what are you saying?" I asked, wondering if I had woken up in an alternate universe.

"I am saying that you have inherited a fortune, and when you turn twenty-one, you will take control of it. The condition under which John Marchessa gave your mother the estate and Eronel, was that in the event of her death, everything would be passed down to her firstborn child— as long as the child is of sound mind, of course. If there was no child, or in the event of the child's death, all ownership would revert back to him."

"You're kidding."

"No. Lenore—your *mother*, promised me she would have this condition removed when you were born, but she never did. So I have fought against this matter in court for years, but as of last week, I've officially lost."

The bitterness in his voice was obvious. I pinched myself discreetly under the blanket to see if I was awake, but the feeling of shock, much like that of being submerged in ice-cold water, had already taken my breath away. I was completely and unfortunately awake.

Dad sighed. "So, that leaves you in the middle of a war. As long as you're alive and able to take control when you turn twenty-one, Eronel Industries and the estate will be yours to do with what you choose. But, if you die before then, John Marchessa will get it all back—which is exactly what he wants."

So that was it in a nutshell. A slippery, withered, rotten-in-the-middle nutshell. I was only protected for the sake of the business. For the money. *For greed.* I squeezed my eyes shut against the painful answer to the burning question that had been in my mind for so long. "All this time I thought Granddad just wanted revenge on you," I said, gulping as tears pushed against my eyelids.

Henry laughed. "Well, yes, he wants that too, but, mostly he's a money hungry bastard just like the rest of us. I turned Eronel into a force to be reckoned with. The failing dump of a company he gave to your mother is now a powerhouse. A game changer. He knows our research is close to giving us—and by *us* I mean *me and you*, Kaya—the control of…"

"Whoa!" I said, almost bolting off the bed. "What if I don't want control… of *anything?*" A crazy grin inched across his face—it was that evil, lopsided one that revealed his true nature. "Then, you can sign it all over to me, and you can walk away," he said smugly.

Sign it all over to him and walk away. That was exactly what he wanted. The need oozed from his repulsive pores and glowed like a radioactive dollar sign hovering over where his heart should have been. I was only important to him so that one day I could give him complete control and ownership of the business he loved more than me.

I bit my lip too hard and tasted blood. "What if, when I turn twenty-one, I keep it all for myself and decide to have nothing to do with you?" I said harshly. "What if I don't approve of your research, and instead I want to make, oh I dunno, lipstick? What if I shut down the company and turn the entire estate into a pet shelter?"

This rattled him down to his one-hundred-dollar socks. His Adam's apple bobbed a few times, and his lips thinned into a tight line. "No one could stop you," he said, "it really is all yours. But I have faith that you will make the right choice."

Well how about that. I held the keys. I could toss them over a cliff if I wanted to. We were staring at each other like gladiators in battle, and he blinked first.

"Please sign this at the bottom and initial here and here," Dad said, producing a thick batch of papers from his suit jacket. "This is to acknowledge that you understand what I have told you, and that you are aware that this conversation has been recorded."

Recorded? Asshole.

I struggled to pull air into my lungs, and then I scratched my name with his overly ornate pen on the lines he had indicated. I wished that my last name was anything other than Lowen and that my hands would stop shaking from overwhelming feeling of pure hatred I reserved for the man before me.

"You have to know, Kaya," he said and grinned, "that I do love you, and I have been making sure you are safe and properly educated, so that when the time comes, you and I can work side by side. I want that more than anything. You're smart and your ability to see through a lie is a business partner's dream—it's like winning every jackpot in Vegas. Besides, your trust fund alone could bankroll the entire research facility for a lifetime and even build new ones. It would help so many people, and it's what Lenore, your mother, truly wanted."

"Yeah, about that," I said, searching my father's face for a hint of truth, "who exactly is my birth mother?"

"Some things are best left alone," he said.

"Just tell me, who named me Kaya? What was it that Anne was trying to tell me?"

A single bead of sweat broke out on his brow and he wordlessly turned and headed for the door.

"Leave it alone," he warned, "or you could ruin everything."

5

HABITS

I'D BEEN SITTING FOR HOURS ON THE EDGE OF THE BED WHILE Oliver took up the corner of the room in a blue, velvet recliner pretending to not pay attention to me. He was freshly showered, his dark hair still damp and his skin clean and glowing. Radiohead songs were blaring from his earbuds but he was only half listening. He rightly assumed I was still upset about Anne, but I couldn't bring myself to tell him the other reason; my life was worth billions of dollars.

I realized, as I stared out the window as the end-of-summer colors swept the valley, that the small bit of love I had for my dad was now gone. The bars across my windows only cemented that fact. They were a glaring confirmation that I was not his child; I was his possession. I vowed to forever refer to him as Henry from this day forward; he didn't deserve the title of Dad.

When the sky became dark and there was nothing left to look at, I pulled the thick curtains covering my prison window shut. My legs were numb. My head hurt. And suddenly, I had to think about something else before sadness ate me alive and the walls caved in.

"I'm going swimming," I announced.

I hadn't said anything to Oliver for days besides 'leave me alone', so he practically fell out of his chair at my abrupt declaration. Standing, he looked at his watch. "No, it's after seven, and…"

Ignoring him, I grabbed a bathing suit out of my dresser and then stared him down, just *hoping* for an argument. But for the first time in ages, there wasn't.

THE POOL IN DAYLIGHT WAS INCREDIBLE, BUT AT NIGHT, IT WAS AMAZING. Perched high on the cliff next to the second terrace, it was the smallest of the three at the estate. With the blue water shimmering beneath the stars, it was only possible to see a vast expanse of black past the ornamental garden surrounding the perimeter. The sound of the river rushing below and the feel of the cool air coming off the snowy, unseen peaks of the mountains allowed me to pretend to be anywhere. Anne used to bring me here when I was a kid and out-of-control bored. She'd sit on the ledge and nag while I pretended to be a mermaid. We'd spend hours out here at night under the moon, and now, when I dipped in my toes, I could clearly picture her face in the white-and-blue tiles and clouds of steam hovering over the water.

I daydreamed I was far away from here, diving under and savoring the weightlessness of my body. I was so relieved to be alone, but when I came up for air, Oliver was taking off his shirt with the intention of joining me. He stood on the ledge next to the deep end, shivering slightly, with each muscle on his body prominently outlined as if airbrushed. He was so incredibly stunning I couldn't peel my gaze away while he slowly crept into the water. Now, instead of daydreaming, all I could think about was how I had to stay away from him.

After twenty minutes of the two of us swimming laps side by side, I stopped to rest my arms on the ledge of the pool and gently stretch out my legs. Oliver came up beside me and did the same. It was hard to keep my eyes looking straight ahead on the night sky instead of ogling his damp skin, but I figured I better keep them there as well as try to apologize.

"I'm sorry about, well… the way I have acted the last few days," I said softly so my voice wouldn't echo across the pool, "I might have gone a little crazy."

"It's okay," he said.

I contemplated telling him about the discussion I had with Henry— about the inheritance, but I had to come to terms with it first. "I know you're just looking out for me, and I'm grateful for that."

"Listen, Kaya, everyone grieves in their own way. I know you'll work it through, but you can always talk to me, all right?"

"I know. I just had to, um, deal with things. But thanks for being there for me."

He'd barely left my side for even a second. Oliver made me crazy, but at least he actually cared.

"You're most welcome," he replied, rubbing some pool water out of his eyes.

I couldn't help it—I admired the shape of his toned arms and snuck glances at the scars he'd earned by protecting me. Each one was a solid reminder of his dedication, his devotion, and how I owed him my life.

I pried my eyes away.

"Wow, the stars… the moon… they're just so beautiful tonight," I said as I looked up. In the distance, a wolf howled in agreement.

"Hmmm, yeah… very beautiful…" he said, but instead of admiring the night, his eyes were centered on me. He leaned closer, too close, and he reached for my chin, tilting my face toward his. "Kaya, I care about you a lot," he said bluntly.

I wanted to laugh but the look on his face was dead serious.

"I care about you too," I said as politely as I could manage.

"I've wanted to tell you for a long time," he said, his knees now grazing mine. "When I thought I might lose you…" His voice grew quiet, and his fingers gently traced the scar on my neck, sending a jolt down my spine. "I realized *how much* I cared."

I anxiously looked toward the security cameras; were *they* watching? Was Old Carl sitting at his desk, shaking his head and zooming in as to not miss the action? Getting ready to send more guards, or worse yet, file a report to Henry?

Then I noticed that the red lights, the teeny ones on the cameras that always glowed, weren't glowing at all. In seventeen years, I'd never encountered this. Obviously, Oliver noticed too or he wouldn't be acting so boldly. New Guy was parked in a lawn chair a foot from the ledge of the pool, and he seemed oblivious to everything except his phone. We were, for the most part, *alone.*

Oliver's nose was now inches from mine, and a shiver shook my entire body as he reached his hand around and nestled it onto the small of my back. He held me steady, and then carefully pulled me tightly to him. I could barely breathe—this was wrong. Our chests were touching in the water and the heat of his thighs against mine brought out a consuming desire to let my hands wander over his skin. My head was yelling *no*, yet I couldn't convince my body to even *try* to move away.

"Kaya, you need to know this," Oliver said, gulping hard. "I'll protect you and be there for you no matter what. Bodyguard, friend or otherwise… I'm yours. Forever and always."

The intensity of his words rattled my chest. They were real, they were honest, and nobody had ever said anything like that to me before. He had avoided the L-word, but it was implied nonetheless. Before I could stop myself, I nervously uttered the only thing that came to mind. "Oliver, you have—um—a great smile."

His face lit up. "And you… make me crazy."

With a hearty laugh, he picked me up effortlessly, lifted me over his head, and then launched me into the air like a cannonball.

When I came up for air, I saw that the waves had splashed New Guy and his freshly lit smoke. Oliver was grinning ear to ear and dove away, disappearing into the depths of the deep end, while New Guy shook water off his phone and tossed the now-wet cigarette into the shrubs.

"Could you guys be more careful? Man, I've only got four smokes left," he said irritably.

Oliver was swimming back to me, the moonlight reflecting off his back, and I knew I had to get away before I said or did anything more than I already had. So I yelled at New Guy for littering and hopped out of the pool. Throwing on my housecoat, I complained loudly about picking up his trash.

I continued to pretend that I was very concerned about the garbage, effectively avoiding Oliver, and tiptoed across the freezing cement and into the garden. I pushed aside some thick cedar shrubs and found a slew of discarded cigarette butts behind them, the moonlight making the white tubes easy to spot. As I plucked them from between the railings in the old iron fence, I noticed what looked like a hinge with rivets and bubbly orange bits of rust on the thick part of the railing. About one foot up, there was another. Was this a gate? I had been in this place hundreds of times and never noticed one before.

Placing the disgusting butts in my fleece pocket, I glanced behind me. Oliver was still swimming, and New Guy was drying off his phone; they weren't paying attention to me. I reached around the rail and was surprised to find a handle. I gripped it hard and pushed. At first, nothing happened, so I put my shoulder against the metal for more leverage, and sure enough, it opened. No flashing lights or alarms went off so I pushed it all the way open, hoping Oliver didn't hear the whining squeak of the rusty hinges. Carefully and tentatively, I stepped forward and found myself standing on the edge of the cliff looking down at the Bow River shimmering hundreds of feet below—one more step and I'd be fish food. But, I assumed that if I crawled along the fence, carefully, it would lead me into the next garden—the one bordering the north section of the estate. My guess was that this fence probably rounded a corner at some point and ended up squarely in the middle of the L-shaped building. That was an area that was boarded up and strictly off limits because Henry thought it was haunted. Now I realize that was just a story meant to keep me from wanting to investigate as a child. Completely empty and forgotten, it was a strictly forbidden place. I wasn't allowed to set foot anywhere near it.

Huh.

"Kaya, what are you doing over there?" Oliver yelled.

I nearly jumped out of my skin, startled by the sudden attention. For some reason, my discovery felt rather devious. Wheels started turning. Plans started forming. I wondered if this was a way out—a way to escape for an hour or two.

"Kaya!" he yelled again.

"Coming, I'm just getting some leaves for my scrapbook," I replied, and then I pulled the gate shut, letting the shrubs fall back into place.

I SHIVERED UNCONTROLLABLY ON THE LONG WALK BACK TO MY ROOM while Oliver lectured me about wandering off. It went in one ear and out the other. My discovery of the gate and the lingering feeling of how his body felt against mine in the pool pretty much obliterated my defense system. And that was bad, bad, bad.

New Guy was on night duty and stationed in the hall, taking up his favorite spot on the leather couch. He'd just cracked a fresh can of coke when I stopped in front of him before going to my room. "I have a gift for you," I said sweetly, and his eyes widened as I reached into my house-coat pocket. "I picked some nice things out of the shrubs." I placed all his gross cigarette butts in his hand.

"Ugh, so not cool!" he said, completely offended.

"Neither is littering."

He sighed and shook his head. "Point taken."

I was expecting an argument, or swearing, or some sort of heated discussion, but instead, he calmly wiped off his hands and relaxed back into the leather sofa with his iPod. "Iron Maiden's *Piece of Mind*," he said loudly as the voice piping through his ear buds soared into the stratosphere, "the concert was amazing! Man, Kaya, you'd probably love this record."

Oliver found all of this extremely hilarious. I wasn't sure if it was the suggestion that I would like rock music, or that 'Princess Kaya'—a name he called me when I complained about getting my hands dirty—had been picking up garbage. I wanted to ask, but it was so rare to see him smile. He was laughing when I said goodnight and still giggling when he wandered off down the hall. He would be back on duty at midnight.

I had six hours.

I ORDERED STEPHAN A POT OF TEA AND GAVE HIM HIS PAIN MEDS. WITHIN an hour, he was sound asleep and snoring loud as a chainsaw. Using his cell phone, I arranged for a driver to meet me at the old lobby. I told greedy driver Dan—one of the estates oldest employees who was well known for being easily bribed—that there'd be a huge tip in it for him if he kept our outing a secret. In the past, he'd snuck Stephan and me pizza, but it cost us an arm and a leg. I took what cash I had and some jewelry, just in case the cash wasn't enough, and wrapped my purse and shoes in a towel. Then, I put on the longest housecoat I had and snuck out into the hallway. New Guy was still stretched out on the sofa. He was casually blowing smoke out of the window and he bolted straight off the couch when he saw me—I caught him breaking a major house rule. Smoking was instant grounds for getting fired.

His eyes widened in horror. "Uh, hey Kaya, uh… ma'am…" he stuttered and quickly dropped the lit cigarette into his pop can. He'd undone his ponytail and long golden locks flipped up around his shoulders—the feminine hairstyle was such a strange contrast to his unshaven cheeks and tattooed arms. I put my hand up to stop him as his face contorted in an effort to come up with some lame excuse.

"Hey, don't worry about it," I said, and his eyebrows arched. I realized his gross smoking habit and my desire to escape could be mutually beneficial. "How about we give each other a bit of a break with the whole *rules* thing for tonight?" I said deviously.

He eyed me curiously. "What are you proposing?"

"Well, I'm going to go to the pool… again… to meet Oliver. We felt like swimming some more—*alone*. You should probably stay here and watch over Stephan, but make sure to keep it really quiet so he can sleep. I'll only be gone a few hours."

"Meeting Oliver eh?" he said, straightening up with a mischievous glint in his eyes.

"And it's already been cleared with the security office," I lied.

He pulled a fresh smoke from his pack. I lit it for him.

"I think we have an understanding," he said, blowing rings of smoke out the window, "just don't be too long."

Well, that was easy.

The second hall guard's extreme drowsiness and crumpled tissue collection suggested he'd had a little too much cold medicine. He didn't need much convincing. The next two guards questioned why I was alone, so I pulled out the girl card: female issues. Having to change bathing suits because of that time of the month— instant hall pass.

I used Stephan's security code to unlock the pool door and breathed a sigh of relief when it opened. Even though cameras were back on, it was colder now, and steam hung in the air above the water like a thick cloud. I knew from being in the security room as a kid that this greatly obstructed the view.

I stashed my robe and towel under the bench, put on my shoes, and quickly made my way through the shrubs to the gate. It swung open with a gentle shove, and I stepped through—mindful that a crisp breeze could push me to my death—and then I carefully turned around to hold on to the iron bars. Was I crazy? Was this something I really had to do?

A resounding *yes* reverberated in every corner of my mind.

I slowly crept along the edge of the fence, deciding not to look down or behind me. The earth under my feet was becoming narrower the farther I went, and soon I was on my tip toes, dancing on barely an inch of ground and praying none of the rails I was clinging to were loose. My hands had become numb from the cold, and just when I thought I might have to turn back, the fence rounded a corner and I was safely standing in the long-forgotten courtyard. I made my way through patches of overgrown rose bushes that tried to claw at me with every step. Dead flowers pointed eerily toward the ground and were so creepy I began to question my sanity; if anything happened to me, no one would even know where to look.

Once through the garden, I faced the side of the massive stone-walled building that stretched four stories over my head with dark windows that looked like squinting eyes. The rotting boards covering the closest basement window came off with a light pull, and I shone the light from my cell phone into what looked to have been an office. I put my legs through the window, jumped down, and landed on a desk, hoping an animal that was nothing more than a mouse scurried away. Following the exit signs through the carpeted hallways, thick with dust and too many locked doors to count, I made my way to the secondary lobby.

It was creepier than the dead garden.

Moonlight shone through the massive windows, lighting up the marble room where portraits of the frozen faces of relatives past and present hung from the walls. The eyes depicted in each of the paintings appeared as if they were staring down, guarding the hotel. Not one of them was smiling. I shouldn't have been shocked to see my mother's face among them—looking nothing like my own—but the sight still took my breath away. At least the haunting guilt of not feeling any emotion for her was gone. In my heart of hearts, as I stared up at her stone-faced expression, I knew we weren't related.

The outbound lobby doors were impossible to open with thick plywood nailed across them in large sheets, but the small valet parking door was easy to unlock. I slid the deadbolt to the side and headed toward the limo that waited at the bottom of the steps. I knew Dan wouldn't let me down; he was a good old boy from down South—as he loved to say—

and he'd do anything to fund a gambling addiction that was legendary among the other drivers.

"Heyo, Ms. Kaya," he said, winking and tipping his driving hat respectfully.

"Hello, Dan," I replied as confidently as I could, quickly climbing into the back of the car. My heart was racing so fast I thought I might pass out. I half expected the world to come crashing down as I put a hefty wad of bills in his outstretched hand. "Please take me to The Derrick Bar; it's a few blocks from the hospital."

"*The Derrick*? Huh. I thought maybe ya just had a hankering fer some pizza, or be wanting to hit the McD's drive through or som'n." Dan's accent slurred past his broken front teeth as he shoved the money into his shirt. He scratched his balding head and made no effort to move the car forward.

"I'm meeting a friend tonight," I said firmly, my stomach churning from anxiety and the scent of those horrid tree-shaped air fresheners he always had hanging from the rear view mirror. "Take me to The Derrick, please."

He pondered this so hard I thought his brain might catch fire. "Uh, it's not safe fer you to be out by yerself, you bein alone and all. Mr. Oliver would have my head for this."

Funny. Dan was more worried about Oliver's reaction than the wrath of Henry. I pulled out more bills and tossed them onto the front seat. "Don't worry. I'll be fine."

"Did I tell ya that Georgia needs braces?" he said greedily, eyeing the extra cash. "She's so pretty, but she gots them teeth, bad ones, ya know? Poor thing, lips is all sticking out here and there. And Jeremy, well, he's all about the acting; some school in New York has caught his eye."

I opened the clasp to the bracelet I was wearing and slipped it off my wrist. It was a gift from Dad—er, *Henry*—and I couldn't care less about it now. "Here, you can buy braces for all your kids *and* their friends with this," I said, and then I dropped the gold-and-sapphire jewelry onto the seat.

"Whoa there, K, giddy up! Now we're talkin' in the same language," he said happily and radioed security. "Yeah, hey, it's Dan. Can ya open the north gate? I'm a headin' to town for a quick sec. Leah got herself a tummy ache and I gotta check on her. I'll be back in two shakes of a whore's butt."

A familiar voice replied through the car radio—ancient, scratchy— and, apparently, wise to Dan's addictions. "Yeah, fine," said Old Carl. "Just don't spend it all on the slots, okay? Groceries are always a good idea. Kids like to eat."

I pictured Old Carl sitting at his desk in the security office and chewing gum like it was an overcooked steak. His favorite chair would be squeaking and complaining under his weight, and his goofy grin would be shadowed by a fishing cap that was permanently glued to his head.

"Thanks Carl," Dan said with a sly wink as he looked at me in the rear-view mirror.

"Yeah, yeah, whatever." Carl sighed. "Pick me up some smokes and a bag of Doritos. And don't friggin' forget this time."

Dan hung up the radio and started the whisper-quiet engine, and then we were on the highway heading to town.

Easy.

It was amazing how people's bad habits had affected me so positively.

6

So a Girl Walks Into a Bar...

She was impossible to miss with her neon-pink hair styled to stand on end a foot off her head. A man in raw denim was whispering in her ear, and by the way she was tapping her long nails on the bar counter, I could tell she was bored to tears.

Suddenly, I was nervous. I had been so focused on escaping that I didn't give any thought as to what to do once I got to The Derrick. I felt my cheeks flush when I bumped into someone playing pool and made my way through the crowd.

"Hey there," I said, tapping Angela on the shoulder.

She whipped around to see me, grateful for the interruption. I noticed a new tattoo on her neck, a pink cactus the same color as her hair, and as I stared she broke into a huge grin.

"Babes!" she said, followed by a kiss to my cheek, "What took you so long? I've been waiting here for hours. You said you would call if you were gonna be late!"

I looked behind me, wondering if she was talking to someone else. "Huh?" was all I could say.

She grabbed my arm and pulled me to her side. The man in denim, who must have bathed in a lot of cheap cologne, looked as confused as I was.

"Glen, this is my *girlfriend*, Kaya," Angela said.

Glen took a step back to examine me and his hawk-like nose wrinkled. Then I got it; Angela was pretending that she and I were a couple so Glen would leave her alone. I saw this in a movie once, so I had an idea of how to play along. "Hi Glen, nice to meet you," I said, extending my hand.

The jerk completely ignored me. "Angela really, this is your *girlfriend*? As in, you're a *couple*? She doesn't seem like your type," he said, eying my makeup-free skin, lack of tattoos, and ultra-boring T-shirt and jeans. I looked like a napkin standing next to a Picasso.

"She's *exactly* my type," Angela grinned, and then she turned and kissed me full on the lips.

My first thought was that she tasted like cotton candy; my second thought was, *yuck*. I kind of stood there, not sure what to do. I'd never been kissed before—it was disappointing.

Glen shook his head in disbelief, and then he wandered off.

When she pulled away, Angela burst out laughing. "Oh my God! Thanks for playing along. That was hilarious! He was driving me crazy, but I didn't want to hurt his feelings because he's a friend of the boss." She waved at the bartender. Suddenly, a drink was in my hand, and we clinked glasses. "So, you snuck out, huh?" she said with a grin.

"I didn't have to sneak," I said, but I was a bad liar.

"Right," she said with a smirk. "So, what brings you here?"

"Well, you said to come and visit you sometime, so I did."

"Oh yeah, that's right! And Mr. Serious ... where is he tonight?" She scanned the room hopefully.

"Oliver doesn't know I'm here, and he might be a little upset if he found out." I checked my watch, feeling like Cinderella having to be back before midnight.

She lifted her eyebrows. "Upset?"

"Yeah. He's a little bit, um, possessive," I admitted.

"Oh. But I thought you weren't dating..."

"That's right. We're just friends."

She waved at the bartender again for a refill and tossed him a ten-dollar bill. "You know," she said, "I'm a little older than you—been around the block a bunch of times—and I've never seen a man look at a woman the way he looks at you. Surely, you know he's after a lot more than friendship, right? He acts like he owns you. I mean, he seems rather obsessed to be honest... he watches your every move. I don't think you even realize it."

"You got all that from serving us coffee?"

"And reading his body language and gorgeous lips," she sighed.

I downed my drink to try to rid myself of the memory of Oliver, his skin damp in the moonlight at the pool. It didn't work. "So, where are you from?" I asked, changing the subject.

Angela laughed. I guess I amused her. "I'm an Aussie."

"Oh."

She shook her head. "Oh? That's it? What does that mean?"

"Well, you don't talk like one. I mean, you have a bit of a strange accent, but you've never said 'g'day mate', or 'shrimps on the barbie', or anything like that."

She laughed with a snort. "You're hilarious!"

"I'm glad you think so."

"You talk strangely, too," she said with a grin.

"I do?"

"Yeah, sometimes it's like typical teenager vocab, but then you'll completely contradict it with some old-style English. You're like an old broad hiding in a young body. It's weird, but kinda cool."

"Oh." I grinned.

"Half the working population in this town is from Australia. I wanted to be different, fit in to my own category and stand out a bit, you know? So I lost the accent."

I took in the full effect of Angela—head-to-toe polished and shiny with almost every square inch of skin, except her face, decorated with permanent ink. "Yeah, good idea. That pink hair and playboy figure makes you a total wallflower," I said, teasing.

She laughed hard at that, slapping her leg and making an entire table turn around to look at us. "Seriously though, why are you here, hun?" she said when she got control of herself. "Cause it's not to find out where I'm from."

"I just really need someone to talk to," I confided, "I have no one. All my friends are, um... well they are—"

I didn't know how to finish the sentence; all my friends are what? Men? Dead? Hired guards? Or should I admit that I really don't have any at the cost of sounding like a loser? Angela noticed my internal struggle.

"Let me guess, *All Your Friends are Funeral Singers*." She smiled.

I laughed, catching the reference. "Angela Bettis was in that movie! I loved it. I loved *her*. She's so great."

"It's one of my faves, but I've yet to meet someone who's seen it." Angela beamed. "Did you know she was also in *Girl, Interrupted*?"

"She played Janet. It's a classic."

Angela nodded with a gleam in her eyes; we had a connection that was impossible to deny. Never in my life had anything like this that happened to me. I wondered if this easy, relaxed banter and desire to spill one's guts was what it was always like when talking between best friends. I longed for that.

We laughed at our favorite, strange movies and I confessed my love of anything with zombies. She lifted her skirt to show me Bub from *Day of the Dead* tattooed on her thigh.

"Well, we could discuss movies all night, but you have something you need to talk about, and I think it has something to do with your hot *friend* Oliver. So, Docta Angela is in da house. Spill it," she said as she smiled and ordered more drinks.

The lights were dim, the music just loud enough so we wouldn't be overheard, and Angela was willing to listen. I started with light stuff. I got past the who's who and what's what, and then I proceeded to pour my heart out. Once the words started, they were like water flowing from a tap that wouldn't shut off. Of course, I left out my last name and any particulars that would give away who I really was. So as far as Angela knew, I was just an average wealthy brat with daddy issues and boy problems. Her advice was sincere, her reassuring pats on the hand were kind, and when I said I had to leave, she reached for me like a worried sister might.

"You gonna be okay, hun?" she asked.

"Yes. Perfectly fine. "

"Well, come back again. I like you," she said, then wrapped her arms around me.

"I'll try," I said with the dark realization that I'd probably never see her again.

"By the way, Kaya, you do realize there's a difference between obsession and love, right?"

I looked at her questioningly.

"Let's just say that if you go missing, I'll tell the police to check Oliver's freezer."

She had a slight smile on her face, but I knew she was dead serious.

"If I go missing, you can have my backpack and running shoes," I said.

THE DRINKS DIDN'T FULLY HIT UNTIL I CRAWLED INTO BED, AND THEN the room started to spin. I started drifting on imaginary waves into a nightmare...

Angela and I were holding onto each other and laughing as we started our descent on a roller coaster, but this was no theme park. Our hair blew in the wind and we waved our arms recklessly in the air as we sped through caves and up mountains toward Oliver, a growing shadow in the distance. A smile dominated his face and his teeth glowed like diamonds, becoming almost blinding the closer we got. Crashing to a halt, I let go of Angela and dove into his arms, and then I pushed my hands up the back of his shirt. His skin was smooth and firm under my fingertips. He bent down to kiss me, but our lips never touched... he was pulled away and was pushed to his knees. I looked up to see Henry hovering over us, laughing as a hundred men dressed in black opened fire. Suddenly, bullets burst through Oliver's chest and blood, birthday cake, and yellow daisies spewed everywhere. Henry laughed and pointed while Oliver died right before my eyes...

I sat straight up in bed. My face was soaked with tears and sweat.

"Whoa, Kaya, it's okay!" Oliver's hands were on my shoulders. Had he been sitting beside me all night? The window was open and the curtains swayed gently, letting sunlight into the room. The spine of his new book was cracked and laid on the nightstand. "It was just a dream," he said softly.

I stared intently at his face. The gory vision of him dying was so vivid I blinked a few times to make it go away. He wiped my cheek with his sleeve.

"What was it about?" he asked, and then he sat down next to me, the bed drooping under his weight.

"Oh... nothing really. Just a dumb dream."

He wore a concerned expression as his eyes searched mine. "Are you sick, Kaya? It's eleven thirty. You haven't slept this late in years."

Sick? Yes. Maybe that's what I would be today. I forced my eyes to remain locked on his so he wouldn't think I was lying. "Yeah, I don't feel so great. I'll be going to bed early tonight."

I ASKED DAN TO WAIT FOR ME IN THE CAR BEHIND THE DERRICK BAR because it was too busy out front. Every table was occupied, the music was loud, and there were people dancing—I hadn't even noticed there was a dance floor before. Even though it felt like a completely different place, Angela was at her usual spot at the bar with a group of men clinging to her words like the yellow mini dress clinging to her thighs. I wondered how on earth she'd sit down without completely exposing herself, and I'm sure the ogling men thought the same.

"Kaya! You came back!" she said excitedly after I made my way toward her. "Let me introduce you to my friends!"

Introductions were a waste of time. Not one of her admirers averted their eyes long enough to acknowledge my presence. I felt wildly inferior, and Angela noticed.

"Have a drink," she said and handed me a glass of something clear and vile.

I nervously took a big sip, wondering if I'd made a huge mistake by coming here. It was too busy, too loud. What if someone figured out who I was? I had done my best to look as plain as possible, wearing a T-shirt and jeans, black ball cap, no makeup, and hair in a long braid. But standing in front of Angela, I wondered if my choice in disguise had actually made me stick out like a sore thumb. "I didn't think it would be so crowded in here," I said nervously.

"Well, yeah, it's the big after party for The Death Race, the whole town is celebrating," Angela said excitedly.

"The Death Race? Was that today?"

"Man, you really do live under a giant rock, don't you?" she teased. "They've got bands playing at the square, and we might go later. You should come with—" she stopped short and pointed to my stomach. "Hey, you're bleeding from somewhere, hun."

I looked down and saw streaks across the bottom half of my shirt. Before I could say a word, Angela was whisking me off to the bathroom to inspect the damage.

"Geez, did you lose a fight with a cat?" she asked.

I gently pulled my shirt up, discovering scratches that ran from my ribs to my belly button and blood that had dried in crusty, brown patches. "I must have caught myself on a damn rose bush. I can't believe I didn't notice."

I felt like an idiot. Angela dabbed the skin around the wounds with wet paper towel, but her attempt at cleaning me up only turned the shirt into a damp, brown mess and now the scratches were really starting to sting.

"I think I better go home," I said, snatching the paper towel from her hands.

"What? Hey no way! We can fix this!"

"But I shouldn't be here, Angela. There are too many people, and if Oliver found out…"

"Hey, it's all right. Relax. Normally, people get out of their bedrooms once in a while, ya know." She smiled and took hold of my hand, her cold, thin fingers holding mine tightly. "Now c'mon, let's take that fancy ride you used to 'not sneak out' and go to my place. I'll fix you up good as new."

I pulled away. "No, I really shouldn't."

Her silver painted fingernails dug into the skin of my palm. "Kaya," she said, "you have to take *some* control of your life, and you deserve to have fun. Besides, look at these guns…" She flexed her tiny, tattooed biceps. "I'm filling in for Mr. Serious tonight."

AFTER PAYING HIM EVEN MORE TO KEEP HIM QUIET AND DRIVE WITHOUT question, Dan called Old Carl in security and rambled off some incredibly ridiculous excuse for being late getting back to the estate. With the last of my rings in his hand, he reluctantly took us to Angela's apartment, just minutes away. I followed her through dark halls covered in peeling wallpaper and climbed the stairs to her third floor apartment. The smell in the decrepit building was so horrendous I had to convince myself not to turn back. Thankfully, once inside, Angela's suite was nothing like the rest of the building. It was tidy and clean, and she'd done her best to decorate it with yellow paint and flowery-blue curtains.

"Cheers to new friendships," she said, grabbing a clear bottle off a weathered coffee table. She took a long swig, and then she handed it to me. I could barely keep down a sip.

"What is this stuff?" I squeaked out and handed it back.

"Dress remover, life-of-the-party maker, liquid-courage giver, or rosebush-scratch-healer—also known as gin."

My throat was on fire. "It's terrible. Are you sure this isn't the stuff you use to clean the bathroom?"

"Give it time, young grasshopper," she smiled. "Now, let's get you a new outfit!"

She sifted through a massive rack of clothes that took up almost the entire living room—which I soon realized was also the bedroom—and I had the feeling I was about to become a living Barbie doll. It was Stephan's dream to make me look girly with makeup and designer clothes. He'd be all over this like hairspray on a Texas housewife.

"Try this on," Angela ordered, and she tossed me a pretty indigo-blue dress.

I pulled off my jeans, tossed the ripped shirt into her garbage can, and pulled the garment down over my head.

"Whoa, that fits you perfectly," she said happily. "The color compliments your crazy pale skin and makes those green peepers of yours pop. I wonder—black shoes or gold? I'm a size eight, and you look like a seven... and so incredibly fit. You must work out a lot. Running? Pilates? Hiking?"

"Uh huh," I mumbled, only half listening. I was looking out the window while she dug around for accessories to match the dress, and I was mesmerized by the suspicious-looking people on the street below. "Why'd you choose to live here?" I asked.

"Some people aren't as fortunate as you are, Kaya. This is the best I can do right now on my own."

Why did I say that? "Oh my gosh! I'm so sorry; I didn't mean to offend you... I just... well..." I stammered as I tried to pry my foot out of my mouth.

"I get it. You don't know much about the real world, which makes sense. You haven't lived in it," she smiled, holding up a pair of blue stilettos that looked more like death traps than shoes.

I shook my head, silently agreeing with her assumption of me. No, I guess I hadn't.

"Yeah, sometimes I forget what your last name is," she muttered.

What? My heart jumped into my throat. I'd been so careful to not let on who I was, and I knew for a fact I had never said it. There hadn't been a picture taken of me in years, and if you asked most people in town, they thought I was just a myth. Did she know I was Kaya Lowen? I gulped hard and tried to play it cool. "What do mean my *last name?*" I asked carefully.

"Listen darling, five minutes into our conversation last night, I figured out who you were. You spilled your guts to me, remember? And your situations are a bit, *unique.* I may appear a bit, uh… different, but I'm not stupid. Put two and two together and you get… well… Kaya *Lowen.*"

My mind raced and the gin came up in my throat. "Oh my God. I'm not supposed to be out on my own, there are people who… don't like me. You have no idea—"

"You don't have to explain anything to me—you already did that. I had to read between the lines somewhat—but honestly, hun, just so you know, your last name means nothing to me. I liked you the first time we met—when you and Oliver came in the bar that night and you tried to order organic fruit. Now I just feel sorry for you. What you've got going on is no way to live."

She put her hand on my cheek and thoughtfully pushed back my hair, just like Oliver did, only with her it was… nice.

"Now, quit worrying about nothing, and let's go out and have some fun." She grinned.

I was still stunned as she fussed with my hair. All I could think about was how I had given myself away and put her in danger. I liked her. I didn't want her to disappear if Henry thought she was a threat. "You look beautiful," she said as she turned me toward the mirror.

"Angela, please, just don't say anything to anyone, okay? Don't tell anyone you ever met me, or you could—"

She put her finger to my lips, and then she stood beside me. Our reflections were so vastly different. It wasn't just our clothes, body shape, hair, or tattooed skin. It was our attitudes. Angela looked strong and fierce, like she could handle just about anything thrown her way, and I looked fragile. Scared.

"Listen, you have my word, Kaya, as a friend. I promise I won't tell anyone who you are, or say anything about you to anybody, all right?" She handed me the gin with a sly smile. "More importantly though, we could probably use a mixer for this, yeah?"

I nodded, and she wandered off to the fridge. As she dug around in the kitchen, I slipped off my jewelry and placed it on the wobbly coffee table. She could sell the earrings and move out of here if she wanted to, and the bracelet would probably be worth enough to buy a...

"You don't have to bribe me to keep quiet," she said, startling me.

I looked up to see her holding two glasses of orange juice. Her hazel eyes drifted from the jewelry, and then back to me.

"It's not a bribe, honestly, Angela. I just realized how stupid I am and how bad this looks. I told the guards I had swimming lessons so I could sneak out, and here I am wearing jewelry. It would be a dead giveaway if they noticed it when I went back, and I didn't bring a purse, so I really need you to keep this stuff for me. Do you mind?"

I was rambling, fearful I'd offended her. She set the glasses down, and within seconds the cheap, plastic baubles hanging from her ears were tossed into the garbage can and the gold and diamond doves Henry had given me years ago were fastened to her ears. I helped lock a thin band of gold around her wrist and she admired herself in the mirror.

"I suppose I could keep these if you really want me too. Maybe they'll bring me good luck."

"Everyone can use a bit of that," I smiled.

"Is that why you always wear that weird necklace? Is it a good luck charm? Because it doesn't match anything I've seen you wear, except maybe those hideous yoga pants."

I patted the silver pendant on my chest. "It's special, but I don't think it's lucky."

"Well then, here's to friends, faith, zombie movies, and gin," she said, handing me a drink, "things a girl can *really* count on."

DAN'S EYES BULGED WHEN HE SAW ME IN THE TOO TIGHT, TOO SHORT, blue dress, and if it weren't for Angela's encouragement, I never would've gotten out of the car. Like a proud Mama, she re-introduced me to her friends at the bar, and this time, they paid attention. Too much attention. It was strange being noticed for my body because it was so completely new to me, but it did give me a rush of confidence—something I desperately needed.

Eight of us squeezed into a booth meant for four while a cocky man named Barry boasted relentlessly. He was tall and sinewy with a rather sinister look about him, and the tip of his nose moved, much like a rabbit's, when he spoke. He had run The Death Race and wanted everyone to know. I was glued to the conversation.

"Yep, they blew the whistle at nine in the morning yesterday, and man, I gotta tell ya, I was ready. I trained hard. I didn't even have beer for six months! I finished at twelve twenty-five this afternoon. I kicked that race's ass!"

He threw a fist in the air and whooped. Angela yawned.

"Only the bravest and strongest can finish a twenty-four hour race like that," he bragged.

"Only the craziest and dumbest would even enter," said a bearded man from across the table. Barry laughed and *accidently* brushed my chest in an attempt to fist bump him.

"What about women? Were there any who finished?" I asked.

Barry scoffed like I had asked a stupid question. "Oh. I dunno—maybe one or two. It's just not a race for chicks."

Angela snapped. "Barry, you are such a pig-headed jerk! Last year, a woman kicked the crap outta the dudes in that race! Alissa St. Laurent from Edmonton finished first. Show some respect!"

"Yeah, Barry, you pig!" said a blonde I hadn't even realized was at our table.

Barry rolled his eyes—I remembered seeing that exact look on Henry's face years ago when I had asked if I could run in the race. He also told me it was no race for a girl.

I was eager to know more about the race, so I hurled questions at Barry faster than he could answer them. What gear did he take? How often did he rest? How many people finished? What about bears? How did you run in the dark? I was fascinated by his answers, awed by his injuries. I knew the race was an annual event, but I had never talked to someone who'd actually participated. I was so enthralled I barely noticed the group had dissipated, leaving Angela and me alone with Barry. When he pulled off his shoes to show me his bruised, swollen feet and missing toenails, Angela walked away, completely disgusted.

"That must be the most incredible feeling, being on your own and making it to the end with so many odds against you, only relying on yourself," I said.

"Yep, it sure is. But you want to know the best part?" He leaned in close, flexing every muscle as his eyes lingered on the lowest point of my V-neck dress. "I get to hang out with hot chicks like you afterward."

I was interested in what he had to say, but not *him*. I nervously laughed, not sure what else to do. I wanted him to keep talking about

The Death Race, but I didn't want to lead him on. Thankfully, Angela intervened and dragged me to the dance floor. Someone gave me a little glass of an amber-colored liquid that tasted like fire.

"Careful honey, that'll knock you flat on your ass," Angela warned, and then she threw her arms up over her head and howled to the music. I did the same. It felt so good to be free and to let loose. The lights spinning over our heads and the closeness of so many bodies—it was a rush. I danced until beads of sweat dripped down my back. Every once in a while, I noticed Barry's eyes wander down to my hemline, and I remembered to pull down my dress. Music pulsed steadily through the crowed room until a ballad nearly cleared the floor, but Angela and I kept on dancing, giggling, and twirling each other around like arthritic old people.

"Why do you have pink hair?" I slurred into her ear as we swayed.

She laughed. "It's my secret weapon."

"Of course. You know, you were my first kiss," I admitted, shocked how the words just fell out of my mouth.

A sly smile came over Angela's face, and her hands moved down my arms and to my waist, and then she gently pulled my hips toward hers. "First kiss, eh? Well, I could also be your second and third. You know, I kinda like you, Kaya," she said.

She was about to kiss me again, for real, and I panicked. "Oh. I um… I don't like girls. I mean, no, I like girls but not in the way you might like… I mean as friends yeah, but not…"

She laughed, not offended by my jumbled words. "Can't blame a girl for trying," she said sweetly and then twirled me away, accidentally right into Barry's clammy hands.

His breath stunk of beer, and a foul, sweaty odor lurked on his skin. My stomach turned.

"I think I need to sit down," I said.

He pressed his hand into the small of my back, and his mouth grazed my ear. "You're a very pretty girl."

Then his hands wandered toward my butt. I pushed him away. "Listen, I hope I didn't give you the wrong impression when we were talking back there. I was interested in hearing about the race, but I'm not interested in having a boyfriend."

He roughly pulled me back toward him. "And I'm not interested in having a girlfriend, but that doesn't mean we can't fool around."

He hand was on my back again, moving lower and tugging at the hem of my short dress, and before I knew it, his sweaty hand was gripping my butt cheek. I shoved him backward as hard as I could.

"Bitch, you're not going to get any better than tonight!" He hissed, and then he yanked me toward him like I was a rag doll. I stumbled, cursing the high heels, and fell into him, his arms holding me with crushing force. He pressed his groin against me. "Now, let's dance," he ordered.

I could feel the bulge in his pants, and I thought I might throw up. "Stop it," I repeated, cursing the booze for making me weak. I could hear Angela's voice just above the music. She was yelling, but I couldn't make out what she was saying. When Barry turned away in an effort to ignore her, what I saw over his shoulder made my heart stop.

It was Oliver.

In a blur, his hands were around Barry's neck, making the veins in his forehead bulge like skinny worms. Barry was lifted, feet dangling inches off the ground, and now his face had started to turn purple.

"Let him go, Oliver, please!" I begged.

Barry's arms flailed, helpless to stop the assault.

"Please, Oliver… he's just a stupid, harmless jerk. Let him go!"

Oliver shook Barry like a dog might shake a small rodent. His eyes were wild and the muscles in his throat had pulled into tight ropes. Someone yelled for security. The music stopped. The lights went up.

"Oliver Bennet, you let him go right *now!*" I yelled. Oliver blinked rapidly as life was being choked out of Barry. "Or I will never forgive you for as long as I live!" I screamed.

That got his attention.

Barry was dropped to the floor, and Oliver turned to stare at me, his anger lingering just below the surface like a bomb about to blow.

"I'm sorry," I said, fighting back tears.

He was breathing heavily, raising his shoulders up and down, and his hands were balled into fists. "It's not your fault this scumbag can't take no for an answer," he huffed.

Barry got to his feet and, quite ridiculously, decided to reclaim his masculinity, but Oliver blocked what was intended to be a punch. He then used Barry's arm as leverage, slamming him down face-first onto a bar table. As Barry lay semi-conscious, the bar staff surrounded Oliver like a pack of wolves, though wisely cautious about making a move.

"Guys, don't worry about him. It's all good," Angela said nervously. "They're leaving, right, Oliver? You're *leaving*…" she pleaded.

But Oliver's gaze was fixed, and I had never seen him look so terrifying. A horrific smile played across his features as he bent down to hover over Barry—I thought he might kill him.

"I'm leaving!" I yelled and made a beeline for the exit.

Once through the door, I ran out onto the street and into the back alley. It was the only thing I could think of to save Barry's life, and it worked. Within seconds, Oliver's hand was around mine, his grip crushing my fingers as he dragged me toward the car.

"Wait a minute," I said, pulling away, "I'm sorry. Please talk to me."

He stopped and began pacing back and forth like a caged animal, pounding his anger into the pavement with each stride. Without anyone else in the alley, the night had become ours alone, and it had started to snow. I counted twenty-six flakes as they hit the ground before he spoke.

"You can't keep things like this from me. Sneaking out and going to a bar alone? I should go back in there and kill that guy for putting his hands on you!"

Where before I felt worried for Barry, I was now worried for myself.

"No. Come on, Oliver. It's my fault, I'm *so* sorry."

"I'll kill *anyone* who hurts you," he raged.

"You're scaring me, Oliver." My voice was no more than a whisper as I backed up against the brick wall, wishing I could disappear into it.

"Just tell me what's going on in your head, Kaya. No secrets. Hell, I would have snuck you out myself if I'd known that's what you wanted. At least you would have been safe!"

I gulped.

"Promise me," he demanded, eyes still wild.

I had no choice but to comply. "Okay. No secrets, I promise."

His face relaxed, and then his eyes wandered over every inch of the tight blue dress I was wearing. If the wall weren't holding me up, I would have collapsed under the intensity of his gaze. "You scared the hell out of me," he said, face softening.

Yes, I had already guessed that.

"Kaya," he said, moving close and putting his chin an inch from my forehead, "look at me."

I lifted my eyes to meet his, relieved to see they had returned to reflect the Oliver I knew and liked. Angry Oliver was someone I never wanted to meet again.

"You have to let me protect you. I would never forgive myself if something happened. And, I'm so sorry I didn't get here sooner."

Snowflakes landed on his cheeks and lightly dusted his hair. Had he always been this beautiful? "I lied, and you're the one who's sorry?" I said. "You've always treated me perfectly. Even when I was a kid, you put up with me when I was awful to you. You've protected me, you've been my friend, and you've saved my life. Without you, I..." Then, it hit me like a ton of bricks how vastly important he was to me. I owed him everything. I put my hands on his chest. "Please, don't leave me. I'll never lie to you again. I promise."

He laughed softly. "Leave you? Kaya, don't you know? Isn't it obvious that I'm…"

It was difficult for him to say what he was feeling, so instead, he tried to show me. Winding his hands through my hair, he kissed my forehead, but he didn't pull away afterward. His breath was hot as it moved down my cheek and over to my mouth. With his lips barely touching mine, as if waiting for me to pull away, he held my head in his hands, and then he slowly, cautiously, kissed me. I wanted to resist. I wanted to pull away from his body as he pushed harder against me, but the sensation of his pillow-soft mouth parting mine stole all my resolve. Warm and inviting, I found myself kissing him back, growing more eager to know this breath-stealing feeling that was rendering me incapable of all sensible thought. After a moment of pure bliss, he pulled away.

"Girl, I have wanted to do that for so long," he said breathlessly.

The snow was falling harder now and sparkled in the moonlight, melting against him just like I was. When he looked me in the eyes, I knew I was now ready to hear what I'd long suspected.

"Kaya, I'm in love with you."

7

SECOND IMPRESSIONS

"I'M SORRY," I SAID FOR THE FIFTH TIME.

Stephan was brushing and unnecessarily flat ironing my hair into straight, shiny strands with his lips pursed, nostrils flared, and eyebrows drawn together in a look that meant he was very, very angry.

"Stephan, please talk to me," I begged, feeling wretched.

He put the iron down on the antique desk, knocking over the lotions and potions he'd kept so proudly organized. In addition to his duties as guard and nanny, it was our morning routine to have casual conversation while he groomed my unruly hair and tended to my sensitive skin. The door was always closed, and it was blissful—just me and him. I looked forward to it every day. This morning, though, I wished for any disruption so I could just crawl back into bed and hide.

"I'm *really* sorry," I said for the sixth time.

"What you did last night was reckless," he spat, finally acknowledging more than my hair with a voice so icy it felt as if it froze my heart. "You've got to be careful. You can't go sneaking out and wandering around unprotected in public. I thought you were smarter than that!"

I fought back tears. I didn't give a crap about how much trouble I was in or who I'd pissed off, but having Stephan upset with me was torture.

"You've gotta understand, Kaya. You put yourself in danger. And you put Oliver in danger, too. So many things could have gone wrong."

Guilt consumed me as stomach acid rolled up into my throat.

"And what if Henry found out?" he went on, "you'd end up chained to the floor, quite literally. Is that what you want?"

"No." I pulled my housecoat tight and stared at the logs smoldering in the fireplace. The room was always cold, but today it was freezing. Stephan shook his head and leaned down, speaking quietly in my ear like the walls were listening.

"I know how Oliver feels about you, Kaya. We all see it. So I am telling you the honest-to-God truth when I say you have to be very, *very* careful. Your father is a clever and devious man. If you reciprocate Oliver's feelings, and those feelings were discovered, he would think nothing of using it against you."

"What do you mean?" I croaked.

"I am saying love is a wonderful thing, but it can also be a person's greatest weakness. If you truly care about Oliver, you'll do your best to hide it."

He was right, of course. Henry used to threaten me with Stephan's welfare when I was little to get me to behave. I always thought he was slightly kidding, but now I know he wasn't.

My inevitable tears caused Stephan's anger to melt away. He enveloped me with fuzzy, sweater-covered arms, and I melted into his chest, safely tucked under his beard, where I could hear his still-healing heartbeat.

"I know this last while has been really tough on you, kiddo," he said. "Just know I am here for you, all right?"

"I love you, Stephan," was all I could manage to say.

His arms tightened around me. "And I love you too, kiddo. And hey, I promise that if I find anything about your mother, I will tell you. You have my word. We haven't talked about it since that day—and…" he gulped, the sound of it loud in his chest, "Anne *may* have been right, but I can't say for sure. That's why I never said anything. There is simply no evidence, only speculation. Now I know I should have shared these suspicions with you, even if that's all they are, and I'm sorry. So, listen, no more secrets from me, and none from you either, okay?"

Yet again, I pledged my allegiance to the No More Secrets Club, but I did so with my fingers crossed. I couldn't tell Stephan that I would soon inherit the estate and Henry's precious company. For all he knew, Henry's visit to my room after Anne died was just a father checking in on his grieving daughter. His true intentions were ones I would keep to myself. For now.

A light knock at the door interrupted our hug, and an irritated Stephan opened the door. New Guy was standing there, cheeks flushed and eyes bloodshot, and for the first time, there was no smug smile on his face. Up until that moment, I'd forgotten I'd involved him in my late-night activities.

"I have something for you," he said with a look of regret as he brushed past Stephan and handed me a brown paper bag. "Sindra wants you to open this right away."

Sindra was my father's bronze-skinned, doe-eyed assistant who was also his right arm. She ran the estate and his life, and she organized my world. I didn't like her, I didn't trust her, and I certainly didn't want anything to do with her. By the look on New Guy's face, he didn't want anything to do with her either. He was only charged with delivering a message from her, and he couldn't get out of my room fast enough.

The paper bag rustled in my hands. Whatever was inside was squishy and soft. I thought of a teddy bear Sindra had one of the guards deliver years ago as a birthday present, but this time I was pretty sure I wasn't going to like this gift. Reaching in the bag, I pulled out a very familiar white shirt. It didn't make sense; it was the one I threw in the garbage last night—the one I wore to Angela's—and then it hit me. My knees went weak with realization and the room started to spin. *Oh my God, Angela...*

Stephan reached for a note neatly tucked into the front pocket. Unfolding it carefully and eyeing my panic-stricken face, he read it aloud.

Kaya,

I will not inform your father of the events that took place last night. It would only worry him needlessly and inhibit your freedom even more. However, consider this a warning. If Stephan and Oliver are unable to manage you, they will be replaced with guards who can. Don't let anything like this happen again. I don't appreciate having to clean up after you.

— Sindra

Stephan tossed the note into the fireplace. Flames swallowed it up and it disappeared, just like I knew Angela had. Just like I knew Stephan and Oliver would if I snuck out again. With a single letter, my walls closed in, and my cage got smaller.

While Stephan stood by the fireplace shaking his head, a maid burst in with clean sheets, and then a porter arrived with the usual tray containing breakfast. My personal space became crowded, and when Oliver appeared in the doorway with the new French tutor, looking like he hadn't gone to bed, my cheeks became hot, feeling like they had caught on fire.

"I need to be alone," I said, and I bolted past all of them, running through the sitting room and out into the hallway.

New Guy was parked on the couch, the window behind him safely closed. He didn't say a word, but his eyes followed my every move as I paced up and down the hall, the thick red carpet under my feet not making a sound, which was oddly infuriating. The sound of my loud, stomping footsteps would have added some validity to my angst.

"Hey, I'm sorry about your friend," New Guy said when I'd marched past him for seemingly the hundredth time. Obviously he'd read the note and knew exactly what Sindra meant by "cleaning up" after me. I dejectedly plunked down on the couch beside him, and he pulled a small flask out of his jacket pocket in response.

"Brandy?" he offered with a grin, "I'm off the smokes now, at least for a bit."

The emotional turmoil I felt pounded relentlessly in my head, so I took a long swig. It was almost as awful as I imagined the bathroom cleaner to be. "I really liked Angela," I said, feeling my throat tighten around the words. "I felt like we could have been good friends."

"Yeah. You don't really have any pals besides us dudes, do ya?" he said.

"Nope."

"Hey, why don't I go to that bar later and see if I can find her? Get a cell number or something. But just keep it between you and me, all righty?"

I looked into his brown eyes, which I had never done before, and was shocked by the kindness in them. His presence had calmed me somewhat—or maybe it was the brandy—but in any case, the compassion he showed did not go unnoticed. Maybe New Guy wasn't so bad after all. "Thank you," I said.

"No problem."

"I'm sorry if I got you in trouble," I said, feeling like an idiot.

"It's okay. No one really said anything to me except Oliver, and he only went crazy and threatened my life, so I just told him you drugged me."

I laughed. "Thanks for that."

"Just doing my job, ma'am."

"Ugh, please don't call me ma'am," I said in annoyance.

The smile left his face. "Oh, okay."

He was just trying to be kind, and I was doing the same thing to him that I had done to Oliver for years; I was being a complete bitch.

"Hey, I'm sorry. Listen, I know I haven't been all that nice to you. It's just that a lot of people come in and out of my life, and I don't want to get attached to the ones who… uh, don't stick around, or—"

"Or die." He grinned, hitting the nail smack dab on the head.

"Uh, yeah, that too."

I kept track of everyone I had lost through the years, and the number was now at fourteen, including Anne.

"Well, I'm not going anywhere. No one besides your crazy father would hire me, and if a life and death situation occurs, I'll just get Command at Starfleet to beam me up."

His goofy sense of humor made me feel even more terrible about the way I'd treated him, and he must have seen the guilt on my face.

"Hey, Kaya, it's all cool. I didn't really give you a fair shake, either. I just automatically assumed you were a spoiled, little, rich bitch. But, you're not... spoiled," he said with a wink, and then he held out his hand. "Whadya say we start over?"

I liked this. I needed this. "Sure," I said, putting my hand in his.

"Hello, I'm Davis." He gave me a polite handshake.

"Nice to meet you Davis, I'm Kaya."

"Cheers, Kaya. To new friendships."

We fist bumped, sat back on the couch, and shamelessly drank the rest of the brandy.

DAVIS KEPT HIS WORD AND SEARCHED FOR ANGELA—HER APARTMENT was empty, her employer had never heard of her, and her landlord wouldn't answer a single question.

Davis then searched for Barry... he was gone too.

It was as if neither of them ever existed.

WINTER

8

'TIS THE SEASON

SNOW COVERED THE GROUND. FOR MOST PEOPLE, THIS WAS AN invitation to jump around and play in it like the world had become a giant feather pillow. To me, it was a devious ice monster with teeth, trapping the unguarded and either freezing or smothering them to death. I hated winter. Storms and howling winds turn me into a fruitcake, and not the yummy white kind soaked in amaretto, but the gross molasses-and-currant kind with green bits of mystery fruit. Add some messed-up feelings for my bodyguard and the constant desire to be as close to him as possible, worry for Stephan every time he coughed, a zillion unanswered questions about my true birth mother, and the super-solid realization that Anne was gone and Angela was missing into the mix… and *voila*! It was the recipe for a full-blown anxiety attack of epic proportions. The first of many to come.

After being coddled, held, pleaded with, and eventually drugged, I woke in the sitting room adjacent to my sleeping quarters on a bitterly cold morning snuggled next to Oliver on the couch. I had no recollection of how I'd gotten there. His breath was slow and even, and his warmth was absolutely blissful as the storm outside began to subside. I was half awake, still partly living in a wonderful dream—running through the forest in bare feet among green trees and blooming flowers—but in reality, it had been two whole months since I'd stepped a foot outside.

"I need to run," I mumbled into Oliver's shirt.

I felt him jerk awake and pull me in closer. His arms were comforting and suffocating all at the same time. The fireplace crackled, and I realized Davis was next to it with a cup of coffee, propped fully upright in an armchair, still sound asleep.

"Yeah, I could use a workout myself," Oliver said with a yawn.

My hand was on his stomach. I moved it slightly, feeling the ripple of his taut muscles under my fingertips. It made me catch my breath. I heard him gulp.

"I need to *run*. I need…" I paused, unsure what my sleepy head was trying to say. The Death Race. That's what I needed to do—run in The Death Race. It had been on my mind since meeting Barry at the bar, and I had been dreaming of entering ever since. It was a solid desire, as was the need to feel Oliver's lips on mine again—

"I need to…" I tried again.

"You need a change of scenery," Oliver said, sitting up. He didn't want to let me go, but he did, and I pried myself away because I didn't trust my hands.

"Ever seen the north section?" I asked deviously.

After a surprisingly small amount of persuasion, we snuck into the boarded-up and strictly off-limits north section of the estate while Davis and Stephan snored longer into the morning. Oliver had never seen the portraits depicting the generations of Lowens in the marble lobby or John Marchessa's face without the slightest trace of warmth hanging beneath the stained glass windows. Our breath made icy clouds in the air as we both stared up at Lenore's thin lips painted red and her corkscrew curls that matched her mother's in the portrait next to her. All the Marchessa women looked the same.

And then, there was me.

A photo from years ago hung slightly off balance. In it, my hair fell down to my waist and had been brushed into shiny, black waves. My eyes were slightly puffy from an allergic reaction I had from strawberries the day before, and Stephan had painted my mouth with deep red lipstick. Where I was fine-boned and pale, the Marchessas were stocky and covered in golden freckles. I was small-nosed and busty, even at fourteen, and the Marchessas had slightly upturned noses and very flat chests, except for Martha, who'd been generously enhanced in her teens.

"You look nothing like any of them," Oliver said, and his voice echoed throughout the vast space.

"I know. Anne was telling the truth." I dragged my feet through the dust on the marble floor, making a huge heart shape, and then I plunked down in the middle. The paintings stared at me while I stared at Oliver.

"Kaya, what do you remember of her?" Oliver asked, still standing before the portrait of Lenore.

"Truthfully? Nothing. Just what Stephan has told me."

While he had his back to me, I let myself freely ogle him without an ounce of shame.

"That's sad," he said, and then he wandered into the middle of my dust heart and sat down next to me. "And the necklace? Wonder what that's about," he said as he reached for it. "Stephan's never said anything?"

"He doesn't know."

Oliver's breath caressed my forehead as he leaned in to inspect the pendant, his fingers grazing my skin purposely. He seemed lost in thought, staring at Lenore Marchessa's initials etched into the silver. I took in a deep breath, and before I could catch myself, I was running my fingers up his forearm. His muscles felt so different than mine—hard, tight—and the skin stretched over them was so smooth—

"I can't take it any longer," he said, and before I even had a chance to react, his mouth was eagerly on mine. His hands moved from my face and down the sides of my body, setting every speck of it on fire as I was pushed down against the cold marble. His breath was heavy as his hand glided over my stomach. I felt like putty beneath him, all my bones melting to jelly against him. His lips moved over mine urgently, roughly, as if no amount of kissing was going to satisfy his intense hunger. His hand moved higher, and then he stopped at my ribcage, his fingers digging in, almost painfully. "I have to stay in control, and it's damn near impossible," he said, breathing hard, and then he pulled away and sat up. I could hear his heart racing—or was it my own?

"But I want you, too," I said, and I crawled onto his lap, draping my arms over his shoulders. All my thoughts foretold one thing: desire. He bent his head forward, and his mouth moved over mine once more, but this time more carefully. He was holding back.

"I love you," he said.

I couldn't say it. I loved him too, but the words seemed to be stuck. Instead, I responded by putting my mouth to his neck and exploring the soft skin there, letting my hands wander over his cheekbones, and then the short hair in tight little curls on the back of his head. He tilted his head back in bliss, and a soft moan came from deep in his throat. I grabbed his shirt and tried to pull it up over his chest.

"No, no Kaya, we can't," he said, catching my hands.

"What?"

"I'm sorry, it's just that—we can't do that yet… I want to—believe me I want to—but we have to wait a bit longer. You're not ready."

"But Oliver—"

He put his finger to my lips. "Patience," he said, "not yet."

I jumped to my feet, hurt and angry. If I couldn't have him now, maybe I didn't want him… ever. I turned away so he wouldn't see the look of childish disappointment on my face, and I skulked over to the lobby desk to hide my red cheeks. As I pretended to busy myself with fixing a dustsheet that had slipped off and exposed the corner, I realized something: we'd be breaking the law. I was still a minor. Also, since he'd subbed for Stephan during my last checkup with the family doctor, he knew everything about me—like the important fact that I wasn't on birth control… yet…

Well, at least one of us had some common sense.

I tried to collect myself by staring blankly at the small section of wall devoted to displaying pictures of celebrities, politicians, and famous artists who had come and gone, but my heart wouldn't stop pounding. I took in a deep breath, trying to quell my emotions from boiling over into what could be another anxiety attack and tried to pull myself together. I counted to ten. I thought of swimming in the lake or anything that might calm my mind, and readied myself to leave. But something caught my eye.

A picture of a woman.

It stole my breath away, and not just because the face staring back at me was so beautiful, but because it was eerily familiar. Also, it was the only one that had been polished. It was without a single speck of dust. Intrigued, I moved behind the desk, reaching for it. The woman smiling down from the wall had pale skin, green eyes, and dark hair—features that matched mine exactly. "Oliver—?"

I didn't have to finish; he was already standing beside me.

My hands started to shake. I pulled at the frame, but it wouldn't budge, Oliver tried as well, but it seemed cemented to the wall. I had the heavy, iron key to the valet door in my pocket, and I held it like a dagger. Before he could protest, I jabbed at the glass as hard as I could, and fragments fell around our feet as the glass instantly shattered. I carefully tapped away the remaining shards and slid the old photograph away from the frame. Oliver smiled, completely amused.

The picture was old. Bits of yellow were creeping in from the edges. As I stared, it suddenly seemed to weigh a hundred pounds. I turned it over, hoping for some sort of clue as to who she was, and found flowing handwriting in indigo ink.

Dearest Henry,

Thank you for the hospitality!

Much love,
—Rayna

"Rayna," I said aloud, and my voice echoed back to me. The connection I felt as I held the portrait was deep. Soul jarring. I knew this woman once. I could feel it in my bones. "It's her, Oliver, I know it. *She's* the one who named me Kaya."

THE EARLY MORNING SUN DIDN'T DO MUCH TO WARM THE HALLWAYS OF the estate, so I held Oliver's hand for warmth—at least, that was my excuse. At the far end of the main lobby, one hundred and seventy-six steps from the big, metal-door-opening guards, was the security room and Old Carl's home away from home. He'd been in the exact same place, every single day, for over forty years. Through renovations, a flood, and a measles outbreak, he hadn't budged. He saw me approach, so I pushed my lips up against the bullet-proof window and made the ugliest face I could. It left behind a greasy mark, earning a scolding from an irritated man who wiped the smudge away.

"Hey, is that like, his *job*?" I asked, glancing at the man holding paper towel like a weapon. "Does he just stand there all day and *guard the glass*?"

"Ah, Kaya, still sassy as ever," Carl laughed and gave me a tight hug.

I loved his spicy cologne and was happy to see the familiar fishing cap he always wore still perched on his head. When I was a kid, it was always a great game to hide it.

"So, only one sidekick with you today? No Davis?"

"He's in the tub."

"And Stephan? He obviously doesn't know you're here, right? Otherwise I would have gotten a call."

I looked at Oliver, who looked at his feet.

"Anyway…" Old Carl said with a grin. "How are things?"

"Um, can I speak to you in private?" I asked, looking around the busy room full of people. "It's a personal matter."

Carl snapped his fingers. Annoyed Assistant made no attempt to challenge his authority, and the room became as quiet as a tomb with the exception of a dozen humming computers. Every square inch of the estate was watched and monitored from here—the gardens, the hallways, the kitchens, the ballrooms, and offices, *the pool.* Carl saw everything.

He pointed toward a chair in the far corner. "You can have a seat over there," he said to Oliver, but as fully expected, Oliver didn't budge an inch from my side. "Like a bloody dog, you are," he muttered under his breath, and then he returned his focus to me. "So, what's up?" he said with a sigh.

I pulled the picture of Rayna out of my pocket, my hand shaking. "I need your help finding someone, and since you've been here since the beginning of time… maybe even longer… I figured you might know who this is."

"Oh I probably do," he said smugly.

When I handed him the photograph, his posture crumpled like I'd punched him in the gut. His voice seemed strained when he spoke. "Nope. Don't know her at all," he said, quickly trying to brush off the subject, and placed the photo back in my hands.

"I think she might be my mother," I said carefully.

Carl cleared his throat like he always did when he was uncomfortable. "What are you talking about, Kaya?"

"This picture was in the north section, in the lobby. Do you know anything about it? Or her? She looks like me."

I held it up next to my face and his skin paled by nearly four shades. "No. I have never seen that woman before."

He was lying.

"How far back do you keep the security tapes?" Oliver asked. "You were here when the hotel was open and operational, right? Wasn't everyone who came and went recorded?"

The bulletproof room suddenly became super stuffy. If Carl wouldn't help me, then I was on my own.

He adjusted his fishing cap in a gesture that usually meant the conversation was over, and then a strange look fell over his grey face. "Actually, maybe she does seem a little familiar," he said, suddenly becoming agreeable. "The tapes are stored in the records room downstairs, although Master Lowen doesn't allow anyone near there. I guess I could see what I could find out, though."

"Thank you," I said, holding back tears of relief.

"It may take a while," he added, "maybe even months. I can't just wander down there whenever I want; it's locked and completely off limits. I have to wait until the time is right. You must have patience."

I nodded and kissed him on the cheek.

When I was about to turn away, he grabbed my hands firmly, his weathered skin rough against my own. "Just don't breathe a word of this to anyone, especially Stephan… You know how he worries—"

"I won't," I said and crossed my fingers behind my back.

"You know, Kaya, some things are best left alone," Carl added, his voice barely more than a whisper.

Henry had said that exact thing, and suddenly, everything about those same words coming from Old Carl made me feel uneasy, like I was Little Red Riding Hood visiting The Big Bad Wolf—but that was ridiculous. Old Carl was gentle, sweet, and had always been good to me.

Oliver whistled an eerie tune as we walked back to my room. It echoed through the banquet halls, and then it got swallowed up in the carpeted walkways. He held my hand tighter than usual, too. "I don't trust that sly old bastard," he mumbled.

And the snowy months crawled by.

SPRING, 2015

9

THE GROUND BENEATH HE OPENED UP

IT TOOK MANY MONTHS TO COME TO TERMS WITH THE FACT THAT I may never know the identity of the woman in the picture. Rayna proved to be elusive—all of my searches for her on the internet yielded no information, and after five months of waiting, Carl turned out to be of no help. Oliver had grown sick of the subject, and I was tired of hiding all of it from Stephan. There was only one piece of the puzzle in my hands, and it wasn't even a corner. So, I decided not to forget about it—because I could *never* forget about it—but to put it aside and occupy my mind with something more tangible.

With a light breeze of spring air wafting through my bedroom window, I right clicked the computer mouse, and then I hit enter, giggling to myself when my laptop made that satisfying little whooshing sound. Within seconds, a message came up on my screen.

Congratulations! You are officially entered into The Death Race.
Train hard!

A buzz of excitement rushed over me. Twenty-four hours of running outside in the mountains on my own—no maids, no guards, no walls—and all I had to do was get Henry to agree. Security was so amped up from recent death threats made towards him I was never sneaking out again, and it was well known that Sindra never made idle threats. If I could get their blessing, it would be a dream come true.

The bedroom door swung open, and a red-faced maid scurried in. I quickly closed the computer. "Whoa, what's the rush?" I asked.

"Too many things to do, not enough time… big party starting soon… lots of work to do, lots and lots…" she mumbled. She then emptied the garbage cans and left as quickly as she came.

Right. My eighteenth birthday party. *Tonight.*

Henry had decided to tempt fate again. After the blood bath during my sixteenth birthday, and John Marchessa's warnings sent in the form of daisies or hit men, I thought the whole idea of a party was pretty risky. But I would go along with it. I would put on a fake smile, say polite things, and be on my best behavior because—more than anything—I needed Henry to be in an agreeable mood when I sprung The Death Race idea on him.

Sindra had picked out my dress for the occasion, and Stephan fussed over my hair and makeup until I looked like a shiny new penny. I felt like a princess as I entered the ballroom, moonlight streaming through the west-facing windows with Davis on one arm and Oliver on the other. The emerald-green satin gown matched my eyes and hugged my body, clinging tight to my hips. It flowed out around my legs so I could walk, and shimmering waves of fabric floated up with every step—it was a far cry from my usual sweat pants and T-shirts. I actually felt pretty, which made me think of Angela. She would have been proud.

We made our way into a crowd of at least two-hundred guests. I smiled. I said hello and good evening. I complimented an older lady on her pink, velvet pantsuit and gave a nod to the chief of police, knowing who he was from his picture in the newspaper this morning. Cocktails were served on silver trays as well as fancy food on sticks. I tasted and sipped, almost happy as I wandered through the chaos, until I realized no one had a clue who I was.

A waiter offered me champagne, and then he wandered off without a word. A group of elderly ladies gave me the once over, and then they whispered among themselves. A few reporters asked me where the birthday girl was, and I jokingly said I didn't know. They believed me.

I was in a room full of people, all here for me, and yet I was a stranger.

Sindra sauntered over in the most revealing dress I had ever seen—some sheer black thing, with just enough sequins to prevent it from being rated X and a neckline plunging so deep I could see her belly button. There wasn't much covering her glittering skin. This would have looked slutty on anyone else, but somehow the mighty Sindra wore it elegantly. She hugged me politely, leaving behind a trail of patchouli-scented oil.

"Did you see that mountain of gifts?" she said excitedly, pointing to the back of the room where a massive, columned archway rose up over a table overflowing with boxes.

My stomach turned. "I told you I didn't want anything," I said, and then I reminded myself that it was important to stay on Sindra's good side.

"Oh come on, Kaya. Every girl likes presents," she said, beaming, her almost-black eyes shining beneath a fringe of thick lashes. She was dripping in diamonds—from her ears, neck, and wrists—making her appear even more beautiful than she already was. But, I knew the tiger underneath the glamorous exterior, the woman who led men around by their noses by day.

"If you don't want *presents,* then what is it that you *do* want?" she asked with an inquisitive head tilt in Oliver's direction.

Was Sindra playing with me? I could never tell if she was actually being nice or if it was part of her professional demeanor to give me a false sense of camaraderie. I shrugged my shoulders at her question, but then I thought, why not tell her? What did I have to lose? I just hoped the noise of the crowd and violins playing Beethoven would keep my words safely from everyone else's ears—especially Oliver's. "I want to compete in The Death Race," I whispered.

Her smile was replaced with a look of shock. Clearly, I hadn't given her the answer she was hoping for. "What? Are you serious?"

"Yes. I really want to do it, Sindra—more than anything."

She gave me an odd smile and shook her head. "I admire your spunk, Kaya. It's good to have dreams, but maybe you should focus on realistic ones, darling—*safe* ones—because you know that little fantasy will *never* happen."

She patted me on the shoulder with a sad little nod, and then she pranced away, her long black hair swinging after her like a horse's tail. I felt like I'd shrunk three feet; if I didn't have Sindra on my side, I would never get Henry to agree. Her influence was paramount.

"What was that about?" Oliver asked.

"Uh, nothing, don't worry about it," I said harshly.

Sindra had me rattled. As I moved mindlessly through the mass of people, anxiety started creeping in. At the far end of the room was a mammoth-sized table of sweets, and I made a beeline for it, hoping to drown my sorrows in chocolate, but Oliver and Davis clung to me as tightly as my green dress. "Maybe you guys could just back off a bit?" I said irritably.

They both nodded and slightly detached themselves from my hip. I turned my attention to the rainbow of pretty confections and tried to ignore the jittery claustrophobic feeling that was beginning to consume me. The desserts were individual works of art in their own right, much like the priceless, gold framed paintings that hung on the ornate walls, but it was the chocolate fountain that caught my eye. An elderly bald man and his wife were dunking in little purple cakes. I reached for an orange slice.

"When is the spoiled little birthday girl going to be here?" the man asked me.

"Who cares?" I said sarcastically.

He laughed like I had told the best joke he'd ever heard, as did his wife—a red-faced hag stuffed into a hideous pink dress. If it burst, I imagined her guts would be nothing but sugar and butter. "We don't care about the brat, either," she snorted, "We're just here for the food. I doubt if Henry even *has* a daughter; he probably hired a professional to act the part, when really he'd made it all up. He's playing the *family man* card to win back support from the community, but he's already got my vote if I can get more of this cake."

"Henry, a family man? Ha!" laughed Baldy who I suddenly discovered was incredibly ugly as the dripping purple mess disappeared into his face. When he spoke, crumbs fell from his mouth. "We even had to bring a present. What the hell do you get an invisible, rich brat… a new servant? A pony?"

"How about a dolphin?" I said flatly.

They roared over that. The hag's over-sprayed hair moved like a helmet as her jowls shook. She mumbled about getting on with dinner between mouthfuls, and I felt the walls close in. A panicked feeling started to build… the people around me became a storm, their voices the howling wind…

I steadied myself against the table; I was about to have an anxiety attack.

I had to get out.

Turning to leave, I walked into a wall of Oliver and Davis, and that was the icing on the proverbial cake. I ran for the garden doors as my lungs started to constrict and bumped into a waiter, spilling the martinis on his precariously balanced tray and almost falling into a table of hideous mermaid ice sculptures. Oliver, of course, was already there to catch me.

"Just get out of my way!" I yelled at him.

He stared, unblinking and unfazed—his usual reaction to my bouts of anxiety. He wrapped his hand tightly around my upper arm as everything in view became hazy and my heart pounded harder. I yelled at the door guards to move aside, but they didn't budge. Oliver's grip tightened and the volume of the string quartet attempted to drown out the desperation in my voice.

"Oliver, let me go! Tell them to move aside… I need to get out for a minute, please!"

I tried to pull free. Guests were starting to stare.

"Just let her go," said Davis, stepping between us to put a hand on

Oliver's arm. "Don't cause a scene, bro."

Oliver hesitantly unwrapped his fingers, and then he nodded to the guards. Seizing my freedom, I burst through the doors and ran out into the warm night. The garden was blooming, and the scent of the newly open blossoms hung heavily in the air. I breathed deeply, trying to calm myself down, as I made my way past heirloom roses, weigela, peonies, and lush flowering trees. The heels of my shoes clicked on the stone path until I came to the end, where a twelve-foot stone fence stood as a barrier between the garden and the steep cliff. Breathless, I looked up. The stars twinkled and shone.

Clear sky. Not even a hint of a cloud. Clear sky. No wind. Everything is perfectly fine... I told myself this, but still, I had to sit down.

The old bench where I'd spent many happy hours with Anne as a child nestled under our favorite Mayday tree, the smell of its flowers heady. I remembered the day Anne pared an apple with a small knife and then carved our initials in the trunk. I reached for the markings that still remained, letting my fingers linger over the crude etching of the letters.

"*What the hell am I doing?*" I said aloud to no one.

Something moved behind the tree. Leaves fluttered, and there was the slightest crunching sound. "Were you talking to me?" said a man's voice.

I jumped up and backed away from the tree, not because my private moment was invaded but because of the timbre of the voice. It sent a strange shiver up my spine. "I thought I was alone. I'm sorry. I was just mumbling to myself," I said into the dark.

"I didn't mean to scare you. Is everything okay?" the man asked, and then he emerged from behind the branches. He moved slowly, as if worried he might scare me even more, and even though I should have been concerned for my safety, I wasn't.

"Yes, everything's all right. Thanks for asking," I said, still trying to catch my breath, "I just had to get away from all the pompous people in that stuffy room."

At that, he laughed. It was a melodic, rich sound that made the hair on my arms rise. Then, I realized he was probably one of the stuffy guests I said I was escaping from. "I didn't mean it that way…"

He took a step closer, but his face was still hidden in the shadows. He was tall—I would guess around six foot three—and of athletic build. I was relieved to see the familiar security card clipped to his jacket, but something about it didn't seem right. "You didn't offend me; I'm just hired help. One of the, uh, new gardeners here," he said.

"And they have you working in the dark while wearing a suit?" I asked, still trying to get my lungs to cooperate. The anxiety had tapered off but not completely.

"You know, big party and all, everyone has to look respectable."

He was lying. I didn't care. He was probably extra undercover security. I tried to make out his features as he stepped out onto the stone path, but the light still missed his face. I continued talking to him, hoping to draw him out even farther into the light, "I have a great respect for gardeners," I said. "They protect and create art with Mother Nature. Her ways are some of the few things I can actually pretend to understand."

I was still breathing fast, like I'd been running, and now my legs had started to shake. I looked up, but it seemed like the sky started to rattle, and shutting my eyes, I stumbled backward. The gardener lunged for my elbow.

"Hey, maybe you should sit down for a minute," he said gently.

My skin tingled beneath his touch. I let him help me to the bench, mostly because passing out would have been super embarrassing.

"Are you sure you're all right?" he asked again.

"Yeah. Probably too much champagne." I rubbed my forehead and realized my hands were shaking; something about this guy made me nervous, but in a good way. I expected him to walk away, but instead, he parked himself on the bench beside me.

"So, you got roped into going to the party?" he asked.

I laughed. "Unfortunately, yes."

Obviously, he didn't know who I was. He picked a blossom with tiny white petals from a branch hanging over our heads and held it out. "A flower for your thoughts?"

As I took it from his hands, my anxiety started to slip away, and something else was taking its place. I slowly turned to look at him, apprehensive about what I might see, and I almost choked—he was stunning. I quickly looked away, hoping he didn't see my jaw drop to the ground.

"Maybe you're a two flower type of girl?" he said and handed me another.

I had to say something--*anything*. My mind reeled. "Do you ever wonder what on earth you are here for? What it is you are meant to do?" I asked bluntly. The question just burst from my mouth without any thought, but it seemed oddly appropriate.

"I know *exactly* why I'm here and what I'm meant to do," he said with so much conviction it gave me goose bumps.

I looked at him again. His eyes—were they blue? So bright, deep, mesmerizing, and perfectly positioned with a nose just the right size between them. His jawline was sharp, perfectly sculpted, and light, golden-brown hair hung loosely around his slightly tanned face where the most perfect, small scar decorated his cheekbone.

He was the most beautiful person I had ever seen.

I begged my mouth not to say this truth out aloud. "I wish I knew what I was meant to do," I managed to say instead.

"One day, you'll discover what to fight for, and when you do, you won't let anything stop you."

His words seemed prophetic. I felt the weight of them settle over me as he took the flowers back from my hands, and I noticed his were covered in cuts and scrapes. They were strong and rugged looking, like hands that had worked hard, but he was young, maybe only in his early twenties. He placed the flowers in the center of his palm and blew on them, sending white petals into the air. Suddenly, a rogue breeze burst through the night, picking up the petals and swirling them madly right before our eyes.

"Well, this is strange," I said in awe.

Then the wind stopped, and the petals drifted to the ground.

"Uh, yeah, really strange," he said, "I wonder if Mother Nature is trying to tell us something."

I didn't know about Mother Nature, but common sense was yelling at me to get up. But when another quick glance at his eyes pulled me in so deep I couldn't look away, I had to confirm their color... blue? Yes. Definitely blue. Like the summer sky.

"Um, may I...?" he said, and he slowly reached for my face to wipe at a tear on my cheek. My breath caught in my throat; I didn't even realize I'd been crying.

"I better go," I said meekly, but I was cemented to the bench.

He glanced at his watch, looked around, and then suddenly became nervous. "Oh, yeah, I better get going, uh, back to work," he said, standing up.

I noticed he was wearing heavy hiking boots, certainly not something a security guard in a suit would wear. "Tell me, who are you *really*? Because you're *definitely* not a gardener."

He looked at me, wide-eyed with shock, and then he shook his head with a smile. "I'm just a regular guy trying to do what's right," he said intensely, and then he took my hand to help me up, but once I was standing, he didn't let go.

One part of me wanted to slap him for being so audacious and the other felt like nothing in the world was more important than allowing my hand to stay in his. I didn't move, didn't speak, and probably didn't breathe, either. This was crazy. If this is what people meant when they described falling for someone, it was certainly an accurate analogy. As I looked in his eyes, it felt like the ground disappeared from under my feet, and there was no stopping the resulting descent into the unknown.

"Please tell me your name," he said quietly.

I thought about it. Maybe I would yell it really loud so that every pretentious guest in that ballroom could hear it, too, but footsteps were approaching. They were heavy, loud, determined, and accompanied by Oliver's agitated voice yelling for Davis.

I quickly pulled my hand away from the stranger's, and then I wished I hadn't.

"Please, just tell me your name." he said urgently as he began backing away.

I looked down the path to see Oliver's shadow. "It's Kaya," I whispered.

But the stranger was already gone.

THE THIEF

10

$\mathcal{P}$OCKET $\mathcal{F}$ULL OF $\mathcal{P}$OSIES

HE FOLLOWED A BLUEPRINT OF THE ESTATE TO THE GIRL'S ROOM. It was tucked away on the fifth floor at the far end of a dark hallway with bars that covered every window. A worn leather couch, its state denoting it must be consistently occupied, was opposite the door. Was there a guard usually posted here, too? He didn't think she'd be that heavily protected.

Thirty-two minutes.

He was overwhelmed by the sheer size of the room. It was more like an apartment suite than a teen's bedroom. There was a sitting area with couches and a fireplace in the middle with a kitchenette off to the side and what looked like a study area next to a balcony. He frantically searched the room, but he found nothing; not a schedule, day planner, phone book, pictures… nothing.

At the far end of the room, there was a single bed next to a massive wall of science-fiction books. This must be where a nanny or another guard slept. There wasn't anything useful there, either. Next to the bookcase, a set of double doors opened into a bedroom where a pristinely made king-sized bed, a vanity table, stone fireplace, and another bathroom were surrounded by red-and-gold wallpaper. He pulled open drawers, looked under the mattress, and searched through the closet for anything that could be of use to him. Did she attend classes somewhere? Visit friends? Have any appointments? Go on holidays? There weren't any diaries or pictures or anything he thought a teenage girl would have. He even went through the medicine cabinet. Inside were painkillers, that pink stuff for acid reflux, heavy sedatives, and a pack of birth control pills that hadn't been opened yet—and not one item had a doctor or patient name. Only a Lowen Pharmaceutical logo was stamped onto the lids.

He started to panic.

Heavy velvet drapes hung ceiling to floor next to the bed, and he pushed them aside to discover more bar-covered windows; this place was more like a prison than a bedroom.

Twenty-six minutes…

He headed back to the desk, thinking maybe he'd missed something, but sheet music and books scattered around a grand piano caught his eye. He flipped through every piece of paper, but they contained nothing but blurs and dots. Frustrated, he tried to access the home screen of a laptop sitting on the piano lid, but it was password protected.

He couldn't go back empty handed, yet there was literally not one personal, useful item of the girl's in the entire suite. Maybe she didn't exist… maybe it was all a big lie…

He turned to leave and accidentally knocked over a cup of pens that had been left haphazardly too close to the edge of the piano lid. Cursing his carelessness, he bent to pick them up and put them back when he noticed a brass key had tumbled to his feet. In a last-ditch effort, he slid the key into the piano bench. The lid popped open.

Jackpot.

It was filled with poems, letters, a photograph of a dark-haired woman too old to be the girl, and little boxes with paper hearts in them. A brochure for something called The Death Race sat on top. Someone had written, "Use the fake name Katy Adams, don't forget!" on the front of it.

He unfolded the slightly tattered paper and read.

Welcome to The Death Race!

Every September in Banff, Alberta, racers come to the Canadian Rockies to cheat death in one of the world's toughest adventure races. Athletes push themselves to the limits of their endurance in a rugged setting with breathtaking scenery. They run a 125 km course over three mountain summits that include 17,000 feet of elevation change and a major river crossing at Hell's Gate, battling heat, cold, altitude, and themselves. There are no big prizes for winning, finishing is hard enough, and the bragging rights are priceless…

He leafed to the back where a paperclip held a registration form.

NAME: ~~Kaya Lowen~~ Katy Adams Age: 18
Height: 5'8" Weight: 110 lbs.
Category: Solo Racer Confirmation: # 6543RET

He couldn't believe his luck; this was exactly what he needed. He memorized every detail on the form, and then he carefully put it back as he'd found it.

Fifteen minutes…

He trekked back through the halls, flashed his fake ID tag to the guards, and gained access once again to the crowded ballroom while smiling and carrying a silver tray loaded with canapés. As casually as possible, he weaved through the over-perfumed and over-made guests, and then made his way out into the garden. At the end of the path, a small door hidden in the stone wall was his escape. He pushed away the tightly woven vines and pulled on the handle—still locked. All his gear for rappelling down to the river below was on the other side of that door. He hoped Seth's fishing buddy would keep his word and open it at the pre-arranged time.

Ten minutes…

The click of fast-approaching footsteps made him duck for cover. Someone stopped a few feet from where he was hiding and began to pace back and forth. He dug out the knife he'd stolen from the kitchen and hoped he wouldn't have to use it.

It was a woman, and she was alone. He peered at her from behind a huge Mayday tree for a better look. A shiny dress hugged her slim body, and long, dark hair fell past her shoulders to a tiny waist. She seemed upset, and her chest heaved slightly as she tried to catch her breath. She paced back and forth, and then she stopped, stared up at the sky, and stumbled backward. He caught a glimpse of milky-white shoulders and a hint of her toned thigh peeking through a slit in the dress. She turned toward him, and he thought he'd been caught. He steadied the knife… but when he saw her face, he forgot why he even had it.

Her features were defined, but the edges were soft. Glowing skin covered high cheekbones, and a hint of pink was noticeable on them even in this light. Her nose was small and dainty, her lips full and berry red, and her wide eyes seemed on the verge of tears, which made them sparkle. She was gorgeous. He was captivated.

The knife fell to the ground.

She said something. Did she speak to him? The whole world seemed to come to a grinding halt—he had to meet her even if it meant risking everything. His body moved toward her like it wasn't his own, and as if in a dream, he found himself sitting next to her, wiping at a tear on her cheek. The heat of her skin under his fingertips and the look in her eyes woke up his heart. Suddenly, he wanted to soothe her, comfort her, and protect her from whatever caused her to run out alone into the night.

He plucked a blossom from the tree and handed it to her, and then watched as the petals got caught up in a sudden mad swirl of wind, rushing and spinning just like the insane feeling starting in his chest. She didn't believe he was a gardener. He liked that. When he spoke to her, he was barely aware of the words coming out of his mouth, and when she responded, his entire body tingled. He was absolutely compelled beyond reason to hold her hand, and when he did, the most startling, earth shattering revelation hit him with full force: *she* was the reason he was here on this earth.

Two minutes…

He didn't believe in luck. He didn't believe in fate. He certainly didn't believe in love at first sight, but there she was, standing in front of him, wearing an emerald dress the same color as her eyes.

Time's up.

KAYA

11

RAT IN A CAGE

"**WELL, IT WAS** A GOOD EVENING, WASN'T IT? A HUGE SUCCESS… and nobody died!"

Henry was so happy his good mood could have been infectious if his mere presence hadn't been such a complete drag.

"Please sit down, darling," he said as he motioned toward the ominous high-backed leather chair in front of his desk.

I had never been in his office at night; it was nice and quiet without the assistants, save Sindra, of course, and the ringing phones. I sat, but my head was in the clouds. The meeting with the stranger in the garden was so surreal—every second of it replayed over and over in my mind. I felt different—*really* different—like a life-changing event had occurred.

"I wanted to give this to you in private," Henry said, fishing something out of his desk drawer.

It was a little blue box with a red bow tied around it. I knew that inside that box would be an investment for him and another piece of useless jewelry for me to add to my wall safe. I noticed Sindra's eyes widen in excitement from her perch on the sofa.

"Wait…" I said to Henry, and I put my hand up, "I have to ask you for something first. I know you might not understand, but please, hear me out."

Sindra rolled her eyes and shook her head as I fished the brochure out of my bra—it had been tremendously difficult getting it out of the piano bench while Oliver and Stephan weren't looking, and since I had no pockets… I tried to straighten it back out, but my hands were shaking, and it didn't help that my skin was still tingling from the stranger's touch. "This is what I want for my birthday. I appreciate all the gifts, I really do, but I really just want to be able to do this," I said, putting the brochure in Henry's hands. *The Death Race* was scrawled across the front in jagged, hand-drawn letters. As Henry looked over the paper, I wished they'd called it something a little less dramatic.

"What the heck is this, Kaya… really?" he said, scanning the crumpled page. "Sindra, is this what you were telling me about earlier?"

"Uh huh," she said sourly.

Henry read the front of the brochure out loud. "The Death Race is a twenty-four hour race through the Rocky Mountains on a 125-kilometer course, and... *blah... blah...* Kaya, this is positively insane!"

"Yes," I said, "which is exactly why I want to do it."

"Why? Why on earth would someone want to put themselves through this?"

"It's good to have goals, purpose, something to work toward. I need to be more than just a rat in your—or I guess it's technically *my* cage. Besides, allowing me to do this might make me feel more agreeable on my twenty-first birthday."

Sindra tried to contain a laugh when, for once, Henry had nothing to say. He just continued reading, shaking his head, while Sindra watched over the rim of her wine glass.

"Please Henr—uh, Dad. Let me do this. I have already entered—under a false name of course—and I'm strong. I'll be totally fine."

I didn't mention that I hadn't even told Oliver or Stephan yet because they most certainly wouldn't have agreed. I needed Henry to back me up first, and then they'd have no choice but to go along with it.

Henry sighed, and then he leaned back against the desk and put down the brochure. "You really want this?"

"Yes."

A sly grin began to spread across his polished face. "I'm sorry," he said.

"Sorry? What... do you mean... *no?*"

"I'm sorry that I have to give you a gift that's a little different than I'd originally planned." He went behind his desk and pushed a piece of wood paneling on the wall. It popped open to reveal a small silver box with metal clasps. Alarm bells went off in my mind. I was pretty sure it wasn't more jewelry when he carefully placed the heavy case in my lap.

"I had this specifically designed for you. I've had it for a while, and I guess now is as good a time as any to give it to you. So here's the deal: you wear this, and you can participate in that Death Trap race."

My skin started to crawl as I tentatively undid the latches. Inside were two items resting on blue satin cushions. One looked like an industrial-strength iPod or minicomputer of some sort, and the other was a thick, gold band in an oval shape with two-half moon etchings carved into the precious metal. It seemed too large to be a bracelet, but it did appear to be jewelry. I picked it up. It was inlaid with strange stones on the inside and little rubies on the outside. It wasn't ugly, but it certainly wasn't the type of jewelry Henry usually bought. I looked at him, completely confused.

"I don't know what—"

He took it from me lovingly, like it was a precious pet. Then, with a small pin, he pushed one of the stones. It clicked and beeped. "Now it's activated," he said.

Sindra faked a cough and looked away when I glanced at her. "Activated? What are you talking about?" I asked, feeling my heart rate speed up.

Henry smiled that lopsided grin I had come to dread. "It's *on*. It's *working*. And once it's on your ankle and locked into place, it will start transmitting. It's a tracking device, Kaya. If you go anywhere outside the estate perimeter, it will alert security. And this..." He took the other piece out of the case. "Will tell us exactly where to look. I will always know where you are. I will always be able to find you."

It felt as if my stomach had risen into my throat. "You can't do this to me!"

He put his hand up. "Oh, yes I can. You *will* wear it, and you will stay safe. Actually, *everyone* around you will stay safe. Do you understand what I mean by *everyone*, Kaya?"

I did. He meant Oliver and Stephan. *Love is a weakness.*

We stared each other down.

This time I blinked first.

"So, what do you say, kiddo? Shall we put on this pretty little trinket? It really is quite in style."

I gulped back all the horrible things I wanted to say as he kneeled before me and locked the device in place around my ankle. "Sindra, why are you letting him do this?" I asked, fighting back tears. She looked uncomfortable, but she didn't respond. I stared at Henry, my *father*, too stunned to fight, too angry to even utter a single word.

"There. See? It's not so bad!" he said, "and indestructible, I might add. I had it made of tungsten at our new lab in Mexico. It's gold plated, and I added some gems so it would look nice."

I wanted to punch him. Just plant one square on his smug jaw and knock that self-satisfied grin right off his face.

"I'm just keeping you safe, Kaya, because I love you." He stood, gave me a kiss on the forehead and added, "And so, your wish is granted, my darling. You are free to enter that race. I don't really agree with it, but Sindra has assured me that you will be safe and heavily escorted. Regardless, there is no possible way you'll last longer than an hour out there, anyway." He lifted a crystal glass to his lips and shot back some amber liquid. "Happy Birthday," he said with a cocky grin and strolled out of the room.

Sindra stood, smoothed her dress, and straightened herself majestically before me. There was a hint of something in her eyes—maybe a touch of guilt or sadness—but she quickly schooled her features. "You're welcome, Cinderella," she said and took off after Henry.

12

OPPORTUNITY KNOCKS

I TRIPPED OVER THE TINIEST ROCK AND HAD TO SLOW TO A walking pace; we were only an hour from the lake, but the anklet was still slowing me down. I had been wearing it for weeks, but I couldn't get over everything it stood for. Sadness weighed heavily on my heart. On top of that, my daydreams had become increasingly distracting. Oliver asked what was wrong, and I blamed my mood on Henry. I couldn't tell him the *whole* truth. I couldn't tell him that along with the extreme anger and hurt I harbored toward my father, I was also constantly thinking of the stranger I'd met in the garden on my birthday. Every time I closed my eyes, even just to blink, I would find myself gazing into his blue eyes…

A slap across the face from a rogue willow branch brought me back to the present—the bright morning, cool breeze, tired legs, and Oliver's voice dripping with concern.

"Whoa, Kaya. Be careful! Come back to earth, darling," he said.

Henry always called me darling—the whole evening that I'd been trying to forget became even clearer. My forehead began to sting, and not just from the willow branch.

"Is there something else on your mind, girl? You're completely in a daze this morning. Wanna talk about it?"

I stopped and looked at Oliver. His cheeks were glowing, and his white T-shirt stretching over his damp skin was an invitation to stare… he was rock-solid perfect. Why would I have anyone else on my mind when I had him?

He plucked a wild daisy from the ground and held it out to me. "A flower for your thoughts?" he said sweetly.

But his words were like a punch in the gut—it was the same thing the stranger had asked me in the garden. I felt the blood drain from my cheeks.

"Kaya, what's wrong?"

"I'm… just a bit dizzy…" I lied.

"Sit down. You've been pushing yourself way too hard the last few weeks."

I did as I was told and sat down on the trail. An ant crawled over my bare leg. I watched him scurry off while I reasoned with myself—Oliver couldn't know what was going on in my mind. Nobody could. Carl had said security was disabled for an hour that night when I confronted him about it, and there wasn't anything on camera when I doubled-checked the footage to make sure he was telling the truth. Besides, I did nothing wrong, I was stressing over literally nothing, and I was feeling guilty over *thoughts* for God's sake. *Thoughts.* "I should run away," I said aloud, but I mostly to myself.

"Huh? What are you talking about? Did that branch rattle your brains?"

"I could leave, couldn't I?" I looked down at the tracking device on my ankle. Despite Stephan's order to leave it alone, I had tried to get it off last night, but it wouldn't budge. Now, a ton of makeup covered horrible bruises. "I think Henry is bluffing."

"I doubt that," he said.

"I want out. You, me, and Stephan—we could all run away together."

Oliver laughed, but then he grew quiet when he realized I was serious. "Is that what you've been thinking about while you've had your head in the clouds lately?"

"Um, yes."

"Are you still dizzy?" he asked.

I shook my head no.

"Come on then, follow me." He stood and pulled me to my feet.

"Where are we going?"

"Well, let's test that anklet. Let's be certain about what we're dealing with so we can put your curiosity to rest. But, Kaya, you know you are only safe *here*, right? Running away is absolutely ludicrous," he said as we wandered off the path into the bush.

I didn't reply. I didn't agree.

We pushed through tall grass and skinny willow trees, carefully parting branches until we came upon an enchanting little clearing. Purple clover and tall wild grass bloomed in small patches, and sunlight shone through breaks in the trees. It seemed too perfect to be real. Bees buzzed and hummed, and one landed on my arm, its pretty yellow-and-black body so fuzzy I had to resist petting it. After a minute, it flew off, soaring up and over Oliver's head. "This is amazing," I said in awe.

Oliver marched out into the middle of the open space, sending butterflies scrambling up and out of the grass. "This should be about the edge of the property. I can hear the highway, and… so far so good," he said, referring to the fact that we were still alone and Lowen Security hadn't swarmed down upon us. There weren't even any flashes of light in the trees—the usual signal we got from *them* to let us know they were near—and they were always near. This was very odd.

"What about *them*?" I asked.

"None here as far as I can tell," Oliver said, looking around curiously. He was about to say something else, but he quickly changed his mind when more blue-and-white wings drifted up out of the clover. A butterfly landed on his hand. He gave it a gentle shake, but it held on.

"I guess it likes you," I laughed.

"And how about you, Kaya Lowen… do you like me, too?" he asked playfully.

"You know it."

His eyes narrowed with intensity. "It has been excruciating not being able to touch you," he said, and then in three eager steps, he was before me, pulling my body to his. His lips brushed my cheek, and then he moved slowly to my mouth—but I didn't want to kiss him back. I suddenly felt apprehensive and had to force myself to respond. Something had changed, and being this close to Oliver didn't feel like it did before. I had been so desperate to have him just weeks ago, and now… not at all. I made my lips move in synch with his anyway, tasting the salt on his skin as his hands moved up the back of my shirt. I had to remind myself that this was okay—this was *Oliver*, the same man who saved my life, sat by my bed, and looked after me when I was sick—but the stranger in the garden was messing with my head. For some twisted reason, I felt like I was cheating… on *him*. Everything was messed up.

"I love you, Kaya," Oliver said, letting go to look into my eyes. Then he got down on his knees before me. "I have been waiting a long time for this moment, and thought about it over and over in my head, praying for the opportunity to make it happen. This might be too soon, but…" he held his breath and stared up at me, brown eyes filling with tears, "I can't live without you. You're everything to me."

My heart was pounding like a jackhammer. He had a tiny box in his hand, and he slowly opened the lid to reveal a shiny gold band covered in pink diamonds. I was speechless. Was he really doing this? Was he *proposing*?

"I want to protect you, make you happy, and I will love you always and forever." He reached for my hand. He was nervous, and I didn't dare move or speak. I just stared at him in disbelief as his voice shook. "Kaya, will you marry me?" he asked.

I fell to my knees before him because they wouldn't hold me up anymore. Marry him? *Marry Oliver?* I'd never entertained even the slightest notion of that happening. I cared about him, and couldn't imagine my life without him, but *marriage?*

I looked at his face and into those blue eyes, pulse fluttering as I reached out to brush away a lock of golden hair that had fallen across the scar over his cheek. A hot feeling bubbled in my chest, then a rush of cold travelled up my spine; I realized I was staring into the face of the stranger, *again.*

I had to end this ridiculous infatuation, and I knew exactly how to do it. "Yes," I said, smiling at Oliver.

"Yes?" he said, seeming shocked and relieved at the same time.

"Yes. I will marry you," I said, but my voice sounded distant and detached to my ears.

The most gorgeous smile came across his face. "Kaya, my girl, I am the luckiest man on earth," he said as he guided the ring onto my finger.

Then his hands were behind my head, winding into my hair, and he kissed me, softly at first, then with more urgency and passion than ever before. I knew there would be no stopping this time. Cars whooshed by on the highway, the meadow hummed with life, and a jet flew over our heads. Oliver's hot breath moved down my neck. His hands were under my shirt, undoing my bra, fingers slipping underneath the fabric and over my bare skin. His breath sped up, and I could feel the heat of him envelope me. I wanted to say no, I wanted to tell him to stop, but my body defied me. My hands were caressing him back, and I heard a soft moan come from my own throat when his mouth found my breast. I silently yelled no when he pushed me down onto the soft clover and eased himself into me. I let him have what he wanted and watched as his eyes fluttered in ecstasy. It was heaven. It was hell. It was my first time.

And I desperately wished it had been with the stranger in the garden.

THE AFTERGLOW DIDN'T LAST LONG.

Guns held by the familiar faces of Lowen Security were pointed at Oliver's forehead, and our beautiful clover patch almost became an execution ground. I was taken back to my room, crying because I'd just gotten engaged, the tracker worked, and Daddy Dearest wasn't bluffing.

I wasn't running away any time soon.

FALL-RACE DAY

13

ON YOUR MARK

GETTING OLIVER TO AGREE TO LET ME RUN **THE DEATH RACE** WAS more of a battle than the race itself was going to be. He was completely beside himself with rage. It was as if the ring on my finger gave him control over my life, and my defiance of his wishes was unthinkable. Stephan played it cool. Part of him was happy to see me following my dreams while the other part was still slightly angry for getting engaged to my bodyguard without passing it by him first. Davis, on the other hand, was ecstatic. About absolutely everything.

So there we were, race *day*, and I was celebrating three things before my feet even touched the starting line. First: just getting here—I kept pinching myself to make sure it was really happening. Second: getting Oliver to agree to it. After much debate, he decided to run with me—really though, was there ever the possibility he'd let me go alone? Nope. And third: I had made it through the first night in three months without having any dreams of the stranger—it had taken eighty-two days of working hard to replace the ache for him with love for Oliver instead. Now, as I stretched and warmed up for the adventure of a lifetime, I could finally let the man in the garden with the blues eyes *go*.

As we gathered at the entrance to Sulphur Mountain, I counted my lucky stars that the weather was perfect, cloudless, and with barely a breeze. It was so beautiful this time of year, too—the vibrant colors of fall painted the landscape in reds and oranges among pines still thick with green. I recognized a few of *them* right away, disguised as runners, and felt slightly deflated for a moment—they were everywhere, watching me and waiting for me to fail so they could report back to Henry. I had to make sure that didn't happen.

"Remember to try and avoid eye contact with them," Stephan reminded me.

He looked so adorable in his 'Go Katy' shirt, playing the role of adoring father, which wasn't a very long stretch. He'd put his ponytail up under a ball cap—something he normally wouldn't be caught dead in—and had trimmed his beard.

Davis was next to him stretching, happy and excited. Gone was the smoker's cough and bit of jelly around his middle. The daily workouts to prepare for the race had turned him into a new man. A Rush concert tee with the sleeves cut off was stretched across his chest, and every pocket of his favorite khaki shorts was stuffed with useless items. If you needed dental floss or a pair of pliers, he had it. Tape? Spare batteries? All there. It had been an all-out war to convince him that he couldn't run in jeans and motorcycle boots, and the sneakers he was proudly displaying were a blinding flash of green and neon orange.

"Wow, those shoes!" I exclaimed, pointing at his feet as the gleam made my eyes water.

"Yep. These babies are all the rage right now," he winked, and then he gave me the once over. "Geez, you should have let me help you shop, though, Kaya, I don't think funeral chic is in this month."

I grinned. I had purposely dressed very plainly. Black tank top, black yoga pants, black ball cap with as much hair stuffed up underneath without having a cone head, and a wind breaker with just a few white strips of piping along the seams.

Stephan laughed. "Looking plain is better than looking like a half-eaten popsicle. What's up with the kiddie shoes, Davis? Henry doesn't pay you enough to buy grown men's footwear?" he teased.

"Yeah, yeah. Hey Stephan, do you even know who the Boston Bruins are, or did you just pick a random cap to wear?"

Stephan smoothed his manicured beard. "Yeah of course. They are a sports team, um, baseball? No… hockey!"

"Stealing from Oliver's closet again, eh?"

While they giggled at each other, Oliver remained straight-faced, glancing around as if a pack of wolves were going to pounce upon us any minute. Davis and Stephan both rolled their eyes.

"Anyway, here are some antacids for your stomach," Stephan said, handing me a little tube of chalky pills.

Oliver zeroed in on me. "What's wrong? Are you sick again?" he asked anxiously.

"No, it's just heartburn, relax." I didn't dare tell him that my throat had been on fire since getting over the flu and I still had a hard time keeping food down, because I wasn't worried. The family doctor did some tests and assured me that all would go back to normal once I quit training so hard.

Brightly colored huts littered the clearing, and people as colorful as the flags and ribbons decorating the beverage tables had lined up to sign in. The lemon-flavored medicine foamed in my mouth while we waited for our turn at the check-in booth. Oliver and Davis breezed through easily enough, but of course, I got held up waiting for an acne-faced boy to find my name on a clipboard. I started feeling anxious as the line grew behind me.

"Adams... Katy Adams..." the boy said as he scanned through dozens of pages, his tight, silver necklace looking like it might choke him. I bit my tongue to stop myself from explaining the concept of 'alphabetical order'. "Katy... I don't see you on here, hmm, oh wait! Yep, yesiree, there you are," he said excitedly, and then he looked up and stared hard at my face. "Oh, damn. Sorry miss, uh Katy, just one sec... I'll be right back, I gotta take this call," he said, and spun around, disappearing into the back of the shack.

I never heard his phone ring. I could hear the feet of the participants impatiently rustle behind me until the boy returned with a flushed look about him. "Yeah, sorry about that. My girlfriend is really sick right now, and the doctor was just giving me an update. Anyway... okay... uh, Katy Adams, right?"

"Yep, still me," I said irritably, "hope your *brother* is all right, are you the eldest?"

He checked off something on his clipboard and reached under the table for my racer package. "Nope younger, and yeah... thanks. He's got appendicitis or something. Anyway, you are number 121. Good luck."

I wondered if Oliver had picked up on the boy's lie, but his stern expression hadn't changed. If I mentioned something seemed out of the ordinary, Oliver would think there was some sort of conspiracy, and I would be delivered home faster than I could blink.

I happily put the racer's bib on over my tank top and number 121 shone in white, reflective numbers. I couldn't conceal my elated grin as a few beads of sweat trickled down my back. I pulled warm, clean mountain air into my lungs and closed my eyes for a minute. This was really happening. I was here. And it was already amazing.

The first group of racers was already off and running, and in ten minutes, it would be our turn to start. As we gathered at the starting line, I noticed a very pretty blonde staring at Oliver. She wasn't just checking him out; she was blatantly and very obviously trying to get his attention, flipping her honey-colored hair and flashing her blinding-white smile. Tiny blue shorts barely covered her butt, and I couldn't help but notice that she was braless—neither could Davis. I felt a tinge of jealousy, even though Oliver was too busy taking in the entire world around him to

packets of orange-flavored gel in my pocket, so I sucked on a few, but my stomach revolted and acid crept up into my throat like a burp of fire.

But I kept moving, jogging at a slower speed while fishing the antacids out of my pocket. As I unraveled the foil around the tube of chalky pills, my eyes left the ground for a second too long and I stumbled off the path. A sharp pain in my foot brought me to a grinding halt. I looked down to see a stick jammed into the side of my shoe, and, in a panic, I bent over and yanked it out. It came away red. I stifled a yelp.

"What's up?" Oliver asked. He'd stopped a few feet ahead.

I couldn't tell him. "Sorry, just dropped my water bottle," I lied.

I jogged up to him, trying not to limp. With each step, it throbbed, and I knew by the wet, sloppy feeling around my toes that it was bleeding a lot. This injury was a legitimate reason for him to take me out of the race. So I faked being more tired than I was, and I carefully stayed a half pace behind him, hoping he wouldn't hear me cursing the increasing pain under my breath.

We came to a fork in the trail, and Davis consulted his map. This was definitely one of many traps we were warned about: two neon markers pointed in opposite directions. If you blindly ran along without checking, you would go in a circle, leading right back to the very point from which you started, adding hours to your time.

Davis led us to the left, and within minutes, we could see the roof of the first check-in hut—four hours down, twenty more to go.

After signing in, I made my way over to Stephan, who had insisted on being shuttled up the old logging road to the checkpoint. This was the last hut he'd have access to; I wouldn't see him again until the end. Collapsing onto a patch of grass next to him, I grinned when I saw the look in his eyes—teary with pride. "How's it going, kiddo? Is everything all right?" he said, and shoved something pasty and sweet in my mouth.

"Oh yeah, I'm tired but I am absolutely loving it! Kinda have a sore foot, though..."

My pink runner had become a muddy brown. He pulled it off and let out a gasp so dramatic I had to laugh. "Something cut your foot right through your shoe!"

"Yeah, I tripped, but it's fine. Just don't say anything to Oliver. He'll freak out," I begged.

"Yeah, yeah. I can't tell how deep it is, though. It could get infected," Stephan said, fussing and rinsing and applying some paste.

"Just please hurry up and cover it before he notices."

Oliver's back was to me, and he was talking to a medic. I noticed that blonde from the starting line purposely changing her shirt as slowly as possible in an effort to get his attention. She was graceful, tanned, pretty… and, thank God, had put on some sort of undergarment. I couldn't tell if he was watching her or not.

"Don't worry, he only has eyes for you," said Stephan, as if reading my mind.

"What? Oh, I'm not jealous. I'm just wondering why he's talking to that medic."

I pulled my soaked T-shirt up over my own head and struggled when it became fused to my sweaty skin. My attempt to be graceful turned embarrassing when I got stuck. My arms were tangled in the shirt above my head, reaching for the sky. I certainly hadn't made a show of it like the blonde, at least one worth watching, anyway.

Stephan, trying not to laugh, came to my rescue. "Well, you're on your own now," he whispered as he freed me from the spandex. "Only volunteers are allowed at the next three check-ins. But our guys are running in relay teams, and there are at least four of them at each station, as well as the ones who have been following you from the start. You've got lots of eyes on ya."

I realized I hadn't seen the ones from the starting line in a long while. They were probably winded and just couldn't keep up. I kept that to myself.

"I've got my ears on ya too; Oliver and Davis are both linked to me as long as we have reception. Oh, and I put two extra shirts and some more protein bars in your backpack." He was rambling, which was his usual approach when worrying about me. "Oh, and more antacids too… and Kaya, even if you don't finish, you've already won, you know. Even making it to the end of this first leg is a victory. You don't have to kill yourself trying to get to the *very* end."

He was so sweet. "Believe me, *Dad*, I'm having a blast. I'm happy about getting this far, but I *know* I can get to the end."

"You're so stubborn," he said and kissed my forehead, his beard making my whole face tickle. He rose to leave, and I dove for him.

"Stephan, wait…" I grabbed him and hugged him tightly, wishing his heart was stronger so he could run with me. I knew that's what he secretly wanted.

"I am so proud of you, kiddo," he whispered and hugged me back, and then, whispering softly in the most sincere and heartfelt tone, he said he loved me.

THE NEXT LEG OF THE RACE WAS TWENTY-SEVEN KILOMETERS. WE HAD six hours to complete it and get to the next check in point. The path was narrow—we were running single file through trees as thick and dense as I imagined the jungle would be. The 'fast pacers' huffed in agitation behind the 'turtles', and when the path widened onto a patch of clover, it became chaos. We passed people gasping for breath while we tried to hang on to our own. I was grateful that I still felt strong and my energy level was good, until out of nowhere, my mouth filled with saliva. The orange gel I'd been cautiously consuming made its way up onto the back of my tongue and my stomach rolled. Only this time, it wasn't teasing—I was going to be sick.

I tried to push the feeling out of my mind, but that seemed to make it worse. Then it came up—everything in my stomach that is—and I had just enough time to take a few steps off the path to hurl orange puke onto a patch of grass in piles. A lady swore at me when she almost collided with my backside, and just as quick as the nausea came, it left. I instantly felt better.

Oliver stopped, bent over and gasping for breath beside me with his hands on his knees. He held out his water bottle. "I think we better go back and get you checked out," he said, still breathing heavily.

"Uh, not in a million years. I'm fine," I replied while I struggled to get control of my breath and straighten myself up.

"But we need to make sure…"

I shushed him. "Oliver, really. People throw up all the time—it's no big deal. And I feel better now. Obviously I can't eat that orange crap."

I forced my feet to get moving again, but I had a hard time getting my rhythm back. My legs had that shakiness one gets after hurling and the race was suddenly becoming just as much a test of will as it was of physical strength. It was getting hot, I had a horrible cramp in my thigh, and each and every muscle ached along with my still-throbbing foot. Positive thinking, pep talks, and bird counting did nothing to subdue my agony… until Davis reminded me that Henry was expecting me to fail.

And that was just the kick in the pants I needed.

AT A HILL COVERED IN LOOSE ROCKS, WE DESCENDED DOWNWARD AS OUR feet slipped out from beneath us. Davis fell and rolled almost all the way to the bottom at one point, unable to stop, and took out a few people in his way. It was like he was tobogganing on rocks—but his rear end was the sled.

At the bottom was a large bog of mud that looked like a river of melted chocolate. Everyone in it seemed to be struggling. Sounds of exhaustion, misery, and anger blended together into one collective voice while volunteers stood by with ropes to rescue those who had given up. I thought it couldn't be that hard—after all, it was only mud.

But as soon as my feet went in, it was as if a thousand pounds of cement clung to them. With every step, the mud got deeper, stickier, and even more determined to keep hold. I was instantly exhausted. Moving forward suddenly became the most difficult thing I had ever done in my life. I lifted my foot, trying to drag it forward, but it barely budged. Each step required maximum effort to cross a minimal distance, and I became stuck—physically and mentally. I began wondering why I had wanted to do this in the first place. I even questioned my very existence. I couldn't go on.

Henry had won.

"I can't do this," I said, even my voice sounded tired. The mud was now up to my thighs. An older woman moved past me, very slowly, but at least she was moving. She cursed and struggled but was not about to let the mud beat her.

"You can do this too, Kaya," Oliver said, and he offered me his hand.

It was the first positive thing to come out of his mouth since we started, yet I refused his help. If I couldn't do this on my own, then why was I even doing it? I didn't budge, and he didn't move from my side. It felt as if an eternity went by as we stood in the brown muck. Finally, staring up at him, I hoped to be greeted by a look that meant he had won and we could go home. "Oliver, I can't do this. I'll admit it. I am too tired, and this is too hard… even my soul hurts. I admit defeat. I quit."

I thought he'd be happy, but instead, he snapped at me like a drill sergeant. "*Nope.* No way are you quitting! You dragged me out here and into this, and if I'm doing it, then so are you. Now, *move your ass!*"

I blinked at him in shock; he'd never talked to me like that before, and I didn't know quite how to process it. Should I be angry, or grateful that he wasn't giving up on me?

He grabbed my hand and looked me square in the eye. "I may not have been supportive before, but we are in this together, and I don't quit. *We* don't quit. Understand? Now take my hand, and get moving."

I pulled up one foot, moved it forward about an inch, and then I plunked it back down. Spurred forward by anger and encouraging words from my guard and fiancé, my desire came back. I rallied every last speck of energy within my cells and made it through the mud, and then I hugged Oliver tightly at the end. We collapsed into a giant messy heap, and I felt like I was going to cry. I rubbed at my face, smearing thick mud from one ear to the next, which caused Davis to burst into laughter. His amusement spread like wildfire, and we rolled on the ground pointing and laughing at each other.

I'd never felt so happy in my entire life.

But soon after, being covered in mud wasn't funny anymore. After a good solid hour of the sun drying it onto our skin, it felt like a thousand mosquito bites. We were so crazed with itch that when Old Man's Creek came into view, we sprinted toward it like bees were chasing us. Black clouds of dirt lifted from our bodies and surrounded us in the water. I rubbed at my face and went completely under, soaking my hair and cooling my overheated body. Afterward, I felt practically brand new.

The sun was now directly overhead, beating down relentlessly and drying our damp clothes as we jogged steadily up Mount Hazel. My lungs burned, and I had a horrible stitch in my side that kept trying to stop me from moving. Oliver's cheeks glowed, and his breathing was loud. Davis however, marched ahead like a machine, barely even sweating—I couldn't believe this former overweight, pack-a-day smoker was kicking our butts.

When the trail ended at a large mound of rock that rose up ominously before us, Davis pulled out the map and confirmed what we all feared—we had to climb. "Once we get to the top, it's about an hour to the next check-in point," he informed us as he carefully re-folded his map.

My legs felt like spaghetti. I waited for my second wind while staring at the rock, hoping there were lots of crevices for footholds and ledges to grasp on to. It didn't seem too steep, but I was tired. I bent over at the waist, willing the stitch in my side to go away, and heard a pained cough and moan from someone on the ground beside me. I looked down to see an elderly man who was sitting cross-legged and looking completely defeated. His knees were bloody, and there was a fresh scrape across his forehead.

"Is everything okay?" I asked.

"Yeah. My legs are strong, but my arms are weak, I wasn't prepared for climbing. I mean, look at that darn rock! Ain't no way around it, either. No ropes, or steps… nothing. I thought this was supposed to be a *running* race."

His voice was so dry and dusty I felt sorry for him. Had he been a bit chubbier, he would have been the spitting image of Old Carl. "There certainly is more to this race than just running, isn't there? I personally wasn't all that fond of the mud."

"Yep. That was bloody awful, too." He nodded in agreement. "I'm Isaac," he said and thrust out a filthy, skinny hand.

I leaned over to shake it. "Nice to meet you, I'm Kaya-uh, Katy."

Oliver leapt to my side as I almost revealed my real name.

"And you are?" Isaac asked, eyeing Oliver's large hand wrapped protectively around mine.

"This is my fiancé," I answered.

Isaac struggled to his feet. "Well, hey big guy, do you think you could you help an old timer like me out?" said Isaac, and he motioned toward the rock. "Maybe give a hand up or a push here and there?"

Oliver's grip on me relaxed. "Yeah, for sure," he said kindly.

"Ah, the strength of youth. What I wouldn't do to have that again," Isaac said as stretched his ancient legs, and I wondered how anyone so old and frail looking could walk let alone run a race.

Isaac started making the climb, his fingers grabbing hold of tree roots, while Oliver followed behind and offered his hand as a foothold. Davis followed, giving me a push once in a while, teasing Oliver by saying he got to feel my butt. I laughed. Of course, Oliver didn't find it funny.

Lush, green moss clinging in sparse patches made some spots slippery. A few times, Isaac lost his footing, and Oliver steadied him. We all waited until he got moving again, ducking from a few stray rocks here as the other racers scurried past. When we were a few feet from the top, Isaac slipped, but this time Oliver didn't have a chance to react. The old man's foot slammed heavily into Oliver's chest with a sickening thud. Oliver lost his footing for a moment, sliding down the rock about a foot and gasping for breath, and I watched helplessly as the old man quickly scrambled the rest of the way up and disappeared over the top.

Davis bolted to Oliver's side and put an arm out to steady him. "Ollie, you okay buddy?" he asked, waiting patiently for Oliver to catch his breath. "Can you climb?"

"Yeah," Oliver choked out. "Man, that—guy got me good—and he was—wearing metal cleats."

"Cleats? What the hell? And the bastard is gone without even thanking you?"

"It's okay… I'll be all right," Oliver said, but he was obviously in pain by the way his right arm was firmly crossed over his chest.

Davis and another racer helped Oliver the rest of the way up, and I was left on my own, or so I thought; I lost my balance and was shocked when a large hand was suddenly steadying me by firmly pushing on my lower back. I knew it had to be one of *them*…

"Careful miss," said a man with steel-grey eyes.

They were eyes I'd never forget. Not because of the squinty shape and odd color, but because they were the eyes of the man that held a gun to Oliver's head the day we tested the tracking device—the day we found the little sanctuary off the trail and got engaged. This man, Mark Reicht, would have had no problem pulling the trigger if he'd been ordered to. No amount of pleading, crying, or screaming would have changed his mind. Only on Sindra's command did he put his gun away and order his men to retreat.

I had the most intense urge to push him backward.

He stuck to me like glue until I was safely at the top, and then he gave me a discreet nod before disappearing. I was glad to be rid of him. Blondie, however, was sprawled out on the grass like a model posing for a beer commercial. It looked like a lightning bolt hit her by the way she sprung to her feet when she saw Oliver.

"What happened?" she asked while Davis eased him to the ground.

"A swift kick to the ribs, and the perp ran off."

"I'm a nurse; let me look at him," she said, her blonde hair falling over her concerned face as she practically shoved Davis and me out of the way.

Oliver glared, his eyes narrowing on her angrily. I knew a wounded Oliver behaved like a wounded dog… you had to approach very, *very* carefully. "I'm fine. Leave me the hell alone," he growled.

But Blondie didn't flinch. Instead, she boldly got up in his face. "Listen sweetheart, even big guys need help once in a while," she said. "Let me at least check the wound."

She called him sweetheart. I decided then and there that I hated her with every fiber of my non-blonde female existence. Then, when Oliver actually let her lift his shirt to inspect the damage, it was all I could do to not rip her face off.

"It's a good scratch; it's not too deep, though," she informed us as she pulled a small plastic box from her pack. "I'll dress it, and he'll be good to go." She pressed a bandage to his ribs, and I noticed him wince, then a horrible cough burst from his lungs. "Drink," she said and put her water bottle to his mouth. He shook his head defiantly. Then another hacking cough erupted, and he lunged for and downed the entire bottle.

Blondie looked a little too pleased.

"Are you all right, Oliver?" I asked, feeling useless beside Davis. "Should we get back to it?"

Oliver looked at me through half-closed eyelids, but didn't reply.

"He needs to rest for a minute," Blondie said, taking his pulse, "I wonder if he might have a bit of altitude sickness."

Oliver mumbled that he was perfectly fine and just needed a minute, then he tipped his face to the sun and closed his eyes.

"I guess we rest for a bit then," I said, outwardly feigning control over the situation while inwardly seething with jealousy.

My own injury was inconveniently bleeding again. While Oliver sat there oblivious to everything around him, I pried off my shoe. The bandage had wiggled its way off, and who knew how much mud and bacteria had worked its way into the wound. Davis intervened, quickly cleaning and wrapping it for me without saying a word.

When Oliver was finally ready to move again, Davis consulted the map and took us on a path that would lead to the summit of Mount Hazel. Here, we struggled with another climb, though thankfully not as difficult as the one before, and then we pushed ourselves up a winding, well-traveled mountainside. Oliver's cough grew worse, but he wouldn't slow down. He was fixated on marching ahead like a machine. Meanwhile, I stopped twice to throw up in the bushes. He didn't even notice.

Once we hit the plateau and our feet were firmly planted on the flat, grassy summit, Davis let out a triumphant wolf howl, and Blondie smiled earring to earring. I did a small happy dance, throwing my arms up like I did the night I danced with Angela, but Oliver's face didn't change. In fact, he looked completely miserable. From up here, there were seemingly endless skies and snow-topped peaks poking up from evergreen valleys for as far as the eye could see. It was completely breathtaking. It was the view that made everything worth it. Oliver barely seemed to notice.

"Hey, you guys, thanks for doing this with me," I choked out between heavy breaths. I was bursting with gratitude for my companions—maybe even the blonde.

Davis's sticky, hot hand grabbed mine, and a slight breeze wafted some of his body odor up my nose. He reeked, but oddly enough, it didn't bother me. "I'm glad you brought me out here, Kaya… this is amazing," he grinned, red-cheeked, bright-eyed, and glowing.

I hugged him. Sometimes I felt like he was the only one who really understood 'this'.

"And you showed him, ya know," he added with a gleam in his eyes.

"Showed who, what?"

"Henry. You've lasted eight times longer than he'd expected… that's a lot of dough for him to lose if he would have bet against ya."

"Yes, you're right!"

I grinned madly with triumphant satisfaction at the thought and went to hug Oliver, but he just looked right through me and marched off with Blondie hot on his heels.

I was dumfounded. In all the years of having him glued to my side, even when I hated him and was horribly nasty to him, he never ignored me like that.

"He's just anxious to get to some sandwiches," Davis said quickly, but he was as shocked at Oliver's behavior as I was.

For the next hour, I chewed antacids like I was gnawing on fake-tanned, blonde, Barbie bones.

JUST WHEN I THOUGHT I COULDN'T TAKE ANOTHER STEP, THE CHECK-IN hut came into view, glowing in the distance like a lighthouse in the twilight. I used my last bit of energy to sprint for it and practically collapsed at the steps from exhaustion and elation. Lit up like a Christmas tree, colored lanterns swung from the railing and the trees, and the fire pits roared with the sound of racers talking as they warmed their hands and sipped their drinks. After the mandatory once over, I was sent to first aid where a very kind woman froze and stitched my foot. I thanked her for the immense relief, and then I stuffed two peanut butter cookies in my mouth and a few in my pocket. I reached for a brownie but stopped when I heard Oliver, angry and slurring, arguing with someone from behind the hut.

"Hey buddy, just chill, all right? Have a seat for a sec like they asked you to," Davis was saying in a firm voice.

I made my way around back to see Oliver wild eyed and confused. His arms swung heavily from his shoulders, and he shook them like he wanted to fight Davis.

A medic spoke calmly, his neon vest displaying the name George in capital letters. He got in between Oliver and Davis with his hands up. "Listen, you might not be getting enough oxygen right now, sir. We're trying to help you," he said, and then firmly grabbed Oliver by the shoulders.

Oliver pulled away and almost tripped backward, rotting deck boards creaking under his weight. When volunteers with radios started to gather around, I could tell by their anxious voices there was something really wrong with Oliver. All the hair on the back of my neck lifted.

"Oliver, listen to them, please…" I begged, and suddenly his eyes snapped into focus on me.

"Let's get goin', Kaya… we've got… race to run…" he said, and then he stumbled forward into my arms. His eyes were wobbling in his head, and a racking cough shook his entire body. Was he drunk? Having a stroke? As Davis and I struggled to keep him upright, someone jabbed a needle into his arm.

"What the hell did you give him?" I asked George the medic when Oliver collapsed onto a stretcher.

George seemed extremely relieved to have Oliver subdued. "Just something to keep him calm so we can get him to town. Pretty sure he's got a touch of altitude sickness. Need medical attention. He's a big guy—if he resists, it might compromise his safety and ours."

People had gathered around us like bugs around a lantern. So many faces staring in our direction stirred up my anxiety. I noticed Mark Reicht's steely stare in the crowd, and I was almost glad I didn't push him off the cliff—almost.

"Kaya, they're—takin' me outta the race," Oliver mumbled. "I'm sorry, baby."

His legs were being safely secured beneath wide straps, so I bent down to get close to his face. I had never seen him weak before. I wanted to be strong and say the right things, but my voice shook with fear. "It doesn't matter; it's just a race. All I care about is you. I'll go with you to the hospital, don't worry. I won't leave your side."

He tried to bolt upright and winced. "No. Don't you dare quit!" he roared. "Kaya, you can do this… you're right, I can't keep you locked up all the time. You gotta keep at it, my girl, and besides—you've got Davis."

"I promise to look after her. You have my word," Davis interjected.

I felt tears coming on and fought desperately to keep them away. I hadn't been anywhere or done anything without Oliver at my side in so long…. "No, I can't just leave you like this," I said, feeling my stomach twist.

"I mean it, Kaya!" Oliver roared with a ferocity that made me jump.

The crowd around us instantly grew silent, and the preparations to extract him came to a grinding halt. I could tell George was contemplating giving Oliver another sedative.

"Oliver, you're hurt, so please relax. I'm tired and was ready to go home, anyway. I won't leave you," I said, trying to reason with him.

His brown eyes fluttered, becoming distant for a moment, and then his hand reached for mine. "No, I'm not hurt. I'm fine. Now, do what you came here to do… or I'll never forgive myself for being the reason you didn't. Promise me you'll keep going."

I squeezed his hand tight. "Yes, I promise," I said with the fingers of my other hand crossed behind my back.

George placed an oxygen mask over Oliver's mouth, and then he offered me his unwanted advice. "I'm sorry miss, but he's right. You should go on and finish. You wouldn't be able to travel down with us, anyway."

Then Oliver was pulled away. I wanted to tell him I loved him and that I couldn't go on without him—but there was no point. His eyes were shut, and he was out cold.

15

ROCK AND ROLL ALL NIGHT

WHILE HOLDING HANDS, DAVIS AND I STUMBLED ACROSS THE third checkpoint at 6:45 pm. After a fist bump and a bear hug, he made his way toward the snack tent, and I plunked myself down on the closest bare patch of earth that looked somewhat comfortable. I was happy to have gotten so far, but I felt lost without Oliver. For years, we had never been apart. He'd become an extension of my body. He called the shots. He made the decisions. Without him, everything seemed uncertain and vast... as if the space around me had been multiplied a thousand times.

I hoped Davis would understand when I told him that I had to leave the race.

He returned wearing what I assumed was orange soda and a trail of blueberry muffin crumbs on his shirt. His clothes had lost their vibrancy from being covered in dirt, yet he still glowed. His brown hair was sticky-looking with bits of mud still clinging to it from the bog, and scrapes covered his knees. I'd never seen anyone happier

"I finally got in contact with Stephan—reception's back," he said and pointed to his earpiece. "He said to tell you that Oliver is just fine and not to worry. He's sleeping off a smidge of altitude sickness. In the morning, he'll be good as new."

A massive wave of relief came over me. If Oliver was okay, then maybe I *could* finish the race. Seeing his proud face when I crossed the finish line on my own would be priceless. And Henry? He could suck it. He could wrap his lips around a great big giant as—

"Everything okay, lil' bud?" asked Davis.

"I'm fine," I smiled. "Just thinking about how amazing it will be to get to the end. And on my own, if you know what I mean."

"I do. And you're gonna make that happen. I know it." He grinned, pulling his hair back into a ponytail. "Maybe you should get that foot checked again, though."

He was right. My once-pink runner was now completely brown

now—and not from mud.

I found a medic to freeze and re-stitch the cut again—which I hoped looked worse than it was. Once it was completely numb, I could shoot bullets into my foot and feel nothing.

The sun was completely gone, and the sky was that ink-black color you only saw in the mountains. The icy air had dropped by about ten degrees just in the last hour, and I could see my breath. Davis and I put on our jackets and we checked the contents of our packs—water, protein bars, dry shirts, headlamps and extra batteries, protective glasses, rain jacket and gloves, sunscreen, band aids, bear spray, bug spray, extra shoes and socks—basically more crap than anyone could possibly use. My pack was heavy, and I contemplated 'accidentally' losing it in the bush somewhere. At least it made a good backrest. Leaning against it, I rubbed my sore legs with one hand and tried to eat a peanut butter sandwich with the other.

"Got you a sandwich, too," I told Davis. "There isn't much protein in those blueberry muffins."

"Thanks," he said with a wink, "I'll need that an hour from now." He wrapped the sandwich carefully in a napkin and put it in his pack. "How's the foot?" he asked.

"Perfect. That freezing is the cat's butt."

"Excellent," he said with a yawn. "Okay, well, I'm just gonna shut my eyes for ten minutes."

Before I could protest, he spread out on the ground and immediately passed out cold. If I didn't know him so well, I would have thought he had died right then and there. I sat beside him and finished my sandwich while he snored for exactly ten minutes.

MY FOOT WAS THE ONLY THING THAT *DIDN'T* HURT WHEN WE STARTED ON the fourth leg of the race. We eased back into a jogging pace with limited visibility. I stumbled a few times, talking myself into making it just to the next tree, and then just to the next rock. I kept this game going, my heart pounding like it might burst out of my chest. Just when I thought I might die of exhaustion, adrenaline kicked in, and a euphoric feeling took over. I became Superwoman conquering the world. My body was an efficient machine—every muscle in sync, lungs powerful, and mind alert and clear. I looked behind often to see the neon vests of the other runners, the lights on their headgear bobbing up and down as hilariously as my own, and realized that *they* were nowhere to be seen. Ha. The Lowen Security losers couldn't keep up.

But… Blondie was back. Like the plague.

Davis puffed out his chest and grinned madly when she ran up beside him. She didn't look dirty or tired or like she'd even broken a sweat—which I thought was odd. Her boobs bounced like basketballs in the tight jacket zipped low enough that I hoped she would get a nasty chest cold.

The light on Davis's hat made it fairly obvious where he was looking. "Hey Barbara," Davis said in his late-night radio DJ voice.

"Hey Ken," she cooed back.

I let loose an involuntary snort; Ken was Davis's alias… Ken and Barbie—hilarious!

"How's your friend, the big guy?" she asked, and I swear she batted her eyelashes.

Davis's tongue was tied up, and his eyeballs were bulging out of his head, so I replied for him. "He's just fine. Go on ahead, and don't worry about us," I said, but, apparently, I was invisible, so my words drifted off into the abyss.

"Hey, thanks again for that sports drink you gave me back there," Davis said to Blondie, "but I hope you don't mind if I gave it away. I just can't do anything grape flavored since grade twelve graduation. Tequila and grape pop—bad combo."

Blondie stumbled and actually seemed offended. Her eyebrows crumpled into what I would imagine sad little caterpillars to look like. "You *gave* it away?" she croaked.

"Yah, some dude looked a little parched, so I offered—"

She came to a grinding halt. Davis did too. His headlamp shone on her wide eyes. "You all right?" he asked her.

"Oh yeah, just got a cramp is all… and I should wait for my, uh, friend… I'll catch up…" she said, sounding strained.

I had to pull a reluctant Davis away. "She's so weird," I said to his red cheeks.

"Yeah, but so damn cute, and that, uh… *jacket*…"

I punched him in the arm as Blondie faded into the background where she belonged.

A BRIGHT, ROUND MOON LIT THE WIDE PATCH OF BARREN TERRAIN WITH an eerie glow. It almost felt like we had landed on Mars. It was flat, dry, dusty, and without a single weed or blade of grass. It made moving fast very easy. We kept an even pace, stopping only to sip water, fix a dying flashlight, and so I could catch my breath twice. Then we were back in the thick of the trees, making it past the escape station at Mount Hamel—the last place you could get off this ride if you wanted too—and finally to the forestry check-in tower in good time. We were both exhausted but elated.

When Davis dropped to the dirt to stretch out, I decided to just rest my muscles for a minute, too, so I lay next to him on the cold ground. I liked Davis's power nap idea but knew I wouldn't wake for hours—there were stories of the cleanup crew finding racers who were sound asleep the next morning. With my luck, I'd be one of them.

So instead, I gazed up at the starry sky and tried to push my mind away from the heaviness in my chest. I thought of Oliver beaming brightly when I made it to the end, and how I would fall into his arms as Stephan grinned madly with that stupid T-shirt on. And then there was the stranger. He was softly smiling, his dreamy, blue eyes blinking slowly while his voice, soft as butter, congratulated me and asked for my name again. No. I already had him out of my head, why was he here? I was telling him to go away, but he wouldn't leave. I tried to push him, but I couldn't reach... *leave me alone... leave me alone...*

Then Davis's booming voice shook the earth, and I bolted upright. "Kaya! Let's rock this!" he yelled, face lit up with more enthusiasm than should be legal.

I swear my heart stopped. Obviously, I'd fallen asleep, and now I was just super aware of how horrible I really felt. Davis stood grinning madly with twigs in his hair, chugging back a cup of coffee with probably twelve spoons of sugar in it. He looked dirty, but brand new. My adrenaline, however, was gone, and in its place was an intense ache and stiffness in every single part of my body. Everything hurt, even my hair. And, on top of that, the vision of the stranger was back.

"I feel like a steaming tower of crap," I admitted.

Davis laughed and handed me a bottle of water. "Well, this is Rockstar Juice. Keeps even the most tired and wasted musician fired up for hours. Tip it back, and you'll be kickin it like Steven Tyler on the *Back in the Saddle Tour.*"

"Who?"

"*Who?*" said Davis incredulously, "Oh my God, Kaya. You're kidding me... only the greatest rock singer in the world! Steven-freaking-Tyler! Rock God of Aerosmith. "Janie's Got A Gun"? "Dream On"? "Sweet Emotion"? The entire *Pump* album?"

I shook my head in tired confusion.

He sighed heavily. "You need a classic rock education... but for now, this drink is the power of positive thinking in a bottle, my friend," he whispered with a sly grin.

I drank the water, wishing it really were magical, because I felt like only a miracle would get me through this. When I was done, Davis widened his stance and grinned madly at my deadpan face.

"Now, are you ready to rock?" he said as he assumed the stance of a man ready to play the guitar solo of his life.

I nodded my head feebly.

"Let me ask you again, Miss *Katy Adams*... are you ready to *ROCK*?" he roared, throwing finger horns to the sky. A woman behind him bolted for the shack.

His excitement was infectious. "Yes, *Ken*, I was born ready." I laughed and returned the rock and roll salute. Then, after our mandatory fist bumps, we were off on the fifth and final leg of the Death Race.

CROSSING THE FINISH BY EIGHT IN THE MORNING WOULD MAKE US winners, and that was a title I wanted more than anything. I just hoped my body wouldn't fall apart. Davis and I adjusted to each other's pace, walking, running, and resting, and encouraging each other along the way. When a massive shadow crossed the path before us and ran off into the trees, Davis assured me it was a unicorn, and it didn't find humans appetizing, I chose to believe him. When he told me the howling wolves were just rogue poodles on the lam from a pet store, I thought that was a little far-fetched.

We pushed ahead, too cold to stop for even a second. Davis was worried about losing me to the night and wanted to rope us together, but I informed him that this was the 'off leash' park. He had a good laugh over that. "We'll be friends for life after this, ya know?" he said, and I happily agreed.

Only the relay racers passed us now, and it often felt like it was just Davis and I out there on the mountain. When we started our descent toward the river and through thick pines, our flashlights barely broke through the darkness. We held on to each other for strength and reassurance. Faced with another fork in the trail, I pulled out my map so Davis could inhale his peanut butter sandwich. "My map says to go straight," I said after careful consideration.

To the right was a loop that would lead us right back to the entrance of the cave, to the left was a trail to nowhere, and the middle was the path to the river and the Ferryman. Two racers passed us and took the path to the left. I was about to yell that they were going the wrong way, but Davis shushed me—he thought it was funny. Another racer didn't bother to look at his map, either, and he also went to the left.

"Dumb kids, they *always* go the wrong way," said a deep, gruff voice from somewhere in the dark.

I steadied my flashlight beam on a man sitting in a lawn chair next to a cooler of water bottles. If he hadn't spoken, we would never have noticed him—his neon vest wasn't bright like the ones the other volunteers wore.

"It's not that hard to follow a map," he said. "Oh well, I guess they'll figure it out when they get down there and have to come all the way back. That's why I'm here with extra water… for the idiots."

"So, the middle path is the one to take?" asked Davis.

"Well, yeah, it says so on your map, doesn't it? And didn't you walk these trails before you came?" he asked in a tone that made us both feel instantly dumb.

"Uh, no, I didn't know you could do that," Davis said with a tinge of embarrassment.

The man rustled around in the cooler, hood slipping slightly to reveal a mass of thinning, grey hair. "Well, here, take some extra H2O and get crackin', then," he said gruffly, holding out two bottles of water.

"Thanks for the tip," I said as I reached for them.

I wished I could see his face a little better, because something about him was familiar, but I didn't want to rudely shine my light into his eyes. Instead, I gratefully downed most of the water he'd given us while Davis tucked his away in his pack.

Then we headed down the middle pathway.

But it felt wrong. Branches whipped our faces. Thankfully, the mandatory protective glasses allowed us to keep our sights on the flashlight beams. As we made our way toward the river, the path thinned and became so overgrown that we had to walk single file. "Maybe that water guy was confused," I said after we had been descending steadily downhill for what seemed like forever. I was starting to feel dizzy, and the freezing in my foot was wearing off. A throb from deep inside the wound was becoming unbearable.

"Nope," Davis said, breathing a little heavier now. "We both read the map, Kaya. We're on the right path. Besides, here's a marker."

A post with neon-orange paint reassured us that we were going the right way, but we still came upon no racers and no one had passed us for at least forty minutes. It just felt all wrong. I was about to suggest that we turn back, but the river came into view, sparkling through the trees in the moonlight.

"See, we made it!" said Davis, just as relieved as I was. "Got your coin?"

I had checked for that coin a thousand times, but I did so again. My fingertips tingled when I handed it to Davis. I was struggling with a feeling of vertigo but didn't want to alarm him. Maybe I was dehydrated; I guzzled the rest of the water.

We made our way across the pebbled riverbed to where a small, yellow dingy was pulled halfway onto the beach. The moon lit up the area and the ominous figure of the Ferryman as he awaited his passengers. A long, black cloak floated around his huge frame, and a hood concealed most of his face.

"This is exciting, Kaya!" said Davis. "I never thought we would get this far, but we are *so* close to the end!"

"I know; I can't believe it. I must admit, I feel like crap mountain, though. Your Rockstar Juice has worn off."

He grabbed my hand, and we dragged our weary bodies up to the boat, the rocks beneath us killing my foot with every step. We eagerly offered our coins to the upturned palm of the Ferryman.

"Here's your fare, sir," said Davis happily.

The Ferryman shone a flashlight onto our faces and the coins were taken from us both. "Only one at a time," he said. "Ladies first."

His voice gave me the chills. It didn't mix well with the fuzzy feeling in my head.

"Uh no, sorry sir, but I travel with her, those are our rules," Davis said.

The boat jiggled slightly as The Ferryman stood straight as an arrow, his large figure looming over us from the boat. "Well you can follow *your* rules and wade across, or follow the rules of the game like everyone else," he said irritably.

"Sorry, the girl stays with me." Davis was adamant. I didn't think he realized how forcefully his fingers were digging into mine. I winced.

"Please, make an exception, sir," I said politely.

The coins were offered back. The Ferryman was taking his volunteer job very seriously, and I didn't want to end up not finishing the race because Davis was stubborn.

"It's okay, Davis. I'll be fine," I said, turning to face Davis, his angst evident in the bright moonlight. "Don't make an issue outta this." His fingers tightened even more around mine. "Really, it's okay. I'm a big girl, ya know. Besides, there are probably a dozen of *them* surrounding us right now," I whispered.

The Ferryman shifted uneasily, and the boat swayed like a big, comfy waterbed. I wanted nothing more than to get in and sit down. My legs were starting to shake.

"Listen, nothing is going to happen to anyone going across," the Ferryman said loudly, "I'll make sure of it. Now, get in lady, and I'll be back for you in five minutes, sir."

Davis reluctantly let go. "Don't you move an inch once you get across. Don't even blink until I'm next to you. Promise me," he said anxiously.

"Yes of course, I promise. Geez, relax." I gave him a quick hug, and then I climbed into the boat, grateful to sit down. My legs were tingling as if they were on pins and needles. I removed my backpack and let it drop to the floor along with the last of my energy.

"So, what's your name, miss?" said the Ferryman as we pushed away from the shore. I caught a glimpse of his cold eyes, and suddenly I felt wildly uneasy… he looked sinister with the moonlight reflecting off the water behind him and the stupid outfit on.

"My name is Katy Adams," I choked out and waved to Davis's fading outline on the shore.

We moved swiftly into the darkness. I thought the boat would just go across the river to the other side, but the Ferryman fired up the motor, and we began moving upstream. I suddenly wished I had stayed with Davis and asked timidly if we were going the right way. The Ferryman laughed, so I told myself I was being silly and worrying about nothing.

I relaxed into the rubber boat and looked up at the stars, wishing Oliver were here to admire them with me. I looked for Orion's Belt, our favorite constellation to gaze upon in the night sky, but I found it hard to focus. The twinkling lights started to blur, and my tongue was tingling too. I fought to keep my eyes open. I was so tired, but it was a strange and dizzy kind of tired…

Something clicked loudly and the floor of the boat quivered. I couldn't focus or move. I couldn't speak, either; my voice seemed to be… stuck. I pried my eyes open just long enough to see the Ferryman coming toward me with something in his hands. There was a sharp pain in my arm, and then the stars disappeared completely.

OLIVER

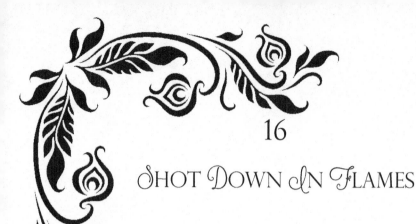

16

ᏚHOT ᎠOWN ᏐN ᎭLAMES

"OLIVER BENNET—SIR, PLEASE WAKE UP," SAID AN IMPATIENT, squeaky voice, and the acrid smell of tobacco breath wafted up my nose. I opened my eyes to a pimply faced girl staring at me with a clipboard in her hand. She was chewing gum and making that disgusting popping sound with her tongue. "Mr. Bennet, you may leave now."

Leave? I was wildly disoriented. I tried to sit up, but a sharp pain in my ribs stole my breath.

The girl adjusted her cat-eye glasses, and then she handed me a piece of paper. "The doctor has given you a prescription for pain—take one every four hours, but don't overdo it. Those things can mess ya up if you're not careful," she said, then scurried away.

Mint-green walls, fluorescent lighting, the smell of bleach—I was in a hospital, laying on a bed among many others in a long hallway. A crumpled white sheet partially covered my bare chest, and the pungent smell of antiseptic clung to my skin. A red sign that read "X-Ray" was above a wide door where I vaguely remembered a doctor explaining to me that there was nothing they could do for my cracked rib. I must have passed out again after that.

Wide-strip bandages were wrapped tightly around my chest, and dots of blood had already seeped through. Sitting up wasn't easy; it felt as if an imaginary knife twisted sadistically in my bones. I took in shallow breaths as I put on the shirt that had been neatly laid out at my feet.

At least my lungs were clear and my head didn't feel so strange anymore. I'd hiked in the mountains many times and had experienced altitude sickness—this was different. I knew the insane dizziness and disorientation couldn't have been from that. It was almost like I'd been drugged.

I swung my legs over the side of the bed and steadied myself, blinking at the shiny white floor while trying to put together the events of the last few hours. Bits and pieces were missing after the old man had kicked me in the chest. Mark Reicht had helped Kaya up to the top, and that blonde bandaged me up and gave me water, then everything after that was a blur.

A familiar sound buzzed in my pocket. I fished out the tiny radio link to Davis and clumsily put it in my ear. His voice blasted frantically from the earpiece.

"Oliver, are you there? *Oliver!*"

The stark hallway bustled with action for a brief second—a doctor moving swiftly, a man on a cell phone leaving a room—and then I was alone again. I was relieved to hear Davis' voice. Maybe he could explain a few things. "Hey, yeah, it's me," I replied, suddenly realizing how agonizingly thirsty I was, "how's it going it out there?"

There was an eerie pause before he answered. "Oliver—it's Kaya…"

He sounded scared, like something was wrong. My heart jumped. "Hey, you're breaking up. What's going on? Is she okay?" I asked.

"No." I heard Davis gulp. "I'm *so* sorry, Oliver. She's missing."

Surely, I'd misunderstood him. She couldn't be missing… "What did you say?"

"I think she's—been kidnapped."

There was no misunderstanding that… but it wasn't possible. It couldn't be. I was in a dream. What Davis was saying wasn't real… *Wake up…*

"I let her out of my sight for—I didn't want to, but—" he was saying.

The hallway started to close in, and my head started to spin. I leaned forward to steady myself and my ribs protested, as if screaming in pain. I fought to breathe while Davis kept blathering.

"She had a different map—it led us right to them and into a trap… the blonde… she drugged you, I think, tried to drug me, too—the Ferryman—a boat, and then someone shot me with a tranquilizer—I was out for hours… Henry knows she's missing. I'm almost at the hospital… just wanted to be the one to tell you first."

"How long has she been gone?" I asked through gritted teeth.

"At least four-and-a-half hours."

I pulled out the earpiece and let it drop to the ground. Nothing could have prepared me for this. The thought of Kaya scared, hurt, or being touched by someone else shook me to the core. I sat paralyzed on the edge of the metal bed, staring at the earpiece as it faintly buzzed. The universe began to push down on my shoulders with such crushing force it rendered my body useless. Panic crept in. I had only felt like this once before and was unable to do a damn thing about it; the strength to overcome wasn't in me, and I watched them die—I was frozen with fear as I helplessly watched my whole family die…

Never again would I lose someone I loved.

The thought turned my fear into rage—blood-boiling, blinding rage. It was the simplest and only emotion that would free my mind from this immobilizing state. I stood up and slammed the earpiece with my foot, stomping on it repeatedly until it turned to dust, and then grabbed the arm of a wheelchair, picked it up as if it weighed nothing at all, and threw it down the hall. A satisfyingly loud crash echoed off the walls. I clenched my hands into fists and searched for something else—anything else—to destroy… I would pummel the brick wall until both it and my hands turned to pulp…

"Stop it!" shouted a stern, female voice from behind me.

It was a voice that demanded my full attention. Through the haze of my anger, I turned to see Sindra calmly standing there, hands on her hips, wearing a trench coat wrapped tight around her tiny figure. With all the willpower I could muster, I forced my arms to stay at my sides— this small but mighty woman could end me with a snap of her fingers.

"Hitting things probably isn't a good idea. You might need your hands to find your fiancée," she said, and then she stopped a male nurse from coming to sedate me. "Now stand down, Oliver."

I obediently uncurled my fists—I was programmed to. Sindra, although only a few years older than me, ruled my life with her words. No matter what was going on in my head, I had no choice but to obey her—and I was fine with that.

"Take a deep breath," she said.

I did that too, steadying myself against the metal bed as pain ripped through my chest with each lungful. "You have to get me out there right now, Sindra. I have to find her," I said, unable to stop my voice from cracking.

"Look at me, Oliver."

I tried to focus on her face—dark brown eyes, brown skin, beautiful as if lit by the moon, black hair long and shiny like Kaya's—and a lump rose in my throat. My arms felt like lead, and my eyes fell to my idle hands, fingernails still dirty with mud from the bog.

"Get yourself under control, or I'll sedate you myself," she ordered.

I nodded my compliance.

"Now, Henry is organizing a team, and he wants you involved. Are you well enough to leave here?"

I nodded again. Sindra eyed the prescription given to me by the gum-chewing nurse and tossed it in the trash. "Don't bother with that crap; it wouldn't quell pain for an infant. This is all you need," she said and handed me a little blue bottle with Lowen Pharmaceuticals clearly printed on the cap.

I tipped it to my mouth and crushed the pills violently between my teeth. Sindra looked around, and then in a rare display of weakness, she took a few herself. Leading the way, I followed her blindly to the exit and through the lobby filled with people in wheel chairs and half-open dressing gowns. For a moment, I thought I might be sick, until the cold air wafting through the hospital doors took my breath. Outside, a limo was waiting in the half-empty parking lot, and Davis was leaning on the hood, nervously smoking. The early-morning light illuminated his weary face.

"Please don't beat the crap out of me," he said morosely, blowing a thick, white cloud of cigarette smoke into the air, his eyes brimming with tears.

There was no way I would hurt this man. He had become like a brother to me. I knew in my heart that what happened wasn't his fault, but I had to stay *controllably* angry; it was the only thing keeping me from being completely useless. "I should beat the crap outta you," I growled, cracking my knuckles to keep my hands busy.

He swayed nervously. "I'll do whatever it takes to get her back, Oliver. I love her like a sister." He stomped out the cigarette, and then put a fresh one to his lips with trembling hands. "I'll do anything you want me to do—*anything*." In one long drag, he turned half the cigarette to ash.

"Well first, you can quit with the damn smokes!" I yelled and slapped the cancer stick out of his mouth.

He sighed and tossed the rest of the pack into a garbage can where a man with one shoe promptly fished them out. "Whatever it takes, Oliver. I'll do whatever it takes to find her. I just hope Henry has a plan."

"It doesn't matter. I have my own," I said.

"Which is…"

I stared anxiously at the snowy peaks surrounding the town, the rising sun lighting the tips of them like candles. "I will tear these mountains apart until I find her, or die trying."

Davis put his hand out to shake mine. "I'm down for that."

KAYA

17

BAD MEDICINE

I WASN'T DEAD. I KNEW THIS BECAUSE I WAS FREEZING AND everything hurt—every muscle, bone, and toe—I could feel them, but I couldn't move them. I tried to open my eyes, but they wouldn't budge. It was as if they were glued shut. I tried to raise a hand to pry them open, but my arms wouldn't cooperate. My toes wouldn't wiggle, my knees wouldn't bend, and my tongue wouldn't shift around behind my teeth. What the hell was happening?

Relax. Don't panic. Breathe... that seems to be working just fine... breathe... try again...

Fingers. Toes. Tongue. *Nothing.*

I was paralyzed.

Okay, now panic.

I tried desperately to scream, but I couldn't even swallow. Was this hell, or was I caught in a strange deep sleep that I couldn't wake from? I could tell my body was moving, at least. My arm was swinging, and from the amount of liquid in my nose, I wondered if I was upside down. Maybe I was buried alive. Maybe I couldn't move because the earth was holding me down... but there was heat on my cheek and chest. I would be cold head to toe if I was in the ground.

I'd heard stories about people under anesthesia who could feel everything happening to them, but their bodies were immobilized—was that happening to me? Was I in surgery? There were people around me, for sure; I heard their heavy breathing, and I could smell them. I could hear the swishing sound of jacketed arms, the crunching of debris under heavy footsteps, and a cell phone ringing.

A voice reverberated in my ears so loud it was like someone had pointed a megaphone toward my head. "Yeah, I've got her," a gruff man's voice said breathlessly, "but she's out cold. We may have given her too much—she's a fighter. Yeah, probably a half hour."

I recognized the voice of the Ferryman, and it all came crashing back: the boat, waking to feel his hands on my neck, and clawing at him with all the energy I had—at least when they find my body, they'll also find a good amount of the bastard's DNA under my fingernails.

"Your turn to carry her," said the Ferryman to another.

I felt my body floating toward a cleaner smell—toward someone who liked musky cologne and soap. "Damn, she shouldn't still be unconscious," said a male with an English accent.

The heat against my body disappeared. Suddenly, I was freezing, shivering so hard I could feel my teeth knocking together. I was cold right to the pit of my stomach, right to my spine. Not the kind of cold you get from being outside in the snow or getting out of the pool at night, but a snap-your-bones-in-half kind of cold.

"Those drugs should have worn off by now. Hey, open your eyes a bit, darling," said the Englishman.

He slapped my cheek—it stung, but I couldn't respond. I just kept getting colder and colder.

"Uh, Seth," he said, voice full of concern. "We have to stop for a minute; something isn't right with her."

I could tell I was being put down because the liquid in my nose drained. Was I on the ground? My limbs started twitching, and my eyes opened briefly to see a glimpse of a young man staring back at me. A dark wool cap barely contained locks of strawberry-red hair, and his freckled cheeks were slightly sunburned. He shone a light into my eyes as he moved his hand to my neck. It was searing hot. What was he doing? Was he going to kill me? I could feel my heart beating faster and faster in my chest, and I knew I had begun to shake violently. *Keep calm, keep calm,* I kept telling myself, but I heard panic in the voices of my captors, too.

"She's going into convulsions. Damn it, Seth, we can't lose her!" said the Englishman.

"You're the doctor! *Do* something!"

The Ferryman... his name is Seth. I repeated this in my head, held on to it, and focused on it by writing it in jagged letters on an imaginary chalkboard in my mind. The man in the boat with the unshaven face and dark cloak... *his name is Seth... his name is Seth...*

"Get the blanket out of the pack," one of them said.

I could feel hands on my neck again. I was dying. I could tell. A strange calm started to creep over my mind, and the crazy pounding in my chest slowed. As the cold started to ebb, I thought of Davis standing on the other side of the river. *Davis... I'm not there... I can't wait for you... I'm sorry. And Stephan, I love you. And Oliver...*

A blinding light pulsed through my eyelids in short bursts. I counted them—one, two, three—and then the fourth pushed against my pupils, burning like the hot sun... and there he was, standing in front of me and reaching for my hand—the beautiful stranger, the man with the incredible blue eyes with lights surrounding him like a halo. *Don't give up,* he was saying, and I didn't bother pushing him away this time. I even considered moving toward him...letting him hold my hand...

But then the bright light turned muddy grey. Someone's mouth was on mine, pushing their breath into my lungs—warm... soft... and my chest rose up and down, the taste of peppermint gum on my tongue... and then the cold came back with a hard slap. My heart jumped in my chest, crashed around, and then slowed to an even beat. I opened my eyes and stared up at the Englishman's immensely relieved face.

"You had us worried there for a minute. Damn it, girl; it's not your time to die... yet," he said, his cheeks red and eyes wide. I tried to recoil when his fingers pushed on my neck, feeling for my pulse, but my body defied me yet again. The moon had moved to the far corner of the sky behind him, so I stared at it to avoid eye contact. "Can you move?" he asked.

If I could, I would rip your eyes out. I tried to yell, but nothing came out.

Seth leaned over and into my line of sight. His scrubby face was inches from mine, his breath foul and hot, and my ragged fingernail scratches scabbing over across his cheek. "Listen, we're not going to hurt you, I promise. Please don't be scared," he said.

And then I was lifted and floating on imaginary waves in his arms while we moved deeper into the trees.

18

1,968

I WOKE TO SEE SUNLIGHT STRUGGLING TO SHINE THROUGH THE canopy of trees. The morning dew was so thick it dropped off the leaves like rain. I licked some off my lips, finally able to move my tongue, and bit the inside of my cheek when the Englishman stumbled.

"Hey, Regan, you okay?" said Seth. "We better stop for a sec."

Regan. Now I had a name for the clean-smelling man with the peppermint breath. He was carrying me now, and by the amount of sweat pouring down the sides of his red cheeks, had been for some time. I studied his face when he put me down. He was quite beautiful—he looked nothing like what I imagined a kidnapper would look like. He wiped the sweat off his brow, which left behind dirty streaks, and then hunched over on his knees as he struggled to catch his breath.

Seth dropped to the ground, too, and the packs he'd been carrying made a light thud as they fell. Gone was the long cloak, and now a brown ski jacket and jeans hung from his average frame. This new look certainly made him seem far less menacing, even though his haggard face was heavily lined, as if life had already worn him down. His brown hair was tinged with silver around the temples and a gold chain held a small cross tight to his throat. I didn't think he looked like a kidnapper, either.

Twisting off the cap of a metal water bottle, he tipped it to his lips and thirstily gulped. "You need to drink, too," he said, eyeing me.

I was thirsty, but I defiantly pursed my lips together; I didn't want anything from him. What if he was trying to drug me again?

"Listen, girlie. You're gonna drink it, or I'll force it down your throat." He lifted my head up and put the bottle to my mouth. I pretended not to want any, but once a few drops hit my tongue, I couldn't help but guzzle back the cool water. "That's good," he said, "you keep behavin' and things will be easier for all of us."

He sat back and cracked his neck, his knuckles, then gave his back a good twist, which sounded like a dry twig snapping. "Ah crap," he said suddenly, stopping and staring down toward my feet. "Girlie here is bleeding from somewhere, Regan. There's blood on the blanket."

I was swiftly unrolled from my warm cocoon. The cold air hit my damp clothes and instantly penetrated my skin. It felt like needles pricking my whole body. I tried to move to cover myself up, but my arms would barely lift an inch. It was like I was glued to the ground. Did they inject my veins with cement? What the hell was wrong with me?

"It's her foot—the shoe is completely soaked," said Seth.

I panicked—the tracking device was on that ankle and I couldn't let them see it. I tried to pull my foot away, but it was like forcing cooked spaghetti to do jumping jacks. I felt the shoe loosen, and then pain surge up my leg as it was pulled it off. I tried not to cry.

"Ah damn," Regan said, "this is bad. It's gotta get cleaned up."

"Please don't touch me," I managed to say in a pathetically weak voice.

Regan's red hair fell around my face, his eyes cold and calculating. "Listen, it's cut pretty badly and it bled a lot. It's gotta get cleaned. Okay? I'd hate to have to remove your foot out here because of infection."

Seth sighed heavily. "Really, Doctor Death? Amputation? Do you *have* to be so dramatic? She's scared enough already. Apparently, they didn't teach you bedside manner in med school."

Regan sighed and moved his face away from mine. "Didn't need it," he said proudly. "All my patients were already dead."

"I'll fix her up; I don't trust you," said Seth, giving my leg a pat with his repulsive hands. "The poor kid will end up with an appendectomy if I let you anywhere near her."

His hot, dirty fingers started probing around my wounded foot, and I couldn't hold back the tears stinging my eyes. Damn it, I didn't want these bastards to see me cry, especially since the redhead was hovering over me again. I felt like a lab specimen beneath his intent stare.

"She certainly isn't what I expected," he said, his English accent thick.

"What do you mean, 'She's not what you expected?' Is it because she's pretty? Or is it because you have finally realized that we kidnapped an actual human being?"

Seth was rustling around, and I heard something unzip. What was he doing? I was almost blind with panic as I lay completely prone and at the mercy of these two strange men in the middle of nowhere. My mind raced with the possibilities of what was going to happen next when Regan positioned a cell phone over my face. Was he recording this? The sick bastard.

His fingertips brushed my forehead and then ran down the bridge of my nose, the intensity on his face still terrifying me to the core. He found the scar on my neck, and I had no choice but to lay there while he boldly traced its jagged edges.

"What's this scar from?" he asked.

"An asshole like you," I spat out, hoping my voice sounded fiercer than I felt.

He yanked his hand away and everything about his demeanor changed. Gone was the clinical coldness. Suddenly, his behavior matched his boyish, almost angelic, appearance. "I'm not like *that*... really. I'm not going to hurt you," he said softly.

Then a sharp explosion shot up my leg toward my spine. Little black dots blurred my vision, and I couldn't help but scream. I fought to stay conscious.

"Seth! What the hell are you doing?" Regan yelled, still holding the cell phone camera over my face as he kept recording.

Another blast of pain ripped through my foot, and this time, my screams came out only as a gurgle in my throat. More little black dots threatened to take over my sight entirely.

"I'm getting out whatever was left in there—a piece of wood or something... I can't believe whoever stitched her up didn't notice. Idiots. It's worked its way in deep. Broken in pieces. I gotta get it out," Seth replied.

"Well, wait until the freezing sets in! It doesn't work instantly, you know. You're *hurting* her. We just finished promising her we *wouldn't* do that."

"Oh, so now you care about someone other than yourself?" Seth snorted and patted me on the leg again, this time his hand hitting the anklet. Though dizzy, I could sense his intrigue at his discovery. His fingers slid around on my skin, and he lifted my pant leg. Spinning the metal band around, he inspected it thoroughly. "Strange jewelry," he mumbled to himself, and then he abruptly went back to digging around in my foot.

I begged him to stop and leave me alone while Regan wondered out loud about why the freezing wasn't working and kept injecting more of it. The pain was unbearable as it surged up my leg and through every nerve in my body. I tried to ignore it by thinking of anything else, but after what seemed like forever, I couldn't contain the blood-curdling scream that escaped from me, starting from the deepest pit of my stomach. It was then that they stopped. They forced water and some strange pills down my throat. And then they got back at it.

I had to disconnect my consciousness from my body. I stared up, fixating on the trees, searching for any sort of distraction, but they barely swayed, and the blue sky remained endless. I turned my head to the side instead and stared at the thick bush, the green dangling leaves, and the stick-straight poplars. I let my mind move past them and into the thick darkness of the forest to where the outline of a man began to take shape. A dark figure grew larger the harder I stared. Soon, someone was parting the bushes and marching quickly toward us. I clamped my eyes shut in sheer terror.

"What the hell is going on?" the party crasher yelled, and his voice blended with a stirring breeze that came out of nowhere and brushed my hair away from my face. It sounded familiar.

"Luke!" Seth said angrily, "don't bloody sneak up on us like that!"

"What are you doing to her?" the man asked.

I felt like I *knew* that voice. I squeezed my eyed shut even tighter.

"She was hurt pretty badly. We had to stop and patch her up—she was bleeding all over the place and we couldn't risk infection," said Regan.

"Yeah, all fixed, though. Just sewing up the wound now," added Seth, and he drove a needle into my flesh.

I uncontrollably moaned in pain.

"Just stop what you're doing for a second!" yelled the newcomer, and the entire forest became dead silent.

I could feel his presence over me and prayed for the tears to stay away. I tried to get my mind to drift again—to think of swimming, or sitting in front of the fireplace with Oliver—but now the man from the garden was talking to me, and it was just so real.

"Please, open your eyes," he said.

Voice like butter. No. It couldn't be him. I was losing my mind. Maybe I *had* died.

"Please…" he begged, and his breath warmed the air around my face.

I figured I could look. I was dead anyway, so what did it matter? I opened my eyes, and sure enough, it was him—plain as day. I would never forget those blue eyes I'd fallen for on my eighteenth birthday. But my mind was playing tricks. Obviously, I had gone completely mad.

The stranger from the garden fell to his knees with a look of complete horror on his face. I stared as hard as I could, trying to match everything about him to my memories from eighty-two nights ago, hoping for a flaw… but it was becoming difficult to focus again. Obviously, whatever drugs I'd been given were really messing with my mind.

"You're sure you got the right girl?" the stranger asked.

A flower for your thoughts… I know exactly what I'm fighting for…

"What?—yeah Luke, of course!" said Regan defensively. "What's going on? You're freaking us out. You look like you've seen a ghost."

"Why can't she move?" Luke asked, ignoring Regan's mounting anxiety.

"Bad combination of sedatives, but at least she is alert now. She died for almost a full minute, but we got her back."

Luke leapt to his feet and shoved Regan angrily backward. Now I could see more than just his face. A wool cap covered gold-tinged hair that was pulled into a ponytail, a heavy flannel blue shirt and black jeans fit his body perfectly, and hiking boots—the same ones he'd worn that night—had a shoelace ready to come undone.

"What the hell's gotten into you?" Regan yelled, putting up his hands defensively as Luke's cheeks became red with anger.

There was arguing—words were relentlessly tossed between angry men while my world spun and not much of anything made sense. Where was I? Who was with me? How did I get here? The jacket I had been wearing during the race was so thin and damp it did nothing to retain the last of my body heat from being sucked out by the cold ground. I was freezing from the top of my head to my toes, and I tried to say something to that effect, but my mouth filled with water and I thought I might be sick. Then I started to shake uncontrollably again.

The voices quieted, and then they began speaking in collected, efficient tones. My wet jacket was pried off, and I lay helpless in nothing but a tank top and yoga pants. This was a female's worst nightmare. I begged them not to hurt me.

"We are just going to get you warmed up. Nobody will hurt you, I promise," said the stranger. Said *Luke*. He kneeled in front me and gently pulled me up into a sitting position, his arms securing me in place against his chest. I had no choice but to lean forward, barely even able to hold up my own head.

"I am so cold," I muttered through chattering teeth.

"I'm gonna fix that," he said.

He eased my arms into his flannel shirt, and his heart pounded against my cheek. It was melodic, like the most perfect piece of music ever written—my own personal serenade. I drifted... *ka boom, ka boom*... singing, dreaming... I had to be...

"Luke," Regan said in a very careful tone, "we need to get moving."

The arms around me tightened.

"Yeah, we need to get to camp," Seth gently urged.

The serenade stopped, and Luke effortlessly lifted me into his arms. I fought to stay awake so I could stare at him and verify the color of his eyes, the sandy-brown hair, the sharp jawline... And yes, every feature was the same as I remembered. There was no way I was imagining this.

"I'm so sorry," he said, blue eyes vibrant in the morning light and filled with sadness as we moved deeper into the thick pines. "I didn't know... I really had no idea who you were. I won't let any harm come to you. I promise." Remorse dripped from his voice. "My name is Luke, and I'm pretty sure I know who you are, but please, say it. Please, tell me your name."

I debated not answering him. I mean, why would I give this criminal the time of day? But, then again, it was *him*. And *he* was Luke. And *this*... was crazy.

"My name is Kaya, Kaya Lowen. And—I knew you weren't a gardener."

He let out a small laugh. Heat burst from my chest to my fingertips so fast I thought the flannel shirt had caught fire.

"Kaya. Kaya Lowen," he said to himself. "I finally have the name of the girl who has haunted me for the last 1,968 hours..."

I shut my eyes. Warm in his arms, his serenade filled my ears and lulled me into a deep sleep.

19

OVER OUR HEADS

I WOKE TO AN ALL TOO FAMILIAR SMELL, ONE THAT BROUGHT back memories of camping and hating every single minute of it. I knew I was in a tent because that awful, musty, nylon odor had been forever sealed into my senses. I half expected that if I opened my eyes, I would see Stephan and the counselor who claimed she could cure me of my anxiety. Instead, the late morning light cast a glow on my actual tent mates, Regan and Seth. I was sandwiched between them as they snored with their backs to me. It took a minute to remember how I got here. There had been arguing, and then I was pulled from Luke's arms...

Luke.

I heard the crackling of a fire and caught a glimpse of a moving shadow. Was he real? The more I thought about it, the more nothing made sense, so I focused on the only thing that did: escape.

I wiggled out from beneath a heavy wool blanket. My arms felt like they weighed a hundred pounds, and my legs were like jelly. Seth stirred, so I held my breath until he started snoring again. Regan didn't budge.

I slowly pulled myself up into a sitting position, and my heart pounded so hard everything went black. I waited for what seemed like an eternity until my vision came back. Then I bent forward on my hands and knees, praying my elbows wouldn't collapse, and reached for the tent zipper. My fingertips got a hold of it, but a strange sound stopped me from yanking it up.

A large form had risen from beside Seth, and it was inches from my ear. Hot, foul breath brushed my neck, and I slowly turned to be greeted by a mass of huge, razor-sharp teeth. It was all I could do not to scream when a low growl came from a dog with a head so huge it could crack my skull like a nut.

Seth sat up groggily. "Oh, Brutus, quit yer grumblin' and get back to bed."

Fangs and claws retreated with a disgruntled snort, and the dog flopped down a few feet from my knees. I thought right then and there my heart was going to actually explode.

"I see you've met my pal. Don't worry about him. Now, where do you think you're going there, girlie?" Seth asked, rubbing his eyes.

I didn't know what to say or do, so my stomach made the decision for me. "I'm… I'm going to throw up," I choked.

"Whoa, not in the tent!" Seth lunged for the zipper, and in one practiced move, he had the flap open.

My head spun wildly, and I hit the dirt just outside the tent, too weak to even sit up. He got behind me on his knees and wrapped his arms across my chest while I retched for what seemed like forever. A gust of smoke from the fire caught in my throat, and my stomach churned even harder. I felt like death, and I was humiliated that I needed this repulsive man's assistance to keep upright.

To make it worse, we'd woken Regan. He emerged, looking sleepy, with a shiny object in his hands and a determined look in his eyes. "This will fix you up, Kaya," he said, tapping the side of a needle.

"If you come near me with that, I'll kill you!" I yelled as my guts twisted.

Ignoring me, he grinned and jabbed my arm, injecting God knows what into my veins.

"I'm not a pin cushion," I barked, but the nausea instantly subsided and my head stopped spinning. "Have you never heard of just a simple, old fashioned *pill?*"

"You should feel better soon," he said, his accent seeming thicker than before, "I've used this a few times on myself, and it works pretty fast. If it doesn't, I've got something else I can try."

"It worked," I said quickly.

"Good. Let's get back to sleep then," said Seth, still holding me.

His body odor was as foul as the beast's breath, and I had a flash of a vision of those bared teeth and wild eyes staring me down like I was breakfast. I trembled. "No… I can't go back in there with you and that… thing."

"That *thing* is my best pal. And really, you don't have a choice," Seth said flatly and began dragging me toward the tent. I heard the beast panting and fought with all my might. My heart pounded so hard that those little black dots came back into view.

"She's scared of the dog, Seth. Let her go," said Luke.

I turned my head to see two dusty hiking boots planted firmly next to me, the laces now tied tightly. I looked up at the stranger, *at Luke*, and choked. Every feature of his perfect face was perfectly clear from this view. Damn it all to hell—he was beautiful, especially in this morning light. The blue of his eyes was vivid, and the golden tips of his hair surrounded his face like a halo.

"You don't have to go back in there," he said.

Seth sighed and let go. I fell forward onto my palms, and pinecones and small rocks dug into my skin.

"Let me help you up," Luke offered.

His hand was outstretched for me to take, and as much as I yearned to reach for it, that would only show weakness. For the first time in my life, I had to stand on my own.

All those nights dreaming about him and fantasizing about who he might be—an actor, classical pianist, maybe even a teacher or brilliant businessman—were now wasted by the reality that my beautiful stranger was nothing but a criminal. I clung to that anger and disappointment, pleading with my legs to be strong. They argued, making their weakness known, but held me up.

The dog eyed me warily as I struggled to remain upright and take in my surroundings: two green army tents, a small fire with a pot of something bubbling over the rim, and a shirt hanging from a tree branch made up the small camp. Trees so thick that there was nothing but blackness behind them surrounded the small bare patch of earth, and what appeared to be a trail snaked out behind me—I would make a run for that and then disappear into the dark...

"Maybe you *should* go back in the tent and rest," Luke said gently.

His hands were still outstretched, ready to break my fall should I stumble. My head spun. Nothing about the look in his eyes or the tone of his voice seemed even remotely villainous. Then I reminded myself that I was here against my will, he was my abductor, and I had to escape.

"Please, Kaya, go and lay down. You can have that tent all to yourself. I won't let those two, or the dog, anywhere near it."

His accomplices didn't protest. In fact, they seemed a bit wary of him. This only confirmed my instinct to be wary of him, too.

I straightened my back and tried to look as confident as I could, but suddenly my heartbeat throbbed so loud in my ears it shut out all the sounds of the forest. I put my hands to my head, and Luke lunged forward to steady me. As if all my emotions had been poured into my hand, I swung a fist at him with all my might. He caught it easily, as if he'd been expecting it, and seemed completely unfazed.

"Save your energy," he said, fingers clamping firmly around mine.

"What do you want from me?" I asked. My entire body had begun to quiver. His touch was confusing, and the pained look in his eyes was heart wrenching. I was trying to be angry, to hate him, but everything I was feeling was the exact opposite.

"I will explain everything soon. It's—just really complicated right now. But I promise nobody will hurt you, okay? I'll make sure of it. You have my word."

"Your word means *nothing* to me," I spat out.

A look of shock came across his face. *Don't look in his eyes...*

"Your father is not the man you think he is," he said quietly.

"Oh, so you're trying to get to my father through me? Well, news flash—Henry Lowen doesn't give a crap whether I'm alive or dead. He doesn't *care*. You're wasting your time." Saying that hurt because it was true. Henry cared about my *worth*, not *me...*

"You don't know what he's done," Luke said.

Regan and Seth had been standing by quietly, and now they eyed each other. "Don't tell her anything," Regan said carefully.

"Plans have changed," said Luke.

Regan shifted irritably and clenched his jaw. "Nothing changes," he said firmly. "We have risked everything, and we aren't going to throw it away just because you have decided to take pity on a pretty girl."

"Nobody touches her!" Luke roared.

Regan jumped back defensively and the stick Seth was about to throw on the fire remained in his hand. The beast stood, his thick, matted black fur lifting up slightly on his back.

"This is not the time to argue, boys. We need to focus," Seth said, motioning for the beast to relax and lie at his feet. "They will be sending out a search party for her soon. Y'all know what we gotta do."

What the hell do they have to do? I pulled my hand away from Luke's and stepped back a foot. Luke and Regan were staring each other down like bulls about to fight. I gathered my breath.

"You don't understand," Luke said quietly. "She's not the girl I thought she was."

I inched back a bit more. In a few steps, I could make a run for the trees and vanish...

"What do you mean, not *the girl you thought she was?*" Regan asked defensively. "We got the right girl! She is Kaya Lowen!"

"No, I mean... yes that's the right girl but... she is, um—she's..." Luke stammered.

Seth and Regan were staring at Luke in confusion. Nobody was watching me.

Regan threw his arms in the air in sudden realization, "Whoa! Wait a second! Is this the girl you've been talking about? The one you met the night you broke into…"

This was it, now or never.

I gathered every single ounce of energy I had and steadied my mind to ignore the pain in my foot and the dizziness in my head. Then, with everything I had, I turned and bolted toward the dense forest. The darkness instantly enveloped me. I could see well enough not to run into tree trunks, but branches caught me at every turn. My head felt as if it was spinning like a top, but I forced my legs to keep going. I could hear the men's voices yelling at each other in an organized manner.

I tripped and found myself on all fours. *Get up, girl. There's nothing wrong with you—get up…*

I made it a few more steps before my head connected with a blue spruce, and then I collapsed in a pathetic heap. My arms were so wobbly I could barely wipe at the gash across my forehead. My body was completely failing me. I prayed to God that the mutt would just snap my neck and get it over with quickly…

Human footsteps approached. I gulped in some air and tried to push myself up, but the world tipped on its side and I fell with it. Within moments, large hands had my wrists pinned to the ground. I struggled and fought with everything I had left, which wasn't much.

"Stop fighting," he said.

His voice created such confusion inside me. I kicked harder.

"Stop… *please*," he begged.

Luke's body pinned mine to the ground. I could feel tears welling up in my eyes.

"Please, Kaya, trust me. I won't let anyone hurt you, I promise."

I was dizzy but vividly aware of his body as it both warmed and chilled mine. I looked up at him; his eyes were tearing up too. "But you *have* hurt me," I said, "you're not… who I thought you were…"

I instantly regretted saying that. I might as well have admitted I felt something for him. He let go and sat back on his heels. "Kaya, remember when I told you that someday you would find something to fight for? Well, I have that something, and I will never, *ever* give it up… it's just… now it's become a lot more complicated… because of you."

He leaned forward and pressed his sleeve to my bleeding forehead, dabbing and inspecting it closely while I had no choice but to gaze up at him. How could this beautiful man be a kidnapper? It just didn't fit.

"It's just a scratch; no stitches required," he said, voice trailing off as his eyes met mine.

We stayed like that for a while: me on the ground, him kneeling over me, and our line of sight only on each other—until an unmistakable sound broke through the treetops.

"They'll find me," I said softly, wondering if Oliver was in the helicopter circling over our heads.

A puzzled look came over Luke's face. He hadn't expected to be located so fast—obviously, my anklet was still working. "Well, there is nowhere to land, and by the time they do, we'll be long gone." He positioned his arms under my body, and, in one graceful motion, he picked me up and into his arms. "Just don't run. Promise me that, please. I'll keep you safe and get you back home. You have my word. Okay?"

He held me tightly—protectively—waiting eagerly for my reply with turmoil in his blue eyes. My whole body hurt, and admittedly, I couldn't have walked another inch. The wolves or that beast would have got to me long before Oliver would have. I was at my kidnapper's mercy, laying helplessly in his arms and falling harder for him by the second.

"I promise," I said.

LUKE

20

GROUNDLESS

LOUISA IS IN THE KITCHEN, HER NIGHTGOWN THE SAME COLOR AS THE light pink lipstick smeared around her mouth. Her eyes look puffy from lack of sleep, and I can see she is upset about something. I pull her close, and she presses her body tightly against mine.

"You should go to sleep," I say, and she gives me a kiss on the cheek.

I promise her we will get out of here soon, to a safer place, somewhere we will be happy and have dinner together every night. Just one more week.

"I love you, Louisa," I tell her, meaning it so wholeheartedly and completely it hurt.

"I love you, too," she says back.

I hear footsteps from out in the hall, and then suddenly, a loud bang shakes the apartment floor and the flimsy front door crashes down. Two men who I thought I would never see again burst into the room and put a gun to my head. They pull Louisa from my arms, and she starts screaming, terrified, her panic cutting right through to my very soul, but I am helpless...

"Louisa, no! Please don't take her... I'll do anything, whatever you want... just please don't..."

I beg, I plead. I scream her name.

And when I wake up on the kitchen floor in a pool of my own blood, she is gone.

"Louisa!" What have I done? "Louisa!"

"LUKE, IT'S ONLY A DREAM. WAKE UP—EVERYTHING'S OKAY," SAID A sleepy voice from beside me in the dark.

I opened my eyes, wishing it really were just a dream and not a replay of the worst night of my life. The memory held me captive, eating away at my insides and haunting me every time I tried to sleep. It was the sole reason this girl with the emerald eyes was beside me now.

I pushed the inescapable horror away as best I could and turned toward Kaya... Kaya Lowen... God, she was beautiful. While she'd been trying to comfort me, she'd fallen back asleep with her hands curled under her chin. I wanted nothing more than to run my fingers through her ebony hair and feel her cheeks to see if they were as soft as they looked.

I'd fallen for her—hard—but it wasn't just her appearance that had pulled me in. It was her... *everything*. I'd been impossibly obsessed from the moment we first met. After that encounter in the garden, I'd spent countless hours reliving the moment, and then countless more trying to banish it from my mind. Yet still she lingered. I couldn't turn off the constant running tap of her voice trickling through my head. How was it that she was here, lying beside me in the dead of the night, *as my hostage*? What the hell was I doing?

My mission was to get Louisa back, and kidnapping Henry Lowen's daughter was the key to making that happen, but everything had changed. Using Kaya for any reason had become unthinkable. I had to get her out of these mountains and somewhere safe, even if that meant losing Louisa forever—and that was tearing me apart. How could I risk one life for another? How could I live with myself if anything happened to either of them?

I stared hard at Kaya's face, matching her name to her every detail, memorizing and forever burning it into my mind. Then I tried to look away—but it was impossible. I was drawn to her like a magnet, so much so that my chest ached and my heart felt like it might burst. As I lay staring at her while she slept, I asked myself the all-important question; could I risk losing everything for this girl I didn't even know?

Yes. Without a doubt. Without question.

Well, if that wasn't downright terrifying...

I moved my fingertips slowly across her cheek. Her skin was even smoother than I imagined, and my heart raced like I was about to dive off a cliff. When her eyes opened, I pulled my hand away, not wanting to frighten her. She looked up at me, those deep, emerald jewels shining in the dim, moonlit tent, and all the missing parts of my life pulled together, making me completely whole.

She searched my face intently, and then she put her delicate hand on my cheek. "I hope you find her," she said sincerely.

I didn't know what she meant. Her touch was so euphoric; I was lost in it.

"The girl in your dreams, the one you were calling out for... Louisa May? I hope you get her back," she said quietly. "She is what you said you would never, ever, give up on. What you said you were fighting for, right?"

I gulped. That was not all I was fighting for. Not anymore.

THE DAY QUICKLY BECAME LIKE A ROLLER COASTER FROM HELL. WE trudged through the forest, staying hidden under the pines while helicopters flew overhead. I wasn't worried, because even if they got their men to the ground, finding us would still be like finding a needle in a haystack. I was however, worried about Kaya. She seemed so frail. I watched her closely and protected her from every branch or loose rock while she glared at me with hatred. It was killing me. I would have died right there from heartbreak if it weren't for her show of affection last night.

By afternoon, we were all completely exhausted. Kaya insisted she could walk on her own, but she couldn't keep up. It was obvious she was in pain, and she threw up a few times. I kept trying to slow the boys down and offered to carry her, but she pushed me away with contempt and anger. At one point, she tripped, and Regan swiftly picked her up. I didn't like the look on his face when she gave in and almost passed out in his arms.

When the light started to leave the sky, we stopped to make camp. Regan carefully set Kaya down against a tree in a small clearing and bound her hands. We set up for the night under her watchful glare.

"A half day's walk and we'll be outta here," Regan said once the fire was crackling, and a large potato was impaled on the end of his knife. My stomach growled.

I can't figure out how they've got our whereabouts," said Seth, jumping back from a spark, "this isn't going to be as easy as I thought. We are moving at less than half speed cause of girlie here. If they follow us up to the summit, we're screwed."

"I'm not worried; we can fight them off," Regan said, giving me a wink. "We just need to know what you want to do with her, Luke."

I knew what *I had* to do: get her the hell out of here and away from… us. "Just gimme a bit more time to think, okay?" I said.

No reply.

I finished putting up the tent, taking extra care to stake it deeply into the ground, and then I unpacked some bedding and shook it out thoroughly. I felt her eyes on me as I searched for a toothbrush in my backpack, re-folded my clothes, and washed my face. When I had done everything I could think of, I had no choice but to face her accusing stare.

I approached her tentatively under the guise of checking her foot.

The bandage was soaked again, and when I started to unwrap it, she pulled away, but quickly changed her mind when she noticed Regan taking interest.

I pushed her pant leg up a bit to expose the smooth skin of her shin and noticed a gold band around her ankle. Even though it wasn't quite dark yet, I still had to strain to make out the details—sections of the band around the stones had rubbed off to reveal a black metal underneath, and it was scratched and gouged. The weight of it was far too heavy for ordinary jewelry. Her eyes widened when I rolled it around looking for the clasp, and she suddenly became extremely nervous—the waning sound of a helicopter retreating for the night made me realize why.

But I let it go.

"Need some help over there, mate?" Regan asked eagerly.

I gritted my teeth. An insanely protective instinct made me angry that he'd even asked. "Sure don't," I said.

Kaya sighed in relief as I pulled the fabric of her pants back down over the anklet. As Regan watched out of the corner of his eye, I forced myself to get back to business, but it was hard to concentrate. Her skin was so smooth and flawless, and the gentle curve of her ankle fit perfectly in my hand.

"I never did congratulate you on getting as far as you did in that race," I said as I cleaned and wrapped her foot. It looked like it probably needed another stitch or two, but I didn't want to put her through that. I also couldn't bear the thought of Regan touching her any more than he already had. "It takes a lot of courage to even attempt a race like that. You probably could have gotten to the end, you know. What was there, about five hours left? I bet you could have made it... not many people could get that far..." I was rambling, desperate to have her say something.

"Wow, you've got *some nerve*," she said icily. "You stole that accomplishment from me, you know."

"I'm sorry... I—"

"You, what? Figured it was okay to take someone against their will? For what, money? And that all would be forgiven with a few compliments?"

Her anger was a knife in my heart.

"It's not what you think there, girlie," said Seth, stepping in and speaking up for me. "We're not bad people, just folks tryin' to fix a few wrongs."

"Then tell me, for God's sake, tell me why I am here? Give me *one* reason why I shouldn't hate you all any less than I do right now!" she yelled.

The thought that she might actually hate me knocked the wind from my lungs with more force than all the punches I'd ever taken to the gut combined. I had no response.

"Something very precious was taken from all of us," said Regan, setting a frying pan down on a stump, "and your father is responsible. He sold the drug, Cecalitrin, to the public even though he knew the risks. Many people tried to stop him, but it's impossible to win a fight against a man with unlimited resources. But now, *we* finally have the upper hand. *We* have something more precious to him than money: you."

Her mouth widened a bit, and then she laughed. "Ha! *Me? More precious than money?* That's hilarious!"

Regan didn't bat an eye. "You are *very* valuable to him, Kaya Lowen. I haven't figured out why exactly, but I will."

"I know my father is a complicated man," Kaya said firmly, "but I don't think he would ever hurt anyone intentionally."

I got the feeling she really didn't believe her own words. Regan stood and pulled his cap down lower over his forehead. His hate for Henry Lowen oozed out of him. "Oh, he sure would. He administered Cecalitrin to his own wife, and she ended up just like my sister did, like Seth's wife, and like Luke's mom—*all dead.*"

Kaya gasped, and unshed tears sparkled in her eyes. She seemed to be giving her response some thought. "I'm so sorry for all your losses," she said softly. "Truly, I am. I know what it's like to lose someone you love. Henry's methods may be strange, but he's not a monster," she added, stumbling over the words. "I'm sure he didn't plan… he couldn't have…"

Regan stopped her midsentence, his tone not as harsh as before. He was a sucker for female tears. One or two drops from a girl he had an eye on, and he'd hand over his wallet and car keys. "Your mother lost her mind and eventually took her own life, correct? Just like our loved ones did. I lost my best friend—my sister—and Cecalitrin was the cause. *Henry Lowen* was the cause."

"But Henry wouldn't—"

"My cousin worked at lab in Montreal and had proof that Henry paid off people to look the other way when it came to getting the drug ready for market. He had copies of forged legal documents, cash 'donations' to the FDA, along with the laboratory findings confirming the claims against the drug were true. Minutes before that evidence would have been in my hands, the building blew up. My cousin's body was never found."

None of us spoke. Kaya's brow furrowed as she tried to make sense of it all. "But, how can a fertility drug make people commit suicide?" she asked cautiously.

Regan spoke as if he'd already explained it a thousand times. "Cecalitrin is an anti-estrogen drug that causes the hypothalamus and pituitary gland located in the brain to release hormones that stimulate the ovaries to produce eggs. It also causes Craniopharyngiomas—slow-growing tumors—to develop. They push on the hypothalamus, causing hormonal imbalance and chemical disruptions in the brain."

"English please, Doctor Death," Seth interjected.

"Oh for God's sake, the girl isn't stupid!" Regan barked, and then he explained patiently, for Seth's sake. "The pituitary gland controls the levels of hormones made by most endocrine glands in the body. If it is sending the wrong messages, then symptoms of what appears to be hypothyroidism start to present: thinning hair, slurred speech, migraines, edema, as well as psychosis such as obsessions, hallucinations, paranoia, and suicidal ruminations. Eight out of ten women will eventually conceive while taking the drug, but they are unaware of the ticking time bomb in their heads."

"How do you know this?" Kaya asked.

The fire crackled, and Regan rubbed his eyes. "Nine years wasting my time pursuing the dream—I share Henry's passion for treating infertility, too. My sister wanted to conceive and couldn't. Our last hope was Cecalitrin. She took it for five months, and five months later, she died."

The leaves shook in a light breeze, smoke wafted up my nose, and a bird that was sweetly singing stopped.

"I'm so sorry for your loss, Regan," Kaya said sincerely.

"I should have known better. I should have done more research," he muttered.

Regan partly blamed himself for his sister's death, and his own guilt and heartache added fuel to his revenge.

"So, what do you want to do with me?" Kaya asked tentatively.

I looked hard at Regan, silently willing him not to answer that question. But of course, he couldn't keep his mouth shut.

"Well, we are going to use you to get your daddy to give us money so Luke here can get Louisa back, and then we will force him to shut down Eronel."

"He won't," she said flatly.

"He'll have to because he wants you back *so* desperately. Why is that, Kaya? Are you actually made of gold? Care to share?" Regan stared at her hard, but she stayed silent. "Not gonna tell, eh? Well then, here's what's going to happen…"

"Drop it, Regan," I said, shaking my head at him. But he kept talking, ignoring me.

"We're going to hurt Henry where he'll feel it most…"

"That's enough, Regan," warned Seth, but Regan still kept on.

"We are going to film a little documentary for him and show him what happens when we inject you with Cecalitrin. Then we will record you for a few months while you lose your mind and slip into insanity. We'll hand you a knife and watch as you take your own life just like our loved ones did. I'll have the great pleasure of being the director of this movie and performing the autopsy on your body afterward."

Kaya's eyes widened in horror. I jumped to my feet and positioned myself in front of her, feeling the world slow down. "I never agreed to any of that, Regan. No one uses her for *anything*. No harm comes to her," I warned, feeling my blood pump efficiently through my muscles as my heart pounded steadily.

"We have a *plan!*" Regan spat.

"I'll kill you… I'll kill both of you bastards. I swear, I'll rip your heads off if either of you so much as breathes in her direction!"

Regan stepped back from the fire, clearly excited to see the fighter he was always trying to coax out of me. Branches stopped swaying, flames froze mid leap, and Regan and Seth's movements became sloth-like. I didn't want Kaya to see this side of me, but I had no problem using it to protect her.

"Luke, relax," Seth said, putting his hands up.

Regan grinned. "Yeah, take it easy there, little buddy," he said, but his eyes were shining with exhilaration, "I'm just joking around."

Joking around or not, I lunged for Regan and put my hands around his throat. His excitement to see the fighter in me instantly turned to fear. This wasn't like those times in the bar when I was saving his ass—he was about to have his handed to him on a platter. I tightened my grip, digging my fingers into the flesh around his esophagus until he tried to choke out an apology.

"Listen, I'm sorry for what I said. Really I am. I won't touch her. Promise."

I let go, and he gasped for breath. The knife he'd been using to cut potatoes with was in my hand before he'd even remembered he'd set it at his feet. Without protest from either of them, I marched over to Kaya and dropped to my knees before her. She shook with fear, her eyes wide as she stared at the blade in my hand. Keeping my composure, I cut the rope from her wrists, her skin red and raw from struggling to get free. She looked at me curiously then shut her eyes tight, as if trying to make us all go away.

"Either you both remain my friends or become my foes," I warned Seth and Regan, and then I stood to face them.

Seth spoke first, clearly rattled. "Geez Luke, relax. Doctor Death is just playing the dramatic, sadistic, vengeful, bastard act. Obviously, he didn't get that part in the school play or something. No harm will come to this girl. You have my word." He moved past the fire, around the sleeping dog, and held out his hand, looking me dead in the eye as I shook it. "On my honor."

Regan let out a heavy sigh and rubbed his throat. "Plans change, I guess."

THE WIND PICKED UP, LIGHTLY PUSHING AROUND THE FIRE AND RUSTLING the pines, and then it grew stronger as a black mass in the sky approached. We moved quickly, securing tents and packing up food while the temperature in the air dropped. The rain came first, a warning that it was about to pour. Seth and Regan piled into their tent, taking Brutus with them, and I called for Kaya to come into mine. She didn't move. She just sat there, shaking like a leaf, even though I knew she heard me. I didn't want to force her, but then again I couldn't leave her to freeze.

"I am going to pick you up, okay?" I said. Reaching under her legs, I pulled her up into my arms, then got back in the tent and secured the flap.

The lantern cast a warm, yellow glow on the makeshift walls as I dug around for warmer clothes. "You're freezing. Put this on," I said, tossing her my cleanest flannel shirt.

She still wouldn't budge. She was scared and upset, and she had every right to be. I knew I had to try to comfort her, but I was part of the problem. "Listen, I am sorry about your dad. I can't imagine what you must be going through—"

"I guess I always sort of—always knew he was that bad," she replied quickly.

The wind blew, the tent shook, and the rain poured. We were going to get hit hard, and there was nothing to do but ride it out. I stretched out on the sleeping bag and put my arm under my head, the weather almost lulling me to sleep, until I realized that the louder it got, the faster Kaya's breathing became. I propped up on an elbow and looked at her eyes, now as wide as saucers. "What's the matter?" I asked and reached over to touch her arm. It was as cold as ice. "Kaya, are you hurt? What's wrong?"

She lunged for the tent flap, and I caught her by the waist.

"I can't let... I have to get out... you can't see me like this," she stammered.

"See you like what? I don't care what you look like, and there's no way you are going out there."

I turned her around to face me. Panic was written all over her face. I had seen my Mum like this a few times when she had anxiety attacks, and I wondered if that's what was going on. It would have been pretty understandable, all things considered. "Everything will be all right," I said gently. "Regan was just trying to scare you. He would never do anything like that, and—"

"No... you don't understand." Tears spilled from her eyes, and her breathing became so fast I was worried she might begin to hyperventilate and pass out. She lunged for the flap again, but I held her back. "Let me go. You don't understand—*let me go!*" she begged.

I held her by the wrists, wrapping my fingers around the same patches of skin where the ropes had dug in. Her bones felt so delicate I was worried I might break them. She winced, and the most sickening feeling came over me; I couldn't cause her more pain. I had to let her go.

Her eyes were wild as she threw weak punches at my chest. I stayed put, allowing her small fists to do as much damage as they could before she scurried backward. She was terrified. Had someone hurt her before? Was she that scared of me?

The howling wind answered my question when it brought a gasp from her lips.

"Kaya, this tent is strong. You don't have to worry, okay? Look at me."

She tried to meet my eyes. "I am... having a bit... terrified sort of anxiety... scared of storms sometimes," she stammered. "And, I'm—sorry... about your mother. I am so very, very, sorry..."

Each tear that rolled down her cheek felt like a stab in the gut. "Hey, *shhh*, it's okay. It's not your fault," I said as the snap of a breaking branch made us both jump. "Listen, if you want to go out there you can, but it will be a whole lot more miserable than being stuck in here with me."

"This just... isn't right, I shouldn't be here—I can't do this," she said, starting to breathe faster again.

"Kaya, let's pretend to be friends for now. I'll look after you, I promise. You'll be all right."

"I am trying so hard to hate you right now," she said, "just trying so...

damn… hard…"

Trying to hate me. So, she didn't yet. Thank you, Lord.

The storm howled and grew louder. "Oh my God," she muttered.

"Kaya, keep looking at me, okay? Take in deep breaths. In, and then out, slowly—c'mon, focus on my eyes—in, now out… you and me, we're friends. Trust me, okay? Breathe in. Now breathe out." I repeated this. I locked eyes with her, and she did exactly as I said. Her breathing started to slow, but her lips had turned blue. "You're cold. I have to get you warm. Come here," I said and held out my arms.

Her mouth parted slightly in confusion. It was pure torture to see her like this and not grab her. I could have pulled her to me and forced my warmth upon her, but she had to come to me on her own. "I won't hold you against your will ever again; every choice you make from here on in will be your own, and I'll fully respect it," I said honestly.

Something on her face changed. She looked at me curiously, and then she slowly crept forward. I felt like my heart was going to explode as I draped my arms around her. "Everything is good. We are warm and safe. Deep breaths still, okay?" I instructed.

At first, I didn't move a muscle, allowing only my voice to comfort her, but soon I couldn't stop my hand from stroking the back of her head. The waves of her hair felt like silk. We stayed like that, kneeling toward each other, until her shivering stopped. Then I pushed my luck.

"We need to sleep now," I said.

I leaned back, holding her close, and lay down on my side while keeping her body tight against mine. She tensed for a brief moment and then seemed to relax. I was vividly aware of every inch of her body and carefully adjusted the blanket around us.

"I'm still angry with you," she said quietly.

"And you have every right to be."

"It's not right to kidnap people."

"I know. I really do. And I'm so sorry. I hope one day you will forgive me," I said.

Her forgiveness was something I would work hard to earn, even if it took forever.

KAYA

21

TEAR US APART

I woke up clinging to him, shocked that I'd even fallen asleep in the first place. He'd talked me out of an anxiety attack under prime *Kaya's gone nuts* conditions. Not even the most high-paid psychologist had been able to pull that off. His voice had cut through what felt like a million cotton balls crammed into my head. When he told me to breathe, my lungs opened up. When he told me I was safe, his arms felt like a fortress. When he said we were friends, the cotton balls turned to dust.

The wind had died, and by the faint morning light, I could see the little clouds my breath made in the freezing-cold air. I pulled my head back and looked up at him, still in awe of how impossibly beautiful and exactly perfect he was. I moved my fingers ever so gently over his Adam's apple, marveling at how the texture of his stubble varied depending on which direction I slid my fingers. I traced his chin, and then my fingers continued to wander up to touch the scar adorning his cheek. The sun had tanned him a light, golden color, but the scar remained a pale white. I wanted to know how he got it. I wanted to wake him, look into his eyes, and ask him that question along with a thousand others, like— where did he live? What was his last name? Favorite color? I wanted to know about Louisa, too. What kind of woman was she to have captured his heart so strongly that he would go to such great lengths to get her back?

That question twisted my stomach with horrific jealousy. Maybe there were some things I was better off not knowing.

I put my head back against his chest. Regardless of the crazy circumstances, it was absolute bliss to be in his arms—to be in arms that didn't belong to Oliver.

Oh my God. *Oliver.*

What was I doing? It was wrong to be snuggled up with this stranger—a man who is *also* taken. Everything I was thinking and feeling was just so very, very wrong. I had to get away…

I carefully placed my hand under Luke's elbow and pushed up to wiggle out from underneath. *I'm engaged* I repeated to myself, because it was absolute torture leaving him and the warm blankets he had constructed into a bed. For a moment, I questioned my sanity. I took one last look at him, slipped on his jacket, and snuck outside.

The world had become a winter wonderland. Snow glistened and clung to the trees, and branches swayed under the weight. It was so calm, clean, and quiet. The tents had held up, although they were a bit haggard looking, but the small clearing for the fire was gone. I figured Seth and Regan were gone too, judging by the two sets of footprints leading off into the trees.

I sat on the stump next to the knife Luke had used to cut the ropes from my wrists. I pulled, using my body weight as leverage to try and get it out, but my hands started to freeze, and it wouldn't budge. I cursed my weakness, and then I tried again, but to no avail. I shoved my frozen hands into the pockets of Luke's jacket and felt a very familiar shape.

A gun.

It could be my ticket out of here. The storm was over. The choppers could fly overhead and I could protect myself with until they found me. I just had to run…

But I didn't. Instead, I looked at the tent. I had made a promise to the man sleeping there and felt compelled to keep it—which was ridiculous. Why did he have such an inexplicable hold on me? I had to chain whatever feelings I had for him to an anchor and allow them to sink to the deepest part of my emotional ocean. He and I were never meant to be. I was engaged to Oliver. I was in love with Oliver.

I toyed with the engagement ring that was a bit too big for my finger. But, was I really *in love* with Oliver? Because, if that was love, then what was *this* feeling I had for Luke?

I guess whatever it was, it didn't matter. I had to do the right thing. I would never be like Henry and hurt and lie to those who loved me.

I put the gun on my lap. It was a titanium Hiezer Defense pistol, and I knew exactly how to use it. I checked the small ports on both sides of the chamber hood—it was loaded, and the button at the base of the grip opened the trapdoor to reveal two .45 Colt cartridges in place for reserve ammo. As I stared at it, lost in thought and completely confused, a loud cracking came from the trees. The heavy pines swayed behind Luke's tent, and I thought I saw something move. A shadow stretched out, and then it disappeared. Snow slid off a giant branch with a loud thud, and Luke bolted out of the tent looking anxious, then smiled with relief when he saw me.

The sleepy look in his eyes and his mussed-up hair made me blush. No human being should look that heart-stopping incredible. He rubbed his hands together, blowing his breath over his fingertips as he came toward me, but stopped when he noticed the gun on my lap. I was so distracted by his appearance I'd forgotten I'd even had it.

"Don't come any closer," I warned, pointing the horrible thing at his feet.

The most heartbreaking look came over his face. I could never fire at him, but he didn't know that.

"Kaya, please, put it down," he said. As he raised his hands slightly, they shook. He was cold and the wool shirt not a thick enough barrier between him and the icy air. I felt bad that I'd stolen his jacket.

"If you come any closer, I'll shoot you. Don't test me," I warned, but my voice was entirely unbelievable.

He stood there motionless. I avoided looking into his sky-blue eyes because they made it impossible to think. I knew that after last night, he could tell me to eat rocks and I'd probably give it a go. If I was going to go through with this, I was just going to have to put my head down and run. But first, I had a question to ask.

"How long have you been plotting to kidnap me?"

"What? I don't know—a while," he answered.

I needed to know. I noticed something move behind the tent again and assumed it was Seth and Regan returning. I felt desperate for an answer. "*How long?*" I demanded.

"Six months, I guess. It took four months to organize the break in, and then we had two months of planning before the race."

"Are you responsible for what happened at the hospital?" I asked.

"Uh…?"

"Did you try to kill me when I was visiting someone there?"

He looked totally confused. "No. Uh… oh my God, *no*."

Damn. If it had been him, it would have been easier to get my feet moving. "Last year, my childhood nanny was shot and killed by someone aiming for me," I said quietly.

His mouth fell open ever so slightly. "I'm sorry, Kaya, but please know that it wasn't me—or any of us. I didn't even know who you were a year ago."

He was telling the truth. I stood up from the stump and backed up toward the bushes. His eyes widened in alarm. "What are you doing?"

Don't look at him! I reminded myself. "I am getting out of here."

"Oh, come on, Kaya, please. There is nowhere for you to go; we are a thousand miles from civilization."

"They'll find me. They'll take me back," I said and looked up at the much-too-quiet sky.

"Take you back where? To your extravagant cage? I saw where you live. How many guards do you have with you all the time? How closely are you watched? Is that any sort of life? Just let me get you to a safe place first, and then you can go wherever—"

I couldn't listen any longer. It was making me weak. I turned and bolted into the trees. My legs were strong again and my head clear, but the snow had made everything a slippery mess. I tripped. I got back up and kept running.

I heard Luke begging me to stop, and the angst in his voice became one-hundred-pound weights around my ankles. He was fast approaching, and his even breathing grew louder until he caught me, grabbed me by the arm of the jacket, and tripped me to the ground. I landed face first in the snow and the gun fell inches out of my reach.

"Let me go!" I yelled.

He flipped me over so we were face to face, his hands gripping my wrists tightly as he sat on my legs, pinning me down—exactly what he said he would never do. I thought my heart would burst inside my chest; I wanted him desperately and had to get away from him all at the same time. "Let me go," I demanded.

A look of turmoil came over him. "I promised myself I wouldn't hold you against your will," he said, "and here I am doing it again."

The look on his face was more crushing than the weight of him. *Oliver. Think of Oliver. Don't let him distract you.* "You have to let me go. This isn't right; I can't be here," I said, but the words weren't even remotely convincing.

His eyes bore into mine. I looked away.

"I can't let you wander off and die," he said with a gulp.

"Henry will find me."

"And what if he doesn't?"

I thought of the tracker on my ankle. "He will."

"Do you really *want* to go back?"

I couldn't be truthful. No, of course I didn't want to go back… but I couldn't tell him that. I pushed hard against him, and he let go. He stood up, backing away a few feet while wrestling with his conscience. I grabbed the gun out of the snow and got onto my knees, pointing it at his torso while catching my breath and trying to calm my pounding heart.

"I don't want to have to hurt you," I said, holding the gun with both hands and reminding myself yet again to not look him in the eyes.

"You might have to," he said, and I noticed something move in the bushes behind him.

I narrowed my eyes on the snow-covered branches and evergreens. A dark shape shifted from the bush as Luke tried to reason with me.

"You can go if you want," he said, "but I'll follow you and make sure you are safe and protect you. Wherever you go, I'll go, and when I know with certainty that you'll be all right, I'll disappear. You'll never see me again."

It moved again. A slight blur, a darkening of the light, and there it was—what had been moving around in the bushes and lurking in the shadows was crouched and ready to kill—a sleek, yellow, mountain lion. It was focused on Luke, tail twitching at its unaware prey. I shifted the gun just slightly up and to the right, but too many branches were in the way of a clear shot. "Do. Not. Move," I said to Luke as firmly as I could.

He froze when I cocked the trigger. The cat was ready to pounce. If I could just get behind Luke, the cat would get to me first, but at least I could shoot it before it got to him...

"I guess you'll have to kill me then, because I'm not leaving you to die out here in these God forsaken mountains," Luke said sadly.

He thought I was pointing the gun at him.

"No, I..." but before I could explain the cat leapt from where it was, and faster than I had anticipated was inches from Luke's back. I aimed and took fire, grazing its shoulder. Luke spun around, and the cat's claws lashed out. I shot again, this time hitting the beast squarely in the head and killing it.

Luke fell to his knees, clutching his chest as the cat lay before him with its brains scattered about. I dropped the gun in shock and practically dove toward him, kicking the slain beast out of the way. "Oh my God, are you okay? Luke... *Answer me!*" I yelled, panicking as blood seeped through his shirt and dripped onto the fresh, white snow.

"Uh, I... am fine," he said with a stunned look on his face.

He pulled his blood-soaked hands away from his chest, looked at them, and then collapsed backward. I tore open the front of his shirt—the cat's claws had made four, long gashes across his torso, and they were bleeding profusely. "I'm so sorry," I said, trembling from head-to-toe, "I tried to get it with the first shot... I should have—"

"Kaya, you saved my life," he said in awe.

And it was then that I finally allowed myself to stare fully into his incredible eyes. I took them in completely, and it hit me: the realization that I would have done anything to save him. I was ready to throw my own body in front of that mountain lion for him, without any hesitation, without any regret. I would have given my life to save his in a heartbeat.

Well… what the hell did that mean?

I put my hands on his cheeks, so incredibly grateful that he was alive. Now, I had to keep him that way. "You're gonna be okay," I said with as much reassurance as I could muster. I pulled off the plaid shirt he had given me last night and pressed the thick, heavy fabric to his wounds. Then I put the jacket back on and retrieved the gun in case there were any more mountain lions around. "We have to get you back to camp. Regan will have something to patch you up with," I said, unable to control the fear choking my throat.

The red snow around Luke made my head woozy. I took in a deep breath and pressed down on the plaid fabric, hoping to slow the bleeding, but blood oozed between my fingers and through the soaked fabric.

"It's just blood, Kaya. Don't pass out on me," he said.

"Can you walk? Luke, I don't know what to do… Are you okay? Oh my God… I'm *so* sorry…" I was rambling and on the edge of an anxiety attack.

He put his hands over mine. "I'm fine. *Really*. I think I'm more in shock over what happened than anything else. You know, you're a pretty good shot."

His voice had taken on that same calm tone it had last night when he was trying to soothe me. I couldn't let my anxiety take over. I had to keep myself together. For him.

"Thank you," he said tilting my chin toward his face.

I saw the world in his eyes, and the sight of it snapped my head into extreme clarity—I could put aside my fears so I could do whatever it took to keep him alive.

"Can you walk?" I asked.

"Yeah, of course," he said and forced himself up.

Blood trickled steadily down his flat stomach toward his belt. He stumbled often as we made our way back to the camp, him dragging the dead cat by the tail in one hand and holding the plaid shirt to his chest with the other. I looked at the trail behind us; our footprints were bloody streaks in the snow. Neon signs couldn't have done a better job of leading anything, or *anyone*, straight to us.

OLIVER

22

𝒫AUSE

SHE HAD BEEN GONE FOR TWENTY-FIVE HOURS. THE MORNING ticked away in the hot, airless room, the tension thicker than the reinforced steel walls.

"They've sent a video," said Old Carl to the group of us gathered in the security office. "I'll put it up on the screen." His withered hands seemed remarkably steady as they moved the mouse, bringing the screen to life. As we all watched, a shaky lens brought the ground into focus. The light was dim, and there was rustling and sniffling, and then Kaya's face appeared. I nearly jumped out of my skin. There were tears pouring from her eyes as she stared past the camera. She appeared to be lying down on a blanket, unrestrained, shaking but not moving. I got a chill so violent my teeth began to throb.

"Looks like they've drugged her with something," Davis said gently, his hand moving to my shoulder.

Henry said nothing. He didn't even flinch. In fact, he seemed calmer than Old Carl as the video showed a man's dirty hand move to his daughter's neck. Staring numbly at the screen, he reacted like he was watching a television ad for dish soap. Stephan, however, looked like he might pass out any second. His nose was fire-engine red and tears were threatening to pour. When a bloodcurdling scream erupted past Kaya's lips, he yelped, and everyone in the room froze.

'*Stop, please stop…*' my girl was begging her captors, tears spilling from her eyes. I put my head in my hands. I had never cried in my life, not even allowing a bit of dampness to cloud my eyes, but watching this brought on the tears. Stephan started to sob. We couldn't tell what was happening to her, but every horrific scenario imaginable flashed through all our minds. Whatever happened while this was filmed, it had been painful.

I would kill them all.

She screamed again. It was the most heartbreaking, gut wrenching sound I'd ever heard. Everyone in the room, even Old Carl, shifted uneasily— only Henry seemed unfazed.

Then the camera panned out and gave us the briefest glimpse of a man crouched at Kaya's feet. When the frame re-focused, the camera was pointed at the ground, but the dirt had been replaced with white, sparkly snow speckled with red. A muffled voice boomed through the speakers.

"As I'm sure you are well aware, we have Kaya Lowen," said a man whose face was kept safely hidden, "and we have no problem torturing her every time we hear your helicopters. In fact, we rather enjoy it."

A knife came into view, the blade of it dripping with what could only be blood. I thought I might be sick.

"Wait," said Davis, leaping out of his chair. "Carl, rewind it a bit, to where we see the glimpse of a man by her feet."

Carl backed up the video.

"Zoom in a bit," Davis said, leaning forward eagerly.

"You can't see his face; he is wearing a hood," Old Carl said with snark in his tone.

"No, zoom in on her feet, yes… there—stop," he said, moving closer to the screen.

"What is it, Davis?" Henry asked, completely agitated by the interruption.

"Huh? Oh, um—well nothing, I guess. I thought maybe I saw something in the background, a clue to her location or something, but I guess I was wrong."

"Well, that doesn't matter, boy. We *know* where she is; we just haven't been able to get there, yet!" Henry bellowed.

"Right, right. Sorry sir, continue on," Davis said, giving me an odd look.

Carl pressed play again, and the kidnapper resumed stating his demands. "Here's the deal: stay away from us, and we will deliver the girl back to you safely. We require two million dollars in cash, divided evenly between two identical backpacks by noon tomorrow, or we will have some more fun with your daughter. You will receive another message shortly with further instructions."

Then the screen went blank.

There was a quiet pause in the room while everyone collected themselves. Henry spoke first, his voice cold, detached, and clinical. "Carl, organize another unit, and get it up there right away. Find out exactly where our men are on foot and how close they are."

I was about to protest, but Carl did it for me. "Sir, with all due respect, sending another chopper will only put her more in danger. We should wait for them to contact us again and follow their instructions."

"They aren't going to kill her," Henry said casually.

"You don't know that—"

"Yes, *I do*. If they were going to kill her, they would have done it by now. She is worth nothing if she's dead. They might inflict some more pain to try and make us sweat a bit, but she's a tough girl, she can handle it."

Everyone in the room gasped in unison. Stephan rose and bolted for the door. Even Sindra balked and turned away. How could a father be so complacent about his child getting hurt?

"Anyway," Henry said nonchalantly, "we have to get her back before John Marchessa finds out she is missing. If he gets to her first, she most certainly *will* be dead." He peered over the shoulder of an assistant who looked like he would rather be anywhere else. "Frank, do we have her location yet?"

It took a second for Frank to find his voice. "Yes. The signal came back just now, sir. I'm not sure why we keep losing it. They don't appear to be moving."

Henry picked up the locater off the assistant's desk and stared at it, absentmindedly running his fingers over the edges of the tiny screen. I wondered if maybe his cool demeanor was just a way of hiding his true feelings—maybe he was just as terrified as I was.

"Sindra, organize the ransom money, and do whatever you have to do to make sure it's kept absolutely quiet," Henry ordered. "I want whoever picks it up followed and "questioned", if you know what I mean. And make sure you clean up after yourself. Don't leave any loose ends."

Sindra nodded and left the room. Henry then turned to me, and when his eyes met mine, I saw the truth in them: he was shaken to his very core. He was just one hell of an actor.

"Oliver," he said firmly holding my gaze, "you are going to take this…" he put the locater in my hands, "and find her. Carl will organize a chopper, and you will take three men with you. Once the money has been exchanged, you will depart."

I fought the urge to take the locater and run out of the room, but only patience and careful planning would bring Kaya back safely.

"Can you do this? Are you well enough?" Henry asked with a glance at my ribs.

"Yeah, of course." I patted the little bottle of pills in my pocket.

"Don't fail me," he said, and his green eyes, the same color as Kaya's, held my gaze firmly. "Don't fail your *fiancée*," he added quietly.

I had no reply. I waited for a lecture, an angry rant, or maybe even a gun to my head for proposing to his daughter, especially without his permission, but instead, he gave me a lopsided grin. "Yes… I knew you were the right one when I picked you out so many years ago," he whispered inches from my face, "you were a good investment."

A good investment?

"You find her. And Oliver… none of those kidnappers live, understand? Whatever you have to do, you make sure you eliminate every single one of them. But let 'em feel it first."

He put out his hand, and I shook it firmly. "That was always the plan, sir."

KAYA

23

INK

I YELLED FOR SETH AND REGAN—WHERE WERE THEY? I HOLLERED again, but then I stopped when I realized I was putting Luke in danger by basically announcing our location.

I grabbed a blanket out of the tent and threw it on the ground, then eased Luke down onto it, his back leaning against a tree. He insisted he was fine, but the color of his face indicated otherwise. I found Regan's medical kit but was barely able to get my fingers to cooperate with the latches. My hands were so cold and sticky with blood that once I got the case open, I spilled most of its contents out onto the blanket. There were scissors, cotton pads, ointments—things I recognized—and then odd things I didn't. I knew a yellow substance in one of the tubes had made its way into my veins a few times.

"You'll be all right," I said, trying to comfort Luke, who was patient while I searched for antiseptic.

"Do you know what you're doing with that stuff?" he asked.

"Sure. Well… no, not really—but I'll figure it out," I said with as calmly as I could manage.

The crumpled plaid shirt he'd been holding over his chest had become unrecognizable—his blood had blended all the colors together into one—and the shirt he was still wearing was shredded and hanging in strips from his shoulder. That's when I noticed another wound.

"That T-shirt needs to come off," I told him.

He laughed, "Yes of course, ma'am."

"Ugh, don't call me ma'am," I said nervously.

He kept pressure on the gouges across his chest while I eased the sticky fabric gently off his wounded arm. On his upper bicep, there was another deep gash. I gulped at the sight, not just because of the wound, but because his glorious, bare skin had been marked by the cat—I would kill that thing a hundred times over if I could.

Stay focused…

Wrapping his arm tightly with more gauze than necessary, I took in a deep breath and steadied myself so I could look at his chest. "Okay, let's see what we're dealing with here…" I carefully pulled the soaked shirt away from his skin, vividly aware of his hot breath on my forehead as I poured water over the wounds. Four, deep cuts ran across his left pectoral, and one almost reached his ribs. They were all bleeding, but the one that had grazed his ribs bled more than the others.

"How bad is it, Doc?" he asked.

"Oh, you'll live," I said, still trying not to freak out.

"That's good, because I have a lot of things to make up to you. I've gotta get you home."

"Don't' worry about me or any of that right now, okay? Just relax."

He was starting to look extremely pale, and the fresh pads of gauze were already soaked through. I told him to take a deep breath, and then I quickly pulled away the gauze and poured what I hoped was antiseptic over the wounds. He gasped in pain. "I'm so sorry," I said, feeling sick as I pressed back down on his chest.

"Kaya, you're gonna have to sew that one up for me," he said, referring to the deepest cut that had revealed a layer of fat, or maybe muscle, under the skin. It was bad—really, *really* bad.

"But I don't know how to—"

"I know. But it's bleeding a bit too much. I kinda need you to do this for me, if you wouldn't mind."

Wouldn't mind? I would throw myself in front of freight train loaded with acid-spitting snakes for you… "Yeah, of course I will," I said casually.

His eyes were getting heavy and his skin paler by the minute; I had to act quickly. I found a needle and eased some black thread through the eye of it. I knew Regan had something for freezing, but I had no idea what it was or how to use it. "I'm sorry, this is really going to hurt," I warned.

He forced a perfect smile. "Just do it, Kaya. It's okay. I trust you."

I pulled the bandage back from the wound a little bit at a time, pouring water over it as I went to wash away the blood. The needle poked through his skin easily. I carefully stuck it through one side of the cut, pulled the wound together, and then tied a knot. It was all I could do to not faint, or cry, or completely lose my mind. I felt like I was torturing him even though he barely made a sound. I detached myself from reality and pretended I was sewing doll clothes—very fragile, lace doll clothes. I managed to get five bits of thread to hold the deepest part of the wound together, but there was still a long way to go.

"Are you okay?" I asked.

Shivering, he looked down and to the side. "Fabulous, couldn't be better," he said bravely.

"Just a few more…"

I pushed the needle through his skin in a daze, and then I added stitches to another gash that needed them. I'd lost count of how many times I'd jabbed him, and when I was done, I realized I'd been pretty much holding my breath the whole time. "Are you okay?" I asked.

"Uh huh," he said sleepily, "a lot of concern from a girl who was running away from me not too long ago."

"Yeah, about that… I won't run again. I promise—for real this time." He raised an eyebrow, as if searching my face for a reason why. "But I will take you up on that offer to get me home."

He nodded, and then his eyes closed.

I squeezed a whole tube of some clear jelly over the crude stitches, allowing my fingers to linger on his skin as long as possible. Then I covered up my handiwork with gauze and medical tape. When there was nothing else I could do, I watched him rest. I let my eyes wander from his perfect face to his collarbone where a little gold maple leaf hung on a chain, and to his chest, then over to his ribs where a large tattoo in black cursive letters said *Louisa May*.

"Hey, Kaya?" he said, catching me staring at him.

"Oh, yeah, um… I was just going to—find you a shirt," I lied and started to rise to my feet. He grabbed my hands, keeping me next to him. "Thank you," he said.

I looked hard at his face, and then before I could think, the words just burst out of my mouth. "Do you love her?" I asked, letting my eyes wander to his ribs and the tattoo.

"Yes. More than anything," he said with such certainty and conviction that it instantly caused a crushing pain in my chest. His love for Louisa was so deep it was permanently etched into his skin, and all I could think was how I wished it were my name he wore so close to his heart.

He squeezed my hands and spoke in a soft voice. "And let me ask you this: do you love *him?*"

His fingers nudged my engagement ring, slippery with his blood. Chills went up my spine. I couldn't look him in the eye—I had to keep it together and turn my emotions *off.* "I have to get you some warm clothes," I said, pulling away, feeling dizzy.

Keep it together…

I was about to go in search of a blanket to warm him up but stopped mid step when the light shifted behind the tent again. Another mountain lion? I crouched in front of Luke and put both hands on the gun, aiming for the trees. He was saying something to me, but I was too focused to listen.

The tent wobbled when something brushed its side, and then from behind it appeared a slow-moving mass of black fur.

The beast. He sniffed the air, and the hair on his back stood straight up, then Seth emerged from the trees with Regan close behind. After a quick glance at Luke on the ground and me covered in blood while aiming a gun at them, their shotguns were pointed at my head.

"It's okay. She saved my life," Luke said, pointing toward the dead cat.

Seth's jaw dropped at the sight of the mangy, yellow beast's corpse sprawled in the snow. "Sweet Jesus!" How the hell…?"

"Two bullets—thankfully the last one was dead on," said Luke weakly. "She's a good shot."

Seth eyed me curiously while Regan dropped his gun and bolted to Luke's side in full panic mode. I felt such an intense relief that they had returned and were able to help that I ran to the bushes to throw up.

"I've got something for that," Regan yelled.

I gave him the finger.

While I waited for my stomach to quiet down, I watched Seth wander off into the trees, dragging the dead cat by its tail. His eyes caught mine, and he gave me a wink. I didn't know what it meant or what was going on in his crazy head. I was just glad he was taking the gross carcass away.

When I returned to Luke, he was covered and flat on his back, his eyes closed, with Regan kneeling next to him. I recognized my backpack underneath his head and felt oddly comforted by its familiarity. Regan was putting his spilled medical kit back together and giving me glances that were impossible to decipher.

"Still nauseated?" he asked.

"*Nope.*"

"Good." He inspected the contents of the kit. "Just wondering, did you use antiseptic?" he asked sarcastically, holding up the almost-empty bottle.

"Oh, yeah. Sorry about that."

"Whatever. You did a good job."

"Thanks."

I got down on my knees across from him, Luke laying quietly between us and thankfully not quite so pale.

"It's kind of remarkable, really," Regan said.

"What is?"

"That you patched the boy up."

"Uh, why?"

He laughed. "Because you're, well… you. A spoiled girl who knows nothing of medicine. It's amazing that you didn't faint or run off crying."

"Did I have a choice?" I said, glancing down at the beautiful man before me.

Regan stopped what he was doing. "Uh… well, yes," he said quietly, "yes, you actually *did* have a choice. You could have left him to die."

Luke's eyes popped open like a lightning bolt had hit him. His fingers wrapped around mine, and I heard him take in a deep breath. Yup… Regan had pretty much said it all. I tried to pull away, but I couldn't. My hand was cemented to the ground, held tightly by the man I'd fallen in love with.

Regan pulled out a needle and filed it up from a little vial of yellow stuff. "Hey Luke, I'm going to give you some painkillers and antibiotics, okay?"

My fingers tightened around Luke's and a wildly protective urge came over me. I didn't trust Regan, or what was in the vial. "Don't touch him," I growled as I felt for the gun in my pocket with my other hand.

Regan eyed me warily. I knew I had a crazed look on my face, because I *felt* crazed. I'd do anything to protect the man lying between us. I wondered if this was the way Oliver felt all those years while being my guard. It was all consuming. It was a rage I'd never known.

Regan cleared his throat. "I would never hurt Luke. Never in a million years," he said most sincerely. "Of that, you can be assured."

I'd been expecting a fight from the strange redhead, and his show of affection for Luke caught me off guard. I realized something as I stared hard at him and at his hand resting gently on Luke's arm. Regan had a thing for Luke. Still though, I had to turn away when he filled Luke's veins with something scary looking.

"We'll give him an hour to recover, but then we have to get moving," Regan said when Luke's eyes grew heavy.

"An hour? But he needs to rest."

"We can't stay here. We're sitting ducks, and there are probably more of those cats around. When Seth gets back, we'll be off."

"Where did Seth go?" I asked.

"To check on our traps and make sure your daddy's pals don't find us, if there are any of them left."

My pulse sped up. "What do you mean, *any of them left?*"

"Nothing, other than we just took care of them," Regan said harshly.

My heart felt as if it had dropped into my stomach. I knew in my heart Oliver was looking for me… I had to put my free hand to the ground to steady myself. "Tell me Regan, what happened? What did you do? Did you… *kill someone?*" I asked frantically and on the verge of a full-blown meltdown. "Who did you *take care of?* What did he look like?"

"Tall," Regan laughed.

I felt tears burst forth, and I had absolutely zero control of them. I pictured Oliver, dead, and I couldn't hold back. Rivers poured from my eyes as the world came crashing down around me. Regan seemed startled by this. He shook his head, and all the callousness of his tone left his voice. "Kaya, honestly, we didn't kill anyone. Don't cry, for goodness' sake, everything is fine. We're not bloody savages."

As tears kept rolling, Regan's tough-guy image crumbled, and he then spoke to me like a brother might to a scared little sister. "Really, it's all right. We just set up a few traps to slow them down and covered our tracks. They'll be going in circles for a while, that's all. Chillax. Everything's fine."

"So, nobody's hurt then?" I asked through sniffles, feeling embarrassed over my meltdown.

"Well, maybe a few bunnies," he said sweetly.

Regan was definitely not a killer. That was now blatantly obvious. As I watched him fuss over Luke and move about cleaning up camp, I wondered if maybe I should be more worried about *them*… about Oliver… who, at any given moment, could come out of the trees, hell bent on retrieving me, and completely unable to listen to logic. Then what would I do? What if he was ordered to release his fury on my captors? His anger would make him completely unreasonable. Pulling the trigger on the cat was easy, but Oliver? That was just too horrible to imagine.

With every shifting of the breeze, my heart sped up. Every shadow made me jump. The small fire crackled and smoked, playing with my vision.

"It's him, isn't it?" Luke said quietly. He had woken up and thankfully didn't seem to be in so much pain. "Your fiancé… you think he's out there somewhere?"

"Yes. Henry would have sent him."

"Why?"

"Because he will stop at nothing to get me back."

"But the sky has been quiet for a while," Luke said softly.

I looked up. There hadn't been the sound of helicopters this morning, even though the sky was vibrant blue above the treetops.

"Do you really love this guy?" Luke asked softly, and I heard him hold his breath.

I forced my head to nod. "Yes."

He closed his eyes tightly, as if my answer pained him horribly, and then he raised himself up on his elbows. "Hey, Regan?" he said. "Promise me you won't go firing at Henry's men."

Regan was taking down the tents and dropped the muddy stakes in dismay. "What? Have you lost your mind? You know damn well they'll blast us to bits the first chance they get. I mean, what if they were to come out of the trees right now and—"

"I don't care what they do. You can scare them or slow them down, but that's where it ends." Regan was about to protest, but Luke's voice boomed through the quiet forest, making us both jump. "*Promise me!*" he yelled.

Regan gritted his teeth. "Fine! Okay fine! You've lost your mind completely, but what-the-hell-ever!"

Luke was trying to protect my fiancé. His bad-guy image was crumbling rapidly before my eyes. He looked hard into my eyes before lying back down. "I'll make you the same promise, too: you have my word that I won't hurt him," he said.

I adjusted the blanket around him and stayed by his side, on the edge of my nerves, while he slept. I kept an eye on the bushes and the gun ready in my hands.

24

ᴀGENDA

I PRACTICALLY INHALED MY SECOND PORTION OF OATMEAL, thinking it was the most delicious thing I'd ever eaten. Then, out of nowhere, a massive wave of nausea hit. I doubled over out of reflex, but this time, there was a lower-abdominal pain accompanying the sick feeling.

This was getting embarrassing.

"What's wrong?" Luke asked.

I was the one supposed to be looking after him. The hour of sleep had brought color back to his cheeks, and he was ready to go, while I was turning into a mess.

"Is it your stomach?" he asked.

There was such a powerful twist in my gut I could barely speak. "Just really… upset… I'll be fine," I managed to squeak out.

"This happens to you a lot," he said with concern.

"No. Just this last month. Haven't quite gotten over a flu bug, I guess."

Luke stood there, quietly contemplating this, and then the strangest look came over his face. He suddenly looked pale again.

"Um, are *you* okay?" I asked.

"Of course," he said curtly, and then he turned and walked away.

I didn't know if I said something wrong, or if the pain meds were messing with his head, but his mood had changed drastically. Most likely, he was probably just too proud to admit he was in pain.

The afternoon sun warmed the air and turned the snow to muck. Our packs were heavy, and we slid constantly as we made our way to the river. The beast seemed to be carrying the most weight, and I thought he must be frying hot with his fur coat and so much wrinkly fat around his neck. He still scared me—his sheer mass alone was intimidating—but when one of those shadows shifted in and out of the trees and he growled a deep, menacing warning, I was glad he was on our side.

The pines thinned out a bit as we got closer to the river, letting in a muted, soft sunlight that for the strangest reason felt rather romantic. The smell in the air was incredible, and we were constantly front row and center to an amazing bird concert. I filled my lungs with the cleanest air you could imagine, grateful to be alive, and when we stopped to rest, I almost felt happy.

Until I looked at Luke's face.

There was so much concentration and intensity about him he looked about to crack. When the beast flopped down at his feet, he didn't even notice.

"You okay?" I asked for probably the hundredth time in the last two hours.

Either he didn't hear me, which was virtually impossible, or I was being ignored. "So, what's the dog's name again? I forgot," I asked as casually as I could, dying inside for any response.

He stared at the ground, his jaw clenched.

Seth proudly spoke up. "The dog's name is Brutus. Brutus Jonathan Wayne."

"Wayne? Is that your last name?" I asked, grateful for any casual conversation.

"Nope. John Wayne was a badass cowboy, just like my furry friend here. It suits him, doesn't it?"

"Uh huh," I agreed.

Brutus seemed thirsty. He intently watched as I uncapped my water bottle and tipped it to my mouth. "Does he need water?" I asked.

"Yup. Call him and give him some. He's a good ole boy; he'll listen."

I thought it best to have the beast on my side, and he really didn't seem like he wanted to rip my limbs off. I tentatively called his name and was shocked when he obeyed. I poured water into my hand in a slow stream, and he lapped it up greedily, leaving behind a slime I pretended not to care about. I touched his head and couldn't help but smile when his tail wagged.

"Hey, don't be seducing my dog now, too," said Seth with a smirk on his face.

I laughed, but Luke's expression still didn't change.

"What kind of dog is he?" I asked, determined to avoid the awkward silence.

"He's a Mastiff and Newfoundland mix—had his fifth birthday last week. Was gonna get him a cake, but at 190 pounds, he probably don't need it."

"Yeah, he's huge. Is that normal?"

Seth grinned. "Yeppers, that's why I got him. Having some useless, yappy little thing that just shits and eats is good for nothin'."

Regan spoke, his tone flat. "My dad used to call those kinds of dogs 'kickables'."

"What? Did he actually *kick them*?" I asked.

He seemed to give my question serious thought. "Well, yes—and us kids, too—whenever he had the chance."

I couldn't stop from continuing. "Sounds like your dad was an asshole."

He smiled. "Yep, just like yours. I guess we have something in common, don't we, Kaya?"

His eyes, I realized, changed with his mood. They had become a soft amber now, gold flecks gleaming in the sun like his red hair. "I guess so," I said, actually feeling confident enough to look at him fully. "Although, it would be much cooler if our common ground was something besides having a shitty parent."

"I think we might have more things in common than that," he said with a sneaky glance at Luke's sullen face.

We plodded down an overgrown trail, parting bushes and slipping on muddy patches. Gone was my happy feeling. Luke stayed eerily quiet even after hours had gone by, yet still he stayed close to me, uncomfortably watching my every move and always ready to catch me if I fell. My mind ran wild. What had I said? What had I done? I stumbled, lost in thought, and his arm shot out to steady me.

"Be careful!" he snapped.

I mumbled I was sorry. I was unraveling. The emotional and logical parts of my brain were at war, my foot throbbed, my muscles ached, and my stomach churned. Luke seemed oblivious to his own wounds and was more worried about me falling or breaking a damn fingernail than anything else. Yet his eyes still avoided mine.

The sound of the river hit our ears well before we saw the glow of it, and once there, Seth and Regan went about putting up the tents. Luke built a fire, avoiding me completely, and I was getting nervous. Maybe those *moments* we had were just that: moments. Maybe he had come to his senses and remembered that I was just a pawn in his plan to get Louisa back from wherever she was. Maybe the attraction I thought he had toward me was all in my head.

That thought hurt like hell.

The fire crackled as daylight faded, but the air stayed warm, soft, and perfectly still. The river moved along slowly and waves lapped up onto the rocky shore as two Ospreys dove in and out to catch their dinner. The colors of the setting sun cast orange-and-pink hues behind the trees, and I leaned back against a piece of driftwood to take it all in. Soothed by the peacefulness and mesmerized by the beauty, I decided that whatever was going on in Luke's head was his problem, not mine. I wasn't going to let it get to me. Soon we would be going our separate ways, anyhow.

Regan had started cooking. Things were being chopped, sizzled, smoked, and taste tested over and over. I felt like I was watching one of those outdoor adventure shows on the food network. He seemed so confident and skilled, but what I liked most was how happy he was to do it.

"What is it?" I asked when a portion of his finished creation was carefully lifted out of the frying pan and onto a plate. The most delicious aroma wafted up my nose.

"Paella," he answered, "cooked the traditional way over a fire with pine branches and cones to infuse it with aromatic smoke—otherwise known as good old rabbit and rice."

"What? Like, actual *bunny rabbit*?" I asked while poking what I assumed was a leg.

"Um, yeah. It's good, Kaya. Try it."

He peeled back the steaming meat from the bone, blowing on it to cool it down. I pictured him doing this for his sister—revealing yet another soft side to Regan—and he held out a tiny piece of brown meat to me. My mouth watered.

"I've never eaten anything like this before," I said.

"You mean paella? Well, if we were at my house, I would have added some shrimp, fresh mussels, chicken, a bit of saffron—"

"No, I mean I've never eaten any sort of… *animal*."

All three men stopped what they were doing and looked at me like aliens landed on my head.

"What do you mean?" Regan said, looking completely dumfounded. Apparently, the concept of vegetarianism was new to him.

"Henry never allowed it. Most of our food was grown on the estate or bought locally. I mean, I've had eggs, but I've never eaten the flesh of an animal."

"What about fish?" asked Seth.

"Nope."

"Chicken?"

"Uh, no…"

"Ham!" said Regan excitedly, and I suspected that was his favorite.

"Well, that comes from a pig, so no—"

"Steak? Oh dear lord, please don't tell me you've never had a steak," said Seth in shock.

"Well, no, it was once a living creature that used to eat and breathe—just like us… so—"

"And you do this by choice?" Seth asked incredulously.

"Well, yes…" But then I gave that question some more thought. Did I? No, it wasn't *my* choice. I had been on a strict vegetarian, organic diet my whole life. I hadn't asked for that. It was forced upon me. "Actually, I guess Henry made that decision for me," I said.

Regan shook his head, his expression almost comical. "Well, I'm gobsmacked. What the bloody hell is Henry's problem?"

"He's *obsessed* with my health and always rants on about how chemicals will 'mess up my insides'. He'd go on about it for hours. Chefs were fired if they were caught with even a speck of 'unapproved' foods in the kitchen."

"Ah," Regan said with sudden clarity. He sat back and ate the piece of rabbit that had grown cold in his fingers. "Well, of course. Henry would know better than anyone about the effects of toxins on the human body."

"Why is that?" I dared ask.

"Because Eronel Industries is responsible for some of the most damaging toxins in history, like polychlorinated biphenyls and dioxin, as well as antrixon, a chemical used in pesticides that is linked to female infertility."

"But Eronel makes medicine…"

"It didn't when your granddad ran it. When he gave it to Henry, the company was a smoking gun—about to be exposed to the world for the horrific damages it was causing. I'm sure he never dreamed his son-in-law would bring Eronel up from the ashes and turn it into a billion-dollar corporation aimed at curing the very disease it created." Regan looked at me curiously, as he perfectly arched an auburn eyebrow toward me. "How can you not know this?"

Luke looked up from his plate. I could tell my answer was important. "I just don't. I don't know… I…"

"According to Isaac Asimov, 'the saddest aspect of life is that science gathers knowledge faster than society gathers wisdom,'" Regan said and shoved a heaping spoonful of paella into his mouth.

I felt stupid. I had refused to pay any attention to the news, or any of Henry's business-related rantings because I really just *didn't want* to know. Avoidance was my defense against the hatred aimed toward me because of my family.

Regan piled more food on his plate and kept talking, but all I could hear was Henry's voice churning in my head. The lectures, the lunges at my plate if I'd happened to have been served a piece of bread, the dismissal of the guard who bought me candy at Christmas, him grilling the chef about every ingredient and where it came from before I could even taste the meal that had been prepared. How many times had Henry said to me *your body has to be clean so you can have a child someday*... a thousand? A million?

An Olympic pool sized dose of reality dumped on my stupid head.

Regan had moved on to discuss the health benefits of meat, but I'd tuned him out. Instead, I was feeling the full effect of Luke's gaze from across the fire. His face said it all: everything about Henry was true. Henry *knew* what he was giving those women—what he was selling them. Fertility was his passion, his expertise, his business—and his business was his *everything*. His company had created the illness *and* the remedy. *'I tried to find a cure for the crazy in her head,'* he had said so often of Lenore...

And what were his motivations for expressing such great concern over my reproductive health? What did it matter to him if I ever had a child? Why did he care? Unless, maybe my producing an heir to the family holdings was important somehow...

The inheritance.

I clutched my stomach.

"It's all natural," Regan was saying, "there are no chemicals to worry about out here."

I made a run for the bushes and dropped to my knees. There was no food to bring up, which made the whole process that much more awful. I choked and coughed on stomach acid and thought briefly that I might die. I could see the headline flash before my eyes—girl dies from puking in the bush.

Then, the nausea was gone again as quickly as it had come. Just like that. I stayed on my knees, ignoring the pebbles digging in to my bones and the strange, tall reeds of grass tickling my nose, until I thought it was safe to move. I carefully sat back on my heels, but my muscles felt unsteady. My head was spinning too, not just from retching, but from the horrible confirmation that my father really and truly was a monster.

Luke had made his way over with water. Apparently, he was no longer ignoring me. I took the cool metal bottle from him and forced down a sip to quiet the acid burning in my throat. He knelt beside me and reached for my hand, but I pulled away—I was annoyed with his hot-and-cold behavior.

"Kaya, I've been thinking about this all day, and, well, excuse me for being blunt, but is there any chance you could be, um, you know..." he said, his eyes looking into mine, searching for an answer to an unclear question.

"Could be... what?"

"When was the last time you, uh... when was the date of your last—"

"Good lord! What are you asking me?"

He grabbed my hand and placed it on my stomach. "Think about it," he said softly.

He thought I was pregnant.

"What? Hell no! I started taking the pill a few months ago, and the doctor said I had just missed a few periods from all the training for the race and it was perfectly normal, and—*why the hell am I telling you this anyway?*"

He looked like he'd been hit in the chest with a hammer. "Oh my God, you *are* late—by how much?"

I thought he might pass out right there in front of me. Is this what he had been so moody about all day? Because obviously he'd given the situation a lot of thought.

"Kaya, answer me. How late are you?" he said, his eyes huge.

"This is ridiculous; I can't be. The doctor checked. I had blood tests done a week ago."

"Maybe they were wrong."

"Stop it!" I hissed.

This was insane. I had only slept with Oliver once and I'd been on the pill, so no, I couldn't be. I stood and angrily backed away, almost tripping over my own feet.

"Kaya, wait, I'm sorry."

"Leave me alone!" I snapped, marching off toward the river and cursing my wimpy tears for being so close to surfacing all the time. Me, *pregnant?* There was no way. It wasn't possible. Dr. Ellis put me on the pill, and I was committed to it—never missed a day. I trusted him. He had been my physician since the day I was born, and he was Henry's oldest and dearest friend—Henry's *oldest and dearest friend...*

Oh. My. God.

LUKE

25

Saw Her Standing There

"Soap," she demanded.

With her hands on her hips and her bottom lip jutted out, she reminded me of Louisa.

"Wha—" Regan began to ask.

"I need *soap*," she insisted, clearly upset.

"Um, we don't have any," Regan answered.

She seemed about to break, and I knew it had nothing to do with soap. "I think I might have some," I said and got up to dig around in my backpack. Regan quizzically raised an eyebrow. "You know, for dishes and such," I said defensively.

I put a half-used citrus-scented bar in Kaya's delicate hand; it was the same one I had used at a truck stop a few weeks ago.

"Please save my dinner for me. I'm going to wander down the river bank a ways to wash up first," she said, speaking mostly to the fire, the flames reflecting in her eyes.

"No. It's way too dangerous," Regan said. "There are bears, cougars, possibly men with guns, and who bloody knows what else lurking about."

"Well, it doesn't matter to me. I just don't want to make you all uncomfortable. I'm going in that river to wash up, get completely naked, and scrub off the vomit, the blood, and the dirt…"

"Ooh, show time," said Regan excitedly, giving me a lewd wink.

Even though he was joking, the thought of him or anyone looking at her naked body made me feel insanely crazy. "Listen," I said softly, not wanting to upset her even more, "go ahead, but not too far out of view. Regan is right; it's dangerous." Then I added, "Please?"

Before anyone could protest, she marched off without saying a word. I felt sick. All day long I had thought about the torture I would endure when I had to let her go. Just having her out of my sight for a minute was unbearable. And since I was pretty sure she was pregnant, I felt an even deeper and overwhelming sense of duty to look out for her well-being.

I stared at the flames, the blue and orange licks crackling and fluttering as it sent columns of smoke up to the treetops. The air was still, the birds were singing, and I wished I could take in the beauty of the place—so wild and untouched, not destroyed by human hands—but I was too miserable.

I felt Seth eyeing me. "Everything all right?" he asked in a fatherly way.

"Nope," I said honestly.

"Are you in a lot of pain?"

I put my hand over my heart. "In so many ways."

"The feeling is mutual, you know. The way she looks at you is intense. She was like a mama bear protecting her cub today when we came back to camp. I think she—"

"Don't say it," I said, rudely cutting him off, "it will be easier to let her go if I can convince myself she wants nothing to do with me."

Regan pretended to be pre-occupied with feeding the fire, but he glanced toward the river too often. "Come on, now," he said, "we don't *have* to let her go."

"You can't hold someone against their will, Regan, and it was wrong of us to even try. I promised I would get her back home, and I will do it. Or, I'll at least keep her safe until her fiancé finds her."

Regan's head whipped around to face me, his expression incredulous. "What? Fiancé? *She's engaged?* What the bloody hell! She's only eighteen. She's too young for that. Are you sure?"

"Yes," I said dismally.

"Who the hell to? She is guarded closer than the Crown Jewels."

"Quite conveniently, a bodyguard."

"That guy Oliver she's talked about? The one who she said has been by her side for nine years? I'm gobsmacked. Are you cool with this?"

Obviously, Regan had been listening in to our conversations. "What? No, of course I'm not cool with it, but what can I do? My hands are tied. Anyway, I want to meet him face-to-face. I want to see the man I'm going to lose absolutely everything to."

Seth and Regan exchanged glances. "Is that why you left the tracking device on her ankle?" Seth asked carefully. His pushed his hands deep into his plaid coat and crossed his feet casually like the question was no big deal.

I gulped so hard it hurt. "Yes," I admitted sheepishly. "I'm sorry guys, but my priority right now is to keep her safe. I will lead her right into his arms if that's what I have to do—whatever is necessary to get her back home."

I was proposing throwing them both to the wolves and destroying a plan that, for Seth, had been years in the making and, for Regan, was an all-consuming mission of revenge. Who's to say they wouldn't kill me in my sleep and continue to do what they had originally set out to? With me out of the way, they could hand Kaya over to the real mastermind behind this whole ridiculous plan.

But I had to trust them. If Henry couldn't find Kaya, and I was left on my own, my odds of getting her out of these mountains were slim to none.

"Listen, I never wanted to put you guys in this situation, and I don't expect you to understand or forgive me, but it's just that... I never thought... I didn't realize I would..."

As usual, words failed me.

"Luke," said Seth delicately, "you don't have to explain. Love just happens. It chooses you. It comes crashing in like a herd of jonesing rhinos in a beer store—unexpected, unwanted, uncontrollable, and completely illogical. Regan and I have been there before. We know what it's like to fall that hard for someone. Although, *I* don't necessarily know what it's like to fall for your own *sister...*" Seth turned and looked at Regan accusingly.

"*Not by blood!*" Regan exploded, cheeks instantly turning scarlet, "Not by blood... and if you would have met her, you'd know why!" He rubbed his forehead, his way of calming himself down whenever this particular topic came up. "You know, Kaya kind of reminds me of her—of Miranda. Long, dark hair, tiny waist... strong willed and a fighter but still very naïve in some ways..."

"Miranda sounded like she was an amazing girl," I said.

Regan stared off into the distance, lost in thought, and then he shrugged off his reminiscing and stood, swiping dirt and a few ants off his knees. "There's an old Cherokee Traveler's greeting that's rather fitting right now, and Luke, since we are on the same journey together, here it goes..." He stared uncomfortably into my eyes with the kind of intensity only Regan could possess, then spoke like the words were literally coming from his *soul.*

"I will draw thorns from your feet
We will walk the white path of life together
Like a brother of my own blood I will love you, and
I will wipe tears from your eyes
And when you are sad, I will put your aching heart to rest."

Never had a man quoted poetry to me before. I raised an eyebrow and tried to cover up a smirk with a cough. This redhead was the strangest man I'd ever met.

"In other words, I've got your back, Luke," he said wholeheartedly.

I was really at a loss for words. Seth crinkled up his face and leaned forward with a long piece of grass in his mouth. "I got yer back too, Luke boy. It's all good," he said. "Of course, without all that poetry nonsense and stuff. I mean… we're *dudes*."

I felt a bit choked up from the sincerity of these two odd human beings. They were on my side. "Thanks guys."

Regan nodded, quickly reverting back to his vengeful-doctor character. "Oh, by the way—we've already demanded the ransom money from Henry, and Kaya will not be harmed at all as it seems he has agreed to the terms. So… let's bloody well get Louisa back home where she belongs, all right?"

I cringed and wished the flames would burn away the sound of Louisa's name in my ears. I couldn't get my hopes up of ever seeing her again, and I had already come to terms with the fact that she was probably already dead—it was the only way I could carry on. Every other scenario was just too awful to imagine.

While Seth tossed Brutus doggy treats, Regan whittled away at a stick, and a wolf howled in the distance, I worried madly about the two people I loved—Louisa and Kaya.

"Luke," Seth said loudly, startling me.

"Yeah?"

"Go keep an eye on Kaya," he said, as if he had read my mind.

THE RIVERBED VEERED OFF TO THE RIGHT. I FOLLOWED IT UNTIL I CAME upon her clothes unceremoniously dumped on the ground—she really had taken everything off. The silvery blue light of dusk lit up the river like a sheet of shiny glass, and I could still see the trees on the other side, but Kaya was nowhere to be found. My heart stopped; where was she?

I looked up and down the beach. There was nothing but sunbleached logs, rock, and masses of lush green grass. I was just about to call her name, but then a figure popped up out of the water—Kaya. The twilight surrounded her and water droplets fell from her soaked hair like jewels and sprinkled the air as she dove under again. After what seemed like forever, she broke the surface once more, rose up, and then slowly stood. The water swirled just below her waist, and she dragged her hands back and forth, skimming its surface. Her bare skin shimmered, and her long hair draped down her back like a waterfall. She had the bar of soap in her hands and started lathering it over her face and body. I was mesmerized. A wrecking ball couldn't have moved me.

She dove under. I held my breath and sighed in relief when she reappeared. Then, when she stood and turned toward the shore, I fell to my knees; they'd become useless.

"Luke?"

"Yeah, just making sure you were okay. I wasn't looking, I swear," I lied, forcing my eyes to keep to the ground.

Her pink-painted toes soon appeared inches from mine. "Do you *really* swear?" she said.

Damn. She could always tell when I was lying. I lifted my chin and allowed my eyes to follow. There she stood, soaking wet and naked, yet making no effort to cover herself. Water dripped across her breasts, down her stomach, and over her thighs—and all the air left my lungs—she was heart-achingly beautiful. I took a mental snapshot before struggling to my feet and opening a blanket to wrap it around her shoulders. When she said thank you, her green eyes locked onto mine without a hint of embarrassment.

"How is your chest?" she asked, wiping her face with a corner of the scratchy, wool cloth.

"Amazingly, it feels much better at the moment," I said, wanting to hold her so bad I had to mentally tie my arms to my sides. I cleared my throat and realized I'd better occupy my mind with anything other than what was underneath the blanket. "I'm sorry about earlier—" I started to say.

She shook her head. "I can't think about that right now, okay?"

I didn't push it.

"The water was freezing, but it feels amazing to be clean," she said, and then she ordered me to turn around while she got dressed.

I couldn't help but peek, only this time my knees became weak for a different reason: the large bruises on her back and the massive one running down her thigh were there because of me. Caused by this awful situation I'd put her in—one I would do my damndest to fix, and then spend a lifetime trying to forget.

KAYA

26

ꝺPARKS

I TRIED TO KEEP IT TOGETHER, BUT MY SANITY FELT LIKE IT WAS dangling from a string, swaying back and forth just out of my reach. By the light of the lantern hanging from the roof of the tent, I unbuttoned Luke's shirt while he watched me intently. My mind swam with a thousand questions as I tried to follow Regan's instructions to the letter, busying myself with the task of playing nurse. It seemed like shooting the cat in the morning was a lifetime ago.

Luke barely flinched, so I took my time, probably more than I needed to, and gently dabbed at his wounds with damp cotton to loosen bits of dried blood. His bare skin was so firm, tight, and smooth, and the muscle under it defined. I wanted to let my hands wander over his stomach and up to his glorious neck but was also content with this deeply satisfying action of caring for him.

The sun had left the sky and had taken every speck of heat with it. I'd draped the warm blanket over my shoulders, grateful Luke had hung it by the fire, but my body absorbed all of its heat. I wished my hair would hurry up and finish drying. The tangled mess could stay wet for hours, and it was getting cold. Luke shivered when I eased the shirt down from his shoulder to apply the dressing to his arm, which I now realized probably could have used stitches, too. I placed tape across the cut, pulling it together like Regan had instructed before wrapping it back up.

"Will I live, doc?" he teased when I was done.

"You better," I said far too seriously.

He gave me a sleepy smile and pulled his shirt closed over his chest. I lay down next to him, being careful not to get too close, and arranged the blanket to cover as much of my body as possible, but the air was intent on getting through.

"Listen, I am sorry about earlier. I didn't mean to make you upset," he said.

"It's okay. I just don't wanna talk about it."

"That's fine, I understand. Goodnight Kaya," he said and clicked off the lantern.

I hated the dark but had too much pride to tell him that. Instead, I tried to concentrate on the sounds of the river, the water moving, and the smell of zest soap on my hands, but nothing diverted my mind from the two huge questions I'd been avoiding: the one I had to ask myself, and one I desperately wanted to ask him.

"How much are you paying to get Louisa back?" I asked bluntly.

My question came at him from out of nowhere, only because being concealed in darkness gave me the courage to ask it. I wasn't really concerned with the dollar amount, but I knew his would lead me to what I *really* wanted to know.

"A million," he answered.

"And where is she now?"

"With the sick bastards who took her from me."

I felt the depth of his anger and the pain in his voice. It was like a knife in my chest. "Will you marry her when you get her back?"

"Marry her?" he asked incredulously.

"Um, yeah. You don't have a ring on your finger, so I assume if you're going to such great lengths to rescue a girl, you have intentions of—"

He laughed, cutting me off. "I wanna show you something, okay?" He turned the lantern back on, propped himself up on his elbow, and reached into his shirt pocket. "I want to show you a picture of Louisa May."

He carefully handed me a very worn photograph. It was obvious he'd held it often. I imagined him gazing at it longingly and didn't know if I really wanted to see what she looked like—this woman who he so dearly loved. She was probably incredibly pretty, and I was already sick with jealousy.

"Please, look at it," he said, sensing my apprehension.

I sat up and held the picture under the light. It didn't make sense; Luke was holding a small child, maybe two or three years old, with golden hair and a smile like his. She held a pink stuffed bunny in her arms and was snuggled happily against Luke's chest.

"Louisa May loves bunnies," he said thoughtfully.

"She is... this little girl... this is Louisa May? She is a... you have a child?" I was completely dumbstruck.

"She's my little sister. That picture was taken on her second birthday."

I felt like such an idiot. I was jealous of his baby *sister*. That's who he was fighting for, who he would never give up on! I looked up at him and fully realized my mistake, then fully realized the nightmare he was living—*someone had taken his little sister.*

"She is beautiful," I said as the dam holding back my tears came close to breaking. I was unable to take my eyes away from the photograph even as he took it back and carefully put it in his shirt pocket.

"What happened?" I had to ask.

He lay back and folded his arms under his head so I could freely stare at his profile. "When my mum died, I was left with nothing. They took the house, the furniture—everything. I was nineteen with a one-year-old baby to look after. I had no money and no place to live…" He hesitated.

This was difficult for him to talk about. "I won't judge you, Luke. I promise."

He cleared his throat. "Well, I made friends with a guy who got me involved with a couple of drug dealers—easy jobs, good pay—and eventually, Louisa and I moved in with him. One night, I did a small job on my own and left Louisa with my roommate. When I returned, the music was cranking loud, and all the lights were on. It was after three in the morning, and Louisa was usually in bed by eight. I found my roommate and his friend in the living room totally wasted. I then went to check on Louisa, but she wasn't in our room. They laughed when I asked where she was, and one of the assholes pointed to the kitchen. I walked in to find Louisa sitting in the corner by the stove with her bunny in her arms. Her eyes were huge with the most scared and hurt look I had ever seen on her face—"

He paused, and his voice became so quiet I had to strain to hear him.

"Her nightgown was covered in blood, and a little pool of it was on the floor underneath her when I picked her up. They had…"

He couldn't finish. My hand went to my mouth, and every hair on my body stood on end. He didn't have to complete his sentence—in fact, I didn't want him to. It was too horrible. "Oh my God, Luke. I am *so* sorry."

"I messed them up *bad*. I tried to kill them, and I would have if the guys across the hall hadn't stopped me."

"They deserved it," I said, unable to even imagine the pain he must be dealing with.

"When my roommate got out of the hospital a month later, he convinced the boss I'd stolen from him. I was going to leave that day, take Louisa with me and run. I had enough money saved up for us to live on. I had just finished packing up her bags when they broke in, and instead of killing me, they took her. They told me I would get her back when I paid off my debt."

"Which is why you kidnapped me—" I mumbled.

"I searched for Louisa, but my efforts were futile. I went crazy—drank to numb the guilt, fought to get out the anger, and then wished I were dead because of the pain. The weekly teaser phone call with her voice crying on the other end was the only thing that kept me going, but eventually those calls stopped."

A wolf howled, followed by another, but it was Luke's story that made me shudder. I reached for his hand when he got lost in thought.

"I saw news coverage in a bar one night," he continued, "a protest at a Montreal drug manufacturing plant that had been organized by the Right Choice Group. I listened through my half-drunken state, and I realized the same thing those people claimed happened to their loved ones had happened to my mother, and if she were around, Louisa would be safe and our lives would have been normal. I made my way there to join in and ended up spending the night in jail with Regan. In the morning, he took me home. He sobered me up and gave me hope and purpose. I would be dead without him."

I remembered watching that news clip in the hospital waiting room—the fire burning and members of the Right Choice Group getting arrested while Henry blatantly lied to the public. It was the day Anne died. "So, they've had Louisa for over a *year?*" I asked, and then I wished I hadn't.

"Yes."

"You know it's not your fault; you did everything you could."

He blinked and stared up at the tent roof.

"Everything will work out, Luke. Tomorrow, Henry will hand over the money, because that amount is absolutely nothing to him, and then you can pay off the ransom and get your sister back."

He sighed heavily. He was past having any hope. I could see that. "We *will* get her back," I said again.

"We?" he said questioningly, and then he turned to face me, his blue eyes wide.

"Yes, *we*. If there is anything I can do, I will. I promise."

A smile came across his face, and he put his hand on my cheek. I wanted to grab him, pull him in tight, hold his head to my chest, and smother him with affection, but I couldn't allow myself to go there. I was already in too deep. "Things will be better tomorrow. You'll see."

"You're exhausted, Kaya. You really need to sleep," he said, and then he pulled his hand away, "try and rest, we've got lots of walking tomorrow. We've gotta get you home… right?"

Now I was the one to sigh. "Right."

He turned off the lamp, and this time I was okay with the dark, unable to look at the hurt on his face without reaching for him. I said goodnight, and my stomach rolled and sent a splash of acid into my throat, which brought me to my next question, the one I finally had to ask myself. Was I pregnant with Oliver's child?

Think about it... answer honestly...

Yes. Yes I was. There really was no doubt. I knew it. I had gone over the details, examined the facts, and it most certainly was true.

How did I go from hating Oliver so much to getting engaged to him and becoming pregnant? I cared about him, that was for sure—there was the friendship, the familiarity, and the physical attraction—but all those things didn't come anywhere near the feelings I had for the man sleeping beside me. The man who I would give my life for. The man who I wanted more than anything...

"How far along are you?" he asked gently.

I didn't want to answer. Saying it out loud would be a confirmation of the dreaded truth.

"Kaya, how far along?" he asked again. "Please tell me."

"Fifteen weeks."

He rolled me onto my back and hovered above me. My heart raced.

"May I?" he asked, and then, quite boldly and without waiting for a reply, he put his hand under the blanket and found his way to my stomach. I stopped him, trying to decide if I wanted him to feel it or not... and then I pulled his hand upward and slowly guided it down under the waistband of my pants. I gave him the opportunity to feel my bare skin or pull away if he wanted to. I heard him gulp as he moved toward my pelvis where he stretched his fingers out between my hip bones.

"Fifteen weeks..." he muttered to himself.

His breath brushed my cheek as he moved his fingers in a gentle circle around the edges of the tiny bump. The pure and genuine affection that emanated from him was something I had never felt so deeply from another human being in my entire life.

"I think Henry knows," I said, "I think somehow he was... uh, involved. I mean, I think he somehow planned this. I can just feel it in my bones."

"It's okay. We'll figure it out," Luke said.

"We?" It was amazing how that one word could be so comforting.

"Yes, *we*," he said earnestly.

He moved his hand from my belly to behind my neck, lifting my head slightly toward his so I had no choice but to stare directly into his eyes. Even though the only speck of light came from the moon, his striking features caught my breath. Then his lips were on my forehead, lightly brushing my skin and sending sparks from my nose to my toes.

"I will be here for you… if you want me," he said.

Want him? Yes, that's part of the problem! I yelled in my head.

"Just say the word, and I will do anything for you," he added, looking at me as if seeing right into my soul.

And I for you. Yet another problem!

I said a very polite and reserved 'thank you', and then I forced myself to pull away—which was probably the hardest thing I'd ever done—and curled up on my side. I shivered. Not just because I was cold, but because I had fallen even more hopelessly in love with a man I could never have. And I was pregnant and scared to death.

I felt the tears come on, now worried that I might actually freeze to death, but his warm arms were suddenly wrapping around me, holding me tight in a way that meant there was no way I was going anywhere, even if I wanted to. And, unfortunately, I was okay with that.

OLIVER

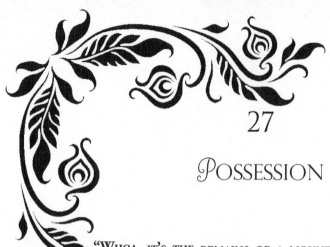

27

$\mathcal{P}$OSSESSION

"**W**HOA, IT'S THE REMAINS OF A MOUNTAIN LION THAT'S BEEN shot in the head." Davis was kicking at a mound of fur, the stink of death pungent around it.

"Just keep an eye out for more of their traps," I reminded him. We'd narrowly escaped the kidnappers' attempts at throwing us off their trail and I hoped the other group going north was just as alert.

"There was only one person here, and there's no sign of Kaya," Davis said, totally in his element out here in the wild. He had a nose like a bloodhound and an uncanny ability for tracking. His instincts led us to the remains of a campfire amidst a small clearing. It was well trodden with footprints, and Kaya's were everywhere. I felt my heart speed up, but what caught my breath was a dark-brown substance dried around the base of a tree. I thought of her screaming in that video.

"What if it's hers?" I said, pointing toward it with shaking hands.

"They don't want to hurt her; I told you that. They didn't show us what they were doing, and she cut her foot open during the race. I have a feeling they were just patching it up. That bit there is most likely blood from that dead cat."

As much as Davis tried, nothing he said eased my mind or alleviated the dread I felt. What if she was dead? What if that cat attacked her? What if…?

"So, tell me Ollie, what are you going to do when you get her back?" Davis asked.

Man, he loved to talk—and talk *and talk*. I wished he would just let me be miserable in peace. His method of diverting my attention in an effort to keep me calm was becoming downright annoying.

"Really, Oliver, what's going to happen?" he pressed.

I hadn't given that any thought past today. "What do you mean?"

"Well, Henry knows you are engaged, right?"

"Yeah, and I have no idea how."

"Well, I never said a thing, I swear," he said, slipping as we descended toward the river and grabbing onto a leafy branch to steady himself. "It's just that... everything is different now, ya know? Is he going to allow you to actually marry her? Will you all live together under his roof? I mean, Henry is—well, um..." He paused, unsure of whether or not to continue.

"He's what?" I asked, curious where Davis was going with this.

"Controlling, conniving, or one could even say manipulative. I don't know, after seeing his blasé reaction to his own daughter screaming in that video, it brought a few things to light."

"Like what?"

"Well, he isn't trying to get Kaya back because he loves her, that's for sure."

"She is his child..."

"Yeah. But... don't you find it strange how she has been so closely guarded all her life, yet lately has been allowed to be alone with you? It's almost as if Henry is encouraging you to... um..."

"To what?"

"*You know.*"

Obviously, Davis had given this a lot of thought. I had just been so excited to be alone with Kaya that it never even occurred to me how it came to happen. I had bought the ring thinking there would never be a good time to give it to her, yet the very next day we'd had a moment to ourselves—the most blissful moment of my life—even if guns were pointed at me afterward. If I thought about it, yes, it was most certainly odd, but I'd chosen to ignore it.

"Do you really think Henry is that evil?" I asked.

Davis quietly considered his answer while concentrating on his footsteps when the trail became steep. "Yeah, I do."

"But how would Kaya and I being together benefit Henry in any way?"

"I have no idea, but I just feel like it does."

If what Davis was hinting at was true, I didn't care. Hell, Kaya was all I ever wanted. Why question it? Henry pulled me off the streets, gave me a home, a job, educated and looked after me, and allowed me to protect his daughter. I had a deep loyalty to Henry, and even though I was starting to see him for what he really was, I couldn't escape the fact that I owed him my life. Some part of me even wanted to defend his treatment of Kaya, even though I knew it was wrong.

We paused to re-hydrate and add on some extra layers of clothing as the air cooled off with the waning sun. The tracker still wasn't working, my ribs were killing me, and I felt as if I'd been moving through quicksand. There would be nothing more satisfying than killing those kidnappers with my bare hands once Kaya was safe and sound.

"Why do you think Henry chose you?" Davis asked, breaking through my thoughts and not giving up on the subject. "I mean, why, out of so many guards, did he decide to pick the one person who Kaya has openly admitted to hating? Why would he do that?"

His yapping was relentless, but the answer was easy, so maybe it would shut him up. "Because he saw right from the beginning that I would fiercely protect her."

"Yeah," said Davis, "or… maybe your love for her was just that obvious. Maybe Henry saw *that* right from the beginning, before *you* even knew it. If there was some way he could use that to his advantage, he would. Just saying."

"It doesn't matter, Davis—who, what, when, where, or why—I don't care about any of that in the least. I will do whatever Henry asks of me on this mission because we both want the same thing: to return Kaya home, safe and sound. That's where she belongs. She's mine, plain and simple. And I am going to get her back."

LISA

28

If I'm the Girl Next Door, You'd Better Move

I HAD TO ADMIT, I LIKED PRETENDING TO BE BARBARA THE NURSE during The Death Race. A normal girl, hitting on cute guys, living a nine-to-five life... and I could have that someday, thanks to Luke. I would do anything for him. But what would I say to Louisa when we were finally face to face? *'Hey baby girl, remember me? I am Lisa, your brother Luke's friend... or um, ex-girlfriend. You and I went on picnics together and to the zoo once, remember? I know your favorite color is purple, and you like bunnies. By the way, you're going to come home with me now, okay?'*

Would she recognize me? What if she cried? Or screamed? What if she caused a huge scene and the police were called... I would lose her and let Luke down. And, I could end up in jail—again.

I made it to the train station a bit early and headed for the bench across from locker number sixteen. If all was right in the world, in that locker would be two identical bags, each containing one million dollars. I just had to wait until the right moment to open it.

There were two big lugs at the far end of the station standing under the departures sign. I laughed at their flowery shirts, shorts, mirrored sunglasses—and no luggage. Two men taking the holiday train from Banff to Hawaii with no bags or sunscreen? Could they be any more obvious? At the opposite end of the platform, standing by the exit doors, were two rather stocky women wearing too much jewelry, designer dresses, and cheap, flat shoes. Their lack of makeup and really bad hair-dye jobs were also a dead giveaway... wow. Lowen Security sure didn't have it together in the disguise department.

The only two patrons I wasn't sure of were the high-looking teenagers hanging out by the washroom. The one with green hair glanced in my direction often, but maybe she thought I was a cop.

The train arrived. People poured into the station in droves, turning the quiet place into a mass of chaos. Under the cover of confusion, I swiftly went to locker sixteen and opened it. There, as promised, were two black, leather bags. I took in a deep breath, grabbed one of the bags, and headed to the handicap stall in the women's washroom. After locking the door with shaking hands, I hesitantly unzipped the bag; stacks of crisp, one-hundred-dollar bills took my breath away. I had fought for every dollar I ever had my entire life and now, without doing a damn thing, there were a million of them in my hands. I could have cried.

Now, to use this money to get Louisa.

I pulled my blonde hair up and stuffed it under a brown, smelly wig I'd bought at a thrift shop, then tied a beige scarf around my neck. The brown windbreaker jacket I'd stuffed in my purse was a crumpled mess and would perfectly complement my disguise. I unfolded the matching tote bag and transferred the money into it, then swung it over my shoulder and stuffed the empty black bag behind the toilet. I swiped on some bronzer, brown lipstick, and thick glasses, and then giggled at my reflection in the mirror. I looked invisible and unmemorable—which was exactly what I wanted.

The station was thinning out again. I quickly placed the brown tote bag into a bottom locker by the pop machine—I would get this money later, under a different disguise. Now to barter with the bag still in locker sixteen, this was exchange money for Louisa.

I sat down next to the teenagers, who didn't even bat an eye at me now. I waited, feigned interest in a brochure, and kept tabs on Henry's men at the exits. Five minutes passed, and then I saw her—little Louisa, the spitting image of her beautiful big brother. My heart rose into my throat; there were shadows under her eyes, and her skin had that grey pallor that screamed neglect and abuse. I knew because I'd looked like that once. Some vile redhead had Louisa's tiny hand in a death grip, and that evil bastard Claude was leading them in my direction. The only satisfying thing to come from the scene was spotting his limp from the two broken legs Luke had given him that never healed right, and his blind, sagging eye. Luke should have killed him. I had a gun. Maybe I would...

I smiled at Louisa when she reached me, and I thought maybe she recognized me by the way her eyes lit up, but the look was fleeting, and she quickly returned to a horrid, vacant stare. I placed a lollipop in her free hand, while the redhead clutched the other, and then passed Claude a note with the combination for locker sixteen—which was still being closely watched by Henry Lowen's holiday boys.

What felt like forever passed while Claude retrieved the money and ducked into the washroom to inspect it. Louisa stared at the floor as the redhead snapped her gum and the poorly disguised, stocky women edged closer. Was Henry's undercover posse interested in me? Or were they concentrating on the man who had taken their money from the locker and waiting for him to come out of the bathroom? My heart pounded so hard it hurt. When Claude returned, he gave the redhead a nod of triumph, and Louisa was shoved in my direction, her tiny hand now blue.

"Have a good vacation with Aunty Kathy," the redhead said loudly, and then she spun on her high heels, following Claude and the money out the door. The teenagers, the stocky women, and the holiday boys all followed suit.

I hoped Henry would be merciless.

I picked up Louisa and held her tiny body tight against mine. She didn't fight or make a sound, so I walked as casually as I could across the tiled floor, through the exit, and then out into the sunshine. Once in the parking lot, I ran.

KAYA

29

ℲOAR

THE SUN WAS RELENTLESS AS WE MARCHED ALONGSIDE THE RIVER.
So was Regan's blabbering. He really, *really,* liked the sound of his
own voice. Good thing at least thirty percent of what he said was
interesting. We had all just endured a lecture on how the Rolling
Stones were the greatest band in the world. I disagreed—because
everyone knows the greatest band in the world is The Beatles—and
he hadn't relented in his retort since.

"Seriously, 'I am the Walrus'? I mean come on… lyrics that don't
make sense, *on purpose*? Elementary penguin? Fly like pigs in the sky?
Sitting on a cornflake? Goo goo b' joob? Utter nonsense."

I gave him no response. It was too hot to argue.

"Now, 'Gimme Shelter' or 'Paint it Black'? That's good stuff!" he
said, and then he sang to himself for a minute. "Man, the weather out
here sure changes in a blink of an eye, doesn't it?" he asked, drastically
changing the subject. "One minute, you're freezing, and the next minute, you're frying like an egg on the hood of my old Chevy."

"You put eggs on your car?" I asked, and then I wished I hadn't.

"Well, yeah. High school stuff. You know how it is."

"Uh no, actually. I don't."

"Bloody hell! Sorry. You never experienced school, or any public in-
stitutions of the sort, right? How sad. No drunken party games for you.
Do you even have friends? Go shopping? Does your fiancé ever let you
out of the cage, or… house?"

I dropped my backpack on the ground, tired of Regan's yapping,
tired of walking, and just plain tired.

"C'mon, girlie, we gotta keep moving. We're a day behind schedule
right now," Seth grumbled politely. He was hot as well, but gone was
that gruff, tough persona. He talked differently to me now—without
any hatred in his voice.

"I'm sweating from places I didn't even know I had. Can't we just
stop for a sec? Please?" I begged all three of them.

Luke happily dropped his pack, Seth threw his hands up in defeat, and Regan started babbling about something I had no interest in. The river was moving slowly, sparkling in the afternoon sun and a family of deer had gathered on the other side. A small fawn tentatively approached the water under the nervous gaze of its mother, and then more of the graceful creatures cautiously came out of the dense bush. The momma deer nudged her baby forward, and I absentmindedly put my hand on my stomach as I watched. The sudden urge to get in the water was suddenly so overpowering I was pulling off my shoes without a second thought.

"Whoa, what's going on, girlie? We don't have time for that," said Seth.

"Please, let's rest and cool off. We all could use it."

As I rolled up my pant legs, Luke sat down on the rocky riverbed, looking amused. His cheeks were red and forehead dripping with sweat. Seth and Regan looked overheated, too.

"You guys should go in as well. You could *really* use a little freshening up," I said to their pink faces.

Seth sniffed his underarm and recoiled. There was no denying that the stink of him was horrendous.

I waded in and wished I was alone so I could take off my clothes and dive under the cool water. Minnows swarmed around my feet, and my stomach growled as I wondered how they might taste cooked over the fire with rice like Regan had prepared the meal we had with rabbit.

"How's the water?" asked Luke.

He looked too good to be true leaning back on his elbows with that relaxed expression on his god-like face, the sun highlighting the gold in his hair and making his blue eyes sparkle.

"Amazing," I replied, wading out a bit deeper and soaking the edges of my pant legs, I was blissfully starting to shiver.

"I'm cold just watching you. How can you stand it?" he asked.

"Easy. I'm Canadian," I yelled proudly.

He laughed. My shivers multiplied.

I pulled off my tank top, grateful for the generous coverage provided by my sports bra, and dipped it into the river to use as a washcloth. Luke watched closely with the same look he had last night when he handed me the blanket. I went to him with the dripping shirt in hand and directed him to put his head back. I wrung water out over his hair and face, pouring it over his skin while being careful not to get the bandages on his chest wet. He reveled in the attention, and I was more than happy to give it. I went back in the water and wet the shirt again, then gently rubbed the back of his neck and squeezed the cloth so little rivers poured down the back of his shirt. The coolness of the water brought down the redness in his cheeks, but the sight of him damp and dewy brought out the scarlet in mine.

The sound of loud shrieks reminded me that we weren't alone. Regan and Seth had made their way into the river, and there they were, butt naked, scrubbing their skin as if their lives depended on it.Seth's body glowed in the sun, his skin paper white with the exception of his arms and head, and Regan was quite impossibly, well... *fit*. Even Brutus was cooling off. Water turned to diamond droplets when he shook his mass of wet fur. I found myself giggling at the whole scene. Their yelps of laughter were so unexpected and so oddly comfortable they made Luke smile too, the most perfect lines around his eyes appearing as he squinted against the sunlight.

"How is your chest?" I asked, needing to pull my gaze away from the river.

Luke shrugged his shoulders.

May I?" I asked, reaching for him.

His grin suggested I could probably do whatever I wanted, so I took my time unbuttoning the front of his shirt. Then I peeked under a bandage—the skin beneath was much too swollen and hot looking. All the hair rose on the back of my neck. Infection was setting in, and that was bad, bad, *bad*... I was about to yell for Regan, but he appeared silently at my side. Thankfully, he was wearing pants.

"I think there might be some infection going on," I said, and every speck of the laughter from a moment ago was replaced with worry.

Regan retrieved his beloved first aid kit and started peeling back the bandages. He dabbed at the wounds with antiseptic, and Luke flinched. I knew if I did it, it wouldn't hurt as much.

"I'll do that," I said, but I was ignored. Luke flinched again, and that crazy, overwhelming feeling to protect him came over me. I clenched my hands into fists and snarled at Regan. "*Back off.*"

Regan put his hands up defensively and eyed me with smug curiosity. "Fine. Make sure you clean the wounds, apply the ointment, and bandage it well. And Luke, you gotta take those antibiotics every four hours. It's a damn good thing we'll be out of here by tonight."

"I'm sorry, Regan. I—I don't know what came over me," I said, trying to apologize.

"It's okay, Kaya. I get it," he said with a discreet wink, and then he walked away.

Holy crap. My head was a mess.

"Well, I'm glad to be on your good side today," Luke said, grinning.

"I have no idea why. You're just a good-for-nothing criminal," I joked.

"I think maybe you might like me, Kaya Lowen." He grinned.

I clamped my mouth shut so I wouldn't reply and continued to carefully tend to his wounds. He closed his eyes and turned his face toward the sun, so I stole as many glances at him as I could, begging my hands not to wander from their task. When finished, I sat down beside him.

"I could stay here forever," I said admiring our surroundings but secretly revealing how I could stay next to him for eternity.

"Not me. I feel like I am in a big, green prison cell," he said, popping some Saskatoon berries in his mouth.

"What? All this space? This beauty? This is the ultimate freedom."

"Yes, it's amazing, but I am a city boy, Kaya. Ultimate freedom to me is driving around for an hour to find the perfect slurpee."

"Slurpee?

"Yeah."

"Um, what on earth is a slurpee?" I asked, feeling dumb.

"You're kidding, right?" he said, straightening up and searching my face to see if I was.

"No. I've never gone out driving around looking for… things like that…"

"A slurpee is a partially frozen beverage, usually made with pop," he said, happy to explain.

"Oh."

"It's sweet and cold and mind blowingly satisfying—as far as beverages go, anyhow—and if you find just the right one, not too frozen and not too melted, it can be the key to the perfect day."

"I don't understand how a drink can make the 'perfect day'."

"It's just one of those 'little things in life', Kaya."

"So… you drive around? Going wherever you want? With no… *plans*?"

He sighed, placed his hand on top of mine, and then picked it up off the pebbled beach. "There are so many things in the world I want to show you. You should let me."

I knew I was supposed to pull away, but I couldn't. His fingers entwined with mine. "Soon, you will be delivering me to my father, and I'm afraid you won't be able to show me anything. I'll never see you again," I reminded him, sadly.

"You don't have to go back, you know."

How could he say that? What else could I do?

"You have a choice," he added.

"Do I?" I had already made a commitment to the man whose child I was carrying, and Henry would never give up looking for me. I stared out at the river with my hand in Luke's and wondered why it felt so right—more right than anything else in this confusing world.

"Kaya," he said after a long pause, "I want to look after you *and* your baby."

He tightened his grip ever so slightly. My heart almost burst.

"I don't even know you—"

"Yes, but we have a connection. You can *feel* it, I know you can. I am trying to be respectful of your, um, situation, and I don't want to push you into anything. And… I promise I will get you back to your family if that's what you want… but you have to know this: you have options. You have a choice."

I didn't at all. My choices had been made for me.

"Besides," he continued, "it will kill me to let you go." He pulled in a lungful of air and slowly poured his sky blue eyes into mine. "There is nothing I want more in the world, than to be with you."

I was at a loss for words. I wanted him too, but if I let him know that, it would hurt him even more when I went back to Oliver—which is what I had to do. So, I was going to have to lie to Luke. Somehow, I was going to have to tell the most beautiful man in the world that he was only a crush. The only person who had calmed my anxiety, been the first to show me respect by letting me make my own decisions, and vowed to protect me even though it went against everything he knew before—the love of my life—was the one I had to let go of.

I gathered my courage. I practiced the lie in my head. But before I could get a word out, Regan's voice boomed through the entire valley.

"*Luke!*" he yelled.

We both jumped to our feet as he ran toward us grinning ear to ear with a cell phone in hand. He looked like a little boy who had gotten a shiny new bike for Christmas. Seth was close behind with just as big of a grin plastered across his face.

"You're not going to believe this!" Regan said, literally trembling with excitement. "I've got Lisa on the phone… and she has Louisa May!"

Luke stared at the phone and stumbled backward. He was tentative and unsure, Regan's words too much to fathom. I reached out and pushed him gently toward Regan's outstretched hand.

"Really Luke, it's her," Regan assured.

With trembling hands, Luke put the phone to his ear, afraid to speak. When he finally did, his voice broke my heart. "Lisa? Yeah, I'm okay. Um—you really did it? Is she all right? You've got her? Could you please, put her on…?" he said, stunned.

We all listened while he held his breath.

"Louisa? Hey sis, it's me, Luke," he said, and tears spilled from his eyes as the little girl's voice on the other end set him free. He dropped to his knees and put his hand over his chest, speaking calmly while trying to hold himself together. I melted as I listened to him—to the way he calmed the crying child, talked to her about bunnies and making a snowman, then promising her he would see her soon.

He would be a great father someday…

When the conversation ended, he stayed on his knees and stared at the phone in disbelief. He gently shook his head, trying to make sense of what had just transpired.

"I owe you guys. I am forever in your debt. Thank you, from the bottom of my heart," he said, struggling to keep from breaking down.

Seth moved toward him, pulled him up off the ground, and gave him a long, silent hug. Regan did the same. Time stopped for a brief moment while the three men reveled in the completion of part of their mission. "Anything for you, my friend," Regan said softly in Luke's ear.

Luke turned to me. The emotion on his face so raw I just wanted to smother him with every ounce of affection I had. "I'm sorry you were used to get my sister back, Kaya, and I hope you can forgive me, forgive *us*."

I didn't have to think too hard about that. "Apology accepted," I said. "I forgive all of you completely. And for the record… I admire what you guys did. I respect you all for never giving up on her."

Luke's jaw dropped slightly. He stood taller and looked me square in the eye, wordlessly telling me that he wasn't giving up on me, either.

THE LONGER WE WALKED, THE LOUDER THE RIVER BECAME, THE increasing rush of water changing from a smooth, purring kitten to a raging, roaring tiger. The rocky beach narrowed into a moss-lined path of flat stones that wound up steep banks. Water swirled and kicked up spray, cooling our skin but also making the ground impossibly slippery. We walked single file with Seth and Brutus leading the way. I didn't want to slow everyone down, so I didn't mention that I was battling dizziness and strange stomach pains. When I stumbled, Regan steadied me from behind.

"You don't want to fall into that," he warned, pointing toward the rushing water beside us. "The rocks will break you in half, and the current will carry you off to only God knows where."

The river had split in two an hour ago, and we had been following the volatile section that contained immense caves and divots lining the canyon walls. It was fascinating, and so was Regan's narrative of Native legends, but I eventually had to give up admiring and listening—it only added to my dizziness.

"How much farther?" I asked, hoping I didn't sound whiny.

Brutus seemed agitated too, growling into the trees and staying glued to Seth's side. "Just before we hit the falls this trail snakes off and heads north. Since I can already hear the falls from here, I'd say we have another hour and a bit to go," Seth yelled over the roar of the water, and then he scolded Brutus for whining.

"And then what?" I asked.

"Well, then we get the hell outta here."

The reality that I would be saying goodbye to Luke by the end of the day was settling over me more and more. He was ahead of me, offering me his hand to pull me up over a slippery patch, and I didn't want to let go.

"What about part two of your plan? Shutting down Eronel?" I asked.

None of them answered.

"I think you should still follow through with it," I said, slipping, and I was thankful yet again for Regan's quick reflexes, "I want you to use me. I want to help."

Seth stopped and turned around, holding on to a tree branch sticking out over the path to steady himself. The whole group came to a screeching halt behind him. "Use you how, exactly?" he asked, intrigued.

Before I could answer, Luke intervened. "No way. Not happening. Nobody is using you for any reason whatsoever," he said, clearly agitated.

"But Luke, I *want* to help. Henry wouldn't even know I was on your side. You all could still get what you want before you have to take me back."

His face paled and he looked like I'd stabbed him. "You're going back?" he said in shock.

"Uh, yes, you know I have to. I'm—"

Regan butted in. "You know Kaya, you're a smart girl, but you can't seem to see what's plain as day and right in front of your face. You were taken advantage of by an older man—someone in a position of trust. That *sick* bodyguard fiancé of yours preyed on you—on a lonesome *teenager*! Besides, you are in love with this guy!" he said loudly and pointed at Luke. "Are you taking crazy pills, or what? Why would you even consider—"

"*Regan*," Luke hissed, but Regan continued.

"I mean, you can go back to that Oliver fellow if you want, out of some stupid sense of duty or commitment, but I think that's wrong when you are clearly in love with someone else."

"I love Oliver. That's why I agreed to marry him in the first place! And what the hell does it matter to you, anyway? You don't care about me," I said fiercely.

"I care about my friend, Luke, and it's just so obvious that the two of you—"

"Regan!" Luke yelled. "Stop it. *She's pregnant.*"

Regan's eyes slowly widened, and his mouth parted in shock. He glanced at my flat stomach and then took a step forward so he was only inches from my nose. Rocks slipped out from under his feet and rolled over the edge into the rolling water.

"Oh my God," he muttered, and it was obvious that something painfully heartbreaking was playing out in his mind. "Miranda wanted a baby so bad—tried everything. She miscarried twice but finally was able to carry to term. The child was stillborn."

"Your sister, right?" I asked, my anger dissolving under the hurt in his eyes.

"Yes."

"Regan, I'm so sorry." I wanted to offer a hug or some kind of comfort, but it just didn't seem appropriate—or safe. The narrow pathway was so steep I might just topple him over. As I searched for something to say, he reached for my face with his big, dirty hands. I felt Luke shift uneasily behind me.

"Kaya, I never would have treated you so badly had I known. All the drugs I gave you—I shouldn't have—oh my God. I'm so sorry." There was a dazed look about him, and I had the feeling he wasn't looking at me, but at the sister he'd lost.

"Regan, let's get moving, okay?" Luke urged gently.

But Regan didn't budge. His face was vacant, eyes distant.

"It's not your fault, Regan. You know that," I said.

My voice brought him back to reality. Startled, he let go of me. "Those injections I gave you… I don't know the side effects. They could interfere with the development of…"

I wasn't listening. A small shadow fell across the path behind him. It was probably just a bird, but it seemed pretty big, and Brutus started to growl.

"…and when your heart stopped…" Regan was saying.

The shadow grew larger. Was it another mountain lion? A bear? "Regan, there's something—"

I didn't finish. Suddenly, there was one of Henry's men standing fifteen feet away, with a rifle aimed at the back of Regan's head. I recognized the steel-grey eyes immediately.

"Put your hands up!" yelled Mark Reicht. His face was bloody and scraped, and his camouflaged clothes were covered in dirt. He looked like he'd been thrown into a blender with a couple of knives and a wasp nest. Regan turned slowly to face him. "I said, *put your hands up!*" Mark demanded again. "All of you! And tell that mutt to stay put, or I'll shoot it!"

Brutus bared his teeth, and Seth ordered him to be quiet.

"Are you all right, Miss Lowen?" Mark asked, his voice slightly less harsh as he addressed me.

The knuckles on his trigger hand were raw, and deep gashes ran up his wrist. I drew in a slow breath and forced myself to be calm; I knew what this man was capable of. "I am perfectly fine," I said. "This is all a misunderstanding. You can put the gun down."

He shook his head. "Nope. Now come over here, and get behind me."

My feet were frozen in place from equal parts shock and fear.

"*Now.* Or you will have the redhead's brains splattered all over your face," Mark said, his crude response serving as a warning.

I slid past Regan, his hands steadying my hips until I was securely past him, but he didn't let go.

"Get your hands off her, or you and your buddies will be dead in two seconds!" Mark yelled.

I looked hard into Regan's eyes, which were now burning with hatred for the man giving him orders. "It's okay. I know him," I muttered, and Regan reluctantly let go.

I inched slowly toward Mark so that I was between him, the gun, and the three men I'd decided to defend. "Mark, they mean me no harm. This is all a misunderstanding. They were actually trying to help me get out of here," I said, trying to sound casual while I was actually terrified.

Mark kept his gun aimed at Regan—the barrel of which now was just inches from my fingertips if I reached...

"I know who they are, Miss Lowen, and I have my instructions. Now get behind me, and close your eyes," Mark ordered.

I gulped. "Your *instructions? Close my eyes?* Why?"

"Just thought I'd spare you the gory details. You've seen enough death. No need for you to see more. I have orders to eliminate them," he said coldly.

Luke must have moved, because suddenly Mark shifted the gun in his direction. I felt the blood drain from my face. "Mark, please, put the gun down," I begged.

Marks steely eyes narrowed into a glare. His intent was obvious. I leaned to the left, getting as dangerously close to the edge of the path as I could without toppling over, and used my body to block his aim at Luke.

"Move away from there," he said nervously.

The spray of the roaring water soaked my cheeks.

"Kaya, you're going to fall. Just listen to him, and do what he says," Luke said.

The obvious panic in Luke's buttery voice made my thoughts that much more clear. I had to save his life, and not because of my selfish love for him, but because he had a little sister who desperately needed her big brother.

I shifted my shoulders, leaning even more toward the river because my feet could go no farther. Another step, and I'd be in the drink. I stared into Mark's robotic eyes, his programming courtesy of the monster who is my father, and saw the same thing I'd seen in Oliver's eyes: the desire to kill. I knew there was no point reasoning.

When Mark returned his aim toward Regan, I knew what I had to do—I swung my arm out against the barrel of the gun and lunged at Mark. The shot fired off into the sky, and we both toppled over the edge into the rushing water.

30

DRIFT

I HEARD THE SOUND OF BONES SNAPPING, BUT THEY WEREN'T mine, and the cold took my breath away. I was pulled under. I fought to get my head up, surfacing only to be pulled under again. I tried to swim, but my arms and legs felt like jelly. Luke's frantic voice and the sound of Brutus barking pulsed in and out of my ears, and then there was screaming… Regan? Something hard hit my head, and a flash of white burst before my eyes.

And then I saw her.

A beautiful baby girl. She was in my arms and laughing as I bent to kiss her soft cheek and peer into her blue eyes. Sandy-brown hair swirled around her forehead… and a white light pulled her away. My head was stinging, my lungs were burning, and I struggled for air. Where was I?

White foam. Cold. Evergreens and beige rock speeding by. The river…

Swim! Keep your head up! Luke was yelling, but the forceful, angry current kept pulling me under and spitting me back up. I was powerless against it. Anne's voice sounded from somewhere in the distance, too… *don't give up,* she whispered…

My hip bone slammed into a rock, and my body stopped moving forward for a second, then I was pushed violently ahead until a sickening blast of fire shot through my arm. I had stopped, but the water continued to rush past me relentlessly. It bashed, pummeled, and tried to pull me under. Whatever was holding my arm had rendered it useless, so I clawed desperately at what was in front of me with the other. A fallen log? I couldn't focus. I tried to keep my head up, tried to get air—but I was so tired—and then I saw her again, the baby. She was crying, but I was helpless to comfort her. I was slipping away from her, sinking down into the darkness…

I COULD HEAR LUKE. HE WAS SAYING MY NAME OVER AND OVER. WHY DID he sound so desperate? I could feel his mouth on mine, his breath moving down my throat and pushing into my lungs, and I looked up at his face as water dripped from his hair and onto my cheeks. His blue eyes were wide and scared. He turned me on my side, and a surge of water erupted from my lungs and my stomach. I puked until I could breathe again, and then he pulled me to his chest.

"I thought I'd lost you," he said breathlessly.

I was so cold. "I saw her," I told him. The vision of the baby in my arms was so vivid—it was the only thing that made sense.

"Her?" he asked.

The world was spinning. I pushed my cheek to his chest, grateful for the beautiful serenade that was his beating heart. "Our baby. Blue eyes—so beautiful... she looked just like you," I said and then everything went black.

THE POUNDING IN MY HEAD PULLED ME FROM UNCONSCIOUSNESS. I TRIED to bring my right hand to my forehead, but it protested in unbearable pain. I tried to swallow, but there was too much liquid in my mouth, and nothing made sense. Bits of blue sky and rolling clouds came in and out of focus.

"Try to stay awake," Luke said anxiously.

His voice sounded strange, but I couldn't make my lips form the words to ask why. Trees swayed against the sky, and I wished they would stop and be still. Something was dripping into my eyes, and I was barely able to get my left hand to my face to rub at the warm, sticky substance that was making the sky turn a funny shade of amber.

"Kaya, listen. I really need you to stay awake, okay?"

"Itz noproblem," I tried to say, wondering why my words were jumbled and slurred.

"Tell me all about the baby girl you saw," he said.

The baby. I felt her. I *knew* her... I wanted to explain—to describe her in detail and tell him about my vision of her—but I couldn't organize my thoughts into words. I watched as he ripped the sleeve of my shirt from wrist to my shoulder, and then he wound fabric tightly around my upper arm like a tourniquet. I wanted to tell him it hurt. I was thirsty. What was he doing?

"Pleeze noneedles..." I begged.

"No, no. No needles, I promise," he said, but his tone implied he had to do something much worse.

"Kaya, I need you to watch for animals, okay? Turn your head a little bit that way..." he grabbed my chin and gently moved my head so I would be facing in the direction of the river. What was he talking about? Watch for what animals? There were just trees and water and clouds...

"See that bird there? The one with the red-and-black feathers? Take a deep breath—"

A searing pain ripped through my body from my arm to my neck, and everything instantly became fuzzy, then black, then fuzzy again. The trees stopped swaying, and the pounding of my heart burst into my ears like a hammer pounding a nail. I wanted to scream, but I couldn't.

"Deep breaths—come on, Kaya... oh my God, I'm sorry—it's almost out... I have to do this... deep breaths—"

I tried to do as he told me, but it felt like he was digging a knife into my arm and prying the bones apart. Spots danced in front of my eyes, and the sounds of the forest funneled in and out of my head. Luke's voice became distant.

"Done," he said quickly as he wrapped something tight around the throbbing part of my arm. "That tree that saved your life—it didn't want to let go."

I watched him move above me frantically. His shirt was off, and he was ripping it into strips. I struggled to stay awake, but my eyes wanted to shut, and it was becoming increasingly hard to fight the urge. I had been so cold, but a strange warmth had begun to creep over me. I knew this feeling; I remembered it from somewhere... my birthday... Oliver's hands around my neck to stop the blood from pouring out of me... Was I dying? What about Luke; was he all right?

"Are *you* okay?" I asked, still unable to fully form words.

I needed to know before I drifted off in case I never came back. He ignored me and continued working on my arm, ripping up more cloth to wrap around it, and then he pulled down my waistband to apply pressure to my hip bone. I gasped at his touch and tried not to yelp from the searing pain.

"Luke," I squeaked out, but he was too anxious to hear me.

"Luke..." I said again. Using my voice required all my energy.

He stopped what he was doing and looked down at me with terror in his eyes. "I'm here, Kaya."

"Are *you* okay?" I asked once more, barely able to focus on his face. My head pounded so hard it seemed as if my own heartbeat flashed before my eyes. He took in a deep breath and forced a smile, holding what was left of his shirt to my head.

"I am perfectly fine, not hurt at all, just worried about you. I've got to stop the bleeding in your arm now, okay?" he said.

"Muh head feel worse than arm."

"There's too much blood, Kaya. I have to stop it somehow."

"I'm sure it… worse than actually…" I couldn't finish what I was trying to say.

"Stay awake, please," he said, but the amber sky disappeared.

LUKE

31

ṢTICKS AND ṢTONES

I BUILT THE FIRE UP TO A MASSIVE ROAR, DESPERATE TO GET HER warm and signal anyone searching for her. Then I pulled off her wet clothes and got them as close to the flames as I could without setting them on fire. I checked her arm again. The bleeding wouldn't stop, the puncture wound too wide and deep.

I kept applying pressure, holding it for what seemed like forever and rewrapping it, but blood continued to ooze, if not pour, from it. I had to stop it.

I put my knife in the fire, my stomach churning as I thought of what I had to do—she would bleed to death if I didn't. She moaned and opened her eyes periodically as I piled up leaves and debris around her lower half, doing what I could to keep her warm. Talking calmly while struggling to keep it together and not lose my mind, I realized I had nothing to numb her pain.

The knife was soon hot, not white or glowing red, but hot enough to sear the skin. I placed a stick between her teeth, unwrapped the cloth around her arm, and then put the bloody bandages around my hand so I could pull the burning blade from the fire.

"Kaya, are you awake?" I asked, hoping she wasn't.

She moaned. Blood gushed from her arm. I steadied myself and told her to bite down. *You have to do this for her,* I told myself and prayed I was doing the right thing.

I picked up the knife, took in a deep breath, and set the blade against her skin. Her eyes jerked open, and a gurgling scream escaped from her throat as I held the hot metal over the wound. The sickening smell of burning flesh wafted up my nose as my own tears fell on my hand. This was the most horrific thing I had ever done.

"Okay baby, I'm sorry—just one more time," I told her, shaking so hard I could barely see straight.

Her eyes rolled back in her head when I repeated the gruesome task. Then, she blacked out.

When the bleeding stopped, I thought my heart might have as well. I had to feel for her pulse to make sure she was alive. "It's okay now; it's over, Kaya. I don't have to do that again."

She mumbled something incoherent.

I covered the wound with strips from the remainder of my shirt, and then I took her wet tank top out of her backpack—the one she had washed us both with earlier—and wiped the blood from her face and eyes. There was a gash on her head that had bled a lot but had finally stopped. I tried to address all the injuries I could see, but I didn't know if there were any internal ones—and those were the ones I was worried about most. What else could I do? I threw leaves on the fire, coaxing it to send plumes of smoke into the air, and tried to comfort her whenever her eyes opened. I felt helpless as she moaned and whimpered in pain.

The wind started to pick up, a clear sign that the weather was about to change, which was the very last thing I needed. The temperature dropped quickly, and a dark mass in the sky approached our makeshift campsite. Kaya was in and out of consciousness and deathly pale. Her bare skin was marked with bruises and scrapes, which I carefully tried to avoid as I dressed her. I eased her legs back into her dry pants, still warm from the fire, and pulled them up and over her hips, pausing to touch the white skin on her stomach… her pregnant stomach…

Getting the dry tank top on her was harder than the pants. Any movement of her arm was excruciating, and tears poured from her eyes. But I had to get her dressed—and fast. The storm was moving in quickly, and all the heat from the fire would soon be useless. I needed to find shelter. We were at the mercy of the elements out here with no tent to hide in or blankets to keep us warm.

"Kaya, we have to move up into the trees. A storm is heading right for us," I told her.

She didn't reply. Her eyes were closed, and she was out cold. I knew that she probably had a concussion on top of the blood loss, and as much as I hated to move her, the impending storm gave me no choice. The dark clouds were approaching, and flashes of light danced in them as the wind started swaying the flames of the fire in every direction. Kaya shivered.

As I collected my thoughts and the backpack from the tree branch, I noticed something coming down the riverbank—something dark and down on all fours. At first, I thought it was a bear, the diminishing light making it hard to tell, but then I realized it was Brutus. The mangy dog launched into a full-out run when he noticed me, and the packs that were strapped to him almost fell off. Never had I been so glad to see a dog in all my life.

"Brutus! Good boy! You found us. Good boy!" I said and threw my arms around him.

He licked my face, and then he went to Kaya and sniffed her all over. He whined, acutely aware there was something wrong.

"I know boy; she's hurt pretty bad," I told him.

I adjusted the straps around his body and removed one of the packs. Seth had obviously sent the dog to find me while he tended to Regan, who was probably dead by now—but I couldn't think about that...

The air was turning to ice, and the wind picked up as the river rushed past us. A flash of lightning burst through the sky, followed a few seconds later by a loud *crack*. Mother Nature wasn't fooling around.

"Kaya, wake up. We have to get out of here." I shook her gently. Her green eyes opened, but they were unsteady.

"Brutus?" she said, noticing the dog.

"Yep, the hairy beast found us."

"Gooboy," she slurred. He licked her face and cleaned up the blood on her neck while I slipped on a shirt I had pulled out from the pack.

"Can you move?" I asked her.

"Uh-huh. I'mkay ta walk."

I pulled her up, getting a bit frantic as the flashes grew more frequent and the cracks that followed were becoming closer. Brutus barked anxiously as she tried to stand, but as soon as she got to her feet, her knees gave out. Thankfully, I caught her before she hit the ground. She was weak, dizzy, and her arm dangled uselessly by her side. Her eyes rolled back in her head. What the heck made me think she could stand?

"Sorry," she muttered as I eased her back down to the ground.

"Don't worry. You're as light as a feather; I'll carry you," I said, but she had already passed out.

I spread my jacket out on the ground and transferred her onto it. Then, as I held her wounded arm across her chest, I brought a sleeve up under her elbow and pulled it securely across her body. I tied the sleeves together to immobilize the wounded arm, and then I fastened the packs tightly to Brutus. As the storm rolled in, I slipped my hands under Kaya's tiny frame and picked her up.

The rocky terrain made it difficult to move quickly, and I struggled. The storm was following close behind us, and the lightning was getting so close my hair started to stand on end. The rain was coming down in full force, and the wind whipped through the trees while the girl in my arms moaned.

"It's okay. Remember what I told you? You are always safe in my arms," I told her breathlessly, ignoring the pain in my chest and the burning in my arms and legs.

I needed to believe my own words, but it was becoming difficult to see. The storm was giving me as good of a beating as any opponent in a street fight ever had. I was becoming exhausted, I was freezing, and my arms had begun to shake. The flashes of the lightning and the cracking sounds that followed were almost even now—the storm was right on top of us. I knew I had to stop though, fearful I might drop Kaya. Sinking to the ground, I cradled her like I had held Louisa when she was scared. She buried her face into my neck, and I wound my hands into her hair to warm them. The rain was sharp, stinging and biting at my bare arms. Brutus whimpered too. There was nothing near us that could offer even the slightest bit of protection from the elements—the trees were so tall their branches jutted out hundreds of feet above our heads, and the forest floor offered no shelter.

Another loud crack sounded through the sky, and a bolt of lightning hit a blue spruce, snapping it in half and blasting pieces of tree into the air. I picked up Kaya and bolted out of the way as the smell of burning wood filled our noses and a loud whooshing sound brushed past our ears.

More ear-deafening booms echoed in the sky, more rain fell, and now a fire raged.

Squinting through the pouring rain, I noticed a shiny surface to the right and headed toward it. Brutus saw it too and ran ahead, barking. We came upon large boulders that were scattered at the base of a massive slab of rock stretching up the mountainside. A part of it jutted out like a nose would on a face, shining like it had been polished, almost glowing in the rain. I ducked down beside it, hoping it might offer some sort of protection, and tried to catch my breath. Brutus was barking into the dark behind me at a space that almost looked like a mouth next to the polished nose. When another blast shot through the sky, he disappeared into it. I followed, hoping I was right to trust the animal's instincts, and moved carefully toward the yellow gleam of his eyes while mine adjusted to the dim light. Miraculously, the dog had found a cave. Without knowing it, he'd probably just saved our lives. "Good job, Brutus," I said breathlessly.

As I neared Brutus, I wondered what other animals might be lurking around, but I suspected the dog would be on edge if there were any, and he only seemed worried about the storm outside. The lightning stayed over our heads. Nature's strobe light pulsed, accompanied by the most deafening sound imaginable. Trees were breaking and snapping, and the rain was coming down in sheets. I held Kaya, my body too numb to move.

"Where are we?" she mumbled, shaking in my arms.

"In some sort of cave."

I was vividly aware of the smell of my soap in her damp hair as I moved some of the strands off her cheeks.

"Everything hurts," she said, her voice catching in her throat.

I told her I would make her better and promised her we would be okay. I repeated this until she fell asleep, and then I gently laid her down.

As I collected whatever dry leaves and twigs I could find in the mouth of the cave, I flicked my lighter on to get a better look at our surroundings. Smooth waves of red rock stretched up about seven feet over our heads and appeared to extend back for a while. My voice echoed off the walls when I said hello into the dark.

I breathed a sigh of relief when the fire caught and began to emit a bit of heat, but it was small and it wouldn't last long. I took the heaviest pack off Brutus and found a flashlight, matches, water, and packets of freeze-dried food, along with two emergency blankets, and thankfully, the medical kit.

I spread one of the blankets out by the fire and eased Kaya onto it. She gasped in pain, and Brutus growled at me while I carefully removed the jacket tied around her that was holding her arm in place. I talked to Brutus like he was my assistant, explaining what I was doing, and he quieted. Damned if the beast didn't understand English.

"I kinda like this dog," Kaya said, awake again.

He stretched his massive body out beside her while I cut the shreds of shirt off her arm. Cleaning the wound caused tears to pour out of her eyes, but she didn't make a sound.

"I'm sorry, but I have to do this, okay?" I didn't know why I was asking her permission to do all the things I needed to do to her to keep her alive, other than I still wanted her to feel like she was in control. Even in this horrible situation, I needed her to know that I would never hurt her purposely.

"Okay," she said in a small voice, running her other hand over Brutus's fur as a distraction. He let out the odd growl at me when I reached for her. "Shh, puppy, Luke's making me all better," she whispered.

The bleeding from her arm had at least stopped, but the skin was red and starting to blister, and I was pretty sure the bone was broken. I wrapped it neatly with fresh bandages, popped some painkillers into her mouth, and then secured her arm to her chest again.

I went about cleaning and applying ointment to her head and ribs, and I warily addressed the large, purple blotch forming around the wound on her hip bone. She winced when I touched it. I found the antibiotics Regan had given me for my chest in my pack. After making her take some of them, I then tended to my own wounds.

The storm raged with flash after flash followed by countless booms while I did everything I could think to do for her. Now there was nothing left to do but to rest. Exhaustion hit me in full force as I lay down beside her and closed my eyes.

"Thank you, Luke," she said softly.

When she reached up and touched my jaw with her knuckles, I took her hand and kissed it, happy to hear the sound of her voice, which, even at a time like this, still made me melt. Back at the river, I didn't know if I would ever hear it again. That vision of her being bashed around in the water, only to be impaled by that tree and thinking she was dead, would haunt me for the rest of my life. But it also confirmed the one thing I knew in my heart I'd really known all along: I could not live in this world without her.

"I thought I had lost you," I choked out.

"That would've sucked," she said weakly.

I couldn't help but let out a small chuckle. "Yes, it would have."

She giggled too, which sounded so strange given the dismal circumstances.

"What's so funny?" I asked.

"Oh… well I'd always wanted to see a cave, but now, not so much."

I turned to face her while she lay on her back staring up into the dark. I could see in her eyes that her laugh was to cover up how scared she really was.

"Don't worry. We'll be all right," I told her.

"Oh, I know," she said, her voice slurring, "but Luke… I really want one of those things you go driving around looking for… what did you call it… a slurpee? Will you take me to get one sometime? I want to just—uh—go for a drive, to nowhere, *no* plans. Just you and me. Do you think they have raspberry? I really *love* raspberry. Itz my favorite flaver."

I had to laugh. The painkillers were working. "Yes, they have every flavor you could dream of, and I promise to take you out for as many slurpees as your heart desires."

I said a silent prayer that I could make that happen. I stroked her cheek until her eyes shut and she passed out again.

I PACED. BRUTUS WATCHED. THERE WAS NOTHING LEFT TO DO BUT WAIT out the storm, which had been raging for hours now. The lightning had almost given up, but the rain was still relentless. I moved Kaya closer to the fire, avoiding the little streams of water rolling in through the cave entrance. She didn't budge or stir even the slightest.

"Kaya, wake up," I said.

She didn't respond.

"I'm just going to look around. I need to find more dry kindling to burn, but I'm not going far."

Brutus was cemented to her side and I knew he would keep watch over her. Shining my flashlight on the smooth surface of the cave roof, I ran my hands up along the stone wall. It felt like one of those worry rocks Mum used to keep in her purse. Soft patterns of orange and beige swirled in the sandstone and played tricks on my eyes. The cave was much larger than it looked, and when I reached the back, the walls came to an end in a smooth arc. There was nothing here but the bones of what had once been a large animal—probably a bear. As my flashlight's beam passed over the remains, I noticed something shiny lay in the rib cage. I moved closer, carefully stepping over the skull for a better look, and realized it was a bullet. As I reached for it, a mouse scurried away, making me nearly jump out of my skin. I kicked at it, sending bones and stones rolling away, but strangely enough, the bones and stones didn't make a stopping sound. I kicked more debris toward the back of the cave, but it all seemed to just disappear into the abyss.

I stepped completely over the dead animal and shone my light around. There was a hole, about three-by-ten feet, perfectly concealed by overlapping panels of flat rock. Clever patterns in the sandstone had created the most brilliant optical illusion to keep the passageway hidden from view. I moved closer and stepped inside, realizing that I couldn't hear anything outside—not the wind, the lightning, or the crackling of the fire. I carefully watched my footing as I moved deeper inside, the ground sloping down and into the earth.

The farther I wandered, the warmer the air became. Then I heard water. The sound grew louder as the sides of the tunnel widened and opened up into a massive cavern. I found myself standing on the edge of an underground cliff, my flash light beam unable to reach the depths where an underground river flowed. This was incredible, but one foot forward and I'd be a goner. What would happen to Kaya if something happened to me?

I turned and made it halfway through the tunnel and back to her when the flashlight flickered and went out. I cursed loud enough for my voice to echo back and slap me in the ears. I couldn't freak out. Not now. Breathing deeply, I reassured myself that everything was fine. I just had to stay calm. I fumbled with the plastic button on the flashlight handle, shaking it and asking it nicely to work, but as my eyes started to adjust to the darkness around me, I realized it wasn't entirely pitch black. There was a dim light to the right that I hadn't noticed before. I moved toward it. Soon, I was able to see the ground clearly under my feet. The closer I got, the brighter the light became, now fire orange and shimmering as if it were dancing off the tunnel walls. The air was getting warmer too—I could bring Kaya here until the rain stopped— but what was it? This strange light… it didn't make any sense. As I slowly crept forward, my mind raced, trying to think of every possible source of what it could be—campers, fire, aliens? I steadied my nerves, took a few more steps forward, and then backed up against a corner of jutting stone from where it seemed a few feet away the light was the strongest. I listened for voices, anything at all, but it just sounded like a kitchen faucet was dripping… I steadied myself and swung my head around, then I almost fell backward in shock of what I saw. What was before my eyes couldn't be real…it was impossible…

OLIVER

32

ANOTHER PILL TO SWALLOW

"I DON'T UNDERSTAND; WE WERE SO CLOSE! I EVEN THOUGHT I heard her voice!" I was livid, gritting my teeth so hard my jaw ached. I hated everything about the tent, the mountains, the trees, the birds, and the entire world around me so much that if I could beat the crap out of it, I would.

Davis gave me a tentative shoulder pat. "Oliver, relax. We'll find her; I'm sure the storm is just interfering with the signal. It'll come back. Deep breaths there, little buddy."

We'd followed Kaya down the river and up into the trees, and then the signal just quit. Henry went crazy, calling every five minutes and screaming death threats at me if I didn't find her. I was going crazy too, stuck in this small tent and unable to do anything but wait out the weather. If the walls around me weren't nylon, I would have driven my fists into them.

"Let's check our supplies; we're getting low on food," Davis said.

He yapped about mashed potatoes and chocolate cake, but all I could think about was Kaya.

"You aren't listening to me, are you?" he said. "She's going to be all right, Oliver. She's the toughest girl I know."

"She's the *only* girl you know."

"Hey, be nice," he said. "Seriously though, you know we need to rest. If we exhaust ourselves, we'll be useless. Also, I'm not particularly interested in getting hit by lightning."

"I know. You're right," I agreed.

Davis was ripping open some instant oatmeal packets. "Dinner's ready, honey," he said with a mischievous glint in his eye.

He handed me a brown paper envelope filled with things I didn't consider to be food, but there was no option of making a fire because of the storm. After 'dinner', I tipped the blue bottle of painkillers to my mouth and chased the pills with a swig of brandy.

"Dessert?" Davis asked.

"Yeah. Sindra gave me these for the pain. They really help."

"I wouldn't take *anything* from that woman."

"Ah, it's just strong aspirin or something."

"Unmarked? You're probably being used as a test subject for some new drug Henry's concocted in his lab. What if it's highly addictive and has nasty side effects?"

"Oh, c'mon. It's perfectly fine."

Even though I said it, I knew it wasn't true. The pills were becoming a bit of a crutch—a means of getting my body, as well as my head, through this hell. They quieted the anger that seemed to consume every part of my mind, but when they wore off, it seemed to be worse than ever... At least my ribs didn't ache as much. As I lay back, feeling the medicine and the brandy mix, a nice heat took over my stomach, the potent combination taming the wretched explosive feeling surging through my veins—if I gritted my teeth any more, I'd wear them down to nothing.

"Oliver?"

"Uh huh," I mumbled.

"When did you realize you were in love with Kaya?"

Davis loved to ask the strangest things right out of the blue. "Really? You want to talk about *that*? *Now*? I'm kinda trying my best to not rip this tent apart and keep myself under control, ya know?"

"I know, but maybe talking about the good things will help ease the pain of the bad."

I remembered the first time I saw her clearly. I knew right then and there she was the one. The moment had been on replay in my head a lot over the last few days.

"*So...*"

Parts of my past were too painful to revisit, but some were the most incredible and precious moments of my life. I looked over at Davis, a man who I considered to be my closest friend, and realized that he was worried too. He was hurting, cold, and hungry, just like I was. Maybe he was the one who needed the distraction

"For a long time, I cared about nothing. I just went numb after my family was... uh... taken. Henry found me and took me in. I could have lived or died; I didn't care. Nothing mattered to me anymore. Then one night, I saw her—this young girl with the most intense emerald-green eyes. She stared at me with what I assumed was hatred, yet I couldn't look away. There was something so different about her. She fired me up and sparked something that had been missing for years, and even though it looked as though she would rather see me dead, I felt alive again."

"So, you fell in love with a little kid? And you're calling *me* a weirdo?" said Davis.

"Ha, no."

"So then, when did you... *know?*"

"I was twenty-three, she was fourteen, and it was Canada Day. I was looking after her while she lay in bed with the chicken pox. I had been her guard for two years by then, and she'd spent that whole time making my life hell, literally being a spoiled brat and doing everything she could to try to make me quit. On this particular evening, she was tormented by horrible itching wounds that I had spent most of the day preventing her from scratching. When her medication was due, I put the sticky syrup on a spoon and held it to her mouth, preparing for the usual fighting and the 'I hate you's', but instead, she looked up at me and very sweetly said 'thank you'. And that was it."

"Um... really?" said Davis.

"What? Yeah."

"Gee, I was kinda hoping for something with a little more glitz and glam. That story is sort of, well... *dull.*" He laughed.

I rolled my eyes.

"Really though, it must have been awful to wait so long to tell her how you feel," he said, reaching for the brandy.

"Yep. That's an understatement. She is everything to me—my love, my life, my family. I couldn't imagine living without her, and I wanted to tell her so for years." I pictured her beautiful face the day in the woods when I put the ring on her finger, which was yet another vision that replayed a lot. I disappeared into those special moments in my mind until I was interrupted by the cell phone buzzing in my pocket. Henry's number flashed on the call display, and I prepared myself for more yelling.

I pressed the answer button.

"Are you any closer?" Henry barked, not even bothering with *hello.*

My anxiety level shot through the roof again. "No. There's zero visibility due to the storm, and it's too dangerous to continue," I replied, and a loud crack of lightning sounded as confirmation.

"*Damn it!* This weather is making a huge mess of things!"

"I'm sorry, sir. As soon as it lets up, we will get back out there. Is there anything showing up on your screen yet?" Even though I knew the answer, I had to ask anyway.

"No, nothing is showing up on the stupid, useless screen. She has *disappeared.*" he yelled, "It's up to you. Do you hear me, Oliver? As soon as you can, you get your ass out there and *find my daughter!*"

I cleared my throat and assured him for the hundredth time I would, but he kept ranting. "I'm the only one who can protect her. You know that. She *has* to be returned to me before the damn wolves sniff her out."

As always, he was worried about the Marchessa 'wolves' while I was worried about real ones. "Listen Henry, there is no way I am finding anything or anybody in this weather," I said firmly.

There was a pause, and then a rather deep and frustrated breath occupied the vast space between us. The tent shook, lightning flashed, and the rain tried to carry Davis and me away.

"Well, maybe I need to light a fire under your ass, *boy*... give you some incentive to move quicker," Henry said darkly.

I waited for him to continue. What more incentive did I need to find Kaya than Kaya herself? Whatever he was about to say wouldn't change a thing. He didn't need to threaten me, and I was just about to tell him so.

"She is carrying your child, Oliver," Henry said. "She is currently about two months pregnant. Yes, you heard me right—*pregnant*. Now, the current environment is *not* the best for a girl in her condition, is it?"

I dropped the phone, and the pills and brandy came back up.

STEPHAN

33

SCARLET PALMS

OVER THE YEARS, I'D ONLY EVER RELIED ON ONE THING TO GET ME through tough times: Scotch. Glenmorangie, eighteen year old, single malt to be specific. It was all I needed to raise Kaya from a child to an adult.

Now, for the first time ever, scotch had failed me.

It was four in the morning. Sleep wouldn't come, and worry wouldn't stop. I knew Henry would still be up, so I made the trek through the building toward his wing of the estate and entered my code into the gate. It didn't work. I tried again, thinking maybe I had entered it wrong, but the iron bars wouldn't budge. I tried a different set of numbers, ones I'd used ages ago that were probably long forgotten, and quite incredibly, it opened.

There wasn't a single guard anywhere to be seen. Maybe they were all still out in those mountains searching for Kaya, which is what I wanted to be doing instead of waiting around uselessly. I needed to convince Henry to let me go out there and help find her, and practiced what I would say to him as I walked through the stone-walled corridors toward his office. It was at the far end of a ballroom across a sea of marble floor surrounded by museum-worthy paintings. Everything was gold—from the ornate moldings around the windows and pillars, to the only four chairs in the room that could have easily seated two hundred. The room glimmered, filled with décor meant to impress—I thought it was all pretentious bullshit.

Light poked out from Henry's office door, and I could hear his voice. I was a foot away but stopped when I heard Lenore's name spewing from his mouth like acid. "That *bitch*!" he roared. "I still to this day can't *believe* she did this to me! If she weren't already dead, I'd shove her off that damn balcony all over again!"

I froze. Was the scotch finally kicking in?

Henry went on, his angry ranting directed at someone else in the room. "In two years, Kaya inherits everything I have worked for, and you've found nothing that can change that?"

"Well, technically, it's not yours, sir. It never was," said a voice I recognized as Henry's lawyer, a sly prick who always wore white cowboy boots and too much jewelry. The scumbag was more snake than human.

"That bitch never intended for me to have a thing." Henry raged.

"Yes. But this baby is the solution, sir," said the snake.

Henry's voice shook with fury. "*Pregnant.* Damn if Doc Ellis conveniently *forgot* to tell me about it until she was in that race. I never would have let her go. If she dies out there, I lose it all!"

What? *My baby girl, pregnant?* I felt dizzy. Maybe this was all some sort of sick joke. Maybe they knew I was here and would burst out in laughter and say *gotcha.* I backed away from the door but kept listening as Henry stomped across the floor in his hard-soled Italian shoes.

"Everything could be fine if Kaya would go along with my plans," Henry said, his voice chilling. "She could live a long, happy life here in paradise. But problem is, the kid has a conscience, and she can see right through my lies. Once she finds out what we've been doing, what we're still doing, she will shut Eronel down. She won't sign anything over."

"That's why we have this backup plan in place," said the snake. "But you know, Daddy Dearest, being sweet as pie won't hurt, either."

"I know that, Michael. Why do you think I let her participate in that stupid race? I was working on a few brownie points. Why don't you tell me something I don't know? Give me something I can actually use!"

I heard the sound of papers rustling, and I pictured the snake's black eyes as he spoke. "Ahem, well that's why I arranged this meeting with you," he said. "You know all that lovely paperwork we get the new trainees to sign?"

Henry didn't answer.

"Anyway, I was going over Oliver's today. When you picked him up, he was underage, and there was a maze of documents exchanged with some agency. As it turns out—"

"*Get to the point!*" yelled Henry.

"Apparently, you are Oliver's legal guardian," the snake hissed. "You are his... *father.*"

"So?"

"So, the baby is Kaya *and* Oliver's. If Kaya dies, everything goes to her child, which, of course was always the plan, so that you could buy more time to figure out—"

"For God's sake, *get to the point!*" Henry barked again.

"Well, if the child dies too, everything would go to its next of kin— the 'baby daddy' if you will. This, quite conveniently, is Oliver. He would inherit everything. Are you with me so far?"

"Yes, damn it. I am not an idiot."

"So, when poor Oliver dies of a broken heart from losing his wife *and* his child, everything he owns—the estate, Eronel, and those love-ly little trust funds—would all go to his next of kin. That, sir, is you. He has no other family… but *you*. The Marchessa's rights at that point would be broken, and you would own everything fully and completely."

I nearly jumped out of my skin when Henry slammed the table in delight. The sweat on my back and forehead had become rivers, and my chest started to ache. I couldn't believe what I was hearing. The vast, glimmering ballroom suddenly became suffocatingly small while I held my breath, waiting for the conversation to continue.

"My God, that's brilliant!" Henry said excitedly. "Although, this might not get me the best parenting award."

"Who cares? You can just buy some new kids if you need 'em," said the snake.

Glasses clinked, and the unity of sick minds rang throughout the ballroom. A deep, stomach-churning shiver rolled up my spine and my knees started to shake.

"Do you believe in destiny, Michael?" Henry asked.

"Sir?"

"Are you one of those 'one door closes and another door opens' kind of guy? Do you think where you end up is pre-planned? Or that it's 'in the cards', or that things are so entirely out of your hands that it's actu-ally the decision of the universe? Or, better yet… that it's *God's plan* for you?"

"All that very well could be true, sir, but I'm not—"

"Weak! Those notions are weak minded! People use them as an ex-cuse for their shitty circumstances, blaming the consequences of their poor choices on destiny. It's pure and utter bullshit. I am where I am because I *put* myself here. I made this fortune out of that dying, pathetic company. *Me*! I made it happen, not bloody destiny!"

I moved away from the door and out of the ballroom, barely able to see through the blinding tears that rolled relentlessly down my cheeks. I considered Kaya to be my child and loved her more than anything. All the scotch in the world wasn't going to help me through this.

The security office was open and completely empty, which I thought was odd, but I didn't question it. Instead, I plunked myself down at Old Carl's desk in complete shock over what I had just heard. *Henry killed Lenore? My Kaya, pregnant? A plan to kill her, the baby, and Oliver?* I could barely wrap my head around this information. All the strange things that had happened over the years suddenly made sense, but along with this new knowledge came the horrific realization that Henry was sick—more so than I'd ever imagined. Greed had made a monster of him.

I didn't want to forget a thing I'd heard. I tried to relay everything in an email to Kaya, wishing I could type a little faster than my two-finger-chicken-peck method allowed. I sent a detailed explanation of what I'd heard to one of her old accounts—a secret one we'd used for a childhood game—and then I prayed to God she'd somehow see it. I told her I loved her. I told her goodbye. And I told her to never, ever, come back here again.

I erased the message from the sent folder and closed out the internet tab. I was numb, dumbstruck, and most definitely sober.

When I restored the computer back to the security settings, I noticed movement on the basement corridor camera. There was a man standing in the back stairwell in an area that was completely off limits. Wiping at my swollen eyes, I realized it was Old Carl, looking nervous and glancing behind often as he quickly walked toward the locked door of the records room. Once inside, he frantically dug through labeled boxes, wiped sweat off his noticeably damp forehead, and mumbled under his breath. When he seemed to find what he was looking for, he grinned madly, and then he plugged a disc into a computer.

I zoomed in on him, able to make out the folders saved on his screen as they popped up and saw he was looking at video security logs—from eighteen years ago.

Carl fast-forwarded through footage of people coming and going when the estate still functioned as a hotel. I'd been a guard for a year by then, after having trained for five beforehand, and remembered that time very well. I'd watched Lenore transform from an incredibly intelligent beauty to a crazed and somewhat violent empty shell of a woman...

Carl studied the screen intently, then pushed pause when the face of a beautiful woman with long, flowing dark hair came into view. The woman, in a long gown and sparkling jewelry, was the spitting image of Kaya. Her arm was linked through Henry's, and he was leading her into the lobby of the now boarded-up north section of the estate. Carl put his hand on the monitor and shook his head, as if saddened by the image, and then fast-forwarded again. He kept searching for something, and when a video of Henry coming out of a hotel room with a baby in his arms popped up, he seemed excited. I zoomed in even closer to see Henry walking swiftly down a hall with a newborn in a flowery baby blanket... and if I hadn't have been sitting down, I might have fallen over—I knew that flowery blanket. The baby was Kaya.

Anne was right.

Now the screen showed the woman with the long, dark hair, her hands bound and mouth gagged, struggling as she was dragged down the dark hallway by a man in a black suit—and that man in the suit was Old Carl.

I pulled out my gun and placed it on his desk, then leaned back and put my feet up. It was about time, after all these years, to get some damn answers.

KAYA

34

ᴵNTO THE ᴰEEP

THE SUN SHONE BRILLIANTLY. WE LAY IN THE GRASS BASKING IN ITS RAYS and watched the small child dance through the sprinkler, her giggles and squeals of happiness giving me warm fuzzies from head-to-toe. She looked exactly like him—like the beautiful man stretched out beside me with the gorgeous grin on his face.

"Kaya..." he said.

The heat of him was glorious. His breath brushed my cheek, and his shirt buttons were smooth under my fingertips. He repeated my name, but I was too cozy and too content to answer. I wiggled my way in as close as I could and heard him laugh—it was that same glorious sound that had captured my heart. If I kept my eyes closed tight, maybe it would echo endlessly... forever...

"Kaya, c'mon, you gotta wake up," he said gently.

A hand was on my shoulder shaking me. The child had disappeared, and so had the sun.

"You've been asleep for over sixteen hours now. Please, wake up, okay? You're starting to freak me out..."

Luke was pleading with me. The concern in his voice flicked on a switch in my head and with it came a dull ache. *Sixteen hours? Asleep?* I opened my eyes to look directly at him. Our noses were almost touching. His cheeks had more stubble than I remembered.

"Hi," he said, looking somewhat relieved.

"Hi," I said, completely confused. Why was I was snuggled up with him? Why was his arm under my head and his hand on my cheek?

"You've had me so worried. How is your head?"

"My head?" The last thing I remembered was lying next to a fire with Brutus, freezing while Luke doctored my arm, which, suddenly started to throb. "My head... I think, is fine... Did I really sleep for sixteen hours?" I asked, my throat scratchy and dry.

"Yes, I woke you up to give you water and more painkillers, but other than that—"

"And you? Did you sleep, too?" I asked, noticing the dark shadows under his eyes.

"Yeah, on and off. Don't worry about me. I'm perfectly fine. All right? Now, do you think you could sit up, Kaya? I want to show you something."

I said yes, but I wasn't really sure.

"Close your eyes." He slowly pulled his arm out from under my head, taking his body heat with him as he sat up. My throbbing arm and hip bone reminded me that the pain had only been subdued by medicine. My ears hurt—so did my neck and my hands. Even my hair hurt. I breathed deeply, managing to adjust myself into a cross-legged position while his hand supported my back.

"Now, open your eyes," he said with a tinge of excitement.

I forced them open. But, I thought maybe I had fallen asleep again. Was this for real? "Uh, Luke, am I awake?"

He laughed, "Yes."

I had died and gone to heaven—it was the only thing that made sense. We were in a huge cavern with massive arches of red-and-white stone hovering above our heads at least ten stories high. At the top, there was a huge crack letting in light. It reflected off a pool of glistening water below, making raindrops sparkle as they poured in.

Impossible.

I blinked a few times, but the image just got better. I ran the palm of my hand gently over the fine grains of sand under my legs—it was dark like charcoal and made a small beach next to the smooth stones that bordered the pool. Was the water bubbling? I took in a gloriously warm breath. Never in my life had I seen a place as magnificent as this.

"Can you believe it? An underground hot spring, untouched by human hands," Luke said.

"If this is a dream, I don't want to wake up."

"It's no dream; it's our paradise. I'm naming it Kayatown," he said with that enchanting smile.

"I think Lukeville has a better ring to it." A small fire gently crackled, and I noticed something cooking over it. My mouth began to salivate, and my stomach groaned.

"Stew—it's instant, but it will be good and hot."

"Oh, wow, I can't believe how hungry I am," I said, and then I noticed that my jaw hurt, too—without those painkillers, I would be in pure agony. "How did you find this place?" I asked, cautiously bending the elbow of my uninjured arm to test it, and then I felt a tender lump on the top of my head beneath some matted, crusty hair.

"At the back of that cave was a tunnel. I carried you here… and you didn't even budge. I was so worried about you. I still am."

"I'm okay," I said. But I was kind of worried about myself, too.

He took his hand slowly away from my back and went about fixing dinner. I blinked often and discreetly pinched myself. This was too good to be real. Everything shined and shimmered—the water, the rocks, the smooth walls—even Luke seemed to glow as he tended the fire.

"Dinner's ready," he said as he pulled two silver packets from the flames, shaking his fingers as the heat threatened to cook them too. I laughed when Brutus bounced up out of a dead sleep and sniffed the air. "You laughing at me, Miss Lowen?"

"Oh no, sir. I would never laugh at someone making me dinner," I joked. Then I coughed and liquid came up. Luke eyed me warily. "I'm okay," I said to his worried face.

He wandered off for a second then returned with a large, rather flat rock. "Our table is ready, madam," he said sweetly, and he plunked the stone down between us.

"Thanks, I thought you might give it to someone else. I didn't make reservations."

He grinned and eased the knife through the foil packets. "Beef stew with potatoes and carrots, but no forks. Damn, this restaurant sucks!"

I liked that he was trying to be light hearted. He stuck the point of the knife it into a brown cube of meat dripping with sauce, and then he blew air on it before he raised it to my lips.

"I've never had beef before," I said, my mouth watering for it.

"That's okay, I've never cooked in a cave before," he smiled.

Henry's ramblings played heavy on my conscience. I wasn't supposed to eat meat—I wasn't *allowed* to eat meat—the rabbit Regan made was delicious, but I'd had to force it down. Luke sensed my conflict. "Kaya, don't worry about other people's opinions. Form your own and do what's best for you. I'll respect your choice, whatever it may be."

I was hungry, but I was so completely satisfied in the knowledge that I was free to make my own choice that it was like I'd experienced an awakening of sorts. I plucked the cube off the knife, held it in my mouth, and then chewed. The texture was unlike anything I'd ever had, and it tasted absolutely delicious. Luke took a bite too, then scooped up some more on the knife and held it out to me. We ate like that, taking turns, him watching me closely.

"That's the best meal I have ever had," I admitted when the packets were almost empty and Brutus begged for the rest.

"Well, I'll make sure to give your compliment to the chef."

"And thank him for taking care of me as well."

"I will."

He lifted an eyebrow in the most charming way. "Someday I would like to cook for you—for real."

"You can actually cook?" I said, taken aback, suddenly realizing how little I really knew about him.

"Can't you?" he asked.

"No. I can make tea."

"Oh. Well, you'll be a blast in the kitchen, then."

I could picture it: him and I standing over pots of boiling water, chopping herbs, tasting tomato sauces off spoons, shiny white cupboards and an old cat sleeping on a rug, blooming flower boxes under every window...

"You're going to be all right, Kaya," he said. "Your father's men are out there. If I can't get you out of these mountains, they will. I'm just surprised they haven't found us yet." He wiped the knife clean, lost in thought for a moment.

I was expecting him to convince me that I shouldn't go back, but here he was comforting me selflessly. Even hurting as much as I was though, I didn't want to be anywhere else than right here with him.

"Hey, let me see your ankle," he said and held his hand out.

I leaned back a bit and carefully placed my foot in his open palm.

"There are a lot of bruises on your upper thigh, but this part of your leg seems fine. The tracking device doesn't seem damaged. Maybe the storm is keeping them away."

"Uh, how do you know what my upper thigh looks like?" I asked.

He had a puzzled look on his face. "Do you remember me pulling you—uh, out of the river?" he asked, gulping hard. I could tell whatever had happened was something he would like to forget.

"No..."

"Do you remember what I had to do to your arm?"

"Vaguely. I remember the smell of skin burning, watching my clothes dangle in the trees, and dreaming of the baby girl with the blue eyes..." That vision was still so vivid—the baby who looked like him, drifting away, and then being carried off toward a white light. I remembered his breath pushing into my lungs, his terrified face as he held his shredded shirt to my head and his heavy breathing as he carried me through the storm... "Oh my God," I said, staring at him in awe.

"What?" his eyes widened.

I couldn't help it. I embarrassingly leaned in and wrapped my functioning arm around him, ignoring my pains and aches to satisfy an overwhelming urge to hug him.

"You saved my life. Without you, I would be dead," I said, close to tears.

He held me, softly wrapping his arms around me and not saying a word. I stayed close to him longer than was appropriate, emotionally and physically unable to pull away. Then, out of nowhere, a pain shot across my abdomen. It was like a sudden jolt, stabbing and steeling my breath. I doubled over in his arms.

"Kaya, what's wrong?"

Then, just as quickly as it had come, the pain was gone.

"Nothing—just a cramp. I probably ate too fast."

"So, how hot is the water?" I asked after waking from a nap on the soft sand.

"Huh? Oh… I don't know," Luke answered.

He seemed distant. Busying himself, but doing nothing. The hug after dinner had made him uncomfortable; I could tell, so I wouldn't do it again. "Would be nice to wash up," I hinted, feeling quite a bit better. The food and rest had done wonders for my throbbing head.

He kneeled down at the water's edge and dipped in his fingers. "It's like a perfectly warm bath. Wow, it's amazing."

I had to see for myself, so I tried to stand but promptly fell back on my butt. "Nothing seems to be working right," I complained.

"Yeah, you got beat up pretty badly. Let me help you."

He guided me carefully to a flat spot next to the water where I could sit and reach in. I couldn't move my wounded arm because he'd wrapped it to my chest, so I used the other to rub the warm, somewhat salty water into my eyes. It was glorious. I tried to get some water on the back of my neck where patches of crusty blood were stuck to my skin, but only having one useable hand made everything nearly impossible. In a matter of minutes, I had become wildly irritated and was desperate to get clean. Luke sensed my frustration.

"I'll go in and scoop up water for you so you can at least wash your face," he said flatly and began unbuttoning his shirt.

I didn't understand why he was affectionate not long ago, holding me tenderly in his arms, and now he seemed cold and detached. Then I noticed the bandages I'd carefully taped across his chest were not even remotely covering his wounds anymore. The skin around the crude stitches was scarlet red and very inflamed looking. Some places had bled again and looked infected. Maybe he was just in a lot of pain.

"Look away…" he said, unzipping his pants.

I was mesmerized by the muscles prominently rippling down his stomach to the flat part just above his belt. If my eyes weren't still so tired, there's no way I would have been able to keep them shut. I heard him move into the water, and soon I felt a damp hand on my knee.

"Okay. It's safe," he said.

His belly button was just above the surface of the steaming pool. I tried to keep focus on his face and nowhere below it. He cupped his hands together and lifted some water up to me.

"Luke, I want to go in, too," I said in an almost-whiny voice.

"I really don't think that's a good idea, Kaya."

"Please…"

"You can't get your arm wet."

"*Please*…" I begged again then playfully batted my eyelashes at him.

"Well, it's fairly shallow right here. I guess we could keep your arm dry if I held you up."

I stuck out my feet out so he could pull off my shoes, and then I leaned back on my elbow so he could wiggle my pants down over my hips. He was very careful to avoid the giant purple bruise, and his face was all business when he came right up the edge of the pool, his head level with my stomach. With shaking hands, he undid the buttons on my shirt. I looked down, grateful I was still wearing the sports bra and underwear and that I wasn't completely naked. I couldn't have cared less, but I knew my bare skin made him nervous.

"Ready?" he asked.

"Yes."

He lifted me off the ledge and into the water with him, his hands staying tight around my waist as he steadied me in the churning pool. Instantly, my aching muscles relaxed—this was glorious. The bubbling, hot water was taking away my aches and pains, but not my worry; Luke's wounds looked bad—scary bad. I overlooked the fact that he was naked and busied myself by dripping water over the patchy sewing job on his chest and gently rubbed away the dried blood. He tensed. "Is everything okay?" I asked.

His eyes met mine. "I'm just… well… yeah. Everything is fine," he said, trying to smile.

I felt the overpowering urge to kiss him, and the look in his eyes said the same thing. "I need to wash my hair," I blurted out.

He laughed. "All right, Princess." He pulled me up into his arms in one fluid motion. "Stay on your side so we can keep your arm dry," he ordered.

I faced him, stomach to stomach, half floating and half supported by him as he ran his fingers gently through my hair. He lightly rubbed the tender spot where the rock had met my skull and released a matted, bloody mess into the water. "Holy…" he said. "If we were in the ocean, we would be shark bait." The water turned deep red then cleared quickly when the bubbles cleared the blotch away, carrying it somewhere deep in the earth.

My body soaked up the salt water, drifting on waves in Luke's arms. He watched me intently, his hands gently moving under my neck, and suddenly, I realized with that look on his face, I would do anything he wanted. I had no defense against the seductive glimmer in his eyes; I had to detach myself, and fast. "I think I can stand on my own. You go ahead and wash up." He was about to protest. "Go on… I'm fine."

I curled my toes over the smooth rock for balance, the mineral-rich water making me extra buoyant, and watched Luke disappear. As he dove under the water, the remainder of his bandages floated up. He reappeared in the middle of the pool under the rain falling in from the crack above, rubbing his hair and holding his mouth open for a drink. I felt wicked watching him, like I was spying on a man in the shower.

He swam back, circling around me like a kid playing shark, then he stood up—water dripped from his skin and he shook off the hair plastered to his face. I could have fainted right there and then… no human being was more beautiful. I was so awestruck I forgot where I was.

"What?" he asked, referring to my dazed expression.

"You, um… you're the most beautiful person I have ever seen in my life," I said before I could stop myself.

He smiled and reached for my waist, his huge hands almost circling it completely, then he pulled me close to his chest with a hungry stare. I couldn't breathe. Or speak. So I pushed him gently away, and then I dropped down under the surface of the water, forgetting about the bandages on my arm, and filled my cheeks with water. I leapt up and spit at him like a fountain. He laughed and splashed me back while halfheartedly giving me heck about my arm.

"It's funny. Even with these injuries and under such strange circumstances, I feel so lucky to be here with you," I said, again without thinking.

"Lucky, eh?"

He pushed me up against the side of the pool. Smooth, hot rock cradled my back as he smiled and moved some damp hair off my face. I felt every part of his naked body next to mine, and my heart felt like it might burst out of my chest. "Luke... I can't..." I said, even though I knew my eyes were saying the opposite of my mouth.

He ignored me and brought his face to mine, and then he gently and perfectly kissed me.

It was just one kiss. But it was *everything*. It sealed the already-blatant confirmation that I was completely, totally, and madly in love with him.

"I don't think I can give you up," he choked out and thankfully didn't push himself on me any further.

"Luke, I..." That sharp pain came back, stabbing my abdomen and stealing my words.

"Kaya, what's wrong?"

The pain grew stronger, wrapping itself around my hips and digging in until I thought I might pass out. Luke gathered me up into his arms when my legs gave out. "I think something's wrong with the baby," I confided.

He put his hand on my stomach then gently over the large patch of red and bruised skin on my hip bone. He was thinking the same, but he didn't say it. I lay in his arms for a long while, neither of us speaking while the water swirled around our bare skin. I rested my head against his chest, getting lost in his heartbeat and listening to the air move in and out of his lungs. "Kaya, I want to look after you," he said softly. "I want you to know I will do anything for you and your baby. You need to know I am—"

I cut him off. I couldn't hear it. I wanted what he was offering, but I knew it would never work. I couldn't lead him on anymore, which was exactly what I was doing by allowing myself to get this close to him. "Luke, I am really confused. I know where my heart is and exactly what it wants, but I absolutely have to do the *right* thing."

He gulped like my words had hit him hard in the stomach. I looked up, stared him straight in the eye, and tried not to look away; he had to know I was serious.

"And doing the *right thing* means going back to Oliver, right?" he said sadly.

The hurt on his face made my chest tighten. I couldn't reply, but I didn't really have to. He already knew the answer, anyway.

"Just tell me, though, please. Never mind what's right or wrong or what you are *supposed* to do. Just tell me what it is that your *heart* wants," he pleaded.

I could see him fill his lungs with air and hold his breath in as he waited for my answer. I had to tell him that what I felt for him was nothing but a crush, a whim, a soon-to-be-fleeting desire… but the ability to pull off such a blatant lie failed me. "It wants you," I confessed.

LUKE

35

ℒET ℐT ℙOUR

AGONY.

I knew every facet of the word inside and out. It was relentless in every miserable and cruel way possible. I felt wide awake yet dead, my body tense yet also pile of mush under her spell.

I was in love with her, yet I was supposed to be fine with her wanting to be with another man.

I wasn't.

I gave her more painkillers and re-bandaged her arm as the tension grew between us.

"Luke, your wounds are looking so much better," she said, attempting small talk. "Your skin isn't nearly as red as it was."

I reached for my shirt and pulled it down over my head.

"There's something strange about that water. I feel about fifty percent better, too. It's amazing. I wonder if it has magical healing qualities," she added, digging for any sort of reply. "I've heard of that before, that the sulfur and magnesium and sometimes the iron in these hot springs…"

Her voice trailed off when she realized I wasn't interested in the topic at hand. The thought of her leaving had become a hammer smashing apart my heart, and before I knew it, words were flying out of my mouth. "You love me, Kaya," I said, and moved onto my knees before her so she had no choice but to look at me. "You love *me*." My tone was more aggressive than I intended. Her eyes widened, her emerald-green irises shining.

"It's not that easy, and you know it."

"But it is. It *really* is. You don't have to go back to him." She bit her lip, and her eyes watered. I should have let it drop, but I didn't. "Tell me the truth. Be honest. Do you love him? Oliver? Are you *in love* with him?"

Tears started rolling down her cheeks and her breathing sped up. "I have known him for years…" she stammered.

"That doesn't answer my question."

"Oliver has looked after me, saved my life, cared for me, and has always been there, so yes. Yes, I do," she said firmly, but she looked down as she said it. She wasn't being truthful with me or herself.

"Kaya, I love Louisa and would do anything for her, but I am not *in love* with her." I was trying to contain my frantic need to make her understand, but my voice was becoming a low roar.

"I made a promise, Luke—and that's important to me, that means something—and... and..." She put her hand on her stomach. "*I'm scared,* okay?" she admitted. "I'm eighteen; what am I going to do with a baby? When I first realized I was pregnant, I was shocked. I didn't want this. But now, I'm terrified that I might lose it. I agreed to marry Oliver, and now I am carrying his child. Doesn't that sort of seal the deal? I mean, do I want to marry him? I guess... not... but what other choice do I have?"

Even with all the horrible things that had happened to her, I had yet to see such agony on her face. I moved forward to comfort her, but she backed away. A look of utter despair and exhaustion came over her face, and I instantly regretted being so persistent. She was tired, injured, and put in this position completely against her will. I was being an ass. When her face paled a few shades, I felt like punching myself in the head.

"I never should have told you," she said, her voice trailing off and her breathing speeding up. Her eyes started to have that same look they did in the tent the night of the storm.

"No, Kaya, I'm glad you told me. If it's him you want, I will honor that. But you have to know that I would treat your child as if it was my own, and to be honest, I wish it was." I was shocked how easily that came out of my mouth. I had never, ever, felt the desire to have a kid of my own, but building a family with her had suddenly become all I could think of. She stared at me in awe, and then out of the blue, she jumped to her feet only to have her knees give out. I caught her before she hit the ground.

"I have to get out of here," she mumbled.

"Hey, it's okay. We won't talk about it anymore. I'm sorry I brought it up."

"I don't even know how to get out... how? How do I get out of here? Where the hell am I?" She was on the verge of an anxiety attack, and the painkillers and exhaustion were messing with her mind. I had to keep her calm.

"Kaya, look, this is a navigational watch. It is the whole reason we haven't gotten lost out here." I put my wrist out before her. "See these numbers? They are the latitude and longitude of where we are."

"I don't know what that means."

"We are fifty-one degrees, thirty-two minutes, and thirty seconds west of the prime meridian on Whaleback Mountain." I spoke slowly, her eyes steady on mine as if memorizing the numbers, the intensity of her gaze making me feel anxious too. "Kaya, take a deep breath, okay? You need to rest. Just listen to my voice."

I told her to lie down, and she did so without protest. I told her to breathe deeply, and as she did, the color started to come back into her cheeks. I knew she would listen to me, and I knew I could take advantage of her any way I wanted, and that thought made me crazy. Did Oliver do that? Did he use his strength to manipulate her? Control her? Did he ever take advantage of this beautiful girl? What kind of man was he?

"I want you to sleep now for a bit. Close your eyes and relax. Listen to the sound of the water," I said, and she obediently squeezed her eyes shut. I talked patiently until her breathing slowed to an even pace, and then, damn it, I couldn't help it. I said what I needed to say. "Kaya, I'll never hold you against your will or force you into doing anything you don't want to do, and I will fiercely protect you from anyone who would. You have to know this; I am in love with you."

She reached for the jacket I'd left on the ground and put it over her head.

And that was that. There was nothing more to say.

I TOOK THE WATER BOTTLES WITH ME. OUTSIDE, THE WIND WAS STILL howling, and the rain fell so hard I was instantly soaked to the bone— good. Maybe it would clear my head. I needed to get myself together. I needed to put away all the emotional crap and get back to my main priority: keeping Kaya safe and alive.

I wedged the bottles between some rocks and waited for them to fill. I was dripping in self-loathing and giving myself a good lecture on how not to be an asshole. Then, I heard a voice over the roar of the wind. *"Did you check it out over there?"* someone yelled. *"Yeah, go do it yourself if you don't trust me,"* yelled another.

I bolted for the darkness of the cave and froze when a figure appeared in the entrance. He shook off the rain like a wet dog then pulled out a flashlight. Was it him? He was tall with a wide stance and a muscular build. He probably had about fifty pounds on me. The whites of his eyes stood out against his dark skin, and he blinked as they adjusted to the dim light. When he wiped at the rain clinging to his forehead, his expression became a mixture of anger and sadness, and when he knelt at our long-dead fire and put his hand in the ash, his posture crumpled in defeat; it was most definitely him.

I felt a pang of guilt. I knew what it was like to have someone you love taken from you and could only imagine what he was going through. I took a few steps back, and his head jerked up, sensing me in the dark. I moved swiftly over the bones and back into the tunnel, struggling with my conscience. Should I announce myself and lead him to her? He could get her to safety—to a hospital and back home—and that's what she wanted… But I was stuck. I was paralyzed with selfish conflictions and doing exactly what I promised myself I would not do.

I silently made my way back through the tunnels. Kaya was curled up on her side, still hiding under my jacket. "You asleep?" I asked, knowing she wasn't.

She didn't answer.

I lay down beside her and put my head under the jacket. Our noses were almost touching. "I saw him," I said.

Her eyes fluttered and her breath caught in her throat. "How did he look?"

I wasn't sure what the right thing was to say. "Um… worried," I confessed.

"Was he alone?"

"No, there was another man with him."

"So close," she said softly.

"Kaya, I'm going to go back and get him. He can get you out of here and to a doctor." I knew this was the right thing to do, but damn did it hurt. "I'm sorry I didn't do it right away, I just…" I took in a deep breath, "I guess I just wanted to say goodbye first."

"No," she choked out. "Not yet. I just… I can't…"

"He can get you out of here faster than I can. You need a doctor."

"No, not yet. Luke. Please," she begged. "I just… I don't—I don't want to go back yet."

"Kaya, this is what's best for you. What if Seth doesn't come for us? What if your tracker fails and Oliver can't find you again? If I can't get you out of here—"

"Shh," she interrupted, putting a finger to my lips. I was suddenly the one to feel a rush of anxiety coming on. "I just need time, Luke, and if we are lost here for a while, under this jacket in a cave… I might not mind that so much."

It was all I could do not to force my mouth upon hers, to hold her as close to me as I could, to love her from head-to-toe… "I have to do what's right," I said to her shining eyes.

"*No*," she said desperately. "I don't want to see him yet, please. I need more time, Luke. *Please.*"

I wiped away a tear on her cheek and let my fingers linger on her soft skin. "Are you sure?" I asked, relieved and conflicted at the same time. "Yes."

She tucked her head down under my chin and we both hid from reality beneath the blue polyester jacket. Here, with the love of my life in my arms, I could have stayed forever.

36

DON'T LET GO

IF THERE HAD BEEN ENOUGH FOOD FOR US AND THE DOG, I probably couldn't have convinced Kaya to leave the cave, even though her stomach pain was getting worse. We avoided the raging river by backtracking to where it was calmer and easy to swim across, but just getting to this point wore her out.

"Tell me about your mother," she said breathlessly.

I laughed. She was very good at changing the subject whenever I had asked how she was feeling. Her freckles had come to life in the afternoon sun, and as I blatantly stared at them, I realized I'd forgotten to answer her question.

"Luke, what did she look like?" she smiled, catching me as my gaze lingered on her face.

"Oh right, my mum. Funny, but I'm always worried I'll forget. She was pretty—small boned, thin. She had thick blonde hair that was always dyed black, and it grazed her shoulders—never longer, never shorter. We had the same color eyes, but hers always had a sparkle in them, even when things were really bad."

I wished I could hear Mum's happy, breathy tone when she called me for dinner, or smell that familiar perfume that wafted around her.

"Name?" Kaya asked when I became lost in thought.

"Monique. She had the biggest heart, rescued every animal and person who needed it. Some of the worst people came in and out of our lives and did awful things, but Mum always gave them the benefit of the doubt. I did awful things, too—Lord knows I put her through hell—yet she never yelled or scolded."

It seemed so right to talk to Kaya like this. My chest didn't hurt like it usually did when I talked about the past. I grabbed her hand to help her over some driftwood, noticing her clothes were still wet and clinging to her body—I had to admire the tufts of grass instead, the gulls dipping into the river, the evergreens towering overhead…

"What did you do? Typical teenage boy stuff?" she asked.

"Um, well… I got in a lot of fights."

"Fights?"

She stopped walking and turned around to stare at me, her emerald eyes flashing a brilliant green.

"Keep moving or I'll have to carry you," I warned.

"Talk. Please, I need to know this," she said moving ahead, stepping carefully over some loose rock.

"My mum did whatever she could to keep me off the streets. We lived in a really rough area—gangs, drugs, you name it—so she put me in martial arts classes. I studied the hell out of it for as long as I can remember. If I wasn't at school, I was at the gym. Mum worked two jobs to keep me there, and the owner liked her, so he took me under his wing and taught me everything he knew."

"You had a smart momma. She obviously adored you. How did you put her through hell, though?"

"When I hit high school, word got around that I was 'martial arts boy', and every jock, dope, and idiot in between wanted a crack at me. I'd get cornered after school or a few blocks from our house or at lunch, and I was constantly getting suspended for defending myself. People got hurt, which is generally what happens when you fight, so it was easiest to blame the guy without a scratch on him. Luckily for me, my math teacher had some pull and found a way to keep me in school and get passing grades. I just had to fight… for him."

"What?"

"Yeah, he was a slimy bastard. He knew my mum was pregnant and on complete bed rest and that we needed the money. He organized a few illegal, back-alley fights through the gangs to fill his pockets, and I got half the cut if I won. I was sixteen and fighting grown men. Sometimes, I got beat up pretty bad."

I caught her eyeing the scar across my cheek. "Oh my God, that's awful," she said softly.

"Yeah. Mum kept little packs of ice in the freezer and tried not to cry when she held them to my face. I always told her it would be the last time, but it never was. I trained harder, the fights got bigger, and I started to win more than I lost. Then I met Claude."

"Claude. The roommate… the one who—?"

"Yeah," I said quickly to cut her off, not wanting her to finish that sentence.

"I can't picture you as the fighting type. You don't seem like you would get angry like that. I'm kinda shocked," she said quietly.

I reached for her hand to help her over another rough patch, but really I just wanted to hold it. "Honestly, anger was never part of the fighting with me. Claude used to say that was why I was good at it. There was nothing clouding up my head or any emotions getting in the way. But I think that it's mostly—and this is the only way I can explain it—like everyone around me is moving really slow, and I'm not."

"Oh, I have heard of that before. That's amazing."

"No. It's weird."

She stopped and turned to face me. "Is that why Regan and Seth always seem a bit fearful of you?"

I had to laugh. "Seth is a retired cop, so I can't imagine him being scared of anyone. But Regan? Yeah. That dumb ass decided to test me one night in a bar and picked a fight with the biggest blokes he could find. I had to save his butt. Now he tries to purposely provoke 'the beast' so he can study it. He is fascinated."

"Ha. Makes sense. I can totally picture him with a notepad, jotting down your every move and analyzing—" She stopped mid-sentence. The pain came back and forced her to her knees. I was worried out of my mind.

"Breathe, Kaya," I said in the calmest voice I could muster and gathered her up into my arms. Marching forward, I dragged my feet, leaving as many clues as I could. Where the hell was Oliver?

"What about your father?" she asked through gritted teeth.

I moved a swiftly as I could without stumbling. "I never knew him," I said, grateful to set foot on a packed animal trail so I could take longer strides.

"And Louisa's father?"

"Somebody named Greg, I think. Mum's boyfriends didn't usually last longer than three months."

"So, why the fertility drugs?"

Kaya was scared. I knew talking made her feel better, so I relived my painful past in order to ease her mind. "A few months after Louisa was born, a lying, cheating prick named Mitchell came into our lives. Mum was crazy about him, even though he would disappear for days at a time and be completely strung out when he returned. He promised her his loyalty and said he would marry her if she had his baby, but they couldn't conceive. Even though she had two kids, Mum was gullible enough to believe him when he said *she* was the problem. I figure the guy knew he was shooting blanks and blamed it on Mum simply because he had nowhere else to go."

Kaya winced, and her arm tightened around my neck. "Whoa, sounds like a great guy."

"Yeah. Stuff started to go missing from the house. I thought it was Mitchell, but then I found out Mum was selling her stuff to buy fertility drugs. Over the course of a year, I watched her turn into a different person—yelling at Louisa, losing her job, and becoming increasingly violent—in the end, she became almost unrecognizable, thin and sickly looking. All her hair fell out, and I thought for sure she had cancer or something. Doctors assured me there was nothing wrong with her. They said it was just *stress*."

"But it was the side effects of the Cecalitrin, right?"

"Regan is positive of that."

A memory of my mum, one that I would happily forget, came to mind. She was standing in front of the bathroom mirror, the lime-green walls casting a sickly hue on her pale face. She was crying and holding handfuls of her black hair. I'd begged her to see another doctor—I had a thousand dollars in my swollen hand, knuckles bleeding from a fight—and for the first time in my life, she yelled at me. I tried to reason with her, but she wouldn't listen. Instead, she slammed her fists into the mirror and sent shards of glass everywhere. When her yelling turned to bone chilling screams of uncontrollable rage, I took Louisa and ran from the house.

"Luke, how did she die?" Kaya asked softly.

I stopped and looked down at the girl in my arms. Never had I uttered a word of this to anyone. Now, after all this time, I *wanted* to talk about it. "Mitchell left her. He took all her money and the last shred of her sanity with him. I came home from the gym one day to find Louisa May screaming in her playpen and there was water flooding the hallway. I knocked on the bathroom door—I could hear the tap running, but there was no answer, and I knew... I mean... I just had that sick feeling you get when something is really wrong. So, I kicked in the door, and there she was, in the bathtub, dead. She'd slit her wrists."

I had to put Kaya down. The memory had made me weak.

"Oh my God, Luke. I'm so sorry."

"I failed her. I did all the wrong things, got mixed up with all the wrong people. Moved in with Claude, for God's sake, he was the devil—"

I felt Kaya's hands on my cheeks. "Hey, you did your best. You can't feel guilty for that. And besides, you fixed it. You got your sister back. Now you can raise her how you want to. I know your mom would be proud of you for that." Her hands slid from my cheeks to the gold chain around my neck. I could feel her breath on my chest, and I had to distract myself by looking at the birds, the trees, the aimless clouds hanging listlessly in the blue sky...

"This necklace, was it hers?" she asked.

I nodded and gulped when her fingers brushed my throat. The little, gold maple leaf charm had never left its permanent place around my neck.

"This was my mom's, too," she said and patted her silver pendant that had miraculously survived the rapids.

"It's strange," I said, brushing her shoulder with my fingertips and watching her cheeks turn pink. "I mean, it's really pretty, but it's not some pricy gem that you'd think a gazillionaire like Lenore Lowen would have owned. It looks like the resin we used in industrial arts class in school. That stuff preserved everything. We'd put bugs in it and make key chains, or—"

She took a step back like I'd shoved her.

"What? Did I say something wrong?" I asked.

Her eyes grew wide, and with a gasp, she turned away from me. "Insurance," she mumbled.

"What? Kaya, I don't understand—"

"Just… just give me a minute to think."

She turned away and stared off, the tone of her voice so strange I did exactly as I was told. I waited. I stood so still a squirrel ran over my feet.

"Luke," she said after a good five minutes had gone by, "I want you to know something." She faced me now, eyes boring into mine so intensely I wavered under the weight of her gaze. "I promise you that no matter what happens, whatever it takes, I will shut Eronel down. I will make Henry pay for what he did to you and your family. I will do this for you, and Louisa May, and your mom."

I couldn't help but smile. Then, I told her to get walking, because all my restraint had crumbled. I guided her along the path—through bushes, over logs and boulders and up hills—and I was barely able to keep it together because in every single way a human could love another human being, I loved her, and I ached with the desire to show her.

"YOU NEED TO REST, LUKE. PUT ME DOWN," SHE DEMANDED.

Brutus brushed up against my legs, as if trying to push me over. I gave in and hit the ground. The pebbles on the riverbed were unexpectedly comfortable, and I stretched out my arms, which felt like spaghetti noodles, as Kaya held a water bottle to my mouth. Brutus panted in my ear.

"Just relax for a sec," she said.

The sky was intensely blue behind her, and the sun was blinding. I had to close my eyes. Something crawled over my hand, but I didn't care.

Suddenly, the sound of a shrieking hawk startled me, and I woke up. How much time had passed? Damn it, I'd fallen asleep.

I raised my head up and slowly inched up to position myself onto my elbows. Every muscle ached and screamed at me to lie back down. Kaya was sitting a few feet away, her legs crossed, and she was staring off into the distance. I could see the outline of her face and she seemed slightly on edge, her shoulders rigid and her breath forcibly even. My gun was on her lap—she was protecting me while I slept. Brutus sat next to her, his rear end at my feet, protectively keeping watch over the both of us. The sight made me smile.

"How long was I out?" I asked, making her jump.

"Oh, you startled me. Uh, I dunno. Maybe a half hour?" Judging by the position of the sun, I had slept longer. "You needed the rest," she added, and then she carefully handed me back the gun.

"What were ya going to do with that?" I asked with a grin.

"Um, maybe hunt some rabbits? Thought I might try Regan's paella recipe."

Regan. I didn't want to tell her that I thought he might be dead. I watched his leg break clean in half, blood flowing out of him like a fountain after he jumped into the rapids to try to rescue her…

"I figured we would have an appetizer first, though," Kaya said, and she put her jacket, which was covered in leaves and berries, on my lap.

"You must be kidding," I laughed, pushing thoughts of Regan out of my mind. "Weeds and berries?"

"Not all food is meat, ya know. Just try some, okay? You need the energy."

"Really, Kaya. You want me to eat flowers?" I sifted through the assortment of yellow petals and pink stems she had shredded into bits and topped with berries.

"Yes—there's fireweed, dandelions, Saskatoon berries, raspberries—and for dessert, we have this lovely orange goo," she said as put a little silver packet in my hand. "I found it in my backpack; it's the last one I have, and it's a pure protein jolt. I promise it's all safe. I spent many hours in the bush, being forced to learn about what you can and can't eat. Had this for dinner many times—still living."

I hoped she wasn't unintentionally poisoning me. The leaves were bitter, but the berries were sweet and the orange goo was a nice chaser. I hoped it would give me the energy I needed to get us to Seth. I offered the leftovers to Brutus, but he turned his head away in complete disgust.

"He's not a fan of your cooking," I joked.

She giggled, and the dog planted a big, wet dog kiss on her face. I wiped the remaining slobber off her cheek out of reflex.

"Thanks," she said sweetly. "I'll admit I didn't know what to think of him at first," she said, still petting the dog but looking directly into my eyes, "but he's not so bad."

She was referring to me; it was written all over her face. "Yeah, he's a good ol' boy," I agreed. The hawk that had flown over us a short while ago let out another shriek as it circled over us, now joined by another. I pointed up. "Look, it has a friend up there."

Kaya tilted her head to the sky. "Those are red-tailed hawks. They mate for life," she said softly.

The birds drifted effortlessly side by side. Although incredible to watch, my focus returned to the beauty beside me. Her dark hair fell in shiny waves, and I imagined it turning grey, her face getting older, her lips still full of that deep red color, and her body a little heavier. I could wake up every morning to that incredible smile. "I can picture the two of us together, forever, like a couple of old birds," I said absently, and before I could stop myself, I added, "I would happily grow old with you."

She looked shocked. "The two of us? You and me? *Growing old together?*" she repeated softly, and everything about her mood changed. The smile left her face, and her eyebrows drew together in concentration. My comment had affected her, and I assumed it was because she saw the future much differently than I did. I desperately wished I could take back what I said, and I wished I didn't mean it.

WE WALKED IN SILENCE NOW, THE SOUNDS OF THE RIVER GROWING louder. Soon, we were at the place Kaya had fallen in, and the swollen, broken body of Henry's guard was caught in a continuous, raging swirl—Regan's body was nowhere to be seen, and I silently prayed that was a good thing.

Kaya gasped at the gruesome sight and grabbed hold of a willow branch to steady herself. She was about to say something, but the words were left on the tip of her tongue when she doubled over instead, clutching her stomach. I put my hand on her back, feeling helpless as tears streamed down her face. We waited for the pain to quit, but it didn't. It was dangerous here, and she was so dizzy I pictured her falling in again… so I lifted her into my arms. She looked extremely pale, and her eyes wavered while I moved as fast as I could alongside the rapids, watching my footing on the slippery rocks. She clung to me, her nails digging into my back as her pain grew worse. Even when she said she was better, I didn't stop. I made it to the falls and turned north, following Seth's trail while ignoring the burning in my arms and legs. I pushed forward and almost cried when Brutus started wildly barking at a figure coming toward us. Although the afternoon light was fading, I could tell it was Seth.

My knees buckled from the relief that washed over me.

Seth, still in the same clothes from a week ago and with a new scrape on his other cheek, took Kaya from my arms. He led the way to a campfire and a small tent nestled next to a towering expanse of rock. This was it—this was the end of the journey.

My muscles felt like they turned to cooked noodles and I collapsed next to the fire. Seth checked Kaya's pulse with his filthy hands. "Didn't think I'd be seeing you two again," he said.

Thanks for coming back for us, Seth," I said, catching my breath. Then, I had to ask, even though I was afraid of the answer, "How's Regan?"

Seth rubbed his forehead. "His leg is broken really bad, he has a concussion, and God knows what else."

"But he's not dead…"

"He should be."

"Why? What happened to him?" Kaya asked.

Seth answered as he ripped open a packet of food for Brutus. "The idiot tried to rescue you by jumping in the rapids. He's lucky he didn't splatter himself all over the rocks like that other guy did."

Kaya's hand flew to her mouth as she gasped.

"Anyway," Seth went on, unfazed by her reaction, "I got him out and back to Lisa, and then I came back for you when the storm cleared. Luke… I'm sorry I couldn't come back for you earlier."

"You have nothing to be sorry for, Seth. I appreciate everything you've done for me."

Seth cleared his throat and shifted uneasily.

"What?" I asked.

"I saw Louisa May."

A shiver ran up my spine and Luke gulped.

"She looks good, Luke. I mean, her eyes are distant and she was terrified of me. It's going to take some time to, well you know… get her back to normal. But she really likes Lisa—won't let go of her. I think the kid is in the absolute best care possible. A female doctor is going to the ranch to check her out today to make sure everything is okay. Lisa stuffed their bedroom with more pink things than you could possibly imagine. I let her run the place for a few weeks, and it has become all girly. It even smells like flowers in there. It's clean, and the fridge is so packed with food I can't find my beer."

"Who's Lisa?" Kaya asked. "And what Ranch?"

"Ah, Luke never mentioned her? She's his ex-girlfriend; a feisty young blonde you'll get to meet at my humble abode soon enough."

Kaya reached for Seth's hand, not bothered in the least by the mention of my ex. "You're a good man, Seth," she said to him sincerely.

I watched every gruff edge Seth fought so hard to maintain disappear. "Well," he said, clearing his throat, "we better get you outta here." He pointed to the top of the towering rock rising up in front of us. "It's not a long climb, but it's a bit difficult once you get close to the top. The chopper is up there, and it will be smooth sailing from then on."

"Chopper, as in *helicopter*?"

"Yep. That's the only place in these god forsaken mountains I could land the thing without getting caught up in trees or discovered by your daddy's posse."

Kaya nodded her head as Seth opened another pack of food for Brutus.

"You can rest here for a few minutes, and then we have to hit the road. Got it, girlie?" he said.

"Got it," Kaya answered bravely.

SETH INSISTED ON HELPING KAYA CLIMB TO THE TOP OF THE RIDGE. I GOT stuck helping the dog.

The rocky incline was full of ledges and jagged points for footholds and handholds, which would have been easy enough for a human, but not so much for a four-legged creature with paws. Brutus struggled and fought against me the whole way. I pulled, ignoring the sweat pouring into my eyes and the rope burning my hands. He whimpered when his harness tightened.

"It's all good, Brutus. We're just about there," I told him as I pulled myself up another foot, dragging the two-hundred-pound dog with me.

Seth was almost at the top. His shirt was drenched in sweat, and he had a vice grip on Kaya's good arm. "I'll get girlie here up, and then I'll help ya with Brutus, all right?"

I nodded as I watched Seth help Kaya get to the top, and then I held my breath until her legs were safely up and over the edge and she was out of my sight.

Then there was nothing. No movement. No sound. Nothing.

The hair on the back of my neck stood on end. Kaya was alone—

with Seth. He could leave me here. He could take her and go through with his original plan, and I had no idea who it was he was supposed to deliver her to. Weeks ago, I didn't care about the details, but now… "Seth!" I yelled.

His head appeared over the edge. "Tie this around the front of Brutus's harness," he yelled and threw down a long rope.

I breathed a sigh of relief, reminding myself to trust him. Brutus however, I had become legitimately wary of. He was suddenly agitated—slobber oozed from his mouth and poured onto the rocks, the fur around his neck stood on end, and his eyes glowed fiercely. He was angry at something, but it wasn't me.

"Okay Brutus, we are pals, remember?" I said, quickly tying the rope through the front of his harness and backing away, highly aware of the teeth that could take off my entire face in a single chomp. Seth pulled from above, and we both struggled until Brutus was at the top. I urged my tired muscles the rest of the way, grateful for a hand from Seth and a pat on the back when my feet were firmly planted on the flat ground. I was thankful that was over, but Brutus continued growling.

"What the hell is your problem, Brutus?" Seth yelled as he shoved the dog into the chopper and slammed the door. "Darn mutt is losing his mind. Anyway, it'll take me a sec to get everything organized, and then we're off."

Seth went about checking the helicopter while Brutus bared his teeth from behind the window. It was so strange to see the shiny, metal bird out in the rugged, pristine setting. To the left of it were miles upon miles of treetops and the sloping cliff we'd just climbed, and straight ahead, the edge of the plateau that fell steeply off and down to the river below. The sky seemingly stretched out for forever, blue and clear with snow-capped mountains reaching toward it. Kaya stood a few feet from me, taking in the view. When she turned to face me, her eyes were wide and her cheeks flushed—all my breath left my lungs. We were surrounded by incredible beauty, yet she completely outshone it with her own.

"This is amazing," she said.

"Uh huh," I muttered, and I moved to stand behind her. She leaned her back against me, as if we were an old couple who had been together forever. I carefully wrapped my arms around her. "Seth is going to take us to his ranch just outside of Revelstoke. From there, it's about a thirty-minute drive to the hospital," I said, and I could feel her heart speed up. I put my face down into her hair, remembering how it looked floating around her when we were in the hot spring. "Soon we'll go our separate ways," I added, the words feeling as though they were barbed wire in my throat, "but I have something I have to say to you first, and this might be my last chance to do it."

"Wait," she said and turned around to face me, her green eyes leveling with mine, "me first…"

"Okay."

She took in a deep breath and bit her lip. "When we saw those hawks in the sky, something that had eluded me my whole life became very clear. Suddenly, I could picture the future; I could actually see a life I might have past what it is today… and it was a life with the two of us growing old together."

I thought my heart might stop. I held my breath, waiting for her to continue.

"And you're right—"

"About what?" I asked, words coming out raspy as I was barely able to speak. Pulling her toward me, I rested one hand on the small of her back and couldn't help the other from cradling her cheek. Her eyes met mine, the liquid green dancing with flecks of gold from the waning sun.

"You said I should…"

She stopped mid-sentence, having become distracted by something behind me. Her mouth parted, and her eyes instantly filled with tears, but I stayed put. I didn't have to turn around to know *he* was there… and it was about damn time.

KAYA

37

WOLF AT THE DOOR

"**OLIVER.**"

His name caught in my throat, and everything about him came flooding back, along with a ton of guilt as I stood in another man's arms with words of betrayal on the tip of my tongue.

He looked like hell—his camouflaged clothes were filthy and torn, and his skin had become darker from being out in the sun. He was breathing heavily, and he looked as if he was ready to tear apart the entire world. He was staring at Luke's back with his gun raised and aimed in the direction of his heart, while carefully avoiding my eyes. He had *that* look on his face.

Davis sauntered out from behind the chopper, holding a gun to Seth's head. "Hey Kaya, what's up?" he said with a crooked smile.

Seth's hands were tied together, and Brutus was now trying to claw through the window to get to his master. I could feel Luke watching my face as I took the whole scene in, but I didn't dare return his gaze. His hands had dropped to his sides, but his fingertips brushed mine. I moved back an inch.

"Let the girl go," Oliver said in a terrifying voice.

Luke turned around slowly to face my enraged fiancé, and I tried to diffuse the situation as my heart tried to beat right out of my chest. "These people mean me no harm, Oliver. You have to trust me," I said in a pathetically wimpy voice. "I am not being held against my will."

His voice erupted, breaking the silence. "Kaya, get away from him, *now!*"

I felt my feet move before my mouth was able to. "Okay, relax," I said as calmly as I could manage. I crept toward Oliver—slowly, carefully—and when I was about a foot away from him, his eyes finally met mine. His expression softened. And then I couldn't help it—I threw my arms around him and heard the air leave his lungs… and Luke's, too.

Oliver's embrace felt incredible. I languished in the familiarity of it and the smell of him mixed with smoke and rain.

"Are you all right?" he asked in his melodically deep timbre.

"Yes," I squeaked out.

"I'm sorry I didn't find you sooner, I tried—"

"Shh, it's okay. I'm fine. Everything is fine. I'm glad you're here. I was worried about you, too."

He stepped back and saw that my arm was wrapped to my chest, and then he ran his fingers over the newly formed scar on my forehead. "I missed you so much," he said, and the direction of the gun in his hand had drifted down to the middle of Luke's torso. "And, I know about... *that*," he softly as he glanced at my stomach, "Henry told me. Don't worry; we'll take care of it when we get back."

Did I hear him right? *Take care of it?* I looked over at Davis when I noticed his head shake in dismay.

Oliver continued, putting his hands on my shoulders and speaking in a whisper. "I'm so sorry. I never wanted *that* to happen. We'll figure out how to fix it."

And then he bent down to kiss me.

I took a step back. Suddenly, everything about being close to him in *that* way became extremely uncomfortable. I unintentionally looked behind me at Luke, and Oliver gritted his teeth in a poor effort to conceal his rage.

"They are my friends," I explained. "I mean—they weren't at first, of course. But I've gotten to know them, Oliver. They have good reason for what they did." Oliver stayed silent, but he was fuming, not buying a single word that was tumbling from my mouth. "Luke there—he uh... he pulled me out of the river, and... well, he saved my life."

"Luke, eh?" Oliver said, glaring and jabbing the gun further in his direction. "One of the same men who kidnapped you also *saved* your life?"

"Uh, yes."

"So, he was... *nice* to you?"

"Well, yes. He's been looking out for me."

"Hmmm, that's interesting. What else did he do, Kaya?"

I could see jealousy seeping into the anger that was consuming Oliver. "I know what you're thinking, and it's not like that. You don't understand—"

"Oh, I think I do!" Oliver bellowed, "Your *pal*, Luke, has brainwashed you into thinking they are the good guys. I have heard of that before. It's called Stockholm syndrome—the abducted start to fall for their captors for some sick, twisted reason. So, I get it Kaya. It's not your fault." He backed away from me and lifted the gun so that it was aimed at Luke's heart. "You! Get on your knees!"

Luke calmly obeyed.

"Whoa there, little buddy!" said Davis nervously. "Let's think this through a bit, okay? Why don't we hear Kaya out and use the radio and tell Henry we've got her? Nobody has to die quite yet, all right?"

Nobody has to die... yet? If killing my captors was a part of Oliver's orders, I knew he would follow through. My mind raced as I started backing away from the man I barely recognized with so much hatred in his eyes.

"You know what we have to do," Oliver hissed at Davis. "Let's get to it."

Seth started struggling against Davis and his restraints, momentarily diverting Oliver's attention away from Luke. So, I did the only thing I could think of—I turned and ran toward Luke, throwing myself at him and almost passing out from the pain that surged through my wounded arm. Luke's expression of shock and worry made his blue eyes slightly grey—I tried to avoid looking at them too long as he gently pulled me up to stand before him.

"What the hell?" Oliver raged. "Get away from him, Kaya! *What are you doing?*"

I turned around and carefully positioned myself between the man I was supposed to be with and the man I wanted to be with—and I was hurting them both. "I'm sorry," I said quietly. "Just drop the gun and kick it away, Oliver. Then, I'll explain everything. Please."

"Not in a million years." Oliver hissed, and his eyes narrowed while he kept the gun pointed in our direction.

I steadied myself and glared back. "Well, if you are that desperate to follow Henry's orders, you'll be killing me in the process because you're going to have to shoot *me* to get to *him*," I said, then added with con-viction, "I'm not moving."

My explanation of the obvious startled him. The struggle to want to follow Henry's orders but not hurt me was evident on his face.

"Just put the gun down and hear me out," I said.

Oliver looked at Davis, who gave him an agreeable nod, then, obvi-ously going against everything he knew, tentatively placed the gun down at his feet. My throat became so dry I could barely swallow. I wanted to be gentle, delicate, and sensitive, but no matter how heartbreaking things are said, they are still heartbreaking.

"They aren't bad people, Oliver," I said as I inched my way back to him, kicking the gun away when I was close enough. I knew what I wanted to tell him, but I stalled, trying to find a way to lightly deliver the heaviest words I would ever say in my life. "I'm sorry. I never meant for this to happen…" I was a foot from him now, and I whispered, so that only he could hear as I motioned discreetly toward Luke, "but I love him."

I was convinced that the only sound that could be heard within a thousand miles was Oliver's shocked inhale. "You slept with him?" he said darkly.

I felt my blood instantly boil. "What? How can you even ask that? You know me. So, *no*." I took a deep breath, trying to stay calm. "I just want you to know why I need you to let him go. Please forget this even happened. I'm honoring the promise I made to you—no secrets—and I'm going home with you. I never had any intention of leaving in the first place, so—"

His nostrils flared. "But you'd thought about it, didn't you?" he interrupted.

"I, uh—"

"*Didn't you!*" he yelled, and then he grabbed me by the hair and roughly pulled me to his side. Oliver had never hurt me before, but now his fingers dinging in to my flesh—it was a complete shock. "What the hell did you do to her?" he yelled accusingly at Luke.

"I didn't do anything," Luke said. "Listen, you have her back now, and she is hurt. You have to get her to a doctor—"

Oliver ignored him, and he pulled my face to his, eyes boring in to mine, as if searching for something. When he didn't see what he wanted, he shook me like one would a bratty kid.

Luke took a few steps closer. "Don't hurt her," he warned.

Oliver laughed. "Hurt her? More than you have?" Oliver's teeth flashed white against his dark skin, and, like a simmering pot, he suddenly boiled over. His resistance finally crumbled. He tossed me aside like a rag doll, then charged toward Luke, swinging out and hitting him square in the jaw. Luke stumbled back, but he made no move to defend himself. Oliver swung again, but Luke just stood there like a punching bag. Why was he letting Oliver hit him? Was all his talk of bar fighting and martial arts training a lie?

Without thinking, I tried to break it up. I dove toward the two men, but Davis caught me by the waist. I begged Oliver to stop, I begged Davis to let me go, and I screamed in horror when blood began to trickle from Luke's nose. "Oliver, stop! You're going to kill him!" I yelled franticly.

The agony in my tone caught Luke's attention. He came out of his daze and rushed toward Oliver, aiming for his knees, knocking him off balance, and swiftly pinning him to the ground. "Chill out, Oliver, please," he said as Oliver struggled beneath him. "I'm not going to fight you, and you are scaring Kaya. She's sick. She has to get to a doctor. You took your anger out on me, and yeah, I deserved it, but enough already."

Oliver's dark eyes looked like black holes. "*I'm going to kill you,*" he said, growling.

Despite the threat, Luke let go and put his hands up in surrender, but Oliver wasn't ready to quit. He threw himself at Luke, wrestled him face first to the ground, and then sat on him, pulling his arms behind his back. Luke lay there calmly, flat on his belly, and didn't even try to get free.

"Okay, Oliver, you got him. Let's tie him up and be done now," said Davis, still holding me tightly. "I've got a burger and fries waiting for me in town."

"Yes, you won Oliver. Just let him go, please," I begged.

But my pleading was like gasoline on the fire. Oliver grinned, and what little light remained had left his eyes completely. Everything about the look on his face meant he had become murderous, and he made sure I was watching as he pulled a knife from his belt. His massive hand grabbed hold of Luke's gold hair and yanked his head up off the ground.

"No! Oh my God, Oliver, stop!"

Oliver's eyes narrowed and sunlight glinted off the knife as he pushed it against Luke's throat. How could he? This was the very same thing that happened to me on my sixteenth birthday... a knife sliced through my skin and tore my neck wide open... Oliver saved the girl he loved... and now he was about to cut the throat of someone I said I loved, and this was much, *much* worse...

Luke didn't struggle. He didn't beg for his life. He just lay there. And then I realized something: he was keeping a promise he'd made to me. The day the mountain lion attacked him, he'd promised me that he wouldn't hurt my fiancé if it ever came to this. Even with his life in danger, he was keeping a *promise he'd made to me...*

"Luke, he is going to kill you!" I yelled desperately. "Get up! I don't want you to keep that promise anymore. I want you... to fight back, please. Fight for *me!*"

And that lit the fire.

It was as if a different creature rose from the ground. In a blur, Luke had tossed Oliver off his back and the knife landed inches from Seth's feet. Luke's face became expressionless—calculated, and his quick-as-lighting reactions blocked every blow Oliver tried to deliver. It became very clear that Oliver was no match for Luke's skill, but he persisted stupidly until a quick strike to the ribs had him doubled over.

As angry as I was, I didn't want anyone hurt. I thought I might throw up.

Oliver was stubborn. He straightened up and charged Luke again but was quickly winded when he took several more blows to the abdomen. He stumbled and fell to his knees, inches from the edge of the plateau. Loose rock gave way. Oliver started slipping backward, and soon his fingers were the only part of him visible from the surface.

Luke and Davis both lunged for him, each one grabbing an arm and pulling until they got him back up. I held my breath the whole time, picturing all three falling to their deaths… and then the pain came back. It pulled across my hips, wrapped around my back, and dug in. I think I might have screamed, because I heard something strange come from my own throat. My legs gave out, and I fell into Seth's arms. As I fought to breathe, I watched Oliver rise to his feet, still wanting to fight. I tried to say something, but the pain had a hold of my voice.

"Are you assholes done yet?" Seth yelled for me.

The pain grew—doubled, tripled—and then I couldn't focus anymore. I dug my nails into Seth's arm, horrified by the smell of him, but comforted by it at the same time.

"Hey!" Seth yelled again, "you aren't going to have a girl to fight over if you both don't kiss and make up right now! She needs a doctor immediately!"

The sound of arguing resonated in my ears, but they were ringing so loud nothing made sense. My muscles pulled tighter and tighter until the world disappeared for a few minutes. Oliver was trying to pull me away, but I clung to Seth for dear life. Commands were issued and Davis murmured something in my ear to persuade me to let go of Seth, then I was carried and placed into the chopper where Brutus's hot, doggy breath brushed my face. We lifted into the air, and I found myself sandwiched between Luke and Oliver in the back of the helicopter. My agony was suddenly not only from the physical ache, or from the dread of losing the baby, but—of all ridiculous things—who to lean on.

Was I going to follow my head, or my heart? Do what *was* right, or what *felt* right? Each had its consequences.

I leaned over and put my head in his lap, breathing a sigh of relief as he caressed my cheek. Then the pain returned, burning and pulling my muscles tighter and tighter until I felt they might break. I pulled my knees up and listened as he told me to breathe. I followed his instructions—letting the air escape when he told me to and moving through the pain while holding on to the sound of his voice. Then, I stared at the split and broken skin on Luke's knuckles until I passed out.

STEPHAN

38

TICK TOCK

I WATCHED THE SUN COME UP UNTIL I FELL ASLEEP AT OLD CARL'S desk. I woke with a killer headache, so I had the kitchen bring me scotch and a sandwich, then napped again. When I dug into a plate of biscuits and a steaming mug of tea, the old boy finally decided to return to the security room late in the afternoon. He wasn't happy to see my crusty old cowboy boots on his desk and the gun beside them covered with crumbs. His withered face turned into a scowl. Shoving his hands into the pockets of his grey pants, he eyed me irritably. "What the hell are you doing, Stephan?"

The computer video feed was off, but I knew he would understand exactly what I was talking about when I got straight to the point and asked, "What's her name?"

"*Who's* name?"

"Kaya's mother."

"Uh, excuse me?"

"Don't play dumb with me, Carl. The name of the woman on that security tape you were watching—the resolution is quite good on your computer screen, by the way—you know, the woman you dragged down the hall, bound and gagged. The woman Henry stole a baby from?"

Carl's haggard face suddenly seemed older, if that were possible. His eyes narrowed until they almost disappeared beneath the fatty folds around his eyes. "You've been waiting at my desk for over twelve hours to ask me that?"

I nodded.

With a heavy sigh, he closed the door to the security room and slid the dead bolt into place. "Kaya's mother is Rayna Claire Gless," he said clearly.

The cold metal room suddenly seemed suffocating. "Rayna Claire Gless, eh? Well, let's chat for a bit about her, shall we?" I said, motioning for him to sit down in an old chair that groaned under his weight. "En-lighten me on a few things. What happened to her—to Rayna? Where did you take her? Is she dead?"

Carl lit a cigarette with an old lighter that had seen better days. "Dead? Hell no—I took her to stay with an old fishin' buddy. Henry wanted me to *get rid* of her, but I couldn't do it. So, I hid her instead." He casually blew circles of smoke in the air like everything he said was no big deal.

I ran my hands absentmindedly through my hair, stomach now not happy with the biscuits. "Why?" I asked, pretending not to be shocked that the jerk was offering up the information so easily.

"Henry got Rayna knocked up, so she took refuge here in the hotel during her pregnancy. She was married to some nasty politician at the time, and Henry went to incredible lengths to make her *disappear...*" Carl's mind wandered off for a moment, and the cigarette ash grew to an alarming length. "Lenore was pregnant, too. She carried the baby to term, but it was stillborn. Henry, always the opportunist, replaced his wife's dead child with Rayna's—a two-week-old baby girl she'd named Kaya. Dr. Ennis made everything look legit on paper."

Dr. Ennis. The sly prick had just given Kaya a checkup a few weeks ago. I shuddered. "Well, that certainly was convenient, wasn't it?"

"Uh huh."

"And evidence of all this is right there in your pocket."

"Yes." Old Carl dropped what was left of the cigarette into a coffee cup. "Listen Stephan, I have lived with guilt over this for a long time, patiently waiting for the day to get back at Henry for the horrible things he has done and for the horrible things he has made me do. I hate him, loathe him, and detest him with every fiber of my very being. And now you can see why—he's a monster."

"So let me guess... you assisted the bastards who kidnapped Kaya to get back at him, right?" I asked, becoming increasingly angry at the entire world.

"Yep. But those Right Choice Group idiots won't hurt her. You have nothing to worry about, I promise."

"Nothing to worry about? Did you know she's pregnant?"

Carl's brow lifted like a missing puzzle piece had fallen into place. "Huh. I guess Henry's little plan worked."

He knew. The growing knot in my stomach tightened, and I wanted nothing more than to rage through the halls, find Henry, and wring his wretched neck. I felt my hands shake, my guts roll, and Carl grinned at me like I'd just joined his 'I Hate Henry' club.

"Listen, Stephan, I promise you Kaya is okay for now. The RCG are a bunch of bleedin' hearts and not interested in killing her; it ain't in 'em. I've known the guy leading them around by the nose for a very long time."

"You put her in the hands of criminals who intend to use her to bargain with Henry for God knows what, and then they're just going to hand her back?"

Carl grinned. "Well, not exactly… but hey, for now, she is fine." He pulled his fishing cap lower over his eyes. I stared at him, speechless and repulsed. "Listen. I need you, Stephan. Things will go a lot smoother with a spy in the house. I have a good, solid plan in place and can get you a fair cut of the deal. When it's done, you could run away with that boy from the kitchen you've been having an affair with all these years—maybe go somewhere warm and tropical. What's his name? William?"

If Carl thought his knowing I was gay was bribe-worthy information, he was sadly mistaken. "All I want is for Kaya to be safe," I said furiously, "and you have proof she isn't of Marchessa bloodline and Lenore isn't her mother. That takes the bounty off her head. She could finally have a normal life and get away from Henry and raise her child wherever she wants without living in fear. That tape in your hands is her *freedom*."

Old Carl waved me off. "Ah, shut up, Stephan. Sometimes you are such an idiot! I stand to make a fortune off this! Besides, I've got orders to follow. I'm not running the show."

"Who is?"

"I can't tell you that."

And then, in the din of my horribly sober mind, it all became crystal clear: RCG. Rayna Claire Gless… *The Right Choice Group.*

"It's her—Rayna. She's got you wrapped around her finger."

Carl rose from the desk and furiously swiped away a stack of files, sending them flying in every direction. He was so mad that I half expected him to pull out the gun he had secured to the back of his pants and blast a hole through me. "She loves me! We would've had a life together if it hadn't been for Henry! Rayna wants her daughter back, and damn it she will have her! It's time to make things right. Now that we have Kaya, we can watch Henry squirm as we use his own kid to bring him to his knees and take everything he cares about. And once we've bled him as much as we can, we will sell Kaya to John Marchessa for a butt load. That will be the final blow to crush him."

"She will end up dead!"

Carl's nostrils flared, and he looked me square in the eye. "Then so be it."

We stared each other down until a soft beeping sound broke the silence. Old Carl bolted to his assistant's computer. "The tracker is working again. Damn it! I've spent the last two days misdirecting Henry's men on the ground and making excuses to not to dispatch the entire army to find her."

Neither of us wanted Henry to find Kaya, but our reasons were completely different.

I picked up my gun, blew off the crumbs, then cocked the trigger and pointed it squarely at Carl's chest. I had to make a decision: was Kaya better off being found by her insane father? Her revenge-seeking mother? Or... should she stay lost with the kidnappers whom Carl claims would never hurt her?

I picked lost.

"Disable the tracker and hand over that tape, Carl."

"Ha! *Nope*. You gotta get in on this, Stephan. How 'bout half a mil as your cut, huh? Take Wee Willy on a cruise; he'd like that. All you gotta do is—"

I realized I had never felt so calm. "Hand that tape over now, or I'll shoot you, Carl," I sighed.

"I know you. You won't do it," he said smugly.

He was testing me. Not the right choice. I warned him again. I told him if he put the tape on the desk, I'd let him walk away. He laughed. So I shot a bullet into his thigh.

Carl reeled back in shock, eyes wide as he fell back onto his butt. "Holy shit! You're an asshole, Stephan! I can't believe you did that!" he gasped as crimson red soaked his pants.

"Why didn't you just listen to me, you old bastard?" I said, feeling a smidge of remorse as the old boy squirmed in pain. Guards had gathered outside the bulletproof glass. They ordered us to unlock the deadbolt. "All is fine!" I yelled as they shook the door.

But it wasn't fine. Carl had tipped his old lighter to the edge of a garbage can, setting fire to the papers inside. "Nobody gets this," he said, and then he dropped Kaya's freedom into the flames.

I dove for the tape, but the old bastard was faster than I anticipated and sent a bullet through my shoulder. It shattered the bone, blinding me with pain. When I refocused, I looked up to see flames leaping out of the metal can and Carl grinning as he fired at me again, this time hitting me just above the knee. Blood poured from my leg like a fountain. Alarms went off. The metal door was shaking. I pointed my gun at the computer to make sure nobody would see Kaya's location, and sent a few rounds into it before falling to the floor.

The world was starting to spin. Carl had fallen unconscious under the window and fire was licking the curtains next to him. I yelled his name, but he didn't move. I watched in horror as the fabric above his head burst into flames, and then his hair disappeared as his old fishing cap melted. Smoke filled the room and unbearable heat stabbed at my skin as I crawled on my belly toward the exit. The heat intensified when the door came down.

I was dragged from the inferno. Carl wasn't so lucky.

LUKE

39

DRIFTING

WE WERE GATHERED ON THE PORCH OF A RANCH HOUSE THAT HAD been in Seth's family for generations while a doctor examined Kaya. The sun was about to disappear between the gentle curves of the mountains in the distance, and the green, flat pasture, munching cows, and patches of sunflowers surrounding the old house would soon be lit only by the moon and strings of porch lanterns swaying in the breeze. A few Elm trees rustled, but that was the only sound for miles. It felt like the calm before the storm.

We all waited.

Oliver sat at the opposite end of the porch on the whitewashed boards, staring at me with pure hatred in his eyes. He had intended to slit my throat only hours ago, yet I didn't feel any anger toward him. Jealousy? Yes… When Kaya practically melted into him on the plateau, it was obvious how much he meant to her. But other than that, I felt completely neutral where he was concerned. Maybe it was from the exhaustion I was experiencing on every level, or because the most important real estate in my brain was occupied with worry about Kaya, or, maybe, because in many ways, I could *relate* to how if felt having her taking up the majority of your thoughts.

Seth sipped beer and chain smoked, Davis fought sleep on an old swing that threatened to break under his weight, and Regan sat in a recliner with his leg elevated, so heavily medicated he could barely speak. Then there was Lisa, my pretty ex-girlfriend, holding my little sister on her lap and lovingly petting her head while Brutus snored at her feet.

It was a sight I couldn't get enough of.

I asked Louisa if she still liked bunnies, and her blue eyes widened in fear. She was different, wary… untrusting. I wanted to explain to her why I had been gone for so long, but she trembled with fear when any attention was directed at her. When I tried to pick her up, she screamed.

Another hour passed.

Regan's redheaded brother Ellis, the one who had been in charge of giving Kaya the fake map at the race, wandered outside and onto the porch with mugs of coffee and plates of sandwiches. I'd been so filled with worry I hadn't realized how hungry I was. The food and beverages were instantly depleted by four starved men, and Lisa ordered Ellis back into the kitchen to make more.

And still we waited.

The sun disappeared, and the moths came out to dance around the porch lights. The wind died down completely, and the stillness of the night stretched my sanity to the breaking point. I couldn't take it any-more—I had to see her. I had to know if she was okay.

I bounced up and out of the plastic lawn chair and moved toward the door.

"Hey!" yelled Lisa, "the doctor ordered everyone to stay out, and you'll damn well listen to her!"

Oliver stood to block me, eager for any reason to start another fight.

"Whoa!" said Davis, jumping to his feet and putting his hands up between us. "I'm *way* too tired for any bullshit from you assholes, all right? Besides, there are more sandwiches coming—"

As if on cue, the porch door opened, but it wasn't Ellis with food. It was the doctor, and the answer to my immediate question was written all over her face.

"Sit down, boys," she said in a tone befitting someone used to giving orders. She brushed nonexistent dirt off an expensive-looking dress and looked down her designer nose at every one of us. "So, who was the father?" she asked.

The word *was,* although spoken quickly, was not missed.

"Me," said Oliver.

"I'm sorry, sir, but Kaya has miscarried," the doctor said mat-ter-of-factly.

I jumped to my feet as a collective moan of grief escaped from ev-eryone except Oliver… he almost looked relieved. Lisa wagged a finger at me to sit back down.

"She really should be at a hospital where we can x-ray her arm," said the doctor.

Oliver spoke up for us all. "No. It's not safe for her there. You have to trust us on that," he said.

The doctor rubbed her forehead in dismay and quickly gave up on the subject—she had been paid very well to overlook a few things. "Kaya has sustained many injuries, and I've tried to treat them all. She needs to heal physically *and* mentally from whatever it was she went through."

I tried to distract myself by counting the geese roaming the yard because I felt my eyes tearing up.

"She has asked to be left alone for a while," the doctor said, addressing Lisa, "and you seem to be the only level-headed one of this bunch—no offense to the rest of you. So, no one but you is allowed to see her for a day or so... okay? Oh, except someone named Davis. She has requested to see him right away."

Davis burst from the swing before anyone could protest and disappeared into the house. The screen door squeaked and bounced off the wood frame behind him.

The doctor turned to me. "Are you the one who pulled her from the river?" she asked.

Oliver's eyes bore into me from across the porch. "Yes," I answered with a gulp.

"That was insane what you did to her arm, but good call. She would have bled to death if you hadn't cauterized the wound. Anyway, I've been told that you have some injuries as well that need to be tended. Apparently an animal attacked you?"

My God. That seemed like a lifetime ago. "Uh yeah. But really, I'm fine Doc, thanks. Just a few scratches."

"I need to assess you, and it's not optional," she said. "Besides, I have some questions. Kaya's wounds have healed remarkably fast, and I need to know what you did to her out there... *exactly*."

Oliver's glare became so intense I half expected to burst into flames—maybe getting away from him for a minute would be a good thing. I stood and the doctor eyed my bloody clothes and black eye.

"Camping trip, my ass," she said perceptively.

We all looked at our feet.

Soon, Davis came flying out the door and back onto the porch, his cheeks red, his eyes glassy. He was vibrating with the energy of a man on a mission. "Hey there, ferry boy," he said pointing at Seth in a rather comedic gesture.

"Uh, excuse me...?" Seth said, clearly offended.

"That's was you, right? You're the ferry dude from the race?"

"Oh, uh yeah," Seth admitted with a smile, "but maybe you could just call me Seth."

Davis cleared his throat, "Well, *Seth*, I need metal cutters, vice grips, pliers, a hacksaw... and maybe some protective eyewear if you've got it."

Seth looked at him vacantly, and then he laughed, stomping his cigarette out and leaving a long black smudge next to many others. "Hell, I got that and more. It's about time we got that damn thing off her leg now, isn't it?"

I slept like I was dead. At least, it's what I'd imagined it would be like—empty, blank, and without dreams—like how I figured life would be without Kaya.

I woke up on a couch in the massive, dusty living room with the curtains drawn and the afternoon sun trying to squeeze through and illuminate the macabre deer and elk heads hanging next to the fireplace. In front were two plaid chairs that looked like they had seen many restless nights. Last I remembered, the doctor was sitting in one, hovering over me and asking a thousand questions. She wanted to know about how I got each wound, the hot spring, and the medicine I had on hand… but all I could think about was Kaya. I couldn't concentrate on anything else. I had tried to be a good patient, but I was losing my mind with worry and unable to lie still. At the end of her exam, she put something under my tongue that knocked me out. That was fifteen hours ago.

Standing up was agony. Every muscle in my body ached and downright throbbed; even my hair hurt. I leaned against the back of the couch for a minute, and then I followed a large hallway toward the sound of muffled voices. I stopped at a slightly ajar door when I heard Kaya and Louisa laughing, the sound making all my achy parts tingle. I held my breath and peeked into the room to see Kaya propped up in bed surrounded by a zillion pillows and Louisa May nestled in beside her. Both of them looked clean and shiny with color in their cheeks. Louisa was grinning madly as Kaya read to her, and both of them giggled. The two people I loved most in the world were together, safe and happy in each other's company—just the thought made my knees so weak I had to steady myself against the wall.

"You're not supposed to be here," whispered Lisa from behind me. She was holding a plate of cookies and her hair was pulled into her '*I'm in charge*' ponytail. "Hey, they are okay, Luke," she added when she saw the look on my face.

I hugged her tightly. "I can't thank you enough," I said softly into her perfumed neck.

"Yeah, yeah, quit with the sappy shit. You know I'd do anything for you," she said with a smile in her voice.

I pulled away to kiss her forehead and the cookies almost hit the floor. Kaya looked up, sensing us there, and I ducked out of sight.

"Listen, go have a shower and clean yourself up," Lisa whispered. "There are some clothes in the bedroom next door that will fit you. And have something to eat; you look like a bag of bones."

I was handed a cookie then gently pushed away.

I showered under the hottest water I could stand until there wasn't a speck of it left in the old taps. The wounds on my chest were a light pink and were healing into some pretty impressive scars, but my hands were a mess. They stung and bled when I washed my hair. I put band-aids on my knuckles and wrapped gauze around my palms once I'd dried off.

I found a neatly folded stack of clothes, all my size and style—T-shirts, jeans, and even a pair of black leather shoes that fit perfectly. I realized when I saw my old backpack hanging from the bedpost that Lisa had gone shopping for me. She knew all I owned was that beat up sack, a few shredded clothes, and a now very precious bar of soap.

I followed my nose to the kitchen where the most wondrous smell drifted from a crock-pot. Dishes shone as they dried on the counter beside a plate of pancakes and cold coffee. I chugged a mug of the black brew like it was a cold beer on a hot day, and then I poured another. Two pancakes were gone in an instant, and then I shoved another in my mouth before bringing two more with me out onto the porch. I leaned back into the same lawn chair I had occupied last night and closed my eyes, savoring every bite.

Then I felt the glare.

Had I known Oliver was there, I would have stayed inside to avoid confrontation. But there he sat on the opposite end of the porch, squished into a plastic chair and facing the pasture just as I was. He looked haggard. Dark circles were visible on his already dark skin, and he was still in the same clothes as yesterday. I wondered if he had moved at all since the night before.

I pretended to be completely busy with my cup of coffee, but it was soon gone.

"Where is everyone?" I asked, not eager to engage in small talk but unable to ignore him any longer.

"That pal of yours, Seth, and Kaya's other guard, Davis, are taking the tracking device to a decoy location," he said as he glanced at a small computer screen in his hands, "it's about four hours from here right now."

I was shocked at his willingness to offer information. "How come Henry didn't swarm us last night?"

Oliver cleared his throat. He spoke slowly, his voice deep and thick. "I have no idea. There's been no communication with him for the last thirty-three hours. If something has happened and security has been compromised, if Kaya's whereabouts have gotten into the wrong hands..."

"You mean, John Marchessa?"

"Yes. I guess she told you about him."

"He is the one you protect her from."

"Him and people like you," he spat out, cracking his knuckles. "I'm only sharing this information with you because if he is out there, I'll need all the help I can get. I only want to protect her."

"Well, I guess we have something in common then."

"Hmm, I guess we do."

I put the empty cup down, craving more, but my muscles were not willing to move from the chair.

"The little girl, Louisa, she is your sister, right? She was taken from you?" Oliver asked.

The directness of the question startled me. Yesterday, he wanted to kill me, and suddenly he wanted to get personal. "Yes," I said, swallowing back the flood of emotion that always came at the mention of her name.

"You did all this... for her?" he asked.

"I had to do whatever it took to get my sister back."

Oliver seemed to ponder my reply. A restless calf called for its mother in the pasture. The breeze picked up. "Did they hurt her?" he asked.

"Yes," I choked out. "In the most horrible way you could ever hurt a child."

"Then I guess, on some level, I have to forgive you."

I looked at him in shock, but was instantly grateful for his forgiveness. "I'm sorry, Oliver... for the hell I put you through. Truly, I'm sorry."

He stood and walked toward the railing, his hands looking like dark chocolate against the white paint. "Understand this, Luke," he said, "that I will do the same for Kaya—whatever it takes."

"Yet another thing we have in common," I said softly.

We both stared off into the distance, quietly contemplating each other until Brutus broke the tension by panting hard and strolling up the steps to drop in an exhausted heap at my feet. When the screen door opened and his tail wagged furiously, I knew who was there.

Kaya tentatively emerged from the house without glancing at either of us. I could detect the scent of soap mixed with something flowery on her skin. The large men's shirt she wore only covered her to the middle of her bare thighs, and although it had probably been thrown on without any thought, she looked incredible. As much as I wanted to grab her, I stayed put. Oliver, however, couldn't contain himself and practically dove at her. She backed away from him like he was the devil while Brutus bared his teeth in her defense.

"Kaya, I'm so sorry about—"

"Stop," she said firmly, putting her hand up, "back up, and just...

stop."

Oliver dropped his arms dejectedly.

"I need to talk to you both. But first, Oliver, you must promise me something." She bit her lip. "*He* is important to me." She made the slightest hand gesture in my direction. "You must promise me that you will never, *ever* try to hurt him again."

"Kaya, it's okay," I said, but she put her hand up to silence me, too.

"Oliver, promise me," she demanded.

Oliver mumbled something incoherent and looked away.

"Oliver, if you don't promise me this, if you *can't* promise me this, then you will *never* be a part of my life from this moment forward."

The pitch of her voice rose with a tinge of unstableness, and she looked as though she might crack. I slowly stood up and moved behind her.

"Okay, yes. I promise!" Oliver said crossly.

She lowered her gaze to her feet and we stood there, the three of us, the tension like a thick haze. Then a phone started ringing in Oliver's pocket. He furrowed his brow in agitation as he fished it out to look at the incoming call. "Kaya, it's Henry," he said, "I haven't heard from him since yesterday morning, and I have to answer it."

When Kaya nodded her head in approval, Oliver put the phone to his ear.

"Where the hell are you, Oliver?" yelled an angry voice clearly audible in the quiet stillness of the afternoon.

Oliver straightened up and turned away from us. "Sir, I have been trying to reach you…"

"Well, we had a slight problem with security here. The control room was completely… *inaccessible* for a while."

Oliver took a step toward the railing, deck boards creaking under him. "Is everything all right now?"

"More or less, we've got it all under control. So, where's Kaya? Where's my daughter?"

I heard Kaya gulp loudly at the mention of her name. I hated the way her father said it with such a cold tone to his voice.

"I have her sir. She is with me, safe and sound," Oliver said.

"Good. I would assume you have eliminated her captors?"

Oliver glared at me. "Yes, as per your request, sir," he lied.

"Excellent," said Henry. "We got rid of the idiots who picked up the ransom money. Got only useless information out of them, though. They claimed they were there to do a deal with someone named Luke and didn't even know who Kaya was. Even as we plucked out his eyeballs, some stupid, French asshole named Claude insisted he knew nothing."

All the air left my lungs, and my head start to spin; Henry had unknowingly either purged me of my past or built me a whole new hornet's nest of problems. His voice continued on, as clear as the blue sky.

"Oliver, I have your location, and I am sending a car for you now." The sound of his assistants jumping into action could be heard in the background.

Oliver turned to stare— Kaya and I were too close together for his liking, and I could see little beads of sweat start to form on his forehead. "Sir, the doctor put Kaya on bed rest for today. I will leave first thing tomorrow morning and bring her back."

"A doctor? You took her to a hospital?" Henry said furiously.

"No, I—"

"Listen, I already have a team heading out. I want her back here, *immediately*. You know how important this is, Oliver, and you know what you are supposed to do!"

Oliver clenched his jaw and pulled the phone away from his ear, clearly struggling with his loyalty. With a heavy breath, he stared hard at Kaya before fumbling for the right words to say to her controlling father. "Sir, with all due respect, it is important to follow the doctor's orders in light of her present condition."

Kaya's head dropped sadly. I knew the loss of the baby weighed heavy on her heart, and I reached for her hand. Oliver's eyes suddenly became darker, his stare sharp, like a dagger pointed in my direction. He began to yell into the phone. "Do you understand, Henry—sir? She is not going anywhere today. Call your men off so they don't waste their time. I'm bringing her back *myself*." With that, he hung up and dropped the phone back into his pocket.

Kaya pulled her hand free of mine and turned to face him. "Just so you know, I'll leave when I'm ready," she stated.

"Which will be *tomorrow*." Oliver replied.

"Uh, no."

Oliver shook his head with a cocky grin. "Listen, Kaya, I am taking you home tomorrow, and that's final."

"It's her choice," I reminded him, feeling my pulse quicken at the potential of an argument.

Oliver laughed arrogantly. "Uh, no, actually it isn't. She is *engaged* to *me*. She *belongs* to *me*, and *I'm* taking her home. *Tomorrow*."

His words made her body sway. They had such a deep emotional pull that they seemed to rob her of whatever strength she had to stand up to him. I put my hand on her shoulder, steadying her, and then stared at the back of her head, hoping for outrage, yelling, tears… any-thing… but she didn't move or speak. The only signal I got that she was still even conscious was her body leaning back into my hand.

Oliver reached out and possessively wrapped his fingers around her arm. Then, he pulled her away.

She didn't resist. My hand dropped from her shoulder.

"We are going home in the morning," he said.

"No. I—"

"There's no arguing, Kaya. You know this is what you have to do."

Her head turned slightly and those dazzling emerald eyes focused on me momentarily. "I can do whatever I choose…"

Oliver looked about to snap. "You are engaged to *me*. You, Kaya Lowen, are *mine,* and you will do as I say."

"Okay," she replied meekly.

My heart felt as if it fell out of my rib cage and splattered onto the porch. "What? What do you mean *okay?*" I repeated, shocked.

"I'm so sorry Luke," she said quietly. "He's right."

A bomb might as well have gone off in my chest. I had braced myself for this, she had *told* me she wasn't going to leave him, but I chose to believe she would follow her heart. Everything she'd said led me to have faith. The world went fuzzy as she walked away with him, my ears filled with the rhythm of my own heartbeat, and I stumbled backward while her voice floated around my head like the moths around the porch lights.

"I'm sorry Luke, so, *so* sorry… but you know this is what I have to do," she said, crying.

Oliver was pulling her away.

"You're killing me, Kaya. Please don't do this… *please…*"

She gave me a fleeting look before Oliver took her inside.

And that was it—it was over.

40

ℐNSIDE ℴUT

I BLINDLY MADE MY WAY OFF THE PORCH AND TOWARD THE OLD barn facing the house, feeling like I was walking in a nightmare. Pacing around a rusty Bronco parked in the middle of the wood floor, my feet sent so much dust into the air I could barely see. There used to be horses in here, but now it was Seth's workshop, filled with things that didn't work—myself included. I slammed my fists onto the hood of the truck and pain surged through my hands. I slammed them again.

"Careful, 'cause it's all yours," said a voice from the door.

Seth.

I tried to say I was sorry, but nothing came out. He handed me a beer and I guzzled it, hoping it would numb any fraction of the heartache.

"I understand Kaya is leaving in the morning. Oliver is inside with that Davis kid making arrangements," he said softly. "You okay?"

He'd just delivered the final blow to the remains of my wishful thinking. "No. No, I'm *not* okay. I can't stand it—I can't stand being... so close—she's right there and knowing I can't—I can't have her... Jesus. I need to get away from here."

Seth gave me a fatherly smile. Light filtered between the planks of the barn walls and lit up the dark shadows under his eyes. "You can take this old girl," he said, patting the Bronco fondly, "she runs well, she just needs that tire put on and some fluid top-offs. I just haven't had the time."

"I can't leave Louisa," I said bitterly.

"Lisa can manage taking care of her for a bit. I'll make sure they are both looked after. You have my word. Just don't go doing anything stupid. That kid needs her brother."

"No, I can't—"

"She'll be fine, Luke. If you gotta go and get your head straight, then go do it. Just do some thinkin' and drinkin', and beat up a few deadbeats while doing both."

Seth seemed eager for me to leave, but maybe I was reading into it. He'd proved time and again he could be trusted. "How can I carry on, Seth? How do I—how am I supposed to… I just can't…" I gave up talking. I didn't even know what I was trying to say.

"Yeah, heartbreak sucks," he said sympathetically.

He was no stranger to it—his ex-wife was a monster.

"I should have let the bastard drop off that cliff," I mumbled.

"Nope. You did the right thing. If Oliver had died, Kaya would have never forgiven you."

He was right, of course.

"Just give it time, Luke. Get some space between the two of ya. Get some perspective. Then you can decide if ya wanna give her up."

"Give her up?" I replied, but he brushed it off.

"Here," he said and held out his hand. In it were the keys to the Bronco and a thick roll of cash. "Your full cut is safely tucked away, so here's a credit card, too. Use it instead of cash whenever you can so I can keep track of things—you know, for accounting purposes and such. Anyway, sign my name when you use it. The limit is high enough that you can buy a darn car with it if ya want too."

Blood money. Everything about it felt so wrong, but I had to take it. I owned nothing. "What about you, Seth? Your, uh, 'boss'—or whoever it was you were supposed to deliver Kaya too—won't he be upset that you've done an about face?"

Seth rubbed his cheek absently where the scars from Kaya's finger-nails were still a deep red. "Oh yeah. She'll be *a little* pissed."

Did I hear him right? "*She?*" I asked.

"Yep… she. The nastiest bitch you'll ever meet." He finished his beer, and then he headed for the door. "Well, you go on and do what you gotta do, kid, and good luck," he said, and then he stopped. "Oh, I almost forgot something… this is yours…" He fished around in his pocket, and then he extended his arm, palm facing up.

I blinked. In his hand was a tooth from the cougar Kaya had shot. I took it from him and rolled it between my fingers, forgetting I'd insisted he go through the trouble of getting it. It seemed so important at the time—so significant. She'd saved me that day, and the look of worry on her face with my blood on her hands as she patched me up was something I never wanted to forget. I knew then and there, at that very moment, when her eyes met mine with the needle in her hands, that she loved me.

But, now the tooth was just a tooth.

"I won't break my promise to you," I said to Seth.

He furrowed his brow questioningly.

"Eronel. Closing it down…"

He looked like he'd forgotten about it.

"I'll help any way I can," I offered, "make a new plan, and I'm in. I'll do anything you want—except kidnap another girl."

Seth embraced me with a quick hug and a pat on the back. "Maybe don't give up on her just yet," he said softly, and then he left.

BETTER TO HAVE LOVED AND LOST THAN NEVER TO HAVE LOVED AT ALL…

That was one of my mum's favorite sayings. Obviously, she'd never experienced true love because that was total bullshit.

I drilled a hole in the tooth and hung it on the chain next to my mum's maple leaf. But I couldn't put the necklace back on; the visual reminder of such an immense loss was too much to take. I would give it to Louisa. She could have something from her mother and a piece of my heart.

Through the murky barn window, I could see her on the porch with Brutus, her golden hair shining and a pink dress puffed up around her legs as Lisa closely watched through the screen door. Like a zombie, I forced my legs to walk toward her, half expecting my feet to hit quick-sand or to be pulled under by the uncut grass and dandelions. I expected her to run from me, too… but she didn't. Brutus's tail slapped loudly on the wood slats as I approached, making her giggle.

"Brutus likes you, Louisa. That's good, because he really needs a friend," I said and crouched down to pet him. We rubbed the dirty dog. It rolled over on its back and put its legs in the air, making Louisa giggle again. The sound was music to my ears.

"He's funny. I like him," she said and scratched his tummy.

Her beautiful little face was shadowed by such deep, underlying sad-ness, but for the time being, she seemed happy. It made everything I did, and every bit of pain I felt, completely worth it. I had to remember why I did all this in the first place—for her. "I have a present for you," I said and held out the necklace. The tooth and leaf made a small clinking sound. I felt a bit sick.

"Oh, thanks," she said sweetly, and then she dangled it over Brutus's nose. "You know my friend—that girl? She is really, really sad," she said and her eyes shined like Mum's did at the prospect of helping someone. "I don't think she has any necklaces. I have lots."

"Oh? Who's your friend?" I asked, assuming it was Lisa.

"The girl with the black hair. My heart loves her," she said.

"You mean… uh *Kaya*?" I asked, barely able to say her name.

"Yes. This is yellow and that's her favorite color. She told me."

"That girl has my heart too," I said, choking on the words. "I think it would be very nice if you gave it to her."

Her face lit up. "It can be from me *and* you."

I nodded in stunned silence as she closed her tiny hand carefully around the gift. "I've missed you, Wheeza," I said, blinking back the stinging feeling of tears in my eyes.

She looked up, her expression dead serious. "I didn't like it there, Luke. I don't wanna go back."

My heart broke into a million pieces. "You will never, ever go back there. I promise. Nobody will ever hurt you again."

She let her hand touch mine and a glimmer of the affectionate little sister I once knew smiled back at me. Then, Oliver opened the door, breaking the spell. He stepped out onto the porch, and Louisa took off, fleeing from him with terror in her eyes and circling back around in a desperate attempt to get back to Lisa. Brutus leapt to his feet, backing up protectively against me.

"Sorry, Luke," Oliver said, his deep voice too thick in my ears, "but I would rather you keep your distance. Maybe head back to that barn over there."

Brutus growled, and I wondered what would happen if I ordered him to chew the triumphant smirk off Oliver's face. My arms started to shake. Never had an ugly feeling come over me like this—I was filling with rage. The world turned scarlet, and then it slowed down, then it almost stopped; I wanted to kill him. *I wanted to kill him…*

Oliver backed away. He could see the hate in my eyes. "Well, it is unfortunate we met under such circumstances," he said carefully.

Three moves, that's all I needed—ribs, then eyes, and then break his neck. All my problems solved…

Oliver put his hands up defensively, sensing my intense urge to fight him—and it would be merciless this time. I was a mere second away from removing the barrier between me and the love of my life, until he said her name.

"Kaya's a great girl, isn't she?" he said softly.

I choked. The rage brought my blood to a rolling boil as her name lingered on his tongue… But it reminded me that I couldn't hurt him— because of her, I couldn't hurt him. She would never forgive me if I did.

A flash of golden sun glinted in his eyes. "Anyway, uh, hey, thanks for not letting me fall back there," he said, clearly uneasy and backing away.

I turned and forced my legs to get moving before I did something stupid. *You're welcome* was not something I could honestly say.

KAYA

41

Wakey Wakey Sugar Cakey

I FELT WRETCHED. I CRIED. I FOUGHT TO BREATHE. I WAS TRYING to do the right thing, but it just didn't feel *right*. Oliver's hold on me was deep. He saved my life, he stuck with me through thick and thin, and he had loved me when Henry didn't. He'd been my best friend… but was I *in love* with him?

Luke had asked me if I was, and I had to think about it—and that, right there, was my answer. Love shouldn't have any doubts, reservations, or questions… it just *is*. You should just *know*. Like I knew with Luke.

Yet I was going home with Oliver tomorrow.

There was a soft knock at the door. I held my breath, hoping whoever it was would just leave, but I could see the shadow of feet lingering in the large gap at the bottom of the doorframe. Something was shoved underneath the door, and it slid across the worn hardwood. I leaned over to try and make sense of what it was, but my eyes were blurry. I rubbed at them, and then, through tears, I recognized the maple leaf… Luke's necklace…

Sparks tingled through all my cells.

I noticed he'd added something to it—a tooth? Why? I reached for it, my hands shaking like it was dust and might disappear if I breathed too hard. Gently, I held it between my fingertips, and suddenly it made sense: the tooth was from that mountain lion.

An overwhelming flood of realization surged through me. I saved him that day, without over thinking, analyzing, pondering or asking myself what the right thing to do was. I just simply saved him. The terror I felt at the thought of him dying and not wanting to live without him hadn't changed since then. The complete realization that I was in love with him hadn't changed either. A life with him was what I wanted, and he was who I truly loved. So what the hell was I doing?

I squeezed the tooth and maple leaf together in my hand between my fingers, gathering strength from it. I made my mind up right then and there, and decided that from now on, the only person I would let decide *my* fate would be *me*.

The light that had once been just a dim dot at the end of the tunnel was now glaring like the afternoon sun.

I wrestled myself into a pair of Lisa's blue jeans and a shirt, cursing my wounded arm for being of no assistance in the process, and then I opened the door to see Louisa standing there. Her pink dress was black all around the bottom, and there was dog hair all over her lace tights.

"These are for you," she said, thrusting forward a bouquet of yellow weeds.

Her angelic face almost fired up my tears again. She was so beautiful; she looked so much like Luke. "Awe, thanks sweetie. They are perfect," I said, and I knelt before her.

"They're for you 'cause you're sad."

"Well, flowers always make me feel better." I opened my palm to display the necklace. "Is this from you too?"

She smiled proudly. "Me and my brother, Luke."

"Oh," I choked, "thank you."

Tiny fingers helped fasten the chain around my neck, and I felt my heart burst with love for the child. With the promise of ice cream, I led her to the kitchen where Lisa stood at the sink elbow deep in dishwater among yellow-painted walls and shining-white counters. She sat Louisa down at a mammoth farm-style table with a vat of maple fudge and a spoon. She'd been keeping an eye on Regan, who was stretched out in an old recliner with his leg elevated, and gave me the nod to try to talk to him.

"Hey," I said softly, and I got on my knees beside him. His beautiful red hair was disheveled, and the mass of freckles across his nose and cheeks stood out in stark contrast to his pale skin. I brushed aside a lock of hair from his cheek. "I hear you tried to rescue me."

His eyes wandered at first then eventually focused on me. "Oh, yeah."

"Thank you," I said.

He forced a smile. "Good thing your knight in shining armor was smarter than me, or you'd be dead."

"Nah, I'm made of steel," I said, quoting Stephan and missing him terribly.

"Apparently, I am too," he said and winced. A thick cast ran from his thigh to his very blue toes on one leg, and the other was wrapped in more bandages than I could count. Thankfully, his perfect face was without a single scratch.

"I'm sorry about the miscarriage," he said, eyes welling up.

There was a part of me that was so empty and so hurting over that loss, I could barely contain the sobs that wanted to burst forth. "You know it's not your fault, Regan. It wasn't the drugs…"

His eyes drifted to his hands and the guilt on his face was heartbreaking, so I changed the subject. "I'm sorry you're hurting so much," I said, wishing there was something I could do to help alleviate his pain.

He faked a smile and coughed. "You risked your life for mine, you stupid girl. Throwing yourself in front of that gun was insane, but brave. I'll never forget it. I would jump into that river all over again for you if I had to."

I was taken aback by the conviction in his voice. "And I the same."

He gulped hard, and his eyes reddened with emotion. "This situation has made me realize a few things, Kaya, one being that… that I—uh, well… I *owe* you."

My throat tightened. "I owe you, too," I said, as I reached for his hand.

"And I've learned my lesson: no more revenge." Then, he added, "And no more dwelling on the past, either. I have to get back to living again, move on and be free of this bullshit. You know, maybe I'll find love again. Nonsense like that."

I nodded and leaned in, kissing his damp forehead. When I rose to leave, he leaned forward and reached for my hand, his grip freakishly strong even though he was drugged. "By the way, have you come to your senses yet?" he asked.

He was of course referring to Luke. I smiled. "Yes."

"Thank heavens, because I'm too tired to give you a lecture."

With that, he drifted back into drugged-out bliss.

Lisa turned to face me. She was scrubbing the stove now, her washing gloves dripping in soap bubbles and her shirt covered in grime, yet she was happy as a clam. The domestic role suited her much better than that of *Nurse Barbie* like she was pretending to be in The Death Race. I knew the moment I met the *real* Lisa—the one who didn't know me from a hole in the ground yet held me in her arms while I bawled my eyes out over the loss of the baby—that I had a friend for life.

"Luke's out in the barn," she said, pointing out the kitchen window with a little smirk.

"Thanks."

I wanted to run to him, to throw myself into his arms and beg him to forgive me, but I had unfinished business to take care of first. "I guess I better talk to Oliver first. I mean, I have to, don't I?" I asked nervously.

"Uh huh," Lisa nodded, "you gotta do it right."

"But how do I say it? How do I tell him?"

Lisa pondered this for a moment. "I don't think it really matters much *how*—he's going to freak out no matter which way you say it. I mean, I gave that guy enough drugs in that race to knock out a horse yet he pushed ahead for hours, *for you.*"

I thought of Angela and her attempt to describe to me the difference between love and obsession. "Well, if I go missing, have a look in the basement freezer," I half-heartedly joked.

OLIVER AND DAVIS WERE IN THE LIVING ROOM, ARGUING IN HUSHED voices. They stopped when I entered the room.

"Well, you look a little better," said Davis, clearing his throat and rising to give me a hug, "not quite like what the cat coughed up anymore." He smiled, but there was still a ton of worry all over his clean-shaven face.

"Yes, it's good to see you've stopped crying, my girl," Oliver said, beaming ear to ear and walking toward me with open arms—I backed away. The antlers of a stuffed elk poked me in the head.

"Uh, I'm gonna see if Lisa needs help," said Davis intuitively, and he fled for the kitchen.

Oliver had on a pair of faded jeans and a white golf shirt that was too tight. Every muscle of his chest was outlined and he looked incredible—as always—but I didn't have even the slightest feeling of desire for him.

"Kaya, I'm sorry about everything that happened back there on the mountain. I hope you can forgive me. I'm sorry about the pregnancy, too—it never should have happened. I don't want you to be sad, but you know it's probably a good thing that it's, uh... *gone.* It will be much easier for me to keep you safe and to protect you. I love you so much. I just want what's best for you."

"I know Oliver. I understand." And I truly did. He wasn't lying. He loved me, and he wanted to keep me safe... because that's what he was programmed to do.

"Henry is breathing down my neck," he said, "and losing his mind. He sent a team to get you, and of course, the anklet led them to the wrong location like we planned. Now he's furious."

"Did you tell him where we really are?"

He held up his phone so I could see; the notifications of missed calls were in the hundreds. "I listened to the first few, and they were all the same—demands, threats—one was Sindra trying the logical approach. I haven't bothered with the rest."

I sat down on the weathered couch and dust floated up. He stood in front of the window, creating a massive shadow across the floor. "Henry is not a good man, Oliver," I said, "I have learned a few things about him. He's not who you think he is."

"He is still your father, Kaya."

"Yes. But you must know by now that the reason he wants me back so badly is not because he loves me." I'd never told Oliver about the inheritance, or breathed a word to anybody. I was glad I'd kept that to myself. "...and, if you look really hard at the circumstances that brought us together, they seem a bit, well... fabricated."

"I know," he sighed.

I was taken aback. "Wait, what? What do you mean, *you know?*"

He cleared his throat and looked rather uncomfortable. "Some things just didn't seem right. Stephan noticed, Davis noticed, but I overlooked it. All I wanted was to be with you and it didn't matter to me how that happened."

I was shocked. He sat down next to me and patted my thigh. I inched away.

"So, the engagement... the—"

"You have to understand, Kaya. I love you. I would do anything for you. Every word I have ever said to you has been my own. The proposal was real—none of my feelings were ever constructed, and nobody ever told me what to do. I am truly, with every fiber of my very being, deeply in love with you."

His face was so sweet, and his words so sincere; they started reeling me back in... and suddenly I was questioning my decision to break off the engagement. He grabbed hold of my hand and brought it to his lips, his big brown eyes staring into mine, seducing—

And then a sicker-than-sick feeling took over; being *with him* was *wrong*.

"Oliver, I'm sorry, but I'm not going back," I said with as much authority and strength as I could muster.

"Okay. I can accept that," he said.

When my jaw almost hit the floor, he quickly noticed my obvious confusion.

"I've thought about it, too," he added, "Davis has agreed, and we've decided that the two of us can keep you safe. We will go to Montreal. Henry has a house there; it's secure and guarded—"

"No, Oliver. I mean I'm not going back *with you*. I can't be with you," I said.

His eyes grew wide. "What are you talking about?"

I swallowed hard in an effort to quell the burning sensation in my chest. "I love you—please don't think for a second that I don't—because you are my best friend, and it's truly killing me to have to make this decision, but—"

"Don't say it!" he yelled and put his hand up.

"Oliver, let me explain."

"No! Don't say another word!"

I twisted the ring off my finger and placed it on the couch next to him. "I don't want to marry you."

His eyes narrowed on me in complete rage and his nostrils flared, then he balled his hands up into fists. "You can't do this, Kaya!" he roared, and then he jumped to his feet. "Is this some sort of a joke? You're not *serious*."

"I am. I know you don't understand, but—"

"No. I *don't* understand," he yelled and the whole house shook.

Davis ran into the living room. I knew he'd been eavesdropping. "Relax, Oliver. Give her some time to think," he said calmly, "she's been through a lot."

I shook my head at Davis, "I'm sorry, but I don't need time to think," I said firmly, "this is what I want."

Oliver cracked his knuckles, his jaw clenched. "Well, if you aren't my fiancée anymore, then all promises are off. I'll *kill him*. I'll *rip him to pieces*." He stormed out of the room with Davis and me running after him. He barged into the kitchen, and Louisa dove under the table. Lisa grabbed a frying pan and held it like a weapon.

"Where is he?" Oliver yelled. "Where is that bastard?"

"Get the hell out of my kitchen," Lisa hissed.

He ignored her, brushing past her and storming out onto the porch. He stomped and paced up and down the boarded deck while Davis pleaded with him to calm down. I strategically placed myself on the steps to create a barrier between Oliver and the barn, but that might as well have been an invitation. His glazed eyes zeroed in on me and sweat broke out on his forehead. "Get out of my way," he ordered, nearly vibrating with anger.

"No. You leave him alone," I said defiantly, standing my ground.

Oliver snarled with a low, guttural sound that lifted all the hair on the back of my neck, and then I watched as his hand flew forward and he shoved me backward. I tried to grab the railing but missed, and I stepped back onto nothing, falling down the steps and landing on my butt.

"What the hell is wrong with you?" Davis hollered as he ran to me.

I was plucked from the ground and cradled against Davis's Iron Maiden T-shirt, shock leaving me without words. I rested against him for a moment, gathering my breath and my thoughts, and then I realized, I was really bloody mad. Really, full on, spitting, *mad*.

In three large and determined steps, I made my way up the steps to stand before Oliver. I glared at him while his eyes darted around wildly.

"I'm sorry," he said robotically. Then, his hands latched onto my arms like vice grips and pulled me toward him. I winced as his fingers dug into the healing hole in my arm, but I tried to stoically stand my ground. "I don't know what came over me," he said flatly.

My mind raced as I tried to find words that would verbally slap him and knock some sense into him, but the anger had left me speechless. As I fished for something to say, anything to let him know how much I hated him right now, the barn doors opened and a truck slowly emerged. Oliver's eyes gleamed, and suddenly, he was crushing his mouth over mine—possessively, fiercely—and the more I resisted, the harder he pressed.

I knew it was all a show for Luke.

I sunk my teeth in, biting hard enough to taste blood, but Oliver didn't even flinch. As the truck sped by, I caught a glimpse of Luke's eyes and the hurt look on his face. Clouds of dust were kicked up from the wheels as it sped toward the highway, and only when it was out of sight did Oliver let me go.

Blood trickled down his chin. He put a finger to his lip, and then he looked at me as if waking from a dream, his face changing from rage to remorse. A look of horror passed over his face when he realized what he'd done. I didn't care. Without hesitation, I raised my hand and slapped him as hard as I could.

"I'm sorry," he said, eyes brimming with tears, his own hand pressed to his stinging cheek. "Oh my God, Kaya, please forgive me."

I was fuming. The Oliver I knew would have never shoved me, or any woman for that matter. Did something happen on that mountain to change him as much as it had changed me? I was about to slap him again, but Davis caught my arm and Seth came around the corner with a shotgun. He aimed it at Oliver's chest, and he cocked the trigger. "You need to take a time out there, boy," he warned. "There'll be none of that bullshit on my property, ya hear?"

Oliver stood, unblinking and unfazed by the gun directed at him. His face was a mixture of denial and complete heartbreak. "You're really leaving me, Kaya?" he choked out.

"*Yes!*" I shouted angrily.

My answer hit him so hard he stumbled backward. He stared vacantly at me for a moment, stunned. "Well, maybe we need some time apart," he said softly, "I guess I can let you go your own way for a little while."

"This is not temporary, Oliver. We're done. "

He shook his head and let out a cocky laugh, like what I'd said was ridiculous. So I poured all of my emotion into four very important words. "*You don't own me!*" I yelled.

The cows stopped grazing. Brutus's hair rose on his back. The world became still.

Oliver sighed. "Fine. I'll allow some separation for now," he said sullenly, "but Lord help that asshole Luke if anything happens to you. Mark my words, Kaya Lowen; I will be back for what's mine—I'm not giving you up."

With that, he turned and marched off across the field.

Davis looked rattled, conflicted over whose side to take. His hand moved to my shoulder. "Something's gotten into him, Kaya. He's not himself. How about you give him another chance?"

I shook my head. "No. Davis, I'm sorry. But this is how it's going to be."

"You're sure about this?" he asked sadly.

"More sure than I've been of anything in my entire life."

He planted a brotherly kiss on my forehead, and then he ran off after Oliver. And that was it. I was alone. Unprotected.

Free.

I took in a deep breath, readjusted the bandage around my arm, and gathered my thoughts while Seth kept his gun aimed at Oliver and Davis until they'd faded into the distance.

"Seth, do you know where Luke went?" I asked, struggling to hold my sanity together.

He didn't answer.

"Seth, tell me, please."

"Listen. You've broken his heart, darlin'. He has to go away and do some forgetting about you," he said, and he pulled out a cigarette from behind his ear. I noticed his fingers were trembling.

"But I made a mistake…"

He lit the cigarette and then slowly blew out a thick plume of smoke. His expression darkened. Everything about him, from his quickening breath to his tongue sliding across his teeth, suddenly made me nervous. He had that same look in his eyes he'd had that night on the boat… and my claw marks on his cheeks were a reminder of what he was capable of.

"Uh, is everything okay?" I asked timidly.

His voice had become cold. "Depends on whether or not you co-operate."

And suddenly, I was face-to-face with the gruff kidnapper who drugged me—the same man who performed surgery on my unfrozen foot and carried my unconscious body over his shoulder like I was a potato sack. I steadied myself against the stair railing. "Seth, what are you doing?" I asked carefully, putting my hands up in defense and wondering if I should run. He moved closer, and now he had the shotgun aimed at me.

"This was supposed to be an easy job. I wasn't supposed to like you. Now it's all too damn complicated. At least I don't have to sneak you out in the middle of the night, because lucky for me, Luke and that dumbass Oliver left you unattended. What *idiots*. They'll never even know you are missing."

"What do you want with me?" I asked.

"I want to hand you over to the bitch who has made my life a living hell for the last eighteen years."

I took a chance. "Your wife, right? Luke told me about her. He said she was, um… dead." I asked while contemplating every escape route I could think of.

"Nope. Unfortunately, the crazy, raving, selfish bitch is still alive. You look like her when she was younger, but you are nothing alike. She would have never have risked her life for another person like you did for Regan. She would have thrown us all to the wolves to save herself."

"She doesn't sound very nice," I said.

"Nope."

"You know, you don't have to do this, Seth. You're being used. And I know exactly how that feels. It sucks."

He laughed. "Ha! Why yes. It does suck."

His gaze drifted to the doorway where Lisa now stood, her hands on her hips as she shook her head back and forth disappointedly, and the sight of her caused an enormous amount of turmoil to take residence on Seth's face. He gulped and looked at his feet for a while, and then he pointed the gun to the ground. "Aw hell. I'm sorry, girlie," he mumbled sheepishly. "I don't know what comes over me sometimes. That bitch wife of mine poisoned me. I'll do what's right from here on in. You can count on it."

I cleared my throat and hoped my voice still worked. "Then can you tell me where Luke went?" I could barely control the trembling in my legs.

"Nope. But I'll help ya find him," he said.

I stared into the eyes of the only person who could help me. I was crazy to trust him. If he wanted me dead or as his hostage, I would be. I forced a smile. "I hope he still wants me."

Seth reached for my hand and pulled me toward his truck a little too eagerly. "Well, let's find out," he said as he opened the passenger door.

I got in without hesitation, because really, I had nothing left to lose.

LUKE

42

A Promise Meant To Be Broken

FIVE MINUTES FROM TOWN, THE BRONCO RAN OUT OF GAS. USING every swear word I could possibly think of, I rolled it off the dark highway and into the ditch. Then, instead of driving, I walked down the middle of the road. I realized that a car could come speeding up behind me at any moment and I could be scattered all over the place—but my heartache would be gone for good. So, I stayed in the middle.

But no noise from car engines broke the night, only a bored dog barking as I made my way past overgrown front yards, chain-link fences, a few trash cans, and a green sign that said 'Welcome to Jude, Population 78'.

I found myself 'downtown'. The convenience store had conveniently closed, and the lights were off in the hardware and grocery stores. I realized, as I passed an hours-of-operation sign at a Laundromat, that I didn't even know what day it was. With the exception of a couple streetlights buzzing, the town was quiet and without a single soul in sight. I longed for a crowd to get lost in or noisy traffic to drown out the pounding in my head. This place made everything that hurt feel so much worse.

I dropped to the curb. The gun in my pocket reminded me that there was a way out—a permanent end to my foreseeable lifetime of misery and heartache. I took the metal beast out of my pocket and pondered the selfish cowardice of ending it all. There was only one bullet left, but that was enough…

Louisa…

No. I finally had her back, and I'd be damned if I would ever let her down again. I had to stick around, *for her.*

So now what? I closed my eyes and took in a deep breath, but the vision of Kaya standing in Oliver's arms kept replaying over and over and was impossible to erase. I couldn't shake it. His hands were on her face, her body pressed tight to his. He had her—he could do whatever he wanted with her—and that killed me over and over… I didn't need that last bullet. I was already dead.

An empty beer bottle rolled down the street. In a daze, I followed it toward a flickering light. The light grew until it became a half-burned-out sign advertising the word 'BAR'. I stopped in front of a windowless, black building with a mass of shiny Harley's angle parked in front. A fair amount of noise snuck out from around a slightly bent door, and someone was singing along to Johnny Cash.

I had a feeling that this place would offer just the kind of distraction I needed.

The door squealed as I opened it, and within two steps, I was standing among a collection of leather-clad men and women. A chubby man with a face only a mother could love stood in my way.

"I ran outta gas a few blocks from here, been having a really crap day. Just need a drink," I said loudly, making sure to address the table of men who looked like they wanted to crush me like a bug, "is that all right?"

I sounded cockier than I'd intended. Ugly Face got the nod of approval from a heavily tattooed bald man in the corner and stepped out of my way.

"Thanks," I said with a forced smile and made my way to the bar.

A bartender strolled over, sweat clinging to his upper lip. "What can I get ya?" he asked.

"Beer—whatever's on tap—and a shot of rye."

"Must be a bad day if you're in here," he said and tilted an icy mug under a running tap.

"Yup."

I got in one sip of the cold brew, barely tasting it, before the empty barstools on either side of me became occupied.

"What's your business here, boy?" asked a man on my right who looked to be in his forties with absolutely no friendliness about him. A dirty bandanna was wrapped around his bald head, and I wondered where the long, grey ponytail at the back was coming from.

"Was just passing through town and ran outta gas. Bad day. Ya know how it is. Drowning my sorrows," I said casually.

"Nobody just passes through this shithole; it's on the way to nowhere. Now, I'll ask you again boy. What's your business here?"

His breath would have peeled the paint off the walls had there been any left. I ordered another shot of rye as I sized up the guy on my left; he would be a handful: tree stumps for arms and a belly that prevented him from getting close to the bar, but Bandanna Man, who was on my right… I could take him out in two moves.

"Whatcha' waiting for, boy?" Bandanna Man said gruffly.

Stumpy's lip curled up at the corner. "Yeah, c'mon and git talking," he ordered.

"Well… it's a bit of a long story…"

"Just give us the short-and-sweet version, asshole. And make it good," said Bandanna Man as he cracked his knuckles.

I took a sip of my beer and cleared my throat. As I eyed my new companions, I decided to start at the beginning—the *very* beginning. It was either that or just start swinging… "Well, when I was nineteen, my mum died and left me to care for my little sister…" I began. I told them about Louisa and my roommate Claude and what he had done to her and how I desperately searched for a way to earn enough money to get her back. The scowl started to leave Bandanna Man's face.

"I'd like to kill that mofo myself," he said.

"Well, now he's dead," I said flatly.

I explained how I conspired to kidnap a girl to get enough ransom money to get my little sister back and seek revenge for my mother's death.

"How much cash are we talking here, boy?" said Stumpy.

"A million," I answered.

"Ooh wee!" he yelped and snapped his fingers at the bartender for another round.

I told Bandana Man and Stumpy that we succeeded—we made it happen—but there was one problem: I fell in love with the girl I'd kidnapped.

My audience had grown in size at this point, and Johnny Cash's "Don't Take Your Guns to Town" had been put on pause. I told them about the mountain lion and I opened my shirt to reveal the wounds for effect; there was a slight gasp from the ladies. I told them how I ran down the side of the rapids and then how I jumped in to fish Kaya out of the water when she had become impaled on a fallen tree, and how I used my knife to cauterize her wound and found a cave to hide in while we waited out a storm. I even told them how I saved her fiancé from falling off a cliff, even though he had tried to slit my throat.

And then I stopped. I stopped because it became too difficult to continue. Now I was at the end of the story: the part where the girl left me. Bandanna Man passed me a sympathy beer. "She is going home tomorrow morning, and I will never see her again," I muttered, my eyes stinging.

Stumpy shook his head like someone who truly understood and not someone who wanted to kill me anymore. Even Ugly Face wandered up and gave me a pat on the back. Their leader, however, the tattooed bald guy in the corner, wasn't having any of it. "I call bullshit!" he barked and stood, letting his chair tip backward and crash to the floor.

The entire room grew quiet as he made a beeline toward me. My audience scattered with the exception of a pretty brunette with fingernails that looked like knives.

"I think your story is bullshit," he said in the deepest, scratchiest voice I had ever heard. Tattoos covered every inch of him except his face. On his bald head were flags, some roses, what seemed to be a dinosaur, and of all things, a giant maple leaf. "Tell the truth," he demanded.

"I am. Why don't you believe me?" I asked as the world around me instinctively slowed down. I calculated the moves I'd need to execute to take him out, but he would get hurt. So would Stumpy and Bandanna Man, and I didn't want that. This big biker stared me straight in the eyes with an unwavering glare, and I stared back, not quite sure what to say.

"You got a death wish, don't ya, kid?" he asked quietly.

I shook my head no. Or, did I?

"I don't get it. You claim you are in love with this girl—that you can't live without her and blah, blah, blah," he said. "Well, if that's the case, then why the hell are you sitting here? Why are you wasting your time in this shithole with a bunch of dickheads like us? Why aren't you going after her?"

I answered him honestly. "Well, because I gave my word that I would honor her decisions."

He studied me for a moment, and then he sucked back his drink. The sweating bartender had another placed in front of him in seconds. "And why are you so intent on keeping your word?" he asked.

That was easy to answer, but hurt to say. "Because it's all I have left."

He rolled his eyes and was about to leave, and then in a complete about face, he turned around and cracked his neck. I rose slightly from the stool, hands ready, but I realized that every speck of ferocity had left his face. If his head wasn't colored like a comic book, I'd think my kind old uncle, Earl, was talking to me now. "You know, kid," he said, "honor, integrity and all that crap is noble and all, but sometimes, promises have to be broken. If keeping your word costs you the one thing you love the most, then what was it even worth keeping in the first place?"

I squeezed my eyes shut. "I just don't know what to do," I confided.

He cleared his throat. "Well, that's easy. Go back and get her," he said, and then he grabbed the brunette by the hair and dragged her outside.

KAYA

43

HEART SPEAKS

I DIALED HENRY FROM SETH'S CELL PHONE WHILE HE LIT HIS third cigarette. The truck sped past the thinning tree line toward town. A deer's eyes flashed in the headlights and an angry voice came on the line just as I was about to hang up.

"Who the hell is…?"

I didn't let him finish. "Henry, it's Kaya."

Dead silence.

"Hello?" I said, wondering if I had lost the signal.

His voice boomed, "Kaya! Are you okay? I've been so worried!"

"Yeah, I'm fine. Never better."

"Where are you?"

"Nowhere. Doesn't matter." I took a deep breath. "Anyway, I'm calling to tell you I'm not coming back."

He laughed nervously. "Don't be ridiculous. This is your home. Stop being silly. You know I'm the only one who can keep you safe. Come home. Now."

"No," I said firmly. Never in my life had that word felt so good to say. Those two letters put together were so powerful. "Listen Henry, regarding my inheritance," I said, forgetting that Seth was within earshot, "when I turn twenty-one, I'll see you again, and we will work it out. If you leave me alone till then, maybe I'll be nice and give you a fair piece of the pie."

Seth's eyebrow rose questioningly. He was now in on my secret, the one Regan was so desperate to uncover.

"That is unacceptable," Henry raged, and I imagined his face turning purple. "You are to come home, *now!*"

"This is *my* life, not yours, and I'm going to live it *exactly* how I want. You are not in control of me any longer."

"Well, then maybe you should talk to Stephan," he said slyly.

Stephan. The only person who could crumble my new found strength to dust. I pondered hanging up, but his deep, slow-as-molasses voice poured into my ear.

"Hello, baby," he said.

Tears instantly gushed forward, and I could barely speak. "Stephan, oh my God, I miss you so much…" I said, trying to contain a full on sob.

"I miss you, too," he said. His voice was strained, like he was in pain.

"Are you okay?" I asked.

"Yep. Never better. For real," he said, but there was still a slight hesitation in his voice. He was lying. "How about you, baby girl, you okay?"

"Yes, perfectly fine," I lied back. There was a long pause. "Stephan, I'm sorry, but I'm not coming back for a while," I choked out.

"It's okay, you go do what you have to," he said quickly. The words were catching in his throat. My big man of steel was crying, and I felt awful.

"Stephan I'm—"

He cut me off. "Wait, listen very, *very* closely; I love you, *Haley Alexandra*."

"Wha…?"

"I'll love you forever and always with cookies on top."

He was using a pretend name and referencing an email game we used to play. Had he sent a message to that old account? Was it something private and not meant for Henry to read? "I love you too, Stevie Muffins," I said, letting him know I understood.

He didn't reply. There was rustling and some muffled arguing in the background.

"…Stephan?"

Henry's voice came back on the line. "Tell me where you are," he said coldly.

"Maybe if you answer my question and are honest with me for once in your life. *You* tell me *this*… who is she?" I said, trying not to sound desperate.

"Who?"

"My mother!"

He swallowed hard. "Your mother is Lenore Lowen," he said stubbornly.

"You're a liar. I think she is someone named Rayna. Rayna Claire Gless."

Seth dropped his cigarette between his legs and almost took the truck off the road. Henry became strangely silent.

"Listen, Henry, you are not going to threaten me or hurt Stephan or anyone else I care about. You also aren't going to try and find me or come anywhere near me, you know why? Because I have a perfectly preserved drop of Lenore's blood in a convenient little silver necklace she gave me for my first birthday. She called it 'insurance'. I call it DNA analysis. Now, I'm sure that John Marchessa would love to get his hands on this and compare his daughter's DNA to mine. That would give him proof that I am not his granddaughter—and you'd lose it all."

I grinned madly to myself, and then I hung up.

Seth cleared his throat and needlessly adjusted the window. "I am proud of you, girlie," he said, rubbing his forehead.

"Thanks."

"Did he take it well, your crazy father?"

"No. And he is not going to give up until he gets me back. I know him. I just pray he doesn't use the one family member I love against me."

"Well, it sounds like you've got some fire power yourself."

"Yeah. But, it's best if we keep that between you and me."

Seth pondered this. "Well, if you don't tell Luke about what happened back at the ranch, I won't breathe a word of this to anyone."

I nodded in agreement.

Cool mountain air brushed my overheated cheeks, and just outside of town, we came upon the Bronco in the ditch. My mouth went dry. "Just ran out of gas is all, he couldn't have gotten far," Seth reassured, "there are probably only four places open in town right now, and he's not playing bingo or doing laundry, so…"

We ended up in front of a bar that Seth said he knew well. I tried to subdue the anxiety about to take over. Every worst-case scenario came to mind, and then escalated, doubled, and multiplied. What if we couldn't find him? What if I never saw him again? What if I was walking into my own death trap? I reminded myself for the hundredth time that I chose to trust Seth. I *had* to trust Seth.

A huge, greasy man with a head full of tattoos and a gorgeous brunette stood outside. The girl was talking on her cell phone and tapping a cigarette with long, silver fingernails, and the big guy was leaning as if he was holding up the wall with a beer in his hand. There were a zillion motorbikes in the parking lot. I stopped dead in my tracks a few feet from the truck, and Seth had to pull me forward.

"Hey!" said the biker as we approached, his aggressive, burly voice frightening, "Seth, you old dawg! I haven't seen you in ages, what brings you here?"

"Just wandering through. Good to see you, too bro," said Seth, giving the big guy a friendly slap on the arm and tipping his hat to the girl on the phone. She flashed a supermodel smile.

"New girlfriend?" the biker asked, eyeing me head-to-toe.

Seth laughed, "Nope. She's way too skinny for me."

I contemplated running.

"I'm here cause I need your help," Seth said when the niceties were out of the way, "a friend of mine is in a bad way. Could be anywhere. I thought you and the boys might have seen him."

"Perhaps," said the biker. "What are the particulars?"

"Well, he's a white male, about six-foot-three, muscular build, young—"

"Blue eyes, light brown hair, and an incredible smile," I interjected.

The biker laughed. The happy sound didn't match his exterior. "I'll ask the guys. It's been pretty quiet around here, though…" he said , and then his gaze fell to the bandage on my arm and his jaw dropped, "whoa, wait a second, are you… *the girl?*"

I backed away instinctively and the brunette almost dropped her phone. "What? No way!" she said excitedly, staring at me like I'd turned into a Jonas Brother.

"What girl? What are you talking about?" I asked as her silver talons pointed at my chest.

"Look at the necklace, it's a mountain lion's tooth!" she said enthusiastically.

The biker shook his head. "Well, damn, he *was* telling the truth. I knew it! You owe me five bucks, Tina!"

"Who was telling the truth? Luke? Is that who you're talking about?" I asked frantically.

The brunette and the biker grinned at each other. It looked so odd. "Ma'am, if you care to follow me, I will take you to whom it is you seek," said the biker, and he opened the bent and battered door and ushered me inside.

"*It's safe,*" Seth mouthed.

I didn't care if I was walking in a room full of snakes and gators. If Luke was in there, I was going in after him. As my eyes adjusted to the dim light and my nose to the smell, my burly host pointed toward a man at the bar.

And there he was. Shoulders slumped, head hanging low, and a biker with a red bandanna talking closely to him and giving him pats on the back. Luke was nodding eagerly, agreeing with whatever the man was saying to him, and then, as if in a hurry, he pushed himself away from the bar. He shook the hand of the man in the bandana, and then he raked his fingers through his golden hair. I was mesmerized, frozen in awe the same way I had been when I'd first laid eyes on him in the garden. Only, now that I knew him, everything about him was even more incredible. He stood confidently, turned, and then he stopped dead in his tracks when his eyes met mine from across the room.

"*Oh my God, I think the story is true,*" I heard someone whisper.

"*Yep, it's really her,*" said the brunette.

The room quieted. I said his name slowly. He seemed very unsure of things—wary of me. Maybe he thought I was coming to say goodbye and twist the knife in a little deeper. "Luke, please forgive me," I said, blocking out everyone but him, "I'm sorry. I was just trying to do what I thought was right." I crossed the room, the ten steps toward him feeling like an epic journey. "I'm not going back," I said, "I told Oliver I wouldn't marry him."

A collective hush settled over the room, but Luke's shocked expression didn't change. I wondered if maybe he didn't hear me, or if maybe he just didn't care. I mustered up a louder voice. "I want to be with you—"

He lunged at me and pulled me tight to him, holding my face in his hands and shaking head-to-toe. My legs went weak as his eyes bore into mine. "I was just coming to get you," he said.

Then he kissed me, fully and completely. I wanted nothing more than to linger against him, but I had to pull away. There was something important I had to tell him—something I had waited too long to say. "Luke, wait," I said breathlessly, "there is something you need to know."

He let go, looking worried, and he let his hands drop to his sides. I hoped he would fully feel the weight of my words—words I could finally say and mean wholeheartedly—words that I knew from now on were what *I* would be fighting for. "I love you," I said.

Tears filled his eyes, and all the air left his lungs. Then he swiftly picked me up and carried me out of the bar to the applause of the bikers. The moonlight shining on the bikes and the blinking neon bar sign was a romantic backdrop as our world stood still. It was as if we were the only ones on the planet, and we were wrapped up in this incredible madness called love. He kissed me hungrily, and I moved my hands up under his shirt to feel that place over his heart. The heat of his body made it hard to breathe, and the desire to know him in every possible way became all consuming. But it was impossible to ignore the fact that someone was clearing their throat and politely trying to get our attention.

"Uh, ahem, hey, kids…" Seth interjected.

We reluctantly pulled away from each other to see him standing on the curb grinning from ear to ear and looking nothing like the man who had held a gun to my chest a few hours ago.

"One brand new Ford F-150, gassed up and ready to go," he said and tossed Luke the truck keys. "The Bronco is going to go home for repairs—I only gave you the old girl 'cause I knew you wouldn't get too far in her. And just so you know, Louisa will be in the best care. You have my word." He gave us both a wink, and then he disappeared down the road.

Rain started to fall, and the night sparkled with endless possibilities.

"Well, the whole world is ours, Kaya," Luke said, pulling me into his arms, "we can go, or do, whatever you want."

I watched as soft drops of water hit his beautiful face. Whatever *I want*.

"So, what'll it be?" he asked with a sly, breathless smile.

I ran my fingers over the scar on his cheek and pushed my body in as close to his as possible. It was pure bliss. It was *home*. "Well," I said happily, "how about we go for a drive and get a couple of slurpees?"

And that was the exact moment, down to the very second, that I started living my own life. My head listened to my heart, and I was relieved of any doubt, uncertainly, or lingering reservation of whether or not I was doing the right thing, because *doing the right thing* didn't matter anymore.

All that mattered was him.

EPILOGUE

THE PHONE WAS RINGING. AGAIN. MY STEAKS WERE ALMOST COOKED TO perfection and two more minutes on the barbeque would ruin them.

"Just answer it," said Lisa.

I sighed. If I didn't do as she said, enduring her wrath would be much worse than talking to the crazy ex-wife calling me. I reluctantly made my way into the hot kitchen and got to the phone on the twelfth, persistent, ring. I didn't bother with hello.

"Are you there?" asked a silky voice.

"Yup. Carl's dead," I said irritably.

"You're sure?"

"Yes."

"Huh. Well, that saves us the trouble of having to deal with him ourselves. He was becoming a pain in the ass. Good riddance to the old prick."

Old Carl had served his purpose and was no longer needed. She said long ago he was the love of her life. Then again, she'd said that about me once as well.

"Where's the girl? You said you had her," she said. "Shouldn't you be on the road delivering her to me right now?"

"I should be, but I'm not. My plans have changed," I said impassively, and I dipped my finger into the coleslaw… darn that Lisa was a good cook; it had the perfect tang.

"What the hell do you mean? We have a deal. Have you lost her?"

I pondered this—lost her? Nope, definitely not. More like saved her. "Listen, I'm done. It's over. I can't go through with this anymore," I said, suddenly feeling happy for the first time in years, "I know exactly where Kaya is, which is far away from Henry *and* you. She's safe, and she is going to stay that way. By the way, I got to know her, and she's a great girl, in case you were wondering. Thank God she's nothing like you."

There was heavy breathing breaking through the white noise. I could picture her petite nostrils flaring and her eyes shining like the devil was in them. "Okay, Seth, joke's over." She laughed sweetly. "You'll get what you want when I see you next. Now, where is she?"

I used to melt into submission at her every request—kneel at her altar, worship the very ground she walked on—but after eighteen years of putting up with planning, hate, and revenge of a woman scorned, I realized it was no longer my burden to bear. Besides, she wasn't ageing well.

"Are we done here? I got steaks cookin'," I said.

"You don't want to cross me. I will bring a war to your doorstep," she hissed.

"Well, Rayna, it will be one hell of a fight then, won't it? That girl isn't going anywhere near you. I am going to make sure your daughter never has to lay eyes on your vile face."

"Then I will find her myself," she spat out, "and I will kill her very slowly in front of you and deliver her in pieces to Henry… and then, my sweet, darling Seth… I will kill you too."

I tossed the phone into the sink. I shouldn't have, because it was brand new and the sink was full of dishwater, but pissing Rayna off made me slightly giddy. I wandered back out onto the porch where I knew he was still watching from afar—the bloke probably never even left—but no matter. Oliver would come in handy when Rayna decided to retaliate. For now, I would just pretend to bask unaware in the bliss of the day, which was easy because Lisa had on that dress I loved and Louisa was giggling while Brutus lay on his back. The cold beer was plentiful, I had cash in the bank, and my new family was happy. Life was good, even though my steaks were choking to death on the barbecue…

ACKNOWLEDGEMENTS

THANK YOU...

THIS BOOK WOULDN'T HAVE BEEN POSSIBLE WITHOUT THE support of my husband, Byran Bueckert, who kept reality in check and looked after life while I wandered about in my dream world. Haley Bueckert—your encouragement, love, and willingness to dream right along with me was more treasured than you will ever know. Emily Bueckert and Josh Bueckert—your extremely honest criticism was so important and so valued—I am grateful for every word you read. Mom—thanks for being there for me, always, and tackling the first mammoth manuscript like a champ. My friend Tammy Wiebe—I felt like you truly believed in me, and that has fueled the fires to keep me going, thank you for the advice and for being there for me in so many ways. Thank you from the bottom of my heart to everyone at Clean Teen Publishing; I am so grateful for all you do! Rebecca Gober, Courtney Knight, Marya Heiman, Melanie Newton, and Wendy Martinez—your patience and guidance through the whole process was amazing. Editor Courtney Whittamore—I am humbled by your wisdom and thankful for the much-needed education. Thank you Clean Teen Street team! And a huge thanks to Shelly Mckenzie, Deirdre Nolan, and Bonnie Cannam for the first read through, and Tina Beattie, Reanne and Kieran Averay-Jones, Grant Tarapacki, Brian Vincent, Erin Greenough, Darrell Newsham, Kourtney Bueckert, Myrna Bueckert, Tennille Sydor and Jaclyn Horne—you were all incredibly positive influences on this journey and for that I am wildly grateful.

About The Author

Photo Credit: Rocco Macri

Heather McKenzie is a Canadian author and Serenade is her first novel. A professional singer/songwriter with five albums to date, she has been telling stories through music for years and pulls from her extraordinary experiences as a musician to fuel her passion for creating Young Adult fiction. A rocker at heart, a mom of three, an aspiring painter, and a lover of animals, she is kept grounded by her husband at their home in Edmonton. You can visit Heather at

WWW.HEATHERMCKENZIE.COM

CPSIA information can be obtained
at www.ICGtesting.com
Printed in the USA
LVOW03s1321290317
528895LV00001B/1/P